Human Intercourse

by

Philip Gilbert Hamerton

Human Intercourse
by Philip Gilbert Hamerton

ISBN: 978-93-59957-61-6

Published by

DOUBLE 9 BOOKS

2/13-B, Ansari Road
Daryaganj, New Delhi – 110002
info@double9books.com
www.double9books.com
Tel. 011-40042856

ABOUT THE AUTHOR

Philip Gilbert Hamerton was born on September 10, 1834, and died on November 4, 1894. Philip Gilbert Hamerton was an English artist, art reviewer, and author. He wrote a lot about the visual arts because he was a big supporter of modern printmaking. He came up with some important ideas about the English Etching Revival. Hamerton was born in Lancashire, England, in the town of Laneside, which is close to Shaw and Crompton. His mother died while giving birth to him, and ten years later, his father died. He moved in with his two aunts at an estate called the Hollins on the edge of Burnley when he was about five years old. He went to Burnley Grammar School there. Hamerton's first attempt at writing, a collection of poems, failed, so he focused on painting landscapes for a while. He camped out in the Scottish Highlands and eventually rented the former island of Inistrynich in Loch Awe, where he settled with his wife Eugénie Gindriez, who was the daughter of a French republican judge, in 1858. After a while, he realized that writing about art was more his forte than painting, so he went to Sens and then to Autun, where he wrote Painter's Camp in the Highlands (1863), a huge hit that paved the way for his famous book Etching and Etchers (1866).

CONTENTS

PREFACE

WHEN this book was begun, some years ago, I made a formal plan, according to which it was to have been one long Essay or Treatise, divided into sections and chapters, and presenting that apparently perfect *ordonnance* which gives such an imposing air to a work of art. I say "apparently perfect *ordonnance*," because in such cases the perfection of the arrangement is often only apparent, and the work is like those formal pseudo-classical buildings that seem, with their regular columns, spaces, and windows, the very highest examples of method; but you find on entering that the internal distribution of space is defective and inconvenient, that one room has a window in a corner and another half a window, that one is needlessly large for its employment and another far too small. In literature the ostentation of order may compel an author to extreme condensation in one part of his book and to excessive amplification in another, since, in reality, the parts of his subject do not fall more naturally into equal divisions than words beginning with different letters in the dictionary. I therefore soon abandoned external rigidity of order, and made my divisions more elastic; but I went still further after some experiments, and abandoned the idea of a Treatise. This was not done without some regret, as I know that a Treatise has a better chance of permanence than a collection of Essays; but, in this case, I met with an invisible obstacle that threatened to prevent good literary execution. After making some progress I felt that the work was not very readable, and that the writing of it was not a satisfactory occupation. Whenever this happens there is sure to be an error of method somewhere. What the error was in this case I did not discover for a long time, but at last I suddenly perceived it. A formal Treatise, to be satisfactory, can only be written about ascertained or ascertainable laws; and human intercourse as it is carried on between individuals, though it looks so accessible to every observer, is in reality a subject of infinite mystery and obscurity, about which hardly anything is known, about which certainly nothing is known absolutely and completely. I found that every attempt to ascertain and proclaim a law only ended, when the supposed law was brought face to face with nature, by discovering so many exceptions that the best practical rules were suspension of judgment and a reliance upon nothing but special observation in each particular case. I found that in real human intercourse the theoretically improbable, or even the theoretically impossible, was constantly happening. I remember a case in real life which illustrates this very forcibly. A certain English lady, influenced by the received ideas about human intercourse which define the conditions of it in a hard and sharp manner, was strongly convinced that it would be impossible for her to have friendly relations with another lady whom she had never seen, but was likely to see frequently. All her reasons would be considered excellent reasons by those who believe in maxims and rules. It was plain that there could be nothing in common. The other lady was neither of the same country, nor of the same religious and political parties, nor exactly of the same class, nor of the same generation. These facts were known, and the inference deduced from them was that intercourse would be impossible. After some time the English lady began to perceive that the case did not bear out the supposed rules; she discovered that the younger lady might be an acceptable friend. At last the full strange truth became apparent,—that she was singularly well adapted, better adapted than any other human being, to take a filial relation to the elder, especially in times of sickness, when her presence was a wonderful support. Then the warmest affection sprang up between the two, lasting till separation by death and still cherished by the survivor. What becomes of rules and maxims and wise old saws in the face of nature and reality? What can we do better than to observe nature with an open, unprejudiced mind, and gather some of the results of observation?

I am conscious of several omissions that may possibly be rectified in another volume if this is favorably accepted. The most important of these are the influence of age on intercourse, and the effects of living in the same house, which are not invariably favorable. Both these subjects are very important, and I have not time to treat them now with the care they would require. There ought also to have been a careful study of the natural antagonisms, which are of terrible importance when people, naturally antagonistic, are compelled by circumstances to live together. These are, however, generally of less importance than the affinities, because we contrive to make our intercourse with antagonistic people as short and rare as possible, and that with sympathetic people as frequent and long as circumstances will permit.

I will not close this preface without saying that the happiness of sympathetic human intercourse seems to me incomparably greater than any other pleasure. I may be supposed to have passed the age of enthusiastic illusions, yet I would at any time rather pass a week with a real friend in any place that afforded simple shelter than with an indifferent person in a palace. In saying this I am thinking of real experiences. One of my friends who is devoted to archæological excavations has often invited me to share his life in a hut or a cottage, and I have invariably found that the pleasure of his society far overbalanced the absence of luxury. On the other hand, I have sometimes endured extreme *ennui* at sumptuous feasts in richly appointed houses. The result of experience, in my case, has been to confirm a youthful conviction that the value of certain persons is not to be estimated by comparison with anything else. I was always a believer, and am so at this day more than ever, in the happiness of genuine human intercourse, but I prefer solitude to the false imitation of it. It is in this as in other pleasures, the better we appreciate the real thing, the less we are disposed to accept the spurious copy as a substitute. By far the greater part of what passes for human intercourse is not intercourse at all, but only acting, of which the highest object and most considerable merit is to conceal the weariness that accompanies its hollow observances.

One sad aspect of my subject has not been touched upon in this volume. It was often present in my thoughts, but I timidly shrank from dealing with it. I might have attempted to show in what manner intercourse is cut short by death. All reciprocity of intercourse is, or appears to be, entirely cut short by that catastrophe; but those who have talked with us much in former years retain an influence that may be even more constant than our recollection of them. My own recollection of the dead is extremely vivid and clear, and I cultivate it by willingly thinking about them, being especially happy when by some accidental flash of brighter memory a more than usual degree of lucidity is obtained. I accept with resignation the natural law, on the whole so beneficent, that when an organism is no longer able to exist without suffering, or senile decrepitude, it should be dissolved and made insensible of suffering; but I by no means accept the idea that the dead are to be forgotten in order that we may spare ourselves distress. Let us give them their due place, their great place, in our hearts and in our thoughts; and if the sweet reciprocity of human intercourse is no longer possible with those who are silent and asleep, let the memory of past intercourse be still a part of our lives. There are hours when we live with the dead more than with the living, so that without any trace of superstition we feel their old sweet influence acting upon us yet, and it seems as if only a little more were needed to give us "the touch of a vanished hand, and the sound of a voice that is still."

Closely connected with this subject of death is the subject of religious beliefs. In the present state of confusion and change, some causes of which are indicated in this volume, the only plain course for honorable men is to act always in favor of truthfulness, and therefore against hypocrisy, and against those encouragers of hypocrisy who offer social advantages as rewards for it. What may come in the future we cannot tell, but we may be sure that the best way to prepare for the future is to be honest and candid in the present. There are two causes which are gradually effecting a great change, and as they are natural causes they are irresistibly powerful. One is the process of analytic detachment, by which sentiments and feelings once believed to be religious are now found to be separable from religion. If a French peasant has a feeling for architecture, poetry, or music, or an appreciation of eloquence, or a desire to hear a kind of moral philosophy, he goes to the village church to satisfy these dim incipient desires. In his case these feelings and wants are all confusedly connected with religion; in ours they are detached from it, and only reconnected with it by accident, we being still aware that there is no essential identity. That is the first dissolving cause. It seems only to affect the externals of religion, but it goes deeper by making the consciously religious state of mind less habitual. The second cause is even more serious in its effects. We are acquiring the habit of explaining everything by natural causes, and of trying to remedy everything by the employment of natural means. Journals dependent on popular approval for the enormous circulation that is necessary to their existence do not hesitate, in clear terms, to express their preference of natural means to the invocation of supernatural agencies. For example, the correspondent of the "Daily News" at Port Said, after describing the annual blessing of the Suez Canal at the Epiphany, observes: "Thus the canal was solemnly blessed. The opinion of the captains of the ships that throng the harbor, waiting until the block adjusts itself, is that it would be better to widen it." Such an opinion is perfectly modern, perfectly characteristic of our age. We think that steam excavators and dredgers would be more likely to prevent blocks in the Suez Canal than a priest reading prayers out of a book and throwing a golden cross into the sea, to be fished up again by divers. We cannot help thinking as we do: our opinion has not been chosen by us voluntarily, it has been forced upon us by facts that we cannot help seeing, but it deprives us of an opportunity for a religious emotion, and it separates us, on that point, from all those who are still capable of feeling it. I have given considerable space to the consideration of these changes, but not a disproportionate space. They have a deplorable effect on human intercourse by dividing friends and families into different groups, and by separating those who might otherwise have enjoyed friendship unreservedly. It is probable, too, that we are only at the beginning of the conflict, and that in years not immeasurably distant there will be fierce struggles on the most irritating of practical issues. To name but one of these it is probable that there will be a sharp struggle when a strong and determined naturalist party shall claim the instruction of the young, especially with regard to the origin of the race, the beginnings of animal life, and the evidences of intention in nature. Loving, as I do, the amenities of a peaceful and polished civilization much better than angry controversy, I long for the time when these great questions will be considered as settled one way or the other, or else, if they are beyond our intelligence, for the time when they may be classed as insoluble, so that men may work out their destiny without bitter quarrels about their origin. The present at least is ours, and it depends upon ourselves whether it is to be wasted in vain disputes or brightened by charity and kindness.

ESSAY I
ON THE DIFFICULTY OF
DISCOVERING FIXED LAWS

A BOOK on Human Intercourse might be written in a variety of ways, and amongst them might be an attempt to treat the subject in a scientific manner so as to elucidate those natural laws by which intercourse between human beings must be regulated. If we knew quite perfectly what those laws are we should enjoy the great convenience of being able to predict with certainty which men and women would be able to associate with pleasure, and which would be constrained or repressed in each other's society. Human intercourse would then be as much a positive science as chemistry, in which the effects of bringing substances together can be foretold with the utmost accuracy. Some very distant approach to this scientific state may in certain instances actually be made. When we know the characters of two people with a certain degree of precision we may sometimes predict that they are sure to quarrel, and have the satisfaction of witnessing the explosion that our own acumen has foretold. To detect in people we know those incompatibilities that are the fatal seeds of future dissension is one of our malicious pleasures. An acute observer really has considerable powers of prediction and calculation with reference to individual human beings, but there his wisdom ends. He cannot deduce from these separate cases any general rules or laws that can be firmly relied upon as every real law of nature can be relied upon, and therefore it may be concluded that such rules are not laws of nature at all, but only poor and untrustworthy substitutes for them.

The reason for this difficulty I take to be the extreme complexity of human nature and its boundless variety, which make it always probable that in every mind which we have not long and closely studied there will be elements wholly unknown to us. How often, with regard to some public man, who is known to us only in part through his acts or his writings, are we surprised by the sudden revelation of characteristics that we never imagined for him and that seem almost incompatible with the better known side of his nature! How much the more, then, are we likely to go wrong in our estimates of people we know nothing about, and how impossible it must be for us to determine how they are likely to select their friends and companions!

Certain popular ideas appear to represent a sort of rude philosophy of human intercourse. There is the common belief, for example, that, in order to associate pleasantly together, people should be of the same class and nearly in the same condition of fortune, but when we turn to real life we find very numerous instances in which this fancied law is broken with the happiest results. The late Duke of Albany may be mentioned as an example. No doubt his own natural refinement would have prevented him from associating with vulgar people; but he readily associated with refined and cultivated people who had no pretension to rank. His own rank was a power in his hands that he used for good, and he was conscious of it, but it did not isolate him; he desired to know people as they are, and was capable of feeling the most sincere respect for anybody who deserved it. So it is, generally, with all who have the gifts of sympathy and intelligence. Merely to avoid what is disagreeable has nothing to do with pride of station. Vulgar society is disagreeable, which is a sufficient reason for keeping aloof from it. Amongst people of refinement, association or even friendship is possible in spite of differences of rank and fortune.

Another popular belief is that "men associate together when they are interested in the same things." It would, however, be easy to adduce very numerous instances in which an interest in similar things has been a cause of quarrel, when if one of the two parties had regarded those things with indifference, harmonious intercourse might have been preserved. The livelier our interest in anything the more does acquiescence in matters of detail appear essential to us. Two people are both of them extremely religious, but one of them is a Mahometan, and the other a Christian; here the interest in religion causes a divergence, enough in most cases to make intercourse impossible, when it would have been quite possible if both parties had regarded religion with indifference. Bring the two nearer together, suppose them to be both Christians, they acknowledge one law, one doctrine, one Head of the church in heaven. Yes, but they do not acknowledge the same head of it on earth, for one accepts the Papal supremacy, which the other denies; and their common Christianity is a feeble bond of union in comparison with the forces of repulsion contained in a multitude of details. Two nominal, indifferent Christians who take no interest in theology would have a better chance of agreeing. Lastly, suppose them to be both members of the Church of England, one of the old school, with firm and settled beliefs on every point and a horror of the most distant approaches to heresy, the other of the new school, vague, indeterminate, desiring to preserve his Christianity as a sentiment when it has vanished as a faith, thinking that the Bible is not true in the old sense but only "contains" truth, that the divinity of Christ is "a past issue,"[1] and that evolution is, on the whole, more probable than direct and intentional creation,—what possible agreement can exist between these two? If they both care about religious topics, and talk about them, will not their disagreement be in exact proportion to the liveliness of their interest in the subject? So in a realm with which I have some acquaintance, that of the fine arts, discord is always probable between those who have a passionate delight in art. Innocent, well-intentioned friends think that because two men "like painting," they ought to be introduced, as they are sure to amuse each other. In reality, their tastes may be more opposed than the taste of either of them is to perfect indifference. One has a severe taste for beautiful form and an active contempt for picturesque accidents and romantic associations, the other feels chilled by severe beauty and delights in the picturesque and romantic. If each is convinced of the superiority of his own principles he will deduce from them an endless series of judgments that can only irritate the other.

Seeing that nations are always hostile to each other, always watchfully jealous and inclined to rejoice in every evil that happens to a neighbor, it would appear safe to predict that little intercourse could exist between persons of different nationality. When, however, we observe the facts as they are in real life, we perceive that very strong and durable friendships often exist between men who are not of the same nation, and that the chief obstacle to the formation of these is not so much nationality as difference of language. There is, no doubt, a prejudice that one is not likely to get on well with a foreigner, and the prejudice has often the effect of keeping people of different nationality apart, but when once it is overcome it is often found that very powerful feelings of mutual respect and sympathy draw the strangers together. On the other hand, there is not the least assurance that the mere fact of being born in the same country will make two men regard each other with kindness. An Englishman repels another Englishman when he meets him on the Continent.[2] The only just conclusion is that nationality affords no certain rule either in favor of intercourse or against it. A man may possibly be drawn towards a foreign nationality by his appreciation of its excellence in some art that he loves, but this is the case only when the excellence is of the peculiar kind that supplies the needs of his own intelligence. The French excel in painting; that is to say, that many Frenchmen have attained a certain kind of excellence in certain departments of the art of painting. Englishmen and Americans who value that particular kind of excellence are often strongly drawn towards Paris as an artistic centre or capital; and this opening of their minds to French influence in art may admit other French influences at the same time, so that the ultimate effect of a love of art may be a breaking down of the barrier of nationality. It seldom happens that Frenchmen are drawn towards England and America by their love of painting, but it frequently happens that they become in a measure Anglicized or Americanized either by the serious study of nautical science, or by the love of yachting as an amusement, in which they look to England and America both for the most advanced theories and the newest examples.

The nearest approach ever made to a general rule may be the affirmation that likeness is the secret of companionship. This has a great look of probability, and may really be the reason for many associations, but after observing others we might come to the conclusion that an opposite law would be at least equally applicable. We might say that a companion, to be interesting, ought to bring new elements, and not be a repetition of our own too familiar personality. We have enough of ourselves in ourselves; we desire a companion who will relieve us from the bounds of our thoughts, as a neighbor opens his garden to us, and delivers us from our own hedges. But if the unlikeness is so great that mutual understanding is impossible, then it is too great. We fancy that we should like to know this or that author, because we feel a certain sympathy with him though he is very different from us, but there are other writers whom we do not desire to know because we are aware of a difference too excessive for companionship.

The only approximation to a general law that I would venture to affirm is that the strongest reason why men are drawn together is not identity of class, not identity of race, not a common interest in any particular art or science, but because there is something in their idiosyncrasies that gives a charm to intercourse between the two. What it is I cannot tell, and I have never met with the wise man who was able to enlighten me.

It is not respect for character, seeing that we often respect people heartily without being able to enjoy their society. It is a mysterious suitableness or adaptability, and _how_ mysterious it is may be in some degree realized when we reflect that we cannot account for our own preferences. I try to explain to myself, for my own intellectual satisfaction, how and why it is that I take pleasure in the society of one very dear friend. He is a most able, honorable, and high-minded man, but others are all that, and they give me no pleasure. My friend and I have really not very much in common, far less than I have with some perfectly indifferent people. I only know that we are always glad to be together, that each of us likes to listen to the other, and that we have talked for innumerable hours. Neither does my affection blind me to his faults. I see them as clearly as if I were his enemy, and doubt not that he sees mine. There is no illusion, and there has been no change in our sentiments for twenty years.

As a contrast to this instance I think of others in which everything seems to have been prepared on purpose for facility of intercourse, in which there is similarity of pursuits, of language, of education, of every thing that is likely to permit men to talk easily together, and yet there is some obstacle that makes any real intercourse impossible. What the obstacle is I am unable to explain even to myself. It need not be any unkind feeling, nor any feeling of disapprobation; there may be good-will on both sides and a mutual desire for a greater degree of intimacy, yet with all this the intimacy does not come, and such intercourse as we have is that of simple politeness. In these cases each party is apt to think that the other is reserved, when there is no wish to be reserved but rather a desire to be as open as the unseen obstacle will allow. The existence of the obstacle does not prevent respect and esteem or even a considerable degree of affection. It divides people who seem to be on the most friendly terms; it divides even the nearest relations, brother from brother, and the son from the father. Nobody knows exactly what it is, but we have a word for it,—we call it incompatibility. The difficulty of going farther and explaining the real nature of incompatibility is that it takes as many shapes as there are varieties in the characters of mankind.

Sympathy and incompatibility,—these are the two great powers that decide for us whether intercourse is to be possible or not, but the causes of them are dark mysteries that lie undiscovered far down in the "abysmal deeps of personality."

ESSAY II
INDEPENDENCE

THERE is an illusory and unattainable independence which is a mere dream, but there is also a reasonable and attainable independence not really inconsistent with our obligations to humanity and our country.

The dependence of the individual upon the race has never been so fully recognized as now, so that there is little fear of its being overlooked. The danger of our age, and of the future, is rather that a reasonable and possible independence should be made needlessly difficult to attain and to preserve.

The distinction between the two may be conveniently illustrated by a reference to literary production. Every educated man is dependent upon his own country for the language that he uses; and again, that language is itself dependent on other languages from which it is derived; and, farther, the modern author is indebted for a continual stimulus and many a suggestion to the writings of his predecessors, not in his own country only but in far distant lands. He cannot, therefore, say in any absolute way, "My books are my own," but he may preserve a certain mental independence which will allow him to say that with truth in a relative sense. If he expresses himself such as he is, an idiosyncrasy affected but not annihilated by education, he may say that his books are his own.

Few English authors have studied past literature more willingly than Shelley and Tennyson, and none are more original. In these cases idiosyncrasy has been affected by education, but instead of being annihilated thereby it has gained from education the means of expressing its own inmost self more clearly. We have the true Shelley, the born Tennyson, far more perfectly than we should ever have possessed them if their own minds had not been opened by the action of other minds. Culture is like wealth, it makes us more ourselves, it enables us to express ourselves. The real nature of the poor and the ignorant is an obscure and doubtful problem, for we can never know the inborn powers that remain in them undeveloped till they die. In this way the help of the race, so far from being unfavorable to individuality, is necessary to it. Claude helped Turner to become Turner. In complete isolation from art, however magnificently surrounded by the beauties of the natural world, a man does not express his originality as a landscape-painter, he is simply incapable of expressing *anything* in paint.

But now let us inquire whether there may not be cases in which the labors of others, instead of helping originality to express itself, act as a check to it by making originality superfluous.

As an illustration of this possibility I may take the modern railway system. Here we have the labor and ingenuity of the race applied to travelling, greatly to the convenience of the individual, but in a manner which is totally repressive of originality and indifferent to personal tastes. People of the most different idiosyncrasies travel exactly in the same way. The landscape-painter is hurried at speed past beautiful spots that he would like to contemplate at leisure; the archæologist is whirled by the site of a Roman camp that he would willingly pause to examine; the mountaineer is not permitted to climb the tunnelled hill, nor the swimmer to cross in his own refreshing, natural way the breadth of the iron-spanned river. And as individual tastes are disregarded, so individual powers are left uncultivated and unimproved. The only talent required is that of sitting passively on a seat and of enduring, for hours together, an unpleasant though mitigated vibration. The skill and courage of the horseman, the endurance of the pedestrian, the art of the paddler or the oarsman, are all made superfluous by this system of travelling by machines, in which previous labors of engineers and mechanics have determined everything beforehand. Happily, the love of exercise and enterprise has produced a reaction of individualism against this levelling railway system, a reaction that shows itself in many kinds of slower but more adventurous locomotion and restores to the individual creature his lost independence by allowing him to pause and stop when he pleases; a reaction delightful to him especially in this, that it gives him some pride and pleasure in the use of his own muscles and his own wits. There are still, happily, Englishmen who would rather steer a cutter across the Channel in rough weather than be shot through a long hole in the chalk.

What the railway is to physical motion, settled conventions are to the movements of the mind. Convention is a contrivance for facilitating what we write or speak by which we are relieved from personal effort and almost absolved from personal responsibility. There are men whose whole art of living consists in passing from one conventionalism to another as a traveller changes his train. Such men may be envied for the skill with which they avoid the difficulties of life. They take their religion, their politics, their education, their social and literary opinions, all as provided by the brains of others, and they glide through existence with a minimum of personal exertion. For those who are satisfied with easy, conventional ways the desire for intellectual independence is unintelligible. What is the need of it?

Why go, mentally, on a bicycle or in a canoe by your own toilsome exertions when you may sit so very comfortably in the train, a rug round your lazy legs and your softly capped head in a corner?

The French ideal of "good form" is to be undistinguishable from others; by which it is not understood that you are to be undistinguishable from the multitude of poor people, but one of the smaller crowd of rich and fashionable people. Independence and originality are so little esteemed in what is called "good society" in France that the adjectives "*indépendant*" and "*original*" are constantly used in a bad sense. "*Il est très indépendant*" often means that the man is of a rude, insubordinate, rebellious temper, unfitting him for social life. "*Il est original*," or more contemptuously, "*C'est un original*," means that the subject of the criticism has views of his own which are not the fashionable views, and which therefore (whatever may be their accuracy) are proper objects of well-bred ridicule.

I cannot imagine any state of feeling more destructive of all interest in human intercourse than this, for if on going into society I am only to hear the fashionable opinions and sentiments, what is the gain to me who know them too well already? I could even repeat them quite accurately with the proper conventional tone, so why put myself to inconvenience to hear that dull and wearisome play acted over again? The only possible explanation of the pleasure that French people of some rank appear to take in hearing things, which are as stale as they are inaccurate, repeated by every one they know, is that the repetition of them appears to be one of the signs of gentility, and to give alike to those who utter them and to those who hear, the profound satisfaction of feeling that they are present at the mysterious rites of Caste.

There is probably no place in the whole world where the feeling of mental independence is so complete as it is in London. There is no place where differences of opinion are more marked in character or more frank and open in expression; but what strikes one as particularly admirable in London is that in the present day (it has not always been so) men of the most opposite opinions and the most various tastes can profess their opinions and indulge their tastes without inconvenient consequences to themselves, and there is hardly any opinion, or any eccentricity, that excludes a man from pleasant social intercourse if he does not make himself impossible and intolerable by bad manners. This independence gives a savor to social intercourse in London that is lamentably wanting to it elsewhere. There is a strange and novel pleasure (to one who lives habitually in the country) in hearing men and women say what they think without deference to any local public opinion.

In many small places this local public opinion is so despotic that there is no individual independence in society, and it then becomes necessary that a man who values his independence, and desires to keep it, should learn the art of living contentedly outside of society.

It has often occurred to me to reflect that there are many men in London who enjoy a pleasant and even a high social position, who live with intelligent people, and even with people of great wealth and exalted rank, and yet who, if their lot had been cast in certain small provincial towns, would have found themselves rigorously excluded from the upper local circles, if not from all circles whatsoever.

I have sometimes asked myself, when travelling on the railway through France, and visiting for a few hours one of those sleepy little old cities, to me so delightful, in which the student of architecture and the lover of the picturesque find so much to interest them, what would have been the career of a man having, for example, the capacity and the convictions of Mr. Gladstone, if he had passed all the years of his manhood in such a place.

It commonly happens that when Nature endows a man with a vigorous personality and its usual accompaniment, an independent way of seeing things, she gives him at the same time powerful talents with which to defend his own originality; but in a small and ancient city, where everything is traditional, intellectual force is of no avail, and learning is of no use. In such a city, where the upper class is an exclusive caste impenetrable by ideas, the eloquence of Mr. Gladstone would be ineffectual, and if exercised at all would be considered in bad taste. His learning, even, would tend to separate him from the unlearned local aristocracy. The simple fact that he is in favor of parliamentary government, without any more detailed information concerning his political opinions, would put him beyond the pale, for parliamentary government is execrated by the French rural aristocracy, who tolerate nothing short of a determined monarchical absolutism. His religious views would be looked upon as those of a low Dissenter, and it would be remembered against him that his father was in trade. Such is the difference, as a field for talent and originality, between London and an aristocratic little French city, that those very qualities which have raised our Prime Minister to a not undeserved pre-eminence in the great place would have kept him out of society in the small one. He might, perhaps, have talked politics in some café with a few shop-keepers and attorneys.

It may be objected that Mr. Gladstone, as an English Liberal, would naturally be out of place in France and little appreciated there, so I will take the cases of a Frenchman in France and an Englishman in England. A brave French officer, who was at the same time a gentleman of ancient lineage and good estate, chose (for reasons of his own which had no connection with social intercourse) to live upon a property that happened to be situated in a part of France where the aristocracy was strongly Catholic and reactionary. He then found himself excluded from "good society," because he was a Protestant and a friend to parliamentary government. Reasons of this kind, or the counter-reasons of Catholicism and disapprobation of parliaments, would not exclude a polished and amiable gentleman from society in London. I have read in a biographical notice of Sidney Dobell that when he lived at Cheltenham he was excluded from the society of the place because his parents were Dissenters and he had been in trade.

In cases of this kind, where exclusion is due to hard prejudices of caste or of religion, a man who has all the social gifts of good manners, kind-heartedness, culture, and even wealth, may find himself outside the pale if he lives in or near a small place where society is a strong little clique well organized on definitely understood principles. There are situations in which exclusion of that kind means perfect solitude. It may be argued that to escape solitude the victim has nothing to do but associate with a lower class, but this is not easy or natural, especially when, as in Dobell's case, there is intellectual culture. Those who have refined manners and tastes and a love for intellectual pursuits, usually find themselves disqualified for entering with any real heartiness and enjoyment into the social life of classes where these tastes are undeveloped, and where the thoughts flow in two channels,—the serious channel, studded with anxieties about the means of existence, and the humorous channel, which is a diversion from the other. Far be it from me to say anything that might imply any shade of contempt or disapprobation of the humorous spirit that is Nature's own remedy for the evils of an anxious life. It does more for the mental health of the middle classes than could be done by the most sublimated culture; and if anything concerning it is a subject for regret it is that culture makes us incapable of enjoying poor jokes. It is, however, a simple matter of fact that although men of great culture may be humorists (Mr. Lowell is a brilliant example), their humor is both more profound in the serious intention that lies under it, and vastly more extensive in the field of its operations than the trivial humor of the uneducated; whence it follows that although humor is the faculty by which different classes are brought most easily into cordial relations, the humorist who has culture will probably find himself à l'étroit with humorists who have none, whilst the cultured man who has no humor, or whose humorous tendencies have been overpowered by serious thought, is so terribly isolated in uneducated society that he feels less alone in solitude. To realize this truth in its full force, the reader has only to imagine John

Stuart Mill trying to associate with one of those middle-class families that Dickens loved to describe, such as the Wardle family in Pickwick.

It follows from these considerations that unless a man lives in London, or in some other great capital city, he may easily find himself so situated that he must learn the art of being happy without society.

As there is no pleasure in military life for a soldier who fears death, so there is no independence in civil existence for the man who has an overpowering dread of solitude.

There are two good reasons against the excessive dread of solitude. The first is that solitude is very rarely so absolute as it appears from a distance; and the second is that when the evil is real, and almost complete, there are palliatives that may lessen it to such a degree as to make it, at the worst, supportable, and at the best for some natures even enjoyable in a rather sad and melancholy way.

Let us not deceive ourselves with conventional notions on the subject. The world calls "solitude" that condition in which a man lives outside of "society," or, in other words, the condition in which he does not pay formal calls and is not invited to state dinners and dances. Such a condition may be very lamentable, and deserving of polite contempt, but it need not be absolute solitude.

Absolute solitude would be the state of Crusoe on the desert island, severed from human kind and never hearing a human voice; but this is not the condition of any one in a civilized country who is out of a prison cell. Suppose that I am travelling in a country where I am a perfect stranger, and that I stay for some days in a village where I do not know a soul. In a surprisingly short time I shall have made acquaintances and begun to acquire rather a home-like feeling in the place. My new acquaintances may possibly not be rich and fashionable: they may be the rural postman, the innkeeper, the stone-breaker on the roadside, the radical cobbler, and perhaps a mason or a joiner and a few more or less untidy little children; but every morning their greeting becomes more friendly, and so I feel myself connected still with that great human race to which, whatever may be my sins against the narrow laws of caste and class, I still unquestionably belong. It is a positive advantage that our meetings should be accidental and not so long as to involve any of the embarrassments of formal social intercourse, as I could not promise myself that the attempt to spend a whole evening with these humble friends might not cause difficulties for me and for them. All I maintain is that these little chance talks and greetings have a tendency to keep me cheerful and preserve me from that moody state of mind to which the quite lonely man exposes himself. As to the substance and quality of our conversations, I amuse myself by comparing them with conversations between more genteel people, and do not always perceive that the disparity is very wide. Poor men often observe external facts with the greatest shrewdness and accuracy, and have interesting things to tell when they see that you set up no barrier of pride against them. Perhaps they do not know much about architecture and the graphic arts, but on these subjects they are devoid of the false pretensions of the upper classes, which is an unspeakable comfort and relief. They teach us many things that are worth knowing. Humble and poor people were amongst the best educators of Shakspeare, Scott, Dickens, Wordsworth, George Eliot. Even old Homer learned from them touches of nature which have done as much for his immortality as the fire of his wrathful kings.

Let me give the reader an example of this chance intercourse just as it really occurred. I was drawing architectural details in and about a certain foreign cathedral, and had the usual accompaniment of youthful spectators who liked to watch me working, as greater folks watch fashionable artists in their studios. Sometimes they rather incommoded me, but on my complaining of the inconvenience, two of the bigger boys acted as policemen to defend me, which they did with stern authority and promptness. After that one highly intelligent little boy brought paper and pencil from his father's house and set himself to draw what I was drawing. The subject was far too difficult for him, but I gave him a simpler one, and in a very short time he was a regular pupil. Inspired by his example, three other little boys asked if they might do likewise, so I had a class of four. Their manner towards me was perfect,—not a trace of rudeness nor of timidity either, but absolute confidence at once friendly and respectful. Every day when I went to the cathedral at the same hour my four little friends greeted me with such frank and visible gladness that it could neither have been feigned nor mistaken. During our lessons they surprised and interested me greatly by the keen observation they displayed; and this was true more particularly of the bright little leader and originator of the class. The house he lived in was exactly opposite the rich west front of the cathedral; and I found that, young as he was (a mere child), he had observed for himself almost all the details of its sculpture. The statues, groups, bas-reliefs, and other ornaments were all, for him, so many separate subjects, and not a confused enrichment of labored stone-work as they so easily might have been. He had notions, too, about chronology, telling me the dates of some parts of the cathedral and asking me about others. His mother treated me with the utmost kindness and invited me to sketch quietly from her windows. I took a photographer up there, and set his big camera, and we got such a photograph as had been deemed impossible before. Now in all this does not the reader perceive that I was enjoying human intercourse in a very delicate and exquisite way? What could be more charming and refreshing to a solitary student than this frank and hearty friendship of children who caused no perceptible hindrance to his work, whilst they effectually dispelled sad thoughts?

Two other examples may be given from the experience of a man who has often been alone and seldom felt himself in solitude.

I remember arriving, long ago, in the evening at the head of a salt-water loch in Scotland, where in those days there existed an exceedingly small beginning of a watering-place. Soon after landing I walked on the beach with no companion but the beauty of nature and the "long, long thoughts" of youth. In a short time I became aware that a middle-aged Scotch gentleman was taking exercise in the same solitary way. He spoke to me, and we were soon deep in a conversation that began to be interesting to both of us. He was a resident in the place and invited me to his house, where our talk continued far into the night. I was obliged to leave the little haven the next day, but my recollection of it now is like the memorandum of a conversation. I remember the wild romantic scenery and the moon upon the water, and the steamer from Glasgow at the pier; but the real satisfaction of that day consisted in hours of talk with a man who had seen much, observed much, thought much, and was most kindly and pleasantly communicative,—a man whom I had never spoken to before, and have never seen or heard of since that now distant but well-remembered evening.

The other instance is a conversation in the cabin of a steamer. I was alone, in the depth of winter, making a voyage by an unpopular route, and during a long, dark night. It was a dead calm. We were only three passengers, and we sat together by the bright cabin-fire. One of us was a young officer in the British navy, just of age; another was an anxious-looking man of thirty. Somehow the conversation turned to the subject of inevitable expenses; and the sailor told us that he had a certain private income, the amount of which he mentioned. "I have exactly the same income," said the man of thirty, "but I married very early and have a wife and family to maintain;" and then—as we did not know even his name, and he was not likely to see us again—he seized the opportunity (under the belief that he was kindly warning the young sailor) of telling the whole story of his anxieties in detail. The point of his discourse was that he did not pretend to be poor, or to claim sympathy, but he powerfully described the exact nature of his position. What had been his private income had now become the public revenue of a household. It all went in housekeeping, almost independently of his will and outside of his control. He had his share in the food of the family, and he was just decently clothed, but there was an end to personal enterprises. The economy and the expenditure of a free and intelligent bachelor had been alike replaced by a dull, methodical, uncontrollable outgo; and the man himself, though now called the head of a family, had discovered that a new impersonal necessity was the real master, and that he lived like a child in his own house. "This," he said, "is the fate of a gentleman who marries on narrow means, unless he is cruelly selfish."

Frank and honest conversations of this kind often come in the way of a man who travels by himself, and they remain with him afterwards as a part of his knowledge of life. This informal intercourse that comes by chance is greatly undervalued, especially by Englishmen, who are seldom very much disposed to it except in the humbler classes; but it is one of the broadly scattered, inestimable gifts of Nature, like the refreshment of air and water. Many a healthy and happy mind has enjoyed little other human intercourse than this. There are millions who never get a formal invitation, and yet in this accidental way they hear many a bit of entertaining or instructive talk. The greatest charm of it is its consistency with the most absolute independence. No abandonment of principle is required, nor any false assumption. You stand simply on your elementary right to consideration as a decent human being within the great pale of civilization.

There is, however, another sense in which every superior person is greatly exposed to the evil of solitude if he lives outside of a great capital city.

Without misanthropy, and without any unjust or unkind contempt for our fellow-creatures, we still must perceive that mankind in general have no other purpose than to live in comfort with little mental exertion. The desire for comfort is not wholly selfish, because people want it for their families as much as for themselves, but it is a low motive in this sense, that it is scarcely compatible with the higher kinds of mental exertion, whilst it is entirely incompatible with devotion to great causes. The object of common men is not to do noble work by their own personal efforts, but so to plot and contrive that others may be industrious for their benefit, and not for their highest benefit, but in order that they may have curtains and carpets.

Those for whom accumulated riches have already provided these objects of desire seldom care greatly for anything except amusements. If they have ambition, it is for a higher social rank.

These three common pursuits, comfort, amusements, rank, lie so much outside of the disciplinary studies that a man of studious habits is likely to find himself alone in a peculiar sense. As a human being he is not alone, but as a serious thinker and worker he may find himself in complete solitude.

Many readers will remember the well-known passage in Stuart Mill's autobiography, in which he dealt with this subject. It has often been quoted against him, because he went so far as to say that "a person of high intellect should never go into unintellectual society, unless he can enter it as an apostle," a passage not likely to make its author beloved by society of that kind; yet Mill was not a misanthropist, he was only anxious to preserve what there is of high feeling and high principle from deterioration by too much contact with the common world. It was not so much that he despised the common world, as that he knew the infinite preciousness, even to the common people themselves, of the few better and higher minds. He knew how difficult it is for such minds to "retain their higher principles unimpaired," and how at least "with respect to the persons and affairs of their own day they insensibly adopt the modes of feeling and judgment in which they can hope for sympathy from the company they keep."

Perhaps I may do well to offer an illustration of this, though from a department of culture that may not have been in Mill's view when he wrote the passage.

I myself have known a certain painter (not belonging to the English school) who had a severe and elevated ideal of his art. As his earnings were small he went to live in the country for economy. He then began to associate intimately with people to whom all high aims in painting were unintelligible. Gradually he himself lost his interest in them and his nobler purposes were abandoned. Finally, art itself was abandoned and he became a coffee-house politician.

So it is with all rare and exceptional pursuits if once we allow ourselves to take, in all respects, the color of the common world. It is impossible to keep up a foreign language, an art, a science, if we are living away from other followers of our pursuit and cannot endure solitude.

It follows from this that there are many situations in which men have to learn that particular kind of independence which consists in bearing isolation patiently for the preservation of their better selves. In a world of common-sense they have to keep a little place apart for a kind of sense that is sound and rational but not common.

This isolation would indeed be difficult to bear if it were not mitigated by certain palliatives that enable a superior mind to be healthy and active in its loneliness. The first of these is reading, which is seldom valued at its almost inestimable worth. By the variety of its records and inventions, literature continually affords the refreshment of change, not to speak of that variety which may be had so easily by a change of language when the reader knows several different tongues, and the other marvellous variety due to difference in the date of books. In fact, literature affords a far wider variety than conversation itself, for we can talk only with the living, but literature enables us to descend, like Ulysses, into the shadowy kingdom of the dead. There is but one defect in literature,—that the talk is all on one side, so that we are listeners, as at a sermon or a lecture, and not sharers in some antique symposium, our own brows crowned with flowers, and our own tongues loosened with wine. The exercise of the tongue is wanting, and to some it is an imperious need, so that they will talk to the most uncongenial human beings, or even to parrots and dogs. If we value books as the great palliative of solitude and help to mental independence, let us not undervalue those intelligent periodicals that keep our minds modern and prevent us from living altogether in some other century than our own. Periodicals are a kind of correspondence more easily read than manuscript and involving no obligation to answer. There is also the great palliative of occasional direct correspondence with those who understand our pursuits; and here we have the advantage of using our own tongues, not physically, but at least in an imaginative way.

A powerful support to some minds is the constantly changing beauty of the natural world, which becomes like a great and ever-present companion. I am anxious to avoid any exaggeration of this benefit, because I know that to many it counts for nothing; and an author ought not to think only of those who have his own mental constitution; but although natural beauty is of little use to one solitary mind, it may be like a living friend to another. As a paragraph of real experience is worth pages of speculation, I may say that I have always found it possible to live happily in solitude, provided that the place was surrounded by varied, beautiful, and changeful scenery, but that in ugly or even monotonous places I have felt society to be as necessary as it was welcome. Byron's expression,—

"I made me friends of mountains,"

and Wordsworth's,

"Nature never did betray
The heart that loved her,"

are not more than plain statements of the companionship that *some* minds find in the beauty of landscape. They are often accused of affectation, but in truth I believe that we who have that passion, instead of expressing more than we feel, have generally rather a tendency to be reserved upon the subject, as we seldom expect sympathy. Many of us would rather live in solitude and on small means at Como than on a great income in Manchester. This may be a foolish preference; but let the reader remember the profound utterance of Blake, that if the fool would but persevere in his folly he would become wise.

However powerful may be the aid of books and natural scenery in enabling us to bear solitude, the best help of all must be found in our occupations themselves. Steady workers do not need much company. To be occupied with a task that is difficult and arduous, but that we know to be within our powers, and to awake early every morning with the delightful feeling that the whole day can be given to it without fear of interruption, is the perfection of happiness for one who has the gift of throwing himself heartily into his work. When night comes he will be a little weary, and more disposed for tranquil sleep than to "danser jusqu' au jour chez l'ambassadeur de France."

This is the best independence,—to have something to do and something that can be done, and done most perfectly, in solitude. Then the lonely hours flow on like smoothly gliding water, bearing one insensibly to the evening. The workman says, "Is my sight failing?" and lo the sun has set!

There is but one objection to this absorption in worthy toil. It is that as the day passes so passes life itself, that succession of many days. The workman thinks of nothing but his work, and finds the time all too short. At length he suddenly perceives that he is old, and wonders if life might not have been made to seem a little longer, and if, after all, it has been quite the best policy always to avoid *ennui*.

ESSAY III
OF PASSIONATE LOVE

THE wonder of love is that, for the time being, it makes us ardently desire the presence of one person and feel indifferent to all others of her sex. It is commonly spoken of as a delusion, but I do not see any delusion here, for if the presence of the beloved person satisfies his craving, the lover gets what he desires and is not more the victim of a deception than one who succeeds in satisfying any other want.

Again, it is often said that men are blinded by love, but the fact that one sees certain qualities in a beloved person need not imply blindness. If you are in love with a little woman it is not a reason for supposing her to be tall. I will even venture to affirm that you may love a woman passionately and still be quite clearly aware that her beauty is far inferior to that of another whose coming thrills you with no emotion, whose departure leaves with you no regret.

The true nature of a profound passion is not to attribute every physical and mental quality to its object, but rather to think, "Such as she is, with the endowments that are really her own, I love her above all women, though I know that she is not so beautiful as some are, nor so learned as some others." The only real deception to which a lover is exposed is that he may overestimate the strength of his own passion. If he has not made this mistake he is not likely to make any other, since, whatever the indifferent may see, or fail to see, in the woman of his choice, he surely finds in her the adequate reason for her attraction.

Love is commonly treated as if it belonged only to the flowering of the spring-time of life, but strong and healthy natures remain capable of feeling the passion in great force long after they are supposed to have left it far behind them. It is, indeed, one of the signs of a healthy nature to retain for many years the freshness of the heart which makes one liable to fall in love, as a healthy palate retains the natural early taste for delicious fruits.

This freshness of the heart is lost far more surely by debauchery than by years; and for this reason worldly parents are not altogether dissatisfied that their sons should "sow their wild oats" in youth, as they believe that this kind of sowing is a preservative against the dangers of pure love and an imprudent or unequal marriage. The calculation is well founded. After a few years of indiscriminate debauchery a young man is likely to be deadened to the sweet influences of love and therefore able to conduct himself with steady worldliness, either remaining in celibacy or marrying for position, exactly as his interests may dictate.

The case of Shelley is an apt illustration of this danger. He had at the same time a horror of debauchery and an irresistible natural tendency to the passion of love.

From the worldly point of view both his connections were degrading for a young gentleman of rank. Had he followed the very common course of a *real* degradation and married a lady of rank after ten years of indiscriminate immorality, is it an unjust or an unlikely supposition that he would have given less dissatisfaction to his friends?

As to the permanence of love, or its transitoriness, the plain and candid answer is that there is no real assurance either way. To predict that it will certainly die after fruition is to shut one's eyes against the evident fact that men often remain in love with mistresses or wives. On the other hand, to assume that love is fixed and made permanent in a magical way by marriage is to assume what would be desirable rather than what really is. There are no magical incantations by which Love may be retained, yet sometimes he will rest and dwell with astonishing tenacity when there seem to be the strongest reasons for his departure. If there were any ceremony, if any sacrifice could be made at an altar, by which the capricious little deity might be conciliated and won, the wisest might hasten to perform that ceremony and offer that acceptable sacrifice; but he cares not for any of our rites. Sometimes he stays, in spite of cruelty, misery, and wrong; sometimes he takes flight from the hearth where a woman sits and grieves alone, with all the attractions of health, beauty, gentleness, and refinement.

Boys and girls imagine that love in a poor cottage or a bare garret would be more blissful than indifference in a palace, and the notion is thought foolish and romantic by the wise people of the world; but the boys and girls are right in their estimate of Love's great power of cheering and brightening existence even in the very humblest situations. The possible error against which they ought to be clearly warned is that of supposing that Love would always remain contentedly in the cottage or the garret. Not that he is any more certain to remain in a mansion in Belgrave Square, not that a garret with him is not better than the vast Vatican without him; but when he has taken his flight, and is simply absent, one would rather be left in comfortable than in beggarly desolation.

The poets speak habitually of love as if it were a passion that could be safely indulged, whereas the whole experience of modern existence goes to show that it is of all passions the most perilous to happiness except in those rare cases where it can be followed by marriage; and even then the peril is not ended, for marriage gives no certainty of the duration of love, but constitutes of itself a new danger, as the natures most disposed to passion are at the same time the most impatient of restraint.

There is this peculiarity about love in a well-regulated social state. It is the only passion that is quite strictly limited in its indulgence. Of the intellectual passions a man may indulge several different ones either successively or together; in the ordinary physical enjoyments, such as the love of active sports or the pleasures of the table, he may carry his indulgence very far and vary it without blame; but the master passion of all has to be continually quelled, the satisfactions that it asks for have to be continually refused to it, unless some opportunity occurs when they may be granted without disturbing any one of many different threads in the web of social existence; and these threads, to a lover's eye, seem entirely unconnected with his hope.

In stating the fact of these restraints I do not dispute their necessity. On the contrary, it is evident that infinite practical evil would result from liberty. Those who have broken through the social restraints and allowed the passion of love to set up its stormy and variable tyranny in their hearts have led unsettled and unhappy lives. Even of love itself they have not enjoyed the best except in those rare cases in which the lovers have taken bonds upon themselves not less durable than those of marriage; and even these unions, which give no more liberty than marriage itself gives, are accompanied by the unsettled feeling that belongs to all irregular situations.

It is easy to distinguish in the conventional manner between the lower and the higher kinds of love, but it is not so easy to establish the real distinction. The conventional difference is simply between the passion in marriage and out of it; the real distinction would be between different feelings; but as these feelings are not ascertainable by one person in the mind or nerves of another, and as in most cases they are probably much blended, the distinction can seldom be accurately made in the cases of real persons, though it is marked trenchantly enough in works of pure imagination.

The passion exists in an infinite variety, and it is so strongly influenced by elements of character which have apparently nothing to do with it, that its effects on conduct are to a great extent controlled by them. For example, suppose the case of a man with strong passions combined with a selfish nature, and that of another with passions equally strong, but a rooted aversion to all personal satisfactions that might end in misery for others. The first would ruin a girl with little hesitation; the second would rather suffer the entire privation of her society by quitting the neighborhood where she lived.

The interference of qualities that lie outside of passion is shown very curiously and remarkably in intellectual persons in this way. They may have a strong temporary passion for somebody without intellect or culture, but they are not likely to be held permanently by such a person; and even when under the influence of the temporary desire they may be clearly aware of the danger there would be in converting it into a permanent relation, and so they may take counsel with themselves and subdue the passion or fly from the temptation, knowing that it would be sweet to yield, but that a transient delight would be paid for by years of weariness in the future.

Those men of superior abilities who have bound themselves for life to some woman who could not possibly understand them, have generally either broken their bonds afterwards or else avoided as much as possible the tiresomeness of a *tête-à-tête*, and found in general society the means of occasionally enduring the ranquil of their home. For short and transient relations the principal charm in a woman is either beauty or a certain sweetness, but for any permanent relation the first necessity of all is that she be companionable.

Passionate love is the principal subject of poets and novelists, who usually avoid its greatest difficulties by well-known means of escape. Either the passion finishes tragically by the death of one of the parties, or else it comes to a natural culmination in their union, whether according to social order or through a breach of it. In real life the story is not always rounded off so conveniently. It may happen, it probably often does happen, that a passion establishes itself where it has no possible chance of satisfaction, and where, instead of being cut short by death, it persists through a considerable part of life and embitters it. These cases are the more unfortunate that hopeless desire gives an imaginary glory to its own object, and that, from the circumstances of the case, this halo is not dissipated.

It is common amongst hard and narrow people, who judge the feelings of others by their own want of them, to treat all the painful side of passion with contemptuous levity. They say that people never die for love, and that such fancies may easily be chased away by the exercise of a little resolution. The profounder students of human nature take the subject more seriously. Each of the great poets (including, of course, the author of the "Bride of Lammermoor," in which the poetical elements are so abundant) has treated the aching pain of love and the tragedy to which it may lead, as in the deaths of Haidée, of Lucy Ashton, of Juliet, of Margaret. In real life the powers of evil do not perceive any necessity for an artistic conclusion of their work. A wrinkled old maid may still preserve in the depths of her own heart, quite unsuspected by the young and lively people about her, the unextinguished embers of a passion that first made her wretched fifty years before; and in the long, solitary hours of a dull old age she may live over and over again in memory the brief delirium of that wild and foolish hope which was followed by years of self-repression.

Of all the painful situations occasioned by passionate love, I know of none more lamentable than that of an innocent and honorable woman who has been married to an unsuitable husband and who afterwards makes the discovery that she involuntarily loves another. In well-regulated, moral societies such passions are repressed, but they cannot be repressed without suffering which has to be endured in silence. The victim is punished for no fault when none is committed; but she may suffer from the forces of nature like one who hungers and thirsts and sees a fair banquet provided, yet is forbidden to eat or drink. It is difficult to suppress the heart's regret, "Ah, if we had known each other earlier, in the days when I was free, and it was not wrong to love!" Then there is the haunting fear that the woful secret may one day reveal itself to others. Might it not be suddenly and unexpectedly betrayed by a momentary absence of self-control? This has sometimes happened, and then there is no safety but in separation, immediate and decided. Suppose a case like the following, which is said to have really occurred. A perfectly honorable man goes to visit an intimate friend, walks quietly in the garden one afternoon with his friend's wife, and suddenly discovers that he is the object of a passion which, until that moment, she has steadily controlled. One outburst of shameful tears, one pitiful confession of a life's unhappiness, and they part forever! This is what happens when the friend respects his friend and the wife her husband. What happens when both are capable of treachery is known to the readers of English newspaper reports and French fictions.

It seems as if, with regard to this passion, civilized man were placed in a false position between Nature on the one hand and civilization on the other. Nature makes us capable of feeling it in very great strength and intensity, at an age when marriage is not to be thought of, and when there is not much self-control. The tendency of high civilization is to retard the time of marriage for men, but there is not any corresponding postponement in the awakening of the passions. The least civilized classes marry early, the more civilized later and later, and not often from passionate love, but from a cool and prudent calculation about general chances of happiness, a calculation embracing very various elements, and in itself as remote from passion as the Proverbs of Solomon from the Song of Songs. It consequently happens that the great majority of young gentlemen discover early in life that passionate love is a danger to be avoided, and so indeed it is; but it seems a peculiar misfortune for civilized man that so natural an excitement, which is capable of giving such a glow to all his faculties as nothing else can give, an excitement which exalts the imagination to poetry and increases courage till it becomes heroic devotion, whilst it gives a glamour of romance to the poorest and most prosaic existence,—it seems, I say, a misfortune that a passion with such unequalled powers as these should have to be eliminated from wise and prudent life. The explanation of its early and inconvenient appearance may be that before the human race had attained a position of any ranquility or comfort, the average life was very short, and it was of the utmost importance that the flame of existence should be passed on to another generation without delay. We inherit the rapid development which saved the race in its perilous past, but we are embarrassed by it, and instead of elevating us to a more exalted life it often avenges itself for the refusal of natural activity by its own corruption, the corruption of the best into the worst, of the fire from heaven into the filth of immorality. The more this great passion is repressed and expelled, the more frequent does immorality become.

Another very remarkable result of the exclusion of passionate love from ordinary existence is that the idea of it takes possession of the imagination. The most melodious poetry, the most absorbing fiction, are alike celebrations of its mysteries. Even the wordless voice of music wails or languishes for love, and the audience that seems only to hear flutes and violins is in reality listening to that endless song of love which thrills through the passionate universe. Well may the rebels against Nature revolt against the influence of Art! It is everywhere permeated by passion. The cold marble warms with it, the opaque pigments palpitate with it, the dull actor has the tones of genius when he wins access to its perennial inspiration. Even those forms of art which seem remote from it do yet confess its presence. You see a picture of solitude, and think that passion cannot enter there, but everything suggests it. The tree bends down to the calm water, the gentle breeze caresses every leaf, the white-pated old mountain is visited by the short-lived summer clouds. If, in the opening glade, the artist has sketched a pair of lovers, you think they naturally complete the scene; if he has omitted them, it is still a place for lovers, or has been, or will be on some sweet eve like this. What have stars and winds and odors to do with love? The poets know all about it, and so let Shelley tell us:—

"I arise from dreams of Thee
In the first sweet sleep of night,
When the winds are breathing low
And the stars are shining bright:
I arise from dreams of thee,
And a spirit in my feet
Has led me—who knows how?—
To thy chamber-window, Sweet!
The wandering airs they faint
On the dark, the silent stream;
The champak odors fail
Like sweet thoughts in a dream;
The nightingale's complaint
It dies upon her heart,
As I must die on thine
O belovèd as thou art!"

ESSAY IV
COMPANIONSHIP IN MARRIAGE

IF the reader has ever had for a travelling-companion some person totally unsuited to his nature and quite unable to enter into the ideas that chiefly interest him, unable, even, to *see* the things that he sees and always disposed to treat negligently or contemptuously the thoughts and preferences that are most his own, he may have some faint conception of what it must be to find one's self tied to an unsuitable companion for the tedious journey of this mortal life; and if, on the other hand, he has ever enjoyed the pleasure of wandering through a country that interested him along with a friend who could understand his interest, and share it, and whose society enhanced the charm of every prospect and banished dulness from the dreariest inns, he may in some poor and imperfect degree realize the happiness of those who have chosen the life-companion wisely.

When, after an experiment of months or years, the truth becomes plainly evident that a great mistake has been committed, that there is really no companionship, that there never will be, never can be, any mental communion between the two, but that life in common is to be like a stiff morning call when the giver and the receiver of the visit are beating their brains to find something to say, and dread the gaps of silence, then in the blank and dreary outlook comes the idea of separation, and sometimes, in the loneliness that follows, a wild rebellion against social order, and a reckless attempt to find in some more suitable union a compensation for the first sad failure.

The world looks with more indulgence on these attempts when it sees reason to believe that the desire was for intellectual companionship than when inconstant passions are presumed to have been the motives; and it has so happened that a few persons of great eminence have set an example in this respect which has had the unfortunate effect of weakening in a perceptible degree the ancient social order. It is not possible, of course, that there can be many cases like that of George Eliot and Lewes, for the simple reason that persons of their eminence are so rare; but if there were only a few more cases of that kind it is evident that the laws of society would either be confessedly powerless, or else it would be necessary to modify them and bring them into harmony with new conditions. The importance of the case alluded to lies in the fact that the lady, though she was excluded (or willingly excluded herself) from general society, was still respected and visited not only by men but by ladies of blameless life. Nor was she generally regarded as an immoral person even by the outer world. The feeling about her was one of regret that the faithful companionship she gave to Lewes could not be legally called a marriage, as it was apparently a model of what the legal relation ought to be. The object of his existence was to give her every kind of help and to spare her every shadow of annoyance. He read to her, wrote letters for her, advised her on everything, and whilst full of admiration for her talents was able to do something for their most effectual employment. She, on her part, rewarded him with that which he prized above riches, the frank and affectionate companionship of an intellect that it is needless to describe and of a heart full of the most lively sympathy and ready for the most romantic sacrifices.

In the preceding generation we have the well-known instances of Shelley, Byron, and Goethe, all of whom sought companionship outside of social rule, and enjoyed a sort of happiness probably not unembittered by the false position in which it placed them. The sad story of Shelley's first marriage, that with Harriett Westbrook, is one of the best instances of a deplorable but most natural mistake. She is said to have been a charming person in many ways. "Harriett," says Mr. Rossetti, "was not only delightful to look at but altogether most agreeable. She dressed with exquisite neatness and propriety; her voice was pleasant and her speech cordial; her spirits were cheerful and her manners good. She was well educated, a constant and agreeable reader; adequately accomplished in music." But in spite of these qualities and talents, and even of Harriett's willingness to learn, Shelley did not find her to be companionable for him; and he unfortunately did discover that another young lady, Mary Godwin, was companionable in the supreme degree. That this latter idea was not illusory is proved by his happy life afterwards with Mary so far as a life could be happy that was poisoned by a tragic recollection.[3] Before that miserable ending, before the waters of the Serpentine had closed over the wretched existence of Harriett, Shelley said, "Every one who knows me must know that the partner of my life should be one who can feel poetry and understand philosophy. Harriett is a noble animal, but she can do neither." Here we have a plain statement of that great need for companionship which was a part of Shelley's nature. It is often connected with its apparent opposite, the love of solitude. Shelley was a lover of solitude, which means that he liked full and adequate human intercourse so much that the insufficient imitation of it was intolerable to him. Even that sweetest solitude of all, when he wrote the "Revolt of Islam" in summer shades, to the sound of rippling waters, was willingly exchanged for the society of the one dearest and best companion:—

"So now my summer-task is ended, Mary,
And I return to thee, mine own heart's home;
As to his Queen some victor Knight of Faëry,
Earning bright spoils for her enchanted dome.
Nor thou disdain that, ere my fame become
A star among the stars of mortal night
(If it indeed may cleave its native gloom),
Its doubtful promise thus I would unite
With thy beloved name, thou child of love and light.

"The toil which stole from thee so many an hour
Is ended, and the fruit is at thy feet.
No longer where the woods to frame a bower
With interlaced branches mix and meet,
Or where, with sound like many voices sweet,
Waterfalls leap among wild islands green
Which framed for my lone boat a lone retreat
Of moss-grown trees and weeds, shall I be seen:
But beside thee, where still my heart has ever been."

It is not surprising that the companionship of conjugal life should be like other friendships in this, that a first experiment may be a failure and a later experiment a success. We are all so fallible that in matters of which we have no experience we generally commit great blunders. Marriage unites all the conditions that make a blunder probable. Two young people, with very little conception of what an unsurmountable barrier a difference of idiosyncrasy may be, are pleased with each other's youth, health, natural gayety, and good looks, and fancy that it would be delightful to live together. They marry, and in many cases discover that somehow, in spite of the most meritorious efforts, they are not companions. There is no fault on either side; they try their best, but the invisible demon, incompatibility, is too strong for them.

From all that we know of the characters of Lord and Lady Byron it seems evident that they never were likely to enjoy life together. He committed the mistake of marrying a lady on the strength of her excellent reputation. "She has talents and excellent qualities," he said before marriage; as if all the arts and sciences and all the virtues put together could avail without the one quality that is *never* admired, *never* understood by others,—that of simple suitableness. She was "a kind of pattern in the North," and he "heard of nothing but her merits and her wonders." He did not see that all these excellencies were dangers, that the consciousness of them and the reputation for them would set the lady up on a judgment seat of her own, from which she would be continually observing the errors, serious or trivial, of that faulty specimen of the male sex that it was her lofty mission to correct or to condemn. All this he found out in due time and expressed in the bitter lines,—

> "Oh! she was perfect past all parallel
> Of any modern female saint's comparison
> ......
> Perfect she was."

The story of his subsequent life is too well known to need repetition here. All that concerns our present subject is that ultimately, in the Countess Guiccioli, he found the woman who had, for him, that one quality, suitableness, which outweighs all the perfections. She did not read English, but, though ignorant alike of the splendor and the tenderness of his verse, she knew the nature of the man; and he enjoyed in her society, probably for the first time in his life, the most exquisite pleasure the masculine mind can ever know, that of being looked upon by a feminine intelligence with clear sight and devoted affection at the same time. The relation that existed between Byron and the Countess Guiccioli is one outside of our morality, a revenge of Nature against a marriage system that could take a girl not yet sixteen and make her the third wife of a man more than old enough to be her grandfather. In Italy this revenge of Nature against a bad social system is accepted, within limits, and is an all but inevitable consequence of marriages like that of Count Guiccioli, which, however they may be approved by custom and consecrated by religious ceremonies, remain, nevertheless, amongst the worst (because the most unnatural) immoralities. All that need be said in his young wife's defence is that she followed the only rule habitually acted upon by mankind, the custom of her country and her class, and that she acted, from beginning to end, with the most absolute personal abnegation. On Byron her influence was wholly beneficial. She raised him from a mode of life that was deplored by all his true friends, to the nearest imitation of a happy marriage that was accessible to him; but the irregularity of their position brought upon them the usual Nemesis, and after a broken intercourse, during which he never could feel her to be really his own, he went to Missolonghi and wrote, under the shadow of Death,—

> "The hope, the fear, the jealous care,
> The exalted portion of the pain
> And power of love, I cannot share,
> But wear the chain."

The difference between Byron and Goethe in regard to feminine companionship lies chiefly in this,—that whilst Byron does not seem to have been very susceptible of romantic love (though he was often entangled in *liaisons* more or less degrading), Goethe was constantly in love and imaginative in his passions, as might be expected from a poet. He appears to have encouraged himself in amorous fancies till they became almost or quite realities, as if to give himself that experience of various feeling out of which he afterwards created poems. He was himself clearly conscious that his poetry was a transformation of real experiences into artistic forms. The knowledge that he came by his poetry in this way would naturally lead him to encourage rather than stifle the sentiments which gave him his best materials. It is quite within the comprehensive powers of a complex nature that a poet might lead a dual life; being at the same time a man, ardent, very susceptible of all passionate emotions, and a poet, observing this passionate life and accumulating its results. In all this there is very little of what occupies us just now, the search for a satisfactory companionship. The woman with whom he most enjoyed that was the Baroness von Stein, but even this friendship was not ultimately satisfying and had not a permanent character. It lasted ten or eleven years, till his return from the Italian journey, when "she thought him cold, and her resource was—reproaches. The resource was more feminine than felicitous. Instead of sympathizing with him in his sorrow at leaving Italy, she felt the regret as an offence; and perhaps it was; but a truer, nobler nature would surely have known how to merge its own pain in sympathy with the pain of one beloved. He regretted Italy; she was not a compensation to him; she saw this, and her self-love suffered."[4] And so it ended. "He offered friendship in vain; he had wounded the self-love of a vain woman." Goethe's longest connection was with Christiane Vulpius, a woman quite unequal to him in station and culture, and in that respect immeasurably inferior to the Baroness von Stein, but superior to her in the power of affection, and able to charm and retain the poet by her lively, pleasant disposition and her perfect constancy. Gradually she rose in his esteem, and every year increased her influence over him. From the precarious position of a mistress out of his house she first attained that of a wife in all but the legal title, as he received her under his roof in defiance of all the good society of Weimar; and lastly she became his lawful wife, to the still greater scandal of the polite world. It may even be said that her promotion did not end here, for the final test of love is death; and when Christiane died she left behind her the deep and lasting sorrow that is happiness still to those who feel it, though happiness in its saddest form.

The misfortune of Goethe appears to have been that he dreaded and avoided marriage in early life, perhaps because he was instinctively aware of his own tendency to form many attachments of limited duration; but his treatment of Christiane Vulpius, so much beyond any obligations which, according to the world's code, he had incurred, is sufficient proof that there was a power of constancy in his nature; and if he had married early and suitably it is possible that this constancy might have stayed and steadied him from the beginning. It is easy to imagine that a marriage with a cultivated woman of his own class would have given him, in course of time, by mutual adaptation, a much more complete companionship than either of those semi-associations with the Frau von Stein and Christiane, each of which only included a part of his great nature. Christiane, however, had the better part, his heartfelt affection.

The case of John Stuart Mill and the remarkable woman by whose side he lies buried at Avignon, is the most perfect instance of thorough companionship on record; and it is remarkable especially because men of great intellectual power, whose ways of thinking are quite independent of custom, and whose knowledge is so far outside the average as to carry their thoughts continually beyond the common horizon, have an extreme difficulty in associating themselves with women, who are naturally attached to custom, and great lovers of what is settled, fixed, limited, and clear. The ordinary disposition of women is to respect what is authorized much more than what is original, and they willingly, in the things of the mind, bow before anything that is repeated with circumstances of authority. An isolated philosopher has no costume or surroundings to entitle him to this kind of respect. He wears no vestment, he is not magnified by any architecture, he is not supported by superiors or deferred to by subordinates. He stands simply on his abilities, his learning, and his honesty. There is, however, this one chance in his favor, that a certain natural sympathy may possibly exist between him and some woman on the earth,—if he could only find her,—and this woman would make him independent of all the rest. It was Stuart Mill's rare good-fortune to find this one woman, early in life, in the person of Mrs. Taylor; and as his nature was intellectual and affectionate rather than passionate, he was able to rest contented with simple friendship for a period of twenty years. Indeed this friendship itself, considered only as such, was of very gradual growth. "To be admitted," he wrote, "into any degree of mental intercourse with a being of these qualities, could not but have a most beneficial influence on my development; though the effect was only gradual, and many years elapsed before her mental progress and mine went forward in the complete companionship they at last attained.

The benefit I received was far greater than any I could hope to give.... What I owe, even intellectually, to her, is in its detail almost infinite."

Mill speaks of his marriage, in 1851 (I use his words), to the lady whose incomparable worth had made her friendship the greatest source to him both of happiness and of improvement during many years in which they never expected to be in any closer relation to one another. "For seven and a half years," he goes on to say, "that blessing was mine; for seven and a half only! I can say nothing which could describe, even in the faintest manner, what that loss was and is. But because I know that she would have wished it, I endeavor to make the best of what life I have left and to work on for her purposes with such diminished strength as can be derived from thoughts of her and communion with her memory.... Since then I have sought for such alleviation as my state admitted of, by the mode of life which most enabled me to feel her still near me. I bought a cottage as close as possible to the place where she is buried, and there her daughter (my fellow-sufferer and now my chief comfort) and I live constantly during a great portion of the year. My objects in life are solely those which were hers; my pursuits and occupations those in which she shared, or sympathized, and which are indissolubly associated with her. Her memory is to me a religion, and her approbation the standard by which, summing up as it does all worthiness, I endeavor to regulate my life."

The examples that I have selected (all purposely from the real life of well-known persons) are not altogether encouraging. They show the difficulty that there is in finding the true companion. George Eliot found hers at the cost of a rebellion against social order to which, with her regulated mind and conservative instincts, she must have been by nature little disposed. Shelley succeeded only after a failure and whilst the failure still had rights over his entire existence. His life was like one of those pictures in which there is a second work over a first, and the painter supposes the first to be entirely concealed, which indeed it is for a little time, but it reappears afterwards and spoils the whole. Nothing could be more unsatisfactory than the domestic arrangements of Byron. He married a lady from a belief in her learning and virtue, only to find that learning and virtue were hard stones in comparison with the daily bread of sympathy. Then, after a vain waste of years in error, he found true love at last, but on terms which involved too heavy sacrifices from her who gave it, and procured him no comfort, no peace, if indeed his nature was capable of any restfulness in love. Goethe, after a number of attachments that ended in nothing, gave himself to one woman by his intelligence and to another by his affections, not belonging with his whole nature to either, and never in his long life knowing what it is to have equal companionship in one's own house. Stuart Mill is contented, for twenty years, to be the esteemed friend of a lady married to another, without hope of any closer relation; and when his death permits them to think of marriage, they have only seven years and a half before them, and he is forty-five years old.

Cases of this kind would be discouraging in the extreme degree, were it not that the difficulty is exceptional. High intellect is in itself a peculiarity, in a certain sense it is really an eccentricity, even when so thoroughly sane and rational as in the cases of George Eliot, Goethe, and Mill. It is an eccentricity in this sense, that its mental centre does not coincide with that of ordinary people. The mental centre of ordinary people is simply the public opinion, the common sense, of the class and locality in which they live, so that, to them, the common sense of people in another class, another locality, appears irrational or absurd. The mental centre of a superior person is not that of class and locality. Shelley did not belong to the English aristocracy, though he was born in it; his mind did not centre itself in aristocratic ideas. George Eliot did not belong to the middle class of the English midlands, nor Stuart Mill to the London middle classes. So far as Byron belonged to the aristocracy it was a mark of inferiority in him, owing to a touch of vulgarity in his nature, the same vulgarity which made him believe that he could not be a proper sort of lord without a prodigal waste of money. Yet even Byron was not centred in local ideas; that which was best in him, his enthusiasm for Greece, was not an essential part of Nottinghamshire common sense. Goethe lived much more in one locality, and even in a small place; but if anything is remarkable in him it is his complete independence of Weimar ideas. It was the Duke, his friend and master, not the public opinion of Weimar, that allowed Goethe to be himself. He refused even to be classed intellectually, and did not recognize the vulgar opinion that a poet cannot be scientific. In all these cases the mental centre was not in any local common sense. It was a result of personal studies and observations acting upon an individual idiosyncrasy.

We may now perceive how infinitely easier it is for ordinary people to meet and be companionable than for these rare and superior minds. Ordinary people, if bred in the same neighborhood and class, are sure to have a great fund of ideas in common, all those ideas that constitute the local common sense. If you listen attentively to their conversations you will find that they hardly ever go outside of that. They mention incidents and actions, and test them one after another by a tacit reference to the public opinion of the place. Therefore they have a good chance of agreeing, of considering each other reasonable; and this is why it is a generally received opinion that marriages between people of the same locality and the same class offer the greatest probability of happiness. So they do, in ordinary cases, but if there is the least touch of any original talent or genius in one of the parties, it is sure to result in many ideas that will be outside of any local common sense, and then the other party, living in that sense, will consider those ideas peculiar, and perhaps deplorable. Here, then, are elements of dissension lying quite ready like explosive materials, and the merest accident may shatter in a moment the whole fabric of affection. To prevent such an accident an artificial kind of intercourse is adopted which is not real companionship, or anything resembling it.

The reader may imagine, and has probably observed in real life, a marriage in which the husband is a man of original power, able to think forcibly and profoundly, and the wife a gentle being quite unable to enter into any thought of that quality. In cases of that kind the husband may be affectionate and even tender, but he is careful to utter nothing beyond the safest commonplaces. In the presence of his wife he keeps his mind quite within the circle of custom. He has, indeed, no other resource. Custom and commonplace are the protection of the intelligent against misapprehension and disapproval.

Marriages of this unequal kind are an imitation of those equal marriages in which both parties live in the local common sense; but there is this vast difference between them, that in the imitation the more intelligent of the two parties has to stifle half his nature. An intelligent man has to make up his mind in early life whether he has courage enough for such a sacrifice or not. Let him try the experiment of associating for a short time with people who cannot understand him, and if he likes the feeling of repression that results from it, if he is able to stop short always at the right moment, if he can put his knowledge on the shelf as one puts a book in a library, then perhaps he may safely undertake the long labor of companionship with an unsuitable wife.

This is sometimes done in pure hopelessness of ever finding a true mate. A man has no belief in any real companionship, and therefore simply conforms to custom in his marriage, as Montaigne did, allying himself with some young lady who is considered in the neighborhood to be a suitable match for him. This is the *mariage de convenance*. Its purposes are intelligible and attainable. It may add considerably to the dignity and convenience of life and to that particular kind of happiness which results from satisfaction with our own worldly prudence. There is also the probability that by perfect courtesy, by a scrupulous observance of the rules of intercourse between highly civilized persons who are not extremely intimate, the parties who contract a marriage of this kind may give each other the mild satisfactions that are the reward of the well-bred. There is a certain pleasure in watching every movement of an accomplished lady, and if she is your wife there may also be a certain pride. She receives your guests well; she holds her place with perfect self-possession at your table and in her drawing-room; she never commits a social solecism; and you feel that you can trust her absolutely. Her private income is a help in the maintenance of your establishment and so increases your credit in the world. She gives you in this way a series of satisfactions that may even, in course of time, produce rather affectionate feelings. If she died you would certainly regret her loss, and think that life was, on the whole, decidedly less agreeable without her.

But alas for the dreams of youth if this is all that is to be gained by marriage! Where is the sweet friend and companion who was to have accompanied us through prosperous or adverse years, who was to have charmed and consoled us, who was to have given us the infinite happiness of being understood and loved at the same time? Were all those dreams delusions? Is the best companionship a mere fiction of the fancy, not existing anywhere upon the earth?

I believe in the promises of Nature. I believe that in every want there is the promise of a possible satisfaction. If we are hungry there is food somewhere, if we are thirsty there is drink. But in the things of the world there is often an indication of order rather than a realization of it, so that in the confusion of accidents the hungry man may be starving in a beleaguered city and the thirsty man parched in the Sahara. All that the wants indicate is that their satisfaction is possible in nature. Let us believe that, for every one, the true mate exists somewhere in the world. She is worth seeking for at any cost of trouble or expense, worth travelling round the globe to find, worth the endurance of labor and pain and privation. Men suffer all this for objects of far inferior importance; they risk life for the chance of a ribbon, and sacrifice leisure and peace for the smallest increase of social position. What are these vanities in comparison with the priceless benefit, the continual blessing, of having with you always the one person whose presence can deliver you from all the evils of solitude without imposing the constraints and hypocrisies of society? With her you are free to be as much yourself as when alone; you say what you think and she understands you. Your silence does not offend her; she only thinks that there will be time enough to talk together afterwards. You know that you can trust her love, which is as unfailing as a law of nature. The differences of idiosyncrasy that exist between you only add interest to your intercourse by preventing her from becoming a mere echo of yourself. She has her own ways, her own thoughts that are not yours and yet are all open to you, so that you no longer dwell in one intellect only but have constant access to a second intellect, probably more refined and elegant, richer in what is delicate and beautiful. There you make unexpected discoveries; you find that the first instinctive preference is more than justified by merits that you had not divined. You had hoped and trusted vaguely that there were certain qualities; but as a painter who looks long at a natural scene is constantly discovering new beauties whilst he is painting it, so the long and loving observation of a beautiful human mind reveals a thousand unexpected excellences. Then come the trials of life, the sudden calamities, the long and wearing anxieties. Each of these will only reveal more clearly the wonderful endurance, fidelity, and fortitude that there is in every noble feminine nature, and so build up on the foundation of your early love an unshakable edifice of esteem and respect and love commingled, for which in our modern tongue we have no single term, but which our forefathers called "worship."

ESSAY V
FAMILY TIES

ONE of the most remarkable differences between the English and some of the Continental nations is the comparative looseness of family ties in England. The apparent difference is certainly very great; the real difference is possibly not so great. It may be that a good deal of that warm family affection which we are constantly hearing of in France is only make-believe, but the keeping-up of a make-believe is often favorable to the reality. In England a great deal of religion is mere outward form; but to be surrounded by the constant observance of outward form is a great practical convenience to the genuine religious sentiment where it exists.

In boyhood we suppose that all gentlemen of mature age who happen to be brothers must naturally have fraternal feelings; in mature life we know the truth, having discovered that there are many brothers between whom no sentiment of fraternity exists. A foreigner who knows England well, and has observed it more carefully than we ourselves do, remarked to me that the fraternal relationship is not generally a cause of attachment in England, though there may be cases of exceptional affection. It certainly often happens that brothers live contentedly apart and do not seem to feel the need of intercourse, or that such intercourse as they have has no appearance of cordiality. A very common cause of estrangement is a natural difference of class. One man is so constituted as to feel more at ease in a higher class, and he rises; his brother feels more at ease in a lower class, adopts its manners, and sinks. After a few years have passed the two will have acquired such different habits, both of thinking and living, that they will be disqualified for equal intercourse. If one brother is a gentleman in tastes and manners and the other not a gentleman, the vulgarity of the coarser nature will be all the more offensive to the refined one that there is the troublesome consciousness of a very near relationship and of a sort of indefinite responsibility.

The frequency of coolness between brothers surprises us less when we observe how widely they may differ from each other in mental and physical constitution. One may be a sportsman, traveller, man of the world; another a religious recluse. One may have a sensitive, imaginative nature and be keenly alive to the influences of literature, painting, and music; his brother may be a hard, practical man of business, with a conviction that an interest in literary and artistic pursuits is only a sign of weakness.

The extreme uncertainty that always exists about what really constitutes suitableness is seen as much between brothers as between other men; for we sometimes see a beautiful fraternal affection between brothers who seem to have nothing whatever in common, and sometimes an equal affection appears to be founded upon likeness.

Jealousy in its various forms is especially likely to arise between brothers, and between sisters also for the same reason, which is that comparisons are constantly suggested and even made with injudicious openness by parents and teachers, and by talkative friends. The development of the faculties in youth is always extremely interesting, and is a constant subject of observation and speculation. If it is interesting to on-lookers, it is still more likely to be so to the young persons most concerned. They feel as young race-horses might be expected to feel towards each other if they could understand the conversations of trainers, stud-owners, and grooms.

If a full account of family life could be generally accessible, if we could read autobiographies written by the several members of the same family, giving a sincere and independent account of their own youth, it would probably be found in most cases that jealousies were easily discoverable. They need not be very intense to create a slight fissure of separation that may be slowly widened afterwards.

If you listen attentively to the conversation of brothers about brothers, of sisters about sisters, you will probably detect such little jealousies without difficulty. "My sister," said a lady in my hearing, "was very much admired when she was young, *but she aged prematurely.*" Behind this it was easy to read the comparison with self, with a constitution less attractive to others but more robust and durable, and there was a faint reverberation of girlish jealousy about attentions paid forty years before.

The jealousies of youth are too natural to deserve any serious blame, but they may be a beginning of future coolness. A boy will seem to praise the talents of his brother with the purpose of implying that the facilities given by such talents make industry almost superfluous, whilst his own more strenuous efforts are not appreciated as they deserve. Instead of soothing and calming these natural jealousies some parents irritate and inflame them. They make wounding remarks that produce evil in after years. I have seen a sensitive boy wince under cutting sarcasms that he will remember till his hair is gray.

If there are fraternal jealousies in boyhood, when the material comforts and the outward show of existence are the same for brothers, much more are these jealousies likely to be accentuated in after-life, when differences of worldly success, or of inherited fortune, establish distinctions so obvious as to be visible to all. The operation of the aristocratic custom by which eldest sons are made very much richer than their brethren can scarcely be in favor of fraternal intimacy. No general rule can be established, because characters differ so widely. An eldest brother *may* be so amiable, so truly fraternal, that the cadets instead of feeling envy of his wealth may take a positive pride in it; still, the natural effect of creating such a vast inequality is to separate the favored heir from the less-favored younger sons. I leave the reader to think over instances that may be known to him. Amongst those known to me I find several cases of complete or partial suspension of intercourse and others of manifest indifference and coolness. One incident recurs to my memory after a lapse of thirty years. I was present at the departure of a young friend for India when his eldest brother was too indifferent to get up a little earlier to see him off, and said, "Oh, you're going, are you? Well, good-by, John!" through his bedroom door. The lad carried a wound in his heart to the distant East.

There is nothing in the mere fact of fraternity to establish friendship. The line of "In Memoriam," —

"More than my brothers are to me,"

is simply true of every real friend, unless friendship adds itself to brotherhood, in which case the intimacy arising from a thousand details of early life in common, from the thorough knowledge of the same persons and places, and from the memories of parental affection, must give a rare completeness to friendship itself and make it in these respects even superior to marriage, which has the great defect that the associations of early life are not the same. I remember a case of wonderfully strong affection between two brothers who were daily companions till death separated them; but they were younger sons and their incomes were exactly alike; their tastes, too, and all their habits were the same. The only other case that occurs to me as comparable to this one was also of two younger sons, one of whom had an extraordinary talent for business. They were partners in trade, and no dissension ever arose between them, because the superiority of the specially able man was affectionately recognized and deferred to by the other. If, however, they had not been partners it is possible that the brilliant success of one brother might have created a contrast and made intercourse more constrained.

The case of John Bright and his brother may be mentioned, as he has made it public in one of his most charming and interesting speeches. His political work has prevented him from laboring in his business, but his brother and partner has affectionately considered him an active member of the firm, so that Mr. Bright has enjoyed an income sufficient for his political independence. In this instance the comparatively obscure brother has shown real nobility of nature. Free from the jealousy and envy which would have vexed a small mind in such a position he has taken pleasure in the fame of the statesman. It is easy to imagine the view that a mean mind would have taken of a similar situation. Let us add that the statesman himself has shown true fraternal generosity of another kind, and perhaps of a more difficult kind, for it is often easier to confer an obligation than to accept it heartily.

It has often been a subject of astonishment to me that between very near relations a sensitive feeling about pecuniary matters should be so lively as it is. I remember an instance in the last generation of a rich man in Cheshire who made a present of ten thousand pounds to a lady nearly related to him. He was very wealthy, she was not; the sum would never be missed by him, whilst to her it made a great difference. What could be more reasonable than such a correction of the inequalities of fortune? Many people would have refused the present, out of pride, but it was much kinder to accept it in the same good spirit that dictated the offer. On the other hand, there are poor gentlefolks whose only fault is a sense of independence, so *farouche* that nobody can get them to accept anything of importance, and any good that is done to them has to be plotted with consummate art.

A wonderful light is thrown upon family relations when we become acquainted with the real state of those family pecuniary transactions that are not revealed to the public. The strangest discovery is the widely different ways in which pecuniary obligations are estimated by different persons, especially by different women. Men, I believe, take them rather more equally; but as women go by sentiment they have a tendency to extremes, either exaggerating the importance of an obligation when they like to feel very much obliged, or else adopting the convenient theory that the generous person is fulfilling a simple duty, and that there is no obligation whatever. One woman will go into ecstasies of gratitude because a brother makes her a present of a few pounds; and another will never thank a benefactor who allows her, year by year, an annuity far larger than is justified by his precarious professional income. In one real case a lady lived for many years on her brother's generosity and was openly hostile to him all the time. After her death it was found that she had insulted him in her will. In another case a sister dependent on her brother's bounty never thanked him or even acknowledged the receipt of a sum of money, but if the money was not sent to the day she would at once write a sharp letter full of bitter reproaches for his neglect. The marvel is the incredible patience with which toiling men will go on sending the fruits of their industry to relations who do not even make a pretence of affection.

A frequent cause of hostility between very near relations is the *restriction* of generosity. So long as you set no limit to your giving it is well, you are doing your duty; but the moment you fix a limit the case is altered; then all past sacrifices go for nothing, your glory has set in gloom, and you will be considered as more niggardly than if you had not begun to be generous. Here is a real case, out of many. A man makes bad speculations, but conceals the full extent of his losses, and by the influence of his wife obtains important sums from a near relation of hers who half ruins himself to save her. When the full disaster is known the relation stops short and declines to ruin himself entirely; she then bitterly reproaches him for his selfishness. A very short time before writing the present Essay I was travelling, and met an old friend, a bachelor of limited means but of a most generous disposition, the kindest and most affectionate nature I ever knew in the male sex. I asked for news about his brother. "I never see him now; a coldness has sprung up between us." — "It must be his fault, then, for I am sure it did not originate with you." — "The truth is, he got into money difficulties, so I gave him a thousand pounds. He thought that under the circumstances I ought to have done more and broke off all intercourse. I really believe that if I had given him nothing we should have been more friendly at this day."

The question how far we are bound to allow family ties to regulate our intercourse is not easily treated in general terms, though it seems plainer in particular cases. Here is one for the reader's consideration.

Owing to natural refinement, and to certain circumstances of which he intelligently availed himself, one member of a family is a cultivated gentleman, whose habitual ways of thinking are of rather an elevated kind, and whose manners and language are invariably faultless. He is blessed with very near relations whose principal characteristic is loud, confident, overwhelming vulgarity. He is always uncomfortable with these relations. He knows that the ways of thinking and speaking which are natural to him will seem cold and uncongenial to them; that not one of his thoughts can be exactly understood by them; that his deficiency in what they consider heartiness is a defect he cannot get over. On the other hand, he takes no interest in what they say, because their opinions on all the subjects he cares about are too crude, and their information too scanty or erroneous. If he said what he felt impelled to say, all his talk would be a perpetual correction of their clumsy blunders. He has, therefore, no resource but to repress himself and try to act a part, the part of a pleased companion; but this is wearisome, especially if prolonged. The end is that he keeps out of their way, and is set down as a proud, conceited person, and an unkind relative. In reality he is simply refined and has a difficulty in accommodating himself to the ways of all vulgar society whatever, whether composed of his own relations or of strangers. Does he deserve to be blamed for this? Certainly not. He has not the flexibility, the dramatic power, to adapt himself to a lower state of civilization; that is his only fault. His relations are persons with whom, if they were not relations, nobody would expect him to associate; but because he and they happen to be descended from a common ancestor he is to maintain an impossible intimacy. He wishes them no harm; he is ready to make sacrifices to help them; his misfortune is that he does not possess the humor of a Dickens that would have enabled him to find amusement in their vulgarity, and he prefers solitude to that infliction.

There is a French proverb, "Les cousins ne sont pas parents." The exact truth would appear to be rather that cousins are relations or not just as it pleases them to acknowledge the relationship, and according to the natural possibilities of companionship between the parties. If they are of the same class in society (which does not always happen), and if they have pursuits in common or can understand each other's interests, and if there is that mysterious suitableness which makes people like to be together, then the fact of cousinship is seized upon as a convenient pretext for making intercourse more frequent, more intimate, and more affectionate; but if there is nothing to attract one cousin to another the relationship is scarcely acknowledged. Cousins are, or are not, relations just as they find it agreeable to themselves. It need hardly be added that it is a general though not an invariable rule that the relationship is better remembered on the humbler side. The cousinly degree may be felt to be very close under peculiar circumstances. An only child looks to his cousins for the brotherly and sisterly affection that fate has denied him at home, and he is not always disappointed. Even distant cousins may be truly fraternal, just as first cousins may happen to be very distant, the relationship is so variable and elastic in its nature.

Unmarried people have often a great vague dread of their future wife's relations, even when the lady has not yet been fixed upon, and married people have sometimes found the reality more terrible even than their gloomy anticipation. And yet it may happen that some of these dreaded new relations will be unexpectedly valuable and supply elements that were grievously wanting. They may bring new life into a dull house, they may enliven the sluggish talk with wit and information, they may take a too thoughtful and studious man out of the weary round of his own ideas. They may even in course of time win such a place in one's affection that if they are taken away by death they will leave a great void and an enduring sorrow. I write these lines from a sweet and sad experience.[5]

Intellectual men are, more than others, liable to a feeling of dissatisfaction with their relations because they want intellectual sympathy and interest, which relations hardly ever give. The reason is extremely simple. Any special intellectual pursuit is understood only by a small select class of its own, and our relations are given us out of the general body of society without any selection, and they are not very numerous, so that the chances against our finding intellectual sympathy amongst them are calculably very great. As we grow older we get accustomed to this absence of sympathy with our pursuits, and take it as a matter of course; but in youth it seems strange that what we feel and know to be so interesting should have no interest for those nearest to us. Authors sometimes feel a little hurt that their nearest relations will not read their books, and are but dimly aware that they have written any books at all; but do they read books of the same class by other writers? As an author you are in the same position that other authors occupy, but with this difference, which is against you, that familiarity has made you a commonplace person in your own circle, and that is a bad opening for the reception of your higher thoughts. This want of intellectual sympathy does not prevent affection, and we ought to appreciate affection at its full value in spite of it. Your brother or your cousin may be strongly attached to you personally, with an old love dating from your boyhood, but he may separate *you* (the human creature that he knows) from the author of your books, and not feel the slightest curiosity about the books, believing that he knows you perfectly without them, and that they are only a sort of costume in which you perform before the public. A female relative who has given up her mind to the keeping of some clergyman, may scrupulously avoid your literature in order that it may not contaminate her soul, and yet she may love you still in a painful way and be sincerely sorry that you have no other prospect but that of eternal punishment.

I have sometimes heard the question proposed whether relations or friends were the more valuable as a support and consolation. Fate gives us our relations, whilst we select our friends; and therefore it would seem at first sight that the friends must be better adapted for us; but it may happen that we have not selected with great wisdom, or that we have not had good opportunities for making a choice really answering to our deepest needs. Still, there must have been mutual affinity of some kind to make a friendship, whilst relations are all like tickets in a lottery. It may therefore be argued that the more relations we have, the better, because we are more likely to meet with two or three to love us amongst fifty than amongst five.

The peculiar peril of blood-relationship is that those who are closely connected by it often permit themselves an amount of mutual rudeness (especially in the middle and lower classes) which they never would think of inflicting upon a stranger. In some families people really seem to suppose that it does not matter how roughly they treat each other. They utter unmeasured reproaches about trifles not worth a moment's anger; they magnify small differences that only require to be let alone and forgotten, or they relieve the monotony of quarrels with an occasional fit of the sulks. Sometimes it is an irascible father who is always scolding, sometimes a loud-tongued matron shrieks "in her fierce volubility." Some children take up the note and fire back broadside for broadside; others wait for a cessation in contemptuous silence and calmly disregard the thunder. Family life indeed! domestic peace and bliss! Give me, rather, the bachelor's lonely hearth with a noiseless lamp and a book! The manners of the ill-mannered are never so odious, unbearable, exasperating, as they are to their own nearest kindred. How is a lad to enjoy the society of his mother if she is perpetually "nagging" and "nattering" at him? How is he to believe that his coarse father has a tender anxiety for his welfare when everything that he does is judged with unfatherly harshness? Those who are condemned to live with people for whom scolding and quarrelling are a necessary of existence must either be rude in self-defence or take refuge in a sullen and stubborn taciturnity. Young people who have to live in these little domestic hells look forward to any change as a desirable emancipation. They are ready to go to sea, to emigrate. I have heard of one who went into domestic service under a feigned name that he might be out of the range of his brutal father's tongue.

The misery of uncongenial relations is caused mainly by the irksome consciousness that they are obliged to live together. "To think that there is so much space upon the earth, that there are so many houses, so many rooms, and yet that I am so unfortunate as to be compelled to live in the same lodging with this uncivilized, ill-conditioned fellow! To think that there are such vast areas of tranquil silence, and yet that I am compelled to hear the voice of that scolding woman!" This is the feeling, and the relief would be temporary separation. In this, as in almost everything that concerns human intercourse, the rich have an immense advantage, as they can take only just so much of each other's society as they find by experience to be agreeable. They can quietly, and without rudeness, avoid each other by living in different houses, and even in the same house they can have different apartments and be very little together. Imagine the difference between two rich brothers, each with his suite of rooms in a separate tower of the paternal castle, and two very poor ones, inconveniently occupying the same narrow, uncomfortable bed, and unable to remain in the wretched paternal tenement without being constantly in each other's way. Between these extremes are a thousand degrees of more or less inconvenient nearness. Solitude is bad for us, but we need a margin of free space. If we are to be crowded let it be as the stars are crowded. They look as if they were huddled together, but every one of them has his own clear space in the illimitable ether.

ESSAY VI
FATHERS AND SONS

THERE is a certain unsatisfactoriness in this relation in our time which is felt by fathers and often avowed by them when they meet, though it does not occupy any conspicuous place in the literature of life and manners. It has been fully treated by M. Legouvé, the French Academician, in his own lively and elegant way; but he gave it a volume, and I must here confine myself to the few points which can be dealt with in the limits of a short Essay.

We are in an interregnum between two systems. The old system, founded on the stern authority of the father, is felt to be out of harmony with the amenity of general social intercourse in modern times and also with the increasing gentleness of political governors and the freedom of the governed. It is therefore, by common consent, abandoned. Some new system that may be founded upon a clear intelligence of both the paternal and the filial relations has yet to come into force. Meanwhile, we are trying various experiments, suggested by the different characters and circumstances of fathers and sons, each father trying his own experiments, and we communicate to each other such results as we arrive at.

It is obvious that the defect here is the absence of a settled public opinion to which both parties would feel bound to defer. Under the old system the authority of the father was efficiently maintained, not only by the laws, but by that general consensus of opinion which is far more powerful than law. The new system, whatever it may be, will be founded on general opinion again, but our present experimental condition is one of anarchy.

This is the real cause of whatever may be felt as unsatisfactory in the modern paternal and filial relations. It is not that fathers have become more unjust or sons more rebellious.

The position of the father was in old times perfectly defined. He was the commander, not only armed by the law but by religion and custom. Disobedience to his dictates was felt to be out of the question, unless the insurgent was prepared to meet the consequences of open mutiny. The maintenance of the father's authority depended only on himself. If he abdicated it through indolence or weakness he incurred moral reprobation not unmingled with contempt, whilst in the present day reprobation would rather follow a new attempt to vindicate the antique authority.

Besides this change in public opinion there is a new condition of paternal feeling. The modern father, in the most civilized nations and classes, has acquired a sentiment that appears to have been absolutely unknown to his predecessors: he has acquired a dislike for command which increases with the age of the son; so that there is an unfortunate coincidence of increasing strength of will on the son's part with decreasing disposition to restrain it on the father's part. What a modern father really desires is that a son should go right of his own accord, and if not quite of his own accord, then in consequence of a little affectionate persuasion. This feeling would make command unsatisfactory to us, even if it were followed by a military promptitude of obedience. We do not wish to be like captains, and our sons like privates in a company; we care only to exercise a certain beneficent influence over them, and we feel that if we gave military orders we should destroy that peculiar influence which is of the most fragile and delicate nature.

But now see the unexpected consequences of our modern dislike to command! It might be argued that there is a certain advantage on our side from the very rarity of the commands we give, which endows them with extraordinary force. Would it not be more accurate to say that as we give orders less and less our sons become unaccustomed to receive orders from us, and if ever the occasion arises when we *must* give them a downright order it comes upon their feelings with a harshness so excessive that they are likely to think us tyrannical, whereas if we had kept up the old habits of command such orders would have seemed natural and right, and would not have been less scrupulously obeyed?

The paternal dislike to give orders personally has had a peculiar effect upon education. We are not yet quite imbecile enough to suppose that discipline can be entirely dispensed with; and as there is very little of it in modern houses it has to be sought elsewhere, so boys are placed more and more completely under the authority of schoolmasters, often living at such a distance from the father of the family that for several months at a time he can exercise no direct influence or authority over his own children. This leads to the establishment of a peculiar boyish code of justice. Boys come to think it not unjust that the schoolmaster should exercise authority, when if the father attempted to exercise authority of equal rigor, or anything approaching it, they would look upon him as an odious domestic tyrant, entirely forgetting that any power to enforce obedience which is possessed by the schoolmaster is held by him vicariously as the father's representative and delegate. From this we arrive at the curious and unforeseen conclusion that the modern father only exercises *strong* authority through another person who is often a perfect stranger and whose interest in the boy's present and future well-being is as nothing in comparison with the father's anxious and continual solicitude.

The custom of placing the education of sons entirely in the hands of strangers is so deadly a blow to parental influence that some fathers have resolutely rebelled against it and tried to become themselves the educators of their children. James Mill is the most conspicuous instance of this, both for persistence and success. His way of educating his illustrious son has often been coarsely misrepresented as a merciless system of cram. The best answer to this is preserved for us in the words of the pupil himself. He said expressly: "Mine was not an education of cram," and that the one cardinal point in it, the cause of the good it effected, was that his father never permitted anything he learnt to degenerate into a mere exercise of memory. He greatly valued the training he had received, and fully appreciated its utility to him in after-life. "If I have accomplished anything," he says, "I owe it, amongst other fortunate circumstances, to the fact that through the early training bestowed on me by my father I started, I may fairly say, with an advantage of a quarter of a century over my contemporaries."

But though in this case the pupil's feeling in after-life was one of gratitude, it may be asked what were his filial sentiments whilst this paternal education was going forward. This question also is clearly and frankly answered by Stuart Mill himself. He says that his father was severe; that his authority was deficient in the demonstration of tenderness, though probably not in the reality of it; that "he resembled most Englishmen in being ashamed of the signs of feeling, and by the absence of demonstration starving the feelings themselves." Then the son goes on to say that it was "impossible not to feel true pity for a father who did, and strove to do, so much for his children, who would have so valued their affection, yet who must have been constantly feeling that fear of him was drying it up at its source." And we probably have the exact truth about Stuart Mill's own sentiments when he says that the younger children loved his father tenderly, "and if I cannot say so much of myself I was always loyally devoted to him."

This contains the central difficulty about paternal education. If the choice were left to boys they would learn nothing, and you cannot make them work vigorously "by the sole force of persuasion and soft words." Therefore a severe discipline has to be established, and this severity is incompatible with tenderness; so that in order to preserve the affection of his children the father intrusts discipline to a delegate.

But if the objection to parental education is clear in Mill's case, so are its advantages, and especially the one inestimable advantage that the father was able to impress himself on his son's mind and to live afterwards in his son's intellectual life. James Mill did not *abdicate*, as fathers generally do. He did not confine paternal duties to the simple one of signing checks. And if it is not in our power to imitate him entirely, if we have not his profound and accurate knowledge, if we have not his marvellous patience, if it is not desirable that we should take upon ourselves alone that immense responsibility which he accepted, may we not imitate him to such a degree as to secure *some* intellectual and moral influence over our own offspring and not leave them entirely to the teaching of the schoolfellow (that most influential and most dangerous of all teachers), the pedagogue, and the priest?

The only practical way in which this can be done is for the father to act within fixed limits. May he not reserve to himself some speciality? He can do this if he is himself master of some language or science that enters into the training of his son; but here again certain difficulties present themselves.

By the one vigorous resolution to take the entire burden upon his own shoulders James Mill escaped minor embarrassments. It is the *partial* education by the father that is difficult to carry out with steadiness and consistency. First, as to place of residence. If your son is far away during his months of work, and at home only for vacation pleasures, what, pray, is your hold upon him? He escapes from you in two directions, by work and by play. I have seen a Highland gentleman who, to avoid this and do his duty to his sons, quitted a beautiful residence in magnificent scenery to go and live in the dull and ugly neighborhood of Rugby. It is not convenient or possible for every father to make the same sacrifice, but if you are able to do it other difficulties remain. Any speciality that you may choose will be regarded by your son as a trifling and unimportant accomplishment in comparison with Greek and Latin, because that is the school estimate; and if you choose either Greek or Latin your scholarship will be immediately pitted against the scholarship of professional teachers whose more recent and more perfect methods will place you in a position of inferiority, instantly perceived by your pupil, who will estimate you accordingly. The only two cases I have ever personally known in which a father taught the classical languages failed in the object of increasing the son's affection and respect, because, although the father had been quite a first-rate scholar in his time, his ways of teaching were not so economical of effort as are the professional ways; and the boys perceived that they were not taking the shortest cut to a degree.

If, to avoid this comparison, you choose something outside the school curriculum, the boy will probably consider it an unfair addition to the burden of his work. His view of education is not your view. *You* think it a valuable training or acquirement; *he* considers it all task-work, like the making of bricks in Egypt; and his notion of justice is that he ought not to be compelled to make more bricks than his class-fellows, who are happy in having fathers too indolent or too ignorant to trouble them. If, therefore, you teach him something outside of what his school-fellows do, he does not think, "I get the advantage of a wider education than theirs;" but he thinks, "My father lays an imposition upon me, and my school-fellows are lucky to escape it."

In some instances the father chooses a modern language as the thing that he will teach; but he finds that as he cannot apply the school discipline (too harsh and unpaternal for use at home), there is a quiet, passive resistance that will ultimately defeat him unless he has inexhaustible patience. He decrees, let us suppose, that French shall be spoken at table; but the chief effect of his decree is to reveal great and unsuspected powers of taciturnity. Who could be such a tyrant as to find fault with a boy because he so modestly chooses to be silent? Speech may be of silver, but silence is of gold, and it is especially beautiful and becoming in the young.

Seeing that everything in the way of intellectual training is looked upon by boys as an unfair addition to school-work, some fathers abandon that altogether, and try to win influence over their sons by initiating them into sports and pastimes. Just at first these happy projects appear to unite the useful with the agreeable; but as the youthful nature is much better fitted for sports and pastimes than middle-age can pretend to be, it follows that the pupil very soon excels the master in these things, and quite gets the upper hand of him and offers him advice, or else dutifully (but with visible constraint) condescends to accommodate himself to the elder man's inferiority; so that perhaps upon the whole it may be that sports and pastimes are not the field of exertion in which paternal authority is most likely to preserve a dignified preponderance.

It is complacently assumed by men of fifty that over-ripe maturity is the superior of adolescence; but an impartial balance of advantages shows that some very brilliant ones are on the side of youth. At fifty we may be wiser, richer, more famous than a clever boy; but he does not care much for our wisdom, he thinks that expenses are a matter of course, and our little rushlights of reputations are as nothing to the future electric illumination of his own. In bodily activity we are to boyhood what a domestic cow is to a wild antelope; and as boys rightly attach an immense value to such activity they generally look upon us, in their secret thoughts, as miserable old "muffs." I distinctly remember, when a boy, accompanying a middle-aged gentleman to a country railway station. We were a little late, and the distance was long, but my companion could not be induced to go beyond his regular pace. At last we were within half a mile, and the steam of the locomotive became visible. "Now let us run for it," I cried, "and we shall catch the train!" Run?—*he* run, indeed! I might as well have asked the Pope to run in the streets of Rome! My friend kept in silent solemnity to his own dignified method of motion, and we were left behind. To this day I well remember the feelings of contemptuous pity and disgust that filled me as I looked upon that most respectable gentleman. I said not a word; my demeanor was outwardly decorous; but in my secret heart I despised my unequal companion with the unmitigated contempt of youth.

Even those physical exertions that elderly men are equal to—the ten miles' walk, the ride on a docile hunter, the quiet drive or sail—are so much below the achievements of fiery youth that they bring us no more credit than sitting in a chair. Though our efforts seem so respectable to ourselves that we take a modest pride therein, a young man can only look upon them with indulgence.

In the mental powers elderly men are inferior on the very point that a young man looks to first. His notion of cleverness, by which he estimates all his comrades, is not depth of thought, nor wisdom, nor sagacity; it is simply rapidity in learning, and there his elders are hopelessly behind him. They may extend or deepen an old study, but they cannot attack a new one with the conquering spirit of youth. *Too late! too late! too late!* is inscribed, for them, on a hundred gates of knowledge. The young man, with his powers of acquisition urging him like unsatisfied appetites, sees the gates all open and believes they are open for him. He believes all knowledge to be his possible province, knowing not yet the chilling, disheartening truth that life is too short for success in any but a very few directions. Confident in his powers, the young man prepares himself for difficult examinations, and he knows that we should be incapable of the same efforts.

Not having succeeded very well with attempts to create intercourse through studies and amusements, the father next consoles himself with the idea that he will convert his son into an intimate friend; but shortly discovers that there are certain difficulties, of which a few may be mentioned here.

Although the relationship between father and son is a very near relationship, it may happen that there is but little likeness of inherited idiosyncrasy, and therefore that the two may have different and even opposite tastes. By the law or accident of atavism a boy may resemble one of his grandfathers or some remoter ancestor, or he may puzzle theorists about heredity by characteristics for which there is no known precedent in his family. Both his mental instincts and processes, and the conclusions to which they lead him, may be entirely different from the habits and conclusions of his father; and if the father is so utterly unphilosophical as to suppose (what vulgar fathers constantly *do* suppose) that his own mental habits and conclusions are the right ones, and all others wrong, then he will adopt a tone of authority towards his son, on certain occasions, which the young man will excusably consider unbearable and which he will avoid by shunning the paternal society. Even a very mild attempt on the father's part to impose his own tastes and opinions will be quietly resented and felt as a reason for avoiding him, because the son is well aware that he cannot argue on equal terms with a man who, however amiable he chooses to be for the moment, can at any time arm himself with the formidable paternal dignity by simply taking the trouble to assume it.

The mere difference of age is almost an insuperable barrier to comradeship; for though a middle-aged man may be cheerful, his cheerfulness is "as water unto wine" in comparison with the merriment of joyous youth. So exuberant is that youthful gayety that it often needs to utter downright nonsense for the relief of its own high spirits, and feels oppressed in sober society where nonsense is not permitted. Any elderly gentleman who reads this has only to consult his own recollections, and ask himself whether in youth he did not often say and do utterly irrational things. If he never did, he never was really young. I hardly know any author, except Shakspeare, who has ventured to reproduce, in its perfect absurdity, the full flow of youthful nonsense. The criticism of our own age would scarcely tolerate it in books, and might accuse the author himself of being silly; but the thing still exists abundantly in real life, and the wonder is that it is sometimes the most intelligent young men who enjoy the most witless nonsense of all. When we have lost the high spirits that gave it a relish, it becomes very wearisome if prolonged. Young men instinctively know that we are past the appreciation of it.

Another very important reason why fathers and sons have a difficulty in maintaining close friendships is the steady divergence of their experience.

In childhood, the father's knowledge of places, people, and things includes the child's knowledge, as a large circle includes a little one drawn within it. Afterwards the boy goes to school, and has comrades and masters whom his father does not personally know. Later on, he visits many places where his father has never been.

The son's life may socially diverge so completely from that of the father that he may really come to belong to a different class in society. His education, habits, and associates may be different from those of his father. If the family is growing richer they are likely to be (in the worldly sense) of a higher class; if it is becoming poorer they will probably be of a lower class than the father was accustomed to in his youth. The son may feel more at ease than his father does in very refined society, or, on the other hand, he may feel refined society to be a restraint, whilst he only enjoys himself thoroughly and heartily amongst vulgar people that his father would carefully avoid.

Divergence is carried to its utmost by difference of professional training, and by the professional habit of seeing things that follows from it. If a clergyman puts his son into a solicitor's office, he need not expect that the son will long retain those views of the world that prevail in the country parsonage where he was born. He will acquire other views, other mental habits, and he will very soon believe himself to possess a far greater and more accurate knowledge of mankind, and of affairs, than his father ever possessed.

Even if the son is in the father's own profession he will have new views of it derived from the time at which he learns it, and he is likely to consider his father's ideas as not brought down to the latest date. He will also have a tendency to look to strangers as greater authorities than his father, even when they are really on the same level, because they are not lowered in his estimate by domestic intimacy and familiarity. Their opinion will be especially valued by the young man if it has to be paid for, it being an immense depreciation of the paternal counsel that it is always given gratuitously.

If the father has bestowed upon his son what is considered a "complete" education, and if he himself has not received the same "complete" education in his youth, the son is likely to accept the conventional estimate of education because it is in his own favor, and to estimate his father as an "uneducated" or a "half-educated" man, without taking into much account the possibility that his father may have developed his faculties by mental labor in other ways. The conventional division between "educated" and "uneducated" men is so definite that it is easily seen. The educated are those who have taken a degree at one of the Universities; the rest are uneducated, whatever may be their attainments in the sciences, in modern languages, or in the fine arts.

There are differences of education even more serious than this, because more real. A man may be not only conventionally uneducated, but he may be really and truly uneducated, by which I mean that his faculties may never have been drawn out by intellectual discipline of any kind whatever. It is hard indeed for a well-educated young man to live under the authority of a father of that kind, because he has constantly to suppress reasons and motives for opinions and decisions that such a father could not possibly enter into or understand. The relationship is equally hard for the father, who must be aware, with the lively suspicion of the ignorant, that his son is not telling him all his thought but only the portion of it which he thinks fit to reveal, and that much more is kept in reserve. He will ask, "Why this reserve towards *me*?" and then he will either be profoundly hurt and grieved by it at times, or else, if of another temper, he will be irritated, and his irritation may find harsh utterance in words.

An educated man can never rid himself of his education. His views of the most ordinary things are different from the views of the uneducated. If he were to express them in his own language they would say, "Why, how he talks!" and consider him "a queer chap;" and if he keeps them to himself they say he is very "close" and "shut up." There is no way out of the dilemma except this, that kind and tender feelings may exist between people who have nothing in common intellectually, but these are only possible when all pretence to paternal authority is abandoned.

Our forefathers had an idea with regard to the opinions of their children that in these days we must be content to give up. They thought that all opinions were by nature hereditary, and it was considered an act of disloyalty to ancestors if a descendant ventured to differ from them. The profession of any but the family opinions was so rare as to be almost inconceivable; and if in some great crisis the head of a family took a new departure in religion or politics the new faith substituted itself for the old one as the hereditary faith of the family. I remember hearing an old gentleman (who represented old English feeling in great perfection) say that it was totally unintelligible to him that a certain Member of Parliament could sit on the Liberal side of the House of Commons. "I cannot understand it," he said; "I knew his father intimately, and he was always a good Tory." The idea that the son might have opinions of his own was unthinkable.

In our time we are beginning to perceive that opinions cannot be imposed, and that the utmost that can be obtained by brow-beating a son who differs from ourselves is that he shall make false professions to satisfy us. Paternal influence may be better employed than in encouraging habits of dissimulation.

M. Legouvé attaches great importance to the religious question as a cause of division between fathers and sons because in the present day young men so frequently imbibe opinions which are not those of their parents. It is not uncommon, in France, for Catholic parents to have unbelieving sons; and the converse is also seen, but more frequently in the case of daughters. As opinions are very freely expressed in France (except where external conformity is an affair of caste), we find many families in which Catholicism and Agnosticism have each their open and convinced adherents; yet family affection does not appear to suffer from the difference, or is, at least, powerful enough to overcome it. In old times this would have been impossible. The father would have resented a difference of opinion in the son as an offence against himself.

A very common cause of division between father and son, in old times, was the following.

The father expressed a desire of some kind, mildly and kindly perhaps, yet with the full expectation that it should be attended to; but the desire was of an exorbitant nature, in this sense, that it involved something that would affect the whole course of the young man's future life in a manner contrary to his natural instincts. The father was then grievously hurt and offended because the son did not see his way to the fulfilment of the paternal desire.

The strongest cases of this kind were in relation to profession and marriage. The father wished his son to enter into some trade or profession for which he was completely unsuited, or he desired him to marry some young lady for whom he had not the slightest natural affinity. The son felt the inherent difficulties and refused. Then the father thought, "I only ask of my son *this one simple thing*, and he denies me."

In these cases the father was *not* asking for one thing, but for thousands of things. He was asking his son to undertake many thousands of separate obligations, succeeding each other till the far-distant date of his retirement from the distasteful profession, or his release, by his own death or hers, from the tedious companionship of the unloved wife. Sometimes the concession would have involved a long series of hypocrisies, as for example when a son was asked to take holy orders, though with little faith and no vocation.

Peter the Great is the most conspicuous example in history of a father whose idiosyncrasy was not continued in his son, and who could not understand or tolerate the separateness of his son's personality. They were not only of independent, but even of opposite natures. "Peter was active, curious, and energetic. Alexis was contemplative and reflective. He was not without intellectual ability, but he liked a quiet life. He preferred reading and thinking. At the age when Peter was making fireworks, building boats, and exercising his comrades in mimic war, Alexis was pondering over the 'Divine Manna,' reading the 'Wonders of God,' reflecting on Thomas à Kempis's 'Imitation of Christ,' and making excerpts from Baronius. While it sometimes seemed as if Peter was born too soon for the age, Alexis was born too late. He belonged to the past generation. Not only did he take no interest in the work and plans of his father, but he gradually came to dislike and hate them.... He would sometimes even take medicine to make himself ill, so that he might not be called upon to perform duties or to attend to business. Once, when he was obliged to go to the launch of a ship, he said to a friend, 'I would rather be a galley-slave, or have a burning fever, than be obliged to go there.'"[6]

In this case one is sorry for both father and son. Peter was a great intelligent barbarian of immense muscular strength and rude cerebral energy. Alexis was of the material from which civilization makes priests and students, or quiet conventional kings, but he was even more unlike Peter than gentle Richard Cromwell was unlike authoritative Oliver. The disappointment to Peter, firmly convinced, as all rude natures are, of the perfection of his own personality, and probably quite unable to appreciate a personality of another type, must have been the more bitter that his great plans for the future required a vigorous, practically minded innovator like himself. At length the difference of nature so exasperated the Autocrat that he had his son three times tortured, the third time in his own presence and with a fatal result. This terrible incident is the strongest expression known to us of a father's vexation because his son was not of his own kind.

Another painful case that will be long remembered, though the character of the father is less known to us, is that of the poet Shelley and Sir Timothy. The little that we do know amounts to this, that there was a total absence of sympathy. Sir Timothy committed the very greatest of paternal mistakes in depriving himself of the means of direct influence over his son by excluding him from his own home. Considering that the supreme grief of unhappy fathers is the feebleness of their influence over their sons, they can but confirm and complete their sorrow by annihilating that influence utterly and depriving themselves of all chance of recovering and increasing it in the future. This Sir Timothy did after the expulsion from Oxford. In his position, a father possessing some skill and tact in the management of young men at the most difficult and wayward period of their lives would have determined above all things to keep his son as much as possible within the range of his own control. Although Shelley afterwards returned to Field Place for a short time, the scission had been made; there was an end of real intercourse between father and son; the poet went his own way, married Harriett Westbrook, and lived through the rest of his short, unsatisfactory existence as a homeless, wandering *déclassé*.

This Essay has hitherto run upon the discouraging side of the subject, so that it ought not to end without the happier and more hopeful considerations.

Every personality is separate from others, and expects its separateness to be acknowledged. When a son avoids his father it is because he fears that the rights of his own personality will be disregarded. There are fathers who habitually treat their sons with sneering contempt. I have myself seen a young man of fair common abilities treated with constant and undisguised contempt by a clever, sardonic father who went so far as to make brutal allusions to the shape of the young man's skull! He bore this treatment with admirable patience and unfailing gentleness, but suffered from it silently. Another used to laugh at his son, and called him "Don Quixote" whenever the lad gave expression to some sentiment above the low Philistine level. A third, whom I knew well, had a disagreeable way of putting down his son because he was young, telling him that up to the age of forty a man "might have impressions, but could not possibly have opinions." "My father," said a kind-hearted English gentleman to me, "was the most thoroughly unbearable person I ever met with in my life."

The frank recognition of separate personality, with all its rights, would stop this brutality at once. There still remains the legitimate power of the father, which he ought not to abdicate, and which is of itself enough to prevent the freedom and equality necessary to perfect friendship. This reason, and the difference of age and habits, make it impossible that young men and their fathers should be comrades; but a relation may be established between them which, if rightly understood, is one of the most agreeable in human existence.

To be satisfactory it must be founded, on the father's side, on the idea that he is repaying to posterity what he has received from his own parents, and not on any selfish hope that the descending stream of benefit will flow upwards again to him. Then he must not count upon affection, nor lay himself out to win it, nor be timidly afraid of losing it, but found his influence upon the firmer ground of respect, and be determined to deserve and have *that*, along with as much unforced affection as the son is able naturally and easily to give. It is not desirable that the affection between father and son should be so tender, on either side, as to make separation a constant pain, for such is human destiny that the two are generally fated to see but little of each other.

The best satisfaction for a father is to deserve and receive loyal and unfailing respect from his son.

No, this is not quite the best, not quite the supreme satisfaction of paternity. Shall I reveal the secret that lies in silence at the very bottom of the hearts of all worthy and honorable fathers? Their profoundest happiness is to be able themselves to respect their sons.

ESSAY VII
THE RIGHTS OF THE GUEST

IF hospitality were always perfectly practised it would be the strongest of all influences in favor of rational liberty, because the host would learn to respect it in the persons of his guests, and thence, by extension of habit, amongst others who could never be his guests.

Hospitality educates us in respect for the rights of others. This is the substantial benefit that the host ought to derive from his trouble and his outlay, but the instincts of uncivilized human nature are so powerful that this education has usually been partial and incomplete. The best part of it has been systematically evaded, in this way. People were aware that tolerance and forbearance ought to be exercised towards guests, and so, to avoid the hard necessity of exercising these qualities when they were really difficult virtues, they practised what is called exclusiveness. In other words, they accepted as guests only those who agreed with their own opinions and belonged to their own class. By this arrangement they could be both hospitable and intolerant at the same time.

If, in our day, the barrier of exclusiveness has been in many places broken down, there is all the greater need for us to remember the true principle of hospitality. It might be forgotten with little inconvenience in a very exclusive society, but if it were forgotten in a society that is not exclusive the consequences would be exactly the opposite of what every friend of civilization most earnestly desires. Social intercourse, in that case, so far from being an education in respect for the rights of others, would be an opportunity for violating them. The violation might become habitual; and if it were so this strange result would follow, that society would not be a softening and civilizing influence, but the contrary. It would accustom people to treat each other with disregard, so that men would be hardened and brutalized by it as schoolboys are made ruder by the rough habits of the playground, and urbanity would not be cultivated in cities, but preserved, if at all, in solitude.

The two views concerning the rights of the guest may be stated briefly as follows:—

1. The guest is bound to conform in all things to the tastes and customs of his host. He ought to find or feign enjoyment in everything that his host imposes upon him; and if he is unwilling to do this in every particular it is a breach of good manners on his part, and he must be made to suffer for it.

2. The guest should be left to be happy in his own way, and the business of the host is to arrange things in such a manner that each guest may enjoy as much as possible his own peculiar kind of happiness.

When the first principle was applied in all its rigor, as it often used to be applied, and as I have myself seen it applied, the sensation experienced by the guest on going to stay in certain houses was that of entirely losing the direction of himself. He was not even allowed, in the middle classes, to have any control over his own inside, but had to eat what his host ordered him to eat, and to drink the quantity of wine and spirits that his host had decided to be good for him. Resistance to these dictates was taken as an offence, as a crime against good fellowship, or as a reflection on the quality of the good things provided; and conversation paused whilst the attention of the whole company was attracted to the recalcitrant guest, who was intentionally placed in a situation of extreme annoyance and discomfort in order to compel him to obedience. The victim was perhaps half an invalid, or at least a man who could only keep well and happy on condition of observing a certain strictness of regimen. He was then laughed at for idle fears about his health, told that he was a hypochondriac, and recommended to drink a bottle of port every day to get rid of such idle nonsense. If he declined to eat twice or three times as much as he desired, the hostess expressed her bitter regret that she had not been able to provide food and cookery to his taste, thus placing him in such a position that he must either eat more or seem to condemn her arrangements. It was very common amongst old-fashioned French *bourgeois* in the last generation for the hostess herself to heap things on the guest's plate, and to prevent this her poor persecuted neighbor had to remove the plate or turn it upside down. The whole habit of pressing was dictated by selfish feeling in the hosts. They desired to see their guests devour voraciously, in order that their own vanity might be gratified by the seeming appreciation of their things. Temperate men were disliked by a generation of topers because their temperance had the appearance of a silent protest or censure. The discomfort inflicted by these odious usages was so great that many people either injured their health in society or kept out of it in self-defence, though they were not sulky and unsociable by nature, but would have been hearty lovers of human intercourse if they could have enjoyed it on less unacceptable terms.

The wholesome modern reaction against these dreadful old customs has led some hosts into another error. They sometimes fail to understand the great principle that it is the guest alone who ought to be the judge of the quantity that he shall eat and drink. The old pressing hospitality assumed that the guest was a child, too shame-faced to take what it longed for unless it was vigorously encouraged; but the new hospitality, if indeed it still in every case deserves that honored name, does really sometimes appear to assume (I do not say always, or often, but in extreme cases) that the guest is a fool, who would eat and drink more than is good for him if he were not carefully rationed. Such hosts forget that excess is quite a relative term, that each constitution has its own needs. Beyond this, it is well known that the exhilaration of social intercourse enables people who meet convivially to digest and assimilate, without fatigue, a larger amount of nutriment than they could in dull and perhaps dejected solitude. Hence it is a natural and long-established habit to eat and drink more when in company than alone, and the guest should have the possibility of conforming to this not irrational old custom until, in Homer's phrase, he has "put from him the desire of meat and drink."

Guests have no right whatever to require that the host should himself eat and drink to keep them in countenance. There used to be a belief (it lingers still in the middle classes and in country places) that the laws of hospitality required the host to set what was considered "a good example," or, in other words, to commit excesses himself that his friends might not be too much ashamed of theirs. It is said that the Emperor William of Germany never eats in public at all, but sits out every banquet before an empty plate. This, though quite excusable in an old gentleman, obliged to live by rule, must have rather a chilling effect; and yet I like it as a declaration of the one great principle that no person at table, be he host or guest, ought to be compelled to inflict the very slightest injury upon his own health, or even comfort. The rational and civilized idea is that food and wines are simply placed at the disposal of the people present to be used, or abstained from, as they please.

It is clear that every invited guest has a right to expect some slight appearance of festivity in his honor. In coarse and barbarous times the idea of festivity is invariably expressed by abundance, especially by vast quantities of butcher's meat and wine, as we always find it in Homer, where princes and gentlemen stuff themselves like savages; but in refined times the notion of quantity has lost its attraction, and that of elegance takes its place. In a highly civilized society nothing conveys so much the idea of festivity as plenty of light and flowers, with beautiful table-linen and plate and glass. These, with some extra delicacy in cookery and wines, are our modern way of expressing welcome.

There is a certain kind of hospitality in which the host visibly declines to make any effort either of trouble or expense, but plainly shows by his negligence that he only tolerates the guest. All that can be said of such hospitality as this is that a guest who respects himself may endure it silently for once, but would not be likely to expose himself to it a second time.

There is even a kind of hospitality which seems to find a satisfaction in letting the guest perceive that the best in the house is not offered to him. He is lodged in a poor little room, when there are noble bedchambers, unused, in the same house; or he is allowed to hire a vehicle in the village, to make some excursion, when there are horses in the stables plethoric from want of exercise. In cases of this kind it is not the privation of luxury that is hard to bear, but the indisposition to give honor. The guest feels and knows that if a person of very high rank came to the house everything would be put at his disposal, and he resents the slight put upon his own condition. A rich English lady, long since dead, had a large mansion in the country with fine bedrooms; so she found a pleasure in keeping those rooms empty and sending guests to sleep at the top of the house in little bare and comfortless chambers that the architect had intended for servants. I have heard of a French house where there are fine state apartments, and where all ordinary guests are poorly lodged, and fed in a miserable *salle à manger*. An aggravation is when the host treats himself better than his guest. Lady B. invited some friends to a country-house; and they drove to another country-house in the neighborhood in two carriages, one containing Lady B. and one friend, the other the remaining guests. Her ladyship was timid and rather selfish, as timid people often are; so when they reached the avenue she began to fancy that both carriages could not safely turn in the garden, and she despatched her footman to the second carriage, with orders that her guests (amongst whom was a lady very near her confinement) were to get out and walk to the house, whilst she drove up to the door in state.

A guest has an absolute right to have his religious and political opinions respected in his presence, and this is not invariably done. The rule more generally followed seems to be that class opinions only deserve respect and not individual opinions. The question is too large to be treated in a paragraph, but I should say that it is a clear breach of hospitality to utter anything in disparagement of any opinion whatever that is known to be held by any one guest present, however humble may be his rank. I have sometimes seen the known opinions of a guest attacked rudely and directly, but the more civilized method is to do it more artfully through some other person who is not present. For example, a guest is known to think, on important subjects, very much as Mr. Herbert Spencer does; then the host will contrive to talk at him in talking about Spencer. A guest ought not to bear this ungenerous kind of attack. If such an occasion arises he should declare his opinions plainly and with firmness, and show his determination to have them respected whilst he is there, whatever may be said against them in his absence. If he cannot obtain this degree of courtesy, which is his right, let him quit the house and satisfy his hunger at some inn. The innkeeper will ask for a little money, but he demands no mental submission.

It sometimes happens that the nationality of a foreign guest is not respected as it ought to be. I remember an example of this which is moderate enough to serve as a kind of type, some attacks upon nationality being much more direct and outrageous. An English lady said at her own table that she would not allow her daughter to be partially educated in a French school, "because she would have to associate with French girls, which, you know, is undesirable." Amongst the guests was a French lady, and the observation was loud enough for everybody to hear it. I say nothing of the injustice of the imputation. It was, indeed, most unjust, but that is not the point. The point is that a foreigner ought not to hear attacks upon his native land even when they are perfectly well founded.

The host has a sort of judicial function in this way. The guest has a right to look to him for protection on certain occasions, and he is likely to be profoundly grateful when it is given with tact and skill, because the host can say things for him that he cannot even hint at for himself. Suppose the case of a young man who is treated with easy and rather contemptuous familiarity by another guest, simply on account of his youth. He is nettled by the offence, but as it is more in manner than in words he cannot fix upon anything to answer. The host perceives his annoyance, and kindly gives him some degree of importance by alluding to some superiority of his, and by treating him in a manner very different from that which had vexed him.

A witty host is the most powerful ally against an aggressor. I remember dining in a very well-known house in Paris where a celebrated Frenchman repeated the absurd old French calumny against English ladies, — that they all drink. I was going to resent this seriously when a clever Frenchwoman (who knew England well) perceived the danger, and answered the man herself with great decision and ability. I then watched for the first opportunity of making him ridiculous, and seized upon a very delightful one that he unwittingly offered. Our host at once understood that my attack was in revenge for an aggression that had been in bad taste, and he supported me with a wit and pertinacity that produced general merriment at the enemy's expense. Now in that case I should say that the host was filling one of the most important and most difficult functions of a host.

This Essay has hitherto been written almost entirely on the guest's side of the question, so that we have still briefly to consider the limitations to his rights.

He has no right to impose any serious inconvenience upon his host. He has no right to disturb the ordinary arrangements of the house, or to inflict any serious pecuniary cost, or to occupy the host's time to the prejudice of his usual pursuits. He has no right to intrude upon the privacy of his host.

A guest has no right to place the host in such a dilemma that he must either commit a rudeness or put up with an imposition. The very courtesy of an entertainer places him at the mercy of a pushing and unscrupulous guest, and it is only when the provocation has reached such a point as to have become perfectly intolerable that a host will do anything so painful to himself as to abandon his hospitable character and make the guest understand that he must go.

It may be said that difficulties of this kind never occur in civilized society. No doubt they are rare, but they happen just sufficiently often to make it necessary to be prepared for them. Suppose the case of a guest who exceeds his invitation. He has been invited for two nights, plainly and definitely; but he stays a third, fourth, fifth, and seems as if he would stay forever. There are men of that kind in the world, and it is one of their arts to disarm their victims by pleasantness, so that it is not easy to be firm with them. The lady of the house gives a gentle hint, the master follows with broader hints, but the intruder is quite impervious to any but the very plainest language. At last the host has to say, "Your train leaves at such an hour, and the carriage will be ready to take you to the station half an hour earlier." This, at any rate, is intelligible; and yet I have known one of those clinging limpets whom even this proceeding failed to dislodge. At the approach of the appointed hour he was nowhere to be found! He had gone to hide himself in a wood with no companion but his watch, and by its help he took care to return when it was too late. That is sometimes one of the great uses of a watch.

ESSAY VIII
THE DEATH OF FRIENDSHIP

A SAD subject, but worth analysis; for if friendship is of any value to us whilst it is alive, is it not worth while to inquire if there are any means of keeping it alive?

The word "death" is correctly employed here, for nobody has discovered the means by which a dead friendship can be resuscitated. To hope for that would be vain indeed, and idle the waste of thought in such a bootless quest.

Shall we mourn over this death without hope, this blank annihilation, this finis of intercourse once so sweet, this dreary and ultimate conclusion?

The death of a friendship is not the death of a person; we do not mourn for the absence of some beloved person from the world. It is simply the termination of a certain degree and kind of intercourse, not of necessity the termination of all intercourse. We may be grieved that the change has come; we may be remorseful if it has come through a fault of our own; but if it is due simply to natural causes there is small place for any reasonable sorrow.

Friendship is a certain *rapport* between two minds during one or more phases of their existence, and the perfection of it is quite as dependent upon what is not in the two minds as upon their positive acquirements and possessions. Hence the extreme facility with which schoolboys form friendships which, for the time, are real, true, and delightful. School friendships are formed so easily because boys in the same class know the same things; and it rarely happens that in addition to what they have in common either one party or the other has any knowledge of importance that is not in common.

Later in life the pair of friends who were once comrades go into different professions that fill the mind with special professional ideas and induce different habits of thought. Each will be conscious, when they meet, that there is a great range of ideas in the other's mind from which he is excluded, and each will have a difficulty in keeping within the smaller range of ideas that they have now in common; so that they will no longer be able to let their *whole* minds play together as they used to do, and they will probably feel more at ease with mere acquaintances who have what is *now* their knowledge, what are now their mental habits, than with the friend of their boyhood who is without them.

This is strongly felt by men who go through a large experience at a distance from their early home and then return for a while to the old place and old associates, and find that it is only a part of themselves that is acceptable. New growths of self have taken place in distant regions, by travel, by study, by intercourse with mankind; and these new growths, though they may be more valuable than any others, are of no practical use, of no social availableness, in the little circle that has remained in the old ways.

Then there are changes of temper that result from the fixing of the character by time. We think we remain the same, but that is one of our many illusions. We change, and we do not always change in the same way. One man becomes mellowed by advancing years, but another is hardened by them; one man's temper gains in sweetness and serenity as his intellect gains in light, another becomes dogmatic, peremptory, and bitter. Even when the change is the same for both, it may be unfavorable to their intercourse. Two merry young hearts may enjoy each other's company, when they would find each other dull and flat if the sparkle of the early effervescence were all spent.

I have not yet touched upon change of opinion as a cause of the death of friendship, but it is one of the most common causes. It would be a calumny on the intelligence of the better part of mankind to say that they always desire to hear repeated exactly what they say themselves, though that is really the desire of the unintelligent; but the cleverest people like to hear new and additional reasons in support of the opinions they hold already; and they do not like to hear reasons, hitherto unsuspected, that go to the support of opinions different from their own. Therefore a slow divergence of opinion may carry two friends farther and farther apart by narrowing the subjects of their intercourse, or a sudden intellectual revolution in one of them may effect an immediate and irreparable breach.

"If the character is formed," says Stuart Mill, "and the mind made up on the few cardinal points of human opinion, agreement of conviction and feeling on these has been felt at all times to be an essential requisite of anything worthy the name of friendship in a really earnest mind." I do not quote this in the belief that it is absolutely true, but it expresses a general sentiment. We can only be guided by our own experience in these matters. Mine has been that friendship is possible with those whom I respect, however widely they differ from me, and not possible with those whom I am unable to respect, even when on the great matters of opinion their views are identical with my own.

It is certain, however, that the change of opinion itself has a tendency to separate men, even though the difference would not have made friendship impossible if it had existed from the first. Instances of this are often found in biographies, especially in religious biographies, because religious people are more "pained" and "wounded" by difference of opinion than others. We read in such books of the profound distress with which the hero found himself separated from his early friends by his new conviction on this or that point of theology. Political divergence produces the same effect in a minor degree, and with more of irritation than distress. Even divergence of opinion on artistic subjects is enough to produce coolness. Artists and men of letters become estranged from each other by modifications of their critical doctrines.

Differences of prosperity do not prevent the formation of friendship if they have existed previously, and can be taken as established facts; but if they widen afterwards they have a tendency to diminish it. They do so by altering the views of one of the parties about ways of living and about the multitude of things involving questions of expense. If the enriched man lives on a scale corresponding to his newly acquired wealth, he may be regarded by the other as pretentious beyond his station, whilst if he keeps to his old style he may be thought parsimonious. From delicacy he will cease to talk to the other about his money matters, which he spoke of with frankness when he was not so rich. If he has social ambition he will form new alliances with richer men, and the old friend may regard these with a little unconscious jealousy.

It has been observed that young artists often have a great esteem for the work of one of their number so long as its qualities are not recognized and rewarded by the public, but that so soon as the clever young man wins the natural meed of industry and ability his early friendships die. They were often the result of a generous indignation against public injustice, so when that injustice came to an end the kindness that was a protest against it ceased at the same time. In jealous natures it would no doubt be replaced by the conviction that public favor had rewarded merit far beyond its deserts.

In the political life of democracies we see men enthusiastically supported and really admired with sincerity so long as they remain in opposition, and their friends indulge the most favorable anticipations about what they would do if they came to power; but when they accept office they soon lose many of these friends, who are quite sure to be disappointed with the small degree in which their excessive hopes have been realized. There is no country where this is seen more frequently than in France, where Ministers are often criticised with the most unrelenting and uncharitable acerbity by the men and newspapers that helped to raise them.

Changes of physical constitution may be the death of friendship in this way. A friendship may be founded upon some sport that one of the parties becomes unable to follow. After that the two men cease to meet on the particularly pleasant occasions that every sport affords for its real votaries, and they only meet on common occasions, which are not the same because there is not the same jovial and hearty temper. In like manner a friendship may be weakened if one of the parties gives up some indulgence that both used to enjoy together. Many a friendship has been cemented by the habit of smoking, and weakened afterwards when one friend gave up the habit, declined the cigars that the other offered, and either did not accompany him to the smoking-room or sat there in open and vexatious nonconformity.

It is well known, so well known indeed as scarcely to require mention here, that one of the most frequent and powerful causes of the death of bachelor friendships is marriage. One of the two friends takes a wife, and the friendship is at once in peril. The maintenance of it depends upon the lady's taste and temper. If not quite approved by her, it will languish for a little while and then die, in spite of all painful and visible efforts on the husband's part to compensate, by extra attention, for the coolness of his wife. I have visited a Continental city where it is always understood that all bachelor friendships are broken off by marriage. This rule has at least the advantage of settling the question unequivocally.

Simple neglect is probably the most common of all causes deadly to friendship,—neglect arising either from real indifference, from constitutional indolence, or from excessive devotion to business. Friendly feelings must be either of extraordinary sincerity, or else strengthened by some extraneous motive of self-interest, to surmount petty inconveniences. The very slightest difficulty in maintaining intercourse is sufficient in most cases to insure its total cessation in a short time. Your house is somewhat difficult of access,—it is on a hill-side or at a little distance from a railway station: only the most sincere friends will be at the trouble to find you unless your rank is so high that it is a glory to visit you.

Poor friends often keep up intercourse with rich ones by sheer force of determination long after it ought to have been allowed to die its own natural death. When they do this without having the courage to require some approach to reciprocity they sink into the condition of mere clients, whom the patron may indeed treat with apparent kindness, but whom he regards with real indifference, taking no trouble whatever to maintain the old connection between them.

Equality of rank and fortune is not at all necessary to friendship, but a certain other kind of equality is. A real friendship can never be maintained unless there is an equal readiness on both sides to be at some pains and trouble for its maintenance; so if you perceive that a person whom you once supposed to be your friend will not put himself to any trouble on your account, the only course consistent with your dignity is to take exactly the same amount of pains to make yourself agreeable to him. After you have done this for a little time you will soon know if the friendship is really dead; for he is sure to perceive your neglect if he does not perceive his own, and he will either renew the intercourse with some *empressement* or else cease from it altogether.

In early life the right rule is to accept kindness gratefully from one's elders and not to be sensitive about omissions, because such omissions are then often consistent with the most real and affectionate regard; but as a man advances towards middle-age it is right for him to be somewhat careful of his dignity and to require from friends, whatever may be their station, a certain general reciprocity. This should always be understood in rather a large sense, and not exacted in trifles. If he perceives that there is no reciprocity he cannot do better than drop an acquaintance that is but the phantom and simulacrum of Friendship's living reality.

It is as natural that many friendships should die and be replaced by others as that our old selves should be replaced by our present selves. The fact seems melancholy when first perceived, but is afterwards accepted as inevitable. There is, however, a death of friendship which is so truly sad and sorrowful as to cast its gloomy shadow on all the years that remain to us. It is when we ourselves, by some unhappy fault of temper that might have been easily avoided, have wounded the kind breast of our friend, and killed the gentle sentiment that was dwelling happily within. The only way to be quite sure of avoiding this great and irretrievable calamity is to remember how very delicate friendly sentiments are and how easy it is to destroy them by an inconsiderate or an ungentle word.

ESSAY IX
THE FLUX OF WEALTH

WE become richer or poorer; we seldom remain exactly as we were. If we have property, it increases or diminishes in value; if our income is fixed, the value of money alters; and if it increased proportionally to the depreciation of money, our position would still be relatively altered by changes in the fortunes of others. We marry and have children; then our wealth becomes less our own after every birth. We win some honor or professional advancement that seems a gain; but increased expenditure is the consequence, and we are poorer than we were before. Amidst all these fluctuations of wealth human intercourse either continues under altered conditions or else it is broken off because they are no longer favorable to its maintenance. I propose to consider, very briefly, how these altered conditions operate.

We have to separate, in the first place, intercourse between individuals from intercourse between families. The distinction is of the utmost importance, because the two are not under the same law.

Two men, of whom one is extremely rich and the other almost penniless, have no difficulty in associating together on terms agreeable to both when they possess intellectual interests in common, or even when there is nothing more than an attraction of idiosyncrasy; but these conditions only subsist between one individual and another; they are not likely to subsist between two families. Intercourse between individuals depends on something in intellect and culture that enables them to understand each other, and upon something in character that makes them love or respect each other. Intercourse between families depends chiefly on neighborhood and similarity in style of living.

This is the reason why bachelors have so much easier access to society than men with wives and families. The bachelor is received for himself, for his genius, information, manners; but if he is married the question is, "What sort of people are *they*?" This, being interpreted, means, "What style do they live in?" "How many servants do they keep?"

Whatever may be the variety of opinions concerning the doctrines of the Church of Rome, there is but one concerning her astuteness. There can be no doubt that she is the most influential association of men that has ever existed; and she has decided for celibacy, that the priest might stand on his merits and on the power of the Church, and be respected and admitted everywhere in spite of notorious poverty.

Mignet, the historian, was a most intimate and constant friend of Thiers. Mignet, though rich in reality, as he knew how to live contentedly on moderate means, was poor in comparison with his friend. This inequality did not affect their friendship in the least; for both were great workers, well qualified to understand each other, though Thiers lived in a grand house, and Mignet in a barely furnished lodging high up in a house that did not belong to him.

Mignet was a bachelor, and they were both childless men; but imagine them with large families. One family would have been bred in the greatest luxury, the other in austere simplicity. Children are keenly alive to these distinctions; and even if there had been neither pride in the rich house nor envy in the poorer one the contrast would have been constantly felt. The historical studies that the fathers had in common would probably not have interested their descendants, and unless there had been some other powerful bond of sympathy the two families would have lived in different worlds. The rich family would have had rich friends, the poorer family would have attached itself to other families with whom it could have exchanged hospitality on more equal terms. This would have happened even in Paris, a city where there is a remarkable absence of contempt for poverty; a city where the slightest reason for distinction will admit any well-bred man into society in spite of narrow means and insure him immunity from disdain. All the more certainly would it happen in places where money is the only regulator of rank, the only acknowledged claim to consideration.

I once knew an English merchant who was reputed to be wealthy, and who, like a true Englishman as he was, inhabited one of those great houses that are so elaborately contrived for the exercise of hospitality. He had a kind and friendly heart, and lived surrounded by people who often did him the favor to drink his excellent wines and sleep in his roomy bedchambers. On his death it turned out that he had never been quite so rich as he appeared and that during his last decade his fortune had rapidly dwindled. Being much interested in everything that may confirm or invalidate those views of human nature that are current in ancient and modern literature, I asked his son how those who were formerly such frequent guests at the great house had behaved to the impoverished family. "They simply avoided us," he said; "and some of them, when they met me, would cut me openly in the street."

It may be said with perfect truth that this was a good riddance. It is certain that it was so; it is undeniable that the deliverance from a horde of false friends is worth a considerable sum per head of them; and that in itself was only a subject of congratulation, but their behavior was hard to bear because it was the evidence of a fall. We like deference as a proof that we have what others respect, quite independently of any real affection on their part; nay, we even enjoy the forced deference of those who hate us, well knowing that they would behave very differently if they dared. Besides this, it is not certain that an impoverished family will find truer friends amongst the poor than it did formerly amongst the rich. The relation may be the same as it was before, and only the incomes of the parties altered.

What concerns our present subject is simply that changes of pecuniary situation have always a strong tendency to throw people amongst other associates; and as these changes are continually occurring, the result is that families very rarely preserve the same acquaintances for more than a single generation. And now comes the momentous issue. The influence of our associates is so difficult to resist, in fact so completely irresistible in the long run, that people belong far less to the class they are descended from than to the class in which they live. The younger son of some perfectly aristocratic family marries rather imprudently and is impoverished by family expenses. His son marries imprudently again and goes into another class. The children of that second marriage will probably not have a trace of the peculiarly aristocratic civilization. They will have neither the manners, nor the ideas, nor the unexpressed instincts of the real aristocracy from which they sprang. In place of them they will have the ideas of the lower middle class, and be in habits and manners just as completely of that class as if their forefathers had always belonged to it.

I have in view two instances of this which are especially interesting to me because they exemplify it in opposite ways. In one of these cases the man was virtuous and religious, but though his ancestry was aristocratic his virtues and his religion were exactly those of the English middle class. He was a good Bible-reading, Sabbath-observing, theatre-avoiding Evangelical, inclined to think that dancing was rather sinful, and in all those subtle points of difference that distinguish the middle-class Englishman from the aristocratic Englishman he followed the middle class, not seeming to have any unconscious reminiscence in his blood of an ancestry with a freer and lordlier life. He cared neither for the sports, nor the studies, nor the social intercourse of the aristocracy. His time was divided, as that of the typical good middle-class Englishman generally is, between business and religion, except when he read his newspaper. By a combination of industry and good-fortune he recovered wealth, and might have rejoined the aristocracy to which he belonged by right of descent; but middle-class habits were too strong, and he remained contentedly to the close of life both in that class and of it.

The other example I am thinking of is that of a man still better descended, who followed a profession which, though it offers a good field for energy and talent, is seldom pursued by gentlemen. He acquired the habits and ideas of an intelligent but dissipated working-man, his vices were exactly those of such a man, and so was his particular kind of religious scepticism. I need not go further into detail. Suppose the character of a very clever but vicious and irreligious workman, such as may be found in great numbers in the large English towns, and you have the accurate portrait of this particular *déclassé*.

In mentioning these two cases I am anxious to avoid misinterpretation. I have no particular respect for one class more than another, and am especially disposed to indulgence for the faults of those who bear the stress of the labor of the world; but I see that there *are* classes, and that the fluctuations of fortune, more than any other cause, bring people within the range of influence exercised by the habits of classes, and form them in the mould, so that their virtues and vices afterwards, besides their smaller qualities and defects, belong to the class they live in and not to the class they may be descended from. In other words, men are more strongly influenced by human intercourse than by heredity.

The most remarkable effect of the fluctuation of wealth is the extreme rapidity with which the prosperous family gains refinement of manners, whilst the impoverished family loses it. This change seems to be more rapid in our own age and country than it has ever been before. Nothing is more interesting than to watch this double process; and nothing in social studies is more curious than the multiplicity of the minute causes that bring it about. Every abridgment of ceremony has a tendency to lower refinement by introducing that *sans-gêne* which is fatal to good manners. Ceremony is only compatible with leisure. It is abridged by haste; haste is the result of poverty; and so it comes to pass that the loss of fortune induces people to give up one little observance after another, for economy of time, till at last there are none remaining. There is the excellent habit of dressing for the evening meal. The mere cost of it is almost imperceptible, except that it causes a small additional expenditure in clean linen; but, although the pecuniary tax is slight, there is a tax on time which is not compatible with hurry and irregularity, so it is only people of some leisure who maintain it. Now consider the subtle influence, on manners, of the maintenance or abandonment of this custom. Where it is kept up, gentlemen and ladies meet in a drawing-room before dinner prepared by their toilet for the disciplined intercourse of well-regulated social life. They are like officers in uniform, or clergymen in canonicals: they wear a dress that is not without its obligations. It is not the luxury of it that does this, for the dress is always plain for men and often simple for ladies, but the mere fact of taking the trouble to dress is an act of deference to civilization and disposes the mind to other observances. It has the further advantage of separating us from the occupations of the day and marking a new point of departure for the gentler life of the evening. As people become poorer they give up dressing except when they have a party, and then they feel ill at ease from the consciousness of a white tie. You have only to go a little further in this direction to arrive at the people who do not feel any inclination to wash their hands before dinner, even when they visibly need it. Finally there are houses where the master will sit down to table in his shirt-sleeves and without anything round his neck. People who live in this way have no social intercourse whatever of a slightly ceremonious kind, and therefore miss all the discipline in manners that rich people go through every day. The higher society is a school of manners that the poor have not leisure to attend.

The downward course of an impoverished family is strongly aided by an element in many natures that the discipline of high life either subdues or eliminates. There are always people, especially in the male sex, who feel ill at ease under ceremonial restraints of any kind, and who find the release from them an ineffably delightful emancipation. Such people hate dressing for dinner, hate the forms of politeness, hate gloves and visiting-cards, and all that such things remind them of. To be rid of these things once for all, to be able to sit and smoke a pipe in an old gray coat, seems to them far greater and more substantial happiness than to drink claret in a dining-room, napkin on knee. Once out of society, such men have no desire to enter it again, and after a very short exclusion from it they belong to a lower class from taste quite as much as from circumstances. All those who have a tendency towards the philosophy of Diogenes (and they are more numerous than we suppose) are of this manner of thinking. Sometimes they have a taste for serious intellectual pursuits which makes the nothings of society seem frivolous, and also consoles their pride for an apparent *déchéance*.

If it were possible to get rid of the burdensome superfluities of high life, most of which are useless encumbrances, and live simply without any loss of refinement, I should say that these philosophers would have reason on their side. The complicated apparatus of wealthy life is not in itself desirable. To convert the simple act of satisfying hunger into the tedious ceremonial of a state dinner may be a satisfaction of pride, but it is assuredly not an increase of pleasure. To receive as guests people whom we do not care for in the least (which is constantly done by rich people to maintain their position) offers less of what is agreeable in human intercourse than a chat with a real friend under a shed of thatch. Nevertheless, to be totally excluded from the life of the wealthy is to miss a discipline in manners that nothing ever replaces, and this is the real loss. The cultivation of taste which results from leisure forms, in course of time, amongst rich people a public opinion that disciplines every member of an aristocratic society far more severely than the more careless opinion of the hurried classes ever disciplines *them*. To know the value of such discipline we have only to observe societies from which it is absent. We have many opportunities for this in travelling, and one occurred to me last year that I will describe as an example. I was boating with two young friends on a French river, and we spent a Sunday in a decent riverside inn, where we had *déjeûner* in a corner of the public room. Several men of the neighborhood, probably farmers and small proprietors, sat in another corner playing cards. They had a very decent appearance, they were fine healthy-looking men, quite the contrary of a degraded class, and they were only amusing themselves temperately on a Sunday morning. Well, from the beginning of their game to the end of it (that is, during the whole time of our meal), they did nothing but shout, yell, shriek, and swear at each other loudly enough to be heard across the broad river. They were not angry in the least, but it was their habit to make a noise and to use oaths and foul language continually. We, at our table, could not hear each other's voices; but this did not occur to them. They had no notion that their noisy kind of intercourse could be unpleasant to anybody, because delicacy of sense, fineness of nerve, had not been developed in their class of society. Afterwards I asked them for some information, which they gave with a real anxiety to make themselves of use. Some rich people came to the inn with a pretty carriage, and I amused myself by noting the difference. *Their* manners were perfectly quiet. Why are rich people quiet and poorer ones noisy? Because the refinements of wealthy life, its peace and tranquillity, its leisure, its facilities for separation in different rooms, produce delicacy of nerve, with the perception that noise is disagreeable; and out of this delicacy, when it is general amongst a whole class, springs a strong determination so to discipline the members of the class that they shall not make themselves disagreeable to the majority. Hence lovers of good manners have a preference for the richer classes quite apart from a love of physical luxury or a snobbish desire to be associated with people of rank. For the same reason a lover of good manners dreads poverty or semi-poverty for his children, because even a moderate degree of poverty (not to speak of the acute forms of it) may compel them to associate with the undisciplined. What gentleman would like his son to live habitually with the card-players I have described?

ESSAY X
DIFFERENCES OF RANK AND WEALTH

THE most remarkable peculiarity about the desire to establish distinctions of rank is not that there should be definite gradations amongst people who have titles, but that, when the desire is strong in a nation, public opinion should go far beyond heralds and parchments and gazettes, and establish the most minute gradations amongst people who have nothing honorific about them.

When once the rule is settled by a table of precedence that an earl is greater than a baron, we simply acquiesce in the arrangement, as we are ready to believe that a mandarin with a yellow jacket is a much-to-be-honored sort of mandarin; but what is the power that strikes the nice balance of social advantages in favor of Mr. Smith as compared with Mr. Jones, when neither one nor the other has any title, or ancestry, or anything whatever to boast of? Amongst the many gifts that are to be admired in the fair sex this seems one of the most mysterious, that ladies can so decidedly fix the exact social position of every human being. Men soon find themselves bewildered by conflicting considerations, but a woman goes to the point at once, and settles in the most definite manner that Smith is certainly the superior of Jones.

This may bring upon me the imputation of being a democrat and a leveller. No, I rather like a well-defined social distinction when it has reality. Real distinctions keep society picturesque and interesting; what I fail to appreciate so completely are the fictitious little distinctions that have no basis in reality, and appear to be instituted merely for the sake of establishing differences that do not naturally exist. It seems to be an unfortunate tendency that seeks unapparent differences, and it may have a bad effect on character by forcing each man back upon the consideration of his own claims that it would be better for him to forget.

I once dined at a country-house in Scotland when the host asked one of the guests this question, "Are you a land-owner?" in order to determine his precedence. It did so happen that the guest owned a few small farms, so he answered "Yes;" but it struck me that the distinction between a man who had a moderate sum invested in land and one who had twice as much in other investments was not clearly in favor of the first. Could not the other buy land any day if he liked? He who hath gold hath land, potentially. If precedence is to be regulated by so material a consideration as wealth, let it be done fairly and plainly. The best and simplest plan would be to embroider the amount of each gentleman's capital in gold thread on the breast of his dress-coat. The metal would be appropriate, the embroidery would be decorative, and the practice would offer unequalled encouragement to thrift.

Again, I have always understood in the most confused manner the distinction, so clear to many, between those who are in trade and those who are not. I think I see the only real objection to trade with the help of M. Renan, who has stated it very clearly, but my difficulty is to discover who are tradesmen, and, still more, who are not tradesmen. Here is M. Renan's account of the matter:—

> "Our ideal can only be realized with a Government that gives some éclat to those who are connected with it and which creates distinctions outside of wealth. We feel an antipathy to a society in which the merit of a man and his superiority to another can only be revealed under the form of industry and commerce; not that trade and industry are not honest in our eyes, but because we see clearly that the best things (such as the functions of the priest, the magistrate, the savant, the artist, and the serious man of letters) are the inverse of the industrial and commercial spirit, the first duty of those who follow them being not to try to enrich themselves, and never to take into consideration the venal value of what they do."

This I understand, provided that the priest, magistrate, savant, artist, and serious man of letters are faithful to this "first duty;" provided that they "never take into consideration the venal value of what they do;" but there are tradesmen in the highest professions. All that can be said against trade is that its object is profit. Then it follows that every profession followed for profit has in it what is objectionable in trade, and that the professions are not noble in themselves but only if they are followed in a disinterested spirit. I should say, then, that any attempt to fix the degree of nobleness of persons by the supposed nobleness of their occupations must be founded upon an unreal distinction. A venal clergyman who does not believe the dogmas that he defends for his endowment, a venal barrister, ready to prostitute his talents and his tongue for a large income, seem to me to have in them far more of what is objectionable in trade than a country bookseller who keeps a little shop and sells note-paper and sealing-wax over the counter; yet it is assumed that their occupations are noble occupations and that his business is not noble, though I can see nothing whatever in it of which any gentleman need be in the slightest degree ashamed.

Again, there seem to be most unreal distinctions of respectability in the trades themselves. The wine trade has always been considered a gentlemanly business; but why is it more respectable to sell wine and spirits than to sell bread, or cheese, or beef? Are not articles of food more useful to the community than alcoholic drinks, and less likely to contribute to the general sum of evil? As for the honesty of the dealers, no doubt there are honest wine-merchants; but what thing that is sold for money has been more frequently adulterated, or more mendaciously labelled, or more unscrupulously charged for, than the produce of European vintages?[7]

Another wonderful unreality is the following. People desire the profits of trade, but are unwilling to lose caste by engaging in it openly. In order to fill their pockets and preserve their rank at the same time they engage in business anonymously, either as members of some firm in which their names do not appear, or else as share-holders in great trading enterprises. In both these cases the investor of capital becomes just as really and truly a tradesman as if he kept a shop, but if you were to tell him that he was a tradesman he would probably resent the imputation.

It is remarkable that the people who most despise commerce are the very people who bow down most readily before the accomplished results of commerce; for as they have an exaggerated sense of social distinctions, they are great adorers of wealth for the distinction that it confers. By their worship of wealth they acknowledge it to be most desirable; but then they worship rank also, and this other cultus goes with the sentiment of contempt for humble and plodding industry in all its forms.

The contempt for trade is inconsistent in another way. A man may be excluded from "good society" because he is in trade, and his grandson may be admitted because the grandfather was in trade, that is, through a fortune of commercial origin. The present Prime Minister (Gladstone) and the Speaker of the House of Commons (Mr. Arthur Peel) and many other men of high position in both Houses may owe their fame to their own distinguished abilities; but they owe the leisure and opportunity for cultivating and displaying those abilities to the wits and industry of tradesmen removed from them only by one or two generations.

Is there not a strange inconsistency in adoring wealth as it is adored, and despising the particular kind of skill and ability by which it is usually acquired? For if there be anything honorable about wealth it must surely be as evidence of the intelligence and industry that are necessary for the conquest of poverty. On the contrary, a narrowly exclusive society despises the virtue that is most creditable to the *nouveau riche*, his industry, whilst it worships his wealth as soon as the preservation of it is compatible with idleness.

There is a great deal of unreal distinction in the matter of ancestry. Those who observe closely are well aware that many undoubted and lineal descendants of the oldest families are in humble social positions, simply for want of money to make a display, whilst others usurp their coats-of-arms and claim a descent that they cannot really prove. The whole subject is therefore one of the most unsatisfactory that can be, and all that remains to the real members of old families who have not wealth enough to hold a place in the expensive modern aristocracy, is to remember secretly the history of their ancestors if they are romantic and poetical enough to retain the old-fashioned sentiment of birth, and to forget it if they look only to the present and the practical. There is, indeed, so little of the romantic sentiment left in the country, that even amongst the descendants of old families themselves very few are able to blazon their own armorial bearings, or even know what the verb "to blazon" means.

Amidst so great a confusion the simplest way would be not to think about rank at all, and to take human nature as it comes without reference to it; but however the ancient barriers of rank may be broken down, it is only to erect new ones. English feeling has a deep satisfaction in contemplating rank and wealth combined. It is that which it likes,—the combination. When wealth is gone it thinks that a man should lock up his pedigree in his desk and forget that he has ancestors; so it has been said that an English gentleman in losing wealth loses his caste with it, whilst a French or Italian gentleman may keep his caste, except in the most abject poverty. On the other hand, when an Englishman has a vast fortune it is thought right to give him a title also, that the desirable combination may be created afresh. Nothing is so striking in England, considering that it is an old country, as the newness of most of the great families. The aristocracy is like London, that has the reputation of being a very ancient city, yet the houses are of recent date. An aristocracy may be stronger and in better repair because of its newness; it may also be more likely to make a display of aristocratic superiorities, and expect deference to be paid to them, than an easy-going old aristocracy would be.

What are the superiorities, and what is the nature of the deference?

The superiority given by title depends on the intensity of title-worship amongst the public. In England that religion is in a very healthy and flourishing state, so that titles are very valuable there; in France the sense of a social hierarchy is so much weakened that titles are of infinitely less value. False ones are assumed and borne with impunity on account of the general indifference, whilst true and authentic titles are often dropped as an encumbrance. The blundering ignorance of the French about our titles, which so astonishes Englishmen, is due to a carelessness about the whole subject that no inhabitant of the British Islands can imagine.[8] In those islands title is of very great importance because the people have such a strong consciousness of its existence. In England, if there is a lord in the room every body is aware of it.

Superiority of family, without title, is merely local; it is not understood far from the ancestral home. Superiority of title is national; it is imperfectly appreciated in foreign countries. But superiority of wealth has the immense advantage over these that it is respected everywhere and can display itself everywhere with the utmost ostentation under pretext of custom and pleasure. It commands the homage of foolish and frivolous people by possibilities of vain display, and at the same time it appears desirable to the wise because it makes the gathering of experience easy and human intercourse convenient.

The rich man has access to an immense range of varied situations; and if he has energy to profit by this facility and put himself in those situations where he may learn the most, he may become far more experienced at thirty-five than a poor man can be at seventy. A poor man has a taste for boating, so he builds a little boat with his own hands, and paints it green and white, with its name, the "Cock-Robin," in yellow. Meanwhile his good wife, in spite of all the work she has to do, has a kindly indulgence for her poor Tom's hobby, thinks he deserves a little amusement, and stitches the sail for him in the evenings. He sails five or six miles up and down the river. Sir Thomas Brassey has exactly the same tastes: he builds the "Sunbeam;" and whilst the "Cock-Robin" has been doing its little trips, the "Sunbeam" has gone round the world; and instead of stitching the sails, the kind wife has accompanied the mariner, and written the story of his voyage. If after that you talk with the owners of the two vessels you may be interested for a few minutes—deeply interested and touched if you have the divine gift of sympathy—with the poor man's account of his doings; but his experience is small and soon told, whilst the owner of the "Sunbeam" has traversed all the oceans and could tell you a thousand things. So it naturally follows in most cases, though the rule has exceptions, that rich men are more interesting people to know than poor men of equal ability.

I remember being forcibly reminded of the narrow experience of the poor on one of those occasions that often happen to those who live in the country and know their poorer neighbors. A friend of mine, with his children, had come to stay with me; and there was a poor woman, living in a very out-of-the-way hamlet on a hill, who had made me promise that I would take my friend and his children to see her, because she had known their mother, who was dead, and had felt for her one of those strong and constant affections that often dwell in humble and faithful hearts. We have a great respect for this poor woman, who is in all ways a thoroughly dutiful person, and she has borne severe trials with great patience. Well, she was delighted to see my friend and his children, delighted to see how well they looked, how much they had grown, and so on; and then she spoke of her own little ones, and showed us the books they were learning in, and described their dispositions, and said that her husband was in full work and went every day to the schist mine, and was much steadier than he used to be, and made her much happier. After that she began again, saying exactly the same things all over again, and she said them a third time, and a fourth time. When we had left, we noticed this repetition, and we agreed that the poor woman, instead of being deficient in intelligence, was naturally above the average, but that the extreme narrowness of her experience, the total want of variety in her life, made it impossible for her mind to get out of that little domestic groove. She had about half-a-dozen ideas, and she lived in them, as a person in a small house lives in a very few rooms.

Now, however much esteem, respect, and affection you may have for a person of that kind, you will find it impossible to enjoy such society because conversation has no aliment. This is the one great reason why cultivated people seem to avoid the poor, even when they do not despise them in the least.

The greater experience of the rich is united to an incomparably greater power of pleasant reception, because in their homes conversation is not interfered with by the multitude of petty domestic difficulties and inconveniences. I go to spend the day with a very poor friend, and this is what is likely to happen. He and I can only talk without interruption when we are out of the house. Inside it his children break in upon us constantly. His wife finds me in the way, and wishes I had not come, because she has not been able to provide things exactly as she desired. At dinner her mind is not in the conversation; she is really occupied with petty household cares. I, on my part, have the uncomfortable feeling that I am creating inconvenience; and it requires incessant attention to soothe the watchful sensitiveness of a hostess who is so painfully alive to the deficiencies of her small establishment. If I have a robust appetite, it is well; but woe to me if my appetite is small, and I must overeat to prove that the cookery is good! If I accept a bed the sacrifice of a room will cause crowding elsewhere, besides which I shall be a nuisance in the early morning hours when nothing in the *ménage* is fit for the public eye. Whilst creating all this inconvenience to others, I suffer the great one of being stopped in my usual pursuits. If I want a few quiet hours for reading and writing there is only one way: I must go privately to some hotel and hire a sitting-room for myself.

Now consider the difference when I go to visit a rich friend! The first delightful feeling is that I do not occasion the very slightest inconvenience. His arrangements for the reception of guests are permanent and perfect. My arrival will scarcely cost his wife a thought; she has simply given orders in the morning for a room to be got ready and a cover to be laid at table. Her mind is free to think about any subject that suggests itself. Her conversation, from long practice, is as easy as the style of a good writer. All causes of interruption are carefully kept in the background. The household details are attended to by a regiment of domestics under their own officers. The children are in rooms of their own with their governesses and servants, and we see just enough of them to be agreeable. If I desire privacy, nothing is more easily obtained. On the slightest hint a room is placed at my disposal. I remember one house where that room used to be a splendid library, full of the books which at that time I most wanted to consult; and the only interruption in the mornings was the noiseless entrance of the dear lady of the house, always at eleven o'clock precisely, with a glass of wine and a biscuit on a little silver tray. It is not the material luxury of rich men's houses that a wise man would desire; but he must thoroughly appreciate their convenience and the varied food for the mind that they afford,—the books, the pictures, the curiosities. In one there is a museum of antiquities that a large town might envy, in another a collection of drawings, in a third a magnificent armory. In one private house in Paris[9] there used to be fourteen noble saloons containing the arts of two hundred years. You go to stay in ten rich houses and find them all different; you enjoy the difference, and in a certain sense you possess the different things. The houses of the poor are all alike, or if they differ it is not by variety of artistic or intellectual interest. By the habit of staying in each other's houses the rich multiply their riches to infinity. In a certain way of their own (it is not exactly the way of the early Christians) they have their goods in common.

There are, no doubt, many guests in the houses of the rich who care little for the people they visit, but much for the variety and accommodation,—guests who visit the place rather than the owner; guests who enjoy the cookery, the wines, the shooting, and who would go to the house if the owner were changed, exactly as they continue to patronize some pleasantly situated and well-managed hotel, after a change of masters. I hardly know how to describe these people in a word, but it is easy to characterize their entertainers. They are unpaid innkeepers.

There are also people, apparently hospitable, who care little for the persons they invite,—so very little, indeed, that we do not easily discover what motive they have for inviting them. The answer may be that they dislike solitude so much that any guest is acceptable, or else that they want admirers for the beautiful arrangements and furniture of their houses; for what is the use of having beautiful things if there is nobody to appreciate them? Hosts of this class are amateur exhibitors, or they are like amateur actors who want an audience, and who will invite people to come and listen, not because they care for the people, but because it is discouraging to play to empty benches.

These two classes of guests and hosts cannot exist without riches. The desire to be entertained ceases at once when it is known that the entertainment will be of a poor quality; and the desire to exhibit the internal arrangements of our houses ceases when we are too poor to do justice to the refinement of our taste.

The story of the rich man who had many friends and saw them fall away from him when he became poor, which, under various forms, reappears in every age and is common to all literatures, is explained by these considerations. Bucklaw does not find Lord Ravenswood a valuable gratuitous innkeeper; and Ravenswood is not anxious to exhibit to Bucklaw the housekeeping at Wolf's Crag.

But quite outside of parasite guests and exhibiting entertainers, there still remains the undeniable fact that if you like a rich man and a poor one equally well, you will prefer the rich man's hospitality for its greater convenience. Nay, more, you will rightly and excusably prefer the rich man's hospitality even if you like the poor man better, but find his household arrangements disagreeable, his wife fagged, worn, irritable, and ungracious, his children ill-bred, obtrusive, and dirty, himself unable to talk about anything rational on account of family interruptions, and scarcely his own better and higher self at all in the midst of his domestic plagues.[10]

There is no nation in the world that has so acute a sense of the value, almost the necessity, of wealth for human intercourse as the English nation. Whilst in other countries people think "Wealth is peace of mind, wealth is convenience, wealth is *la vie élégante*," in England they silently accept the maxim, "A large income is a necessary of life;" and they class each other according to the scale of their establishments, looking up with unfeigned reverence to those who have many servants, many horses, and gigantic houses where a great hospitality is dispensed. An ordinary Englishman thinks he has failed in life, and his friends are of the same opinion, if he does not arrive at the ability to imitate this style and state, at least in a minor degree. I have given the best reasons why it is desired; I understand and appreciate them; but at the same time I think it deeply to be deplored that an expenditure far beyond what can be met by the physical or intellectual labor of ordinary workers should be thought necessary in order that people may meet and talk in comfort. The big English house is a machine that runs with unrivalled smoothness; but it masters its master, it possesses its nominal possessor. George Borrow had the deepest sense of the Englishman's slavery to his big, well-ordered dwelling, and saw in it the cause of unnumbered anxieties, often ending in heart-disease, paralysis, bankruptcy, and in minor cases sacrificing all chance of leisure and quiet happiness. Many a land-owner has crippled himself by erecting a great house on his estate,—one of those huge, tasteless buildings that express nothing but pompous pride. What wisdom there is in the excellent old French adage, "A petite terre, petite maison"!

The reader may remember Herbert Spencer's idea that the display of wealth is intended to subjugate. Royal palaces are made very vast and magnificent to subjugate those who approach the sovereign; and all rich and powerful people use the same means, for the same purpose, though in minor degrees. This leads us to the price that has to be paid for intercourse with persons of great rank and wealth. May we not suspect that there is a heavy price of some kind, since many of the best and noblest minds in the world either avoid it altogether or else accept it cautiously and only with a very few rich men whom they esteem independently of their riches?

The answer is that wealth and rank expect deference, not so much humble and slavish manners as that intellectual deference which a thinker can never willingly give. The higher the rank of the personage the more it is considered ill-bred to contradict him, or even to have an opinion of your own in his presence. This, to a thinker, is unendurable. He does not see that because a person is rich and noble his views on everything must be the best and soundest views.

You, my dear Aristophilus, who by your pleasing manners are so well fitted for the very best society, could give interesting answers to the following questions: Have you never found it advisable to keep silence when your wealthy host was saying things against which you inwardly protested? Have you not sometimes gone a step further, and given a kind of assent to some opinion that was not your own? Have you not, by practice, attained the power of giving a still stronger and heartier assent to what seemed doubtful propositions?

There is one form of this assent which is deeply damaging to character. Some great person, a great lady perhaps, unjustly condemns, in your presence, a public man for whom you have a sincere respect. Instead of boldly defending him, you remain silent and acquiescent. You are afraid to offend, afraid to lose favor, afraid that if you spoke openly you would not be invited to the great house any more.

Sometimes not a single individual but a class is attacked at once. A great lady is reported to have said that she "had a deep objection to French literature in all its branches." Observe that this expression of opinion contains a severe censure on *all* French authors and on all readers of French literature. Would you have ventured to say a word in their defence? Would you have dared to hint, for example, that a serious mind might be none the worse for some acquaintance with Montesquieu and De Tocqueville? No, sir, you would have bowed your head and put on a shocked expression of countenance.

In this way, little by little, by successive abandonments of what we think, and abdications of what we know, we may arrive at a state of habitual and inane concession that softens every fibre of the mind.

ESSAY XI
THE OBSTACLE OF LANGUAGE

THE greatest impediment to free intercourse between nations is neither distance nor the differences of mental habits, nor the opposition of national interests; it is simply the imperfect manner in which languages are usually acquired, and the lazy contentment of mankind with a low degree of attainment in a foreign tongue when a much higher degree of attainment would be necessary to any efficient interchange of ideas.

It seems probable that much of the future happiness of humanity will depend upon a determination to learn foreign languages more thoroughly. International ill-will is the parent of innumerable evils. From the intellectual point of view it is a great evil, because it narrows our range of ideas and deprives us of light from foreign thinkers. From the commercial point of view it is an evil, because it leads a nation to deny itself conveniences in order to avoid the dreaded result of doing good to another country. From the political point of view it is an enormous evil, because it leads nations to make war upon each other and to inflict and endure all the horrors, the miseries, the impoverishment of war rather than make some little concession on one side or on both sides that would have been made with little difficulty if the spirit of the two countries had been more friendly. May we not believe that a more general spirit of friendliness would result from more personal intercourse, and that this would be the consequence of more thorough linguistic acquirement?

It has always seemed to me an inexpressible misfortune to the French that they should not be better acquainted with English literature; and this not simply from the literary point of view, but because on so many questions that interest active minds in France it would be such an advantage to those minds to be able to see how those questions have appeared to men bred in a different and a calmer atmosphere. If the French read English easily they might often avoid (without ceasing to be national) many of those errors that result from seeing things only from a single point of view. I know a few intelligent Frenchmen who do read our most thoughtful writers in the original, and I can see what a gain this enlarged experience has been to them. On the other hand, it is certain that good French literature may have an excellent effect on the literary training of an Englishman. The careful study of that clear, concise, and moderate French writing which is the most perfect flower of the cultivated national mind has been most beneficial to some English writers, by making them less clumsy, less tedious, less verbose.

Of commercial affairs it would be presumptuous in me to say much, but no one disputes that international commerce is a benefit, and that it would not be possible without a class of men who are acquainted with foreign languages. On this class of men, be they merchants or corresponding clerks, the commercial intercourse between nations must depend. I find it stated by foreign tradesmen that if they were better acquainted with the English language much trade that now escapes them might be made to pass through their hands. I have myself often observed, on a small scale, that transactions of an international character have taken place because one of the parties happened to know the language of the other, when they would certainly not have taken place if it had been necessary to make them through an agent or an interpreter.

With regard to peace and war, can it be doubted that the main reason for our peaceful relations with the United States lies in the fact of our common language? We may have newspaper quarrels, but the newspapers themselves help to make every question understood. It is far harder to gain acceptance for English ideas in France, yet even our relations with France are practically more peaceful than of old, and though there is intense jealousy between the two countries, they understand each other better, so that differences which would certainly have produced bloodshed in the days of Pitt, cause nothing worse than inkshed in the days of Gladstone. This happy result may be attributed in great part to the English habit of learning French and going to Paris or to the south of France. We need not expect any really cordial understanding between the two countries, though it would be an incalculable benefit to both. That is too much to be hoped for; their jealousy, on both sides, is too irritable and too often inflamed afresh by new incidents, for neither of them can stir a foot without putting the other out of temper; but we may hope that through the quietly and constantly exerted influence of those who know both languages, war may be often, though perhaps not always, avoided.

Unfortunately an imperfect knowledge of a foreign language is of little use, as it does not give any real freedom of intercourse. Foreigners do not open their minds to one who blunders about their meaning; they consider him to be a sort of child, and address to him "easy things to understand." Their confidence is only to be won by a demonstration of something like equality in intelligence, and nobody can give proof of this unless he has the means of making his thoughts intelligible, and even of assuming, when the occasion presents itself, a somewhat bold and authoritative tone. People of mature and superior intellect, but imperfect linguistic acquirements, are liable to be treated with a kind of condescending indulgence when out of their own country, as if they were as young in years and as feeble in power of thought as they are in their knowledge of foreign languages.

The extreme rarity of that degree of attainment in a foreign language which deserves to be called *mastery* is well known to the very few who are competent to judge. At a meeting of French professors Lord Houghton said that the wife of a French ambassador had told him that she knew only three Englishmen who could speak French. One of these was Sir Alexander Cockburn, another the Duke of Bedford, and we may presume the third to have been Lord Houghton himself. Amongst men of letters Lord Houghton only knew one, Henry Reeve, the editor of the "Edinburgh Review" and translator of the works of De Tocqueville. He mentioned Lord Arthur Russell as an example of accomplishment, but he is "quasi French by *l'esprit*, education, and marriage."

On reading the report of Lord Houghton's speech, I asked a cultivated Parisian lady (who knows English remarkably well and has often been in England) what her own experience had been. After a little hesitation she said it had been exactly that of the French ambassadress. She, also, had met with three Englishmen who spoke French, and she named them. I suggested several others, and amongst them some very learned scholars, merely to hear what she would say, but her answer was that their inadequate power of expression compelled them to talk far below the level of their abilities, so that when they spoke French nobody would suppose them to be clever men. She also affirmed that they did not catch the shades of French expression, so that in speaking French to them one was never sure of being quite accurately understood.

I myself have known many French people who have studied English more or less, including several who read English authors with praiseworthy industry, but I have only met with one or two who can be said to have mastered the language. I am told that M. Beljame, the learned Professor of English Literature at the Sorbonne, has a wonderful mastery of our tongue. Many French professors of English have considerable historical and grammatical knowledge of it, but that is not practical mastery. In general, the knowledge of English attained by French people (not without more labor than the result would show) is so poor and insufficient as to be almost useless.

I remember an accidental circumstance that put into my hands some curious materials for judging of the attainments of a former generation. A

Belgian lady, for a reason that has no concern with our present subject, lent me for perusal an important packet of letters in the French language written by English ladies of great social distinction about the date of Waterloo. They showed a rough familiarity with French, but no knowledge of its finer shades, and they abounded in glaring errors. The effect of this correspondence on my mind was that the writers had certainly used (or abused) the language, but that they had never condescended to learn it.

These and other experiences have led me to divide progress in languages into several stages, which I place at the reader's disposal in the belief that they may be convenient to him as they have been convenient to me.

The first stage in learning a language is when every sentence is a puzzle and exercises the mind like a charade or a conundrum. There are people to whom this kind of exercise is a sport. They enjoy the puzzle for its own sake and without any reference to the literary value of the sentence or its preciousness as an utterance of wisdom. Such people are much better adapted to the early stage of linguistic acquirement than those who like reading and dislike enigmas.

The excessive slowness with which one works in this early stage is a cause of irritation when the student interests himself in the thoughts or the narrative, because what comes into his mind in a given time is so small a matter that it seems not worth while to go on working for such a little intellectual income. Therefore in this early stage it is a positive disadvantage to have eager literary desires.

In the second stage the student can push along with the help of a translation and a dictionary; but this is not *reading*, it is only aided construing. It is disagreeable to a reader, though it may be endured by one who is indifferent to reading. This may be made clear by reference to other pursuits. A man who loves rowing, and who knows what rowing is, does not like to pull a slow and heavy boat, such as an ordinary Scottish Highlander pulls with perfect contentment. So a man who loves reading, and knows what reading is, does not like the heavy work of laborious translation. This explains the fact which is often so unintelligible to parents, that boys who are extremely fond of reading often dislike their classical studies. Grammar, prosody, philology, so far as they are the subjects of *conscious attention* (which they are with all pedagogues), are the rivals of literature, and so it happens that pedagogy is unfavorable to literary art. It is only when the sciences of dissection are forgotten that we can enjoy the arts of poetry and prose.

If, then, the first stage of language-learning requires rather a taste for solving puzzles than a taste for literature, so I should say that the second stage requires rather a turn for grammatical and philological considerations than an interest in the ideas or an appreciation of the style of great authors. The most favorable state of mind for progress in this stage is that of a philologist; and if a man has literary tastes in great strength, and philological tastes in a minor degree, he will do well, in this stage, to encourage the philologist in himself and keep his love of literature in abeyance.

In the third stage the vocabulary has become rich enough to make references to the dictionary less frequent, and the student can read with some degree of literary enjoyment. There is, however, this remaining obstacle, that even when the reader knows the words and can construe well, the foreign manner of saying things still appears *unnatural*. I have made many inquiries concerning this stage of acquirement and find it to be very common. Men of fair scholarship in Latin tell me that the Roman way of writing does not seem to be really a natural way. I find that even those Latin works which were most familiar to me in youth, such as the Odes of Horace, for example, seem unnatural still, though I may know the meaning of every word, and I do not believe that any amount of labor would ever rid me of this feeling. This is a great obstacle, and not the less that it is of such a subtle and intangible nature.[11]

In the fourth stage the mode of expression seems natural, and the words are perfectly known, but the sense of the paragraph is not apparent at a glance. There is the feeling of a slight obstacle, of something that has to be overcome; and there is a remarkable counter-feeling which always comes after the paragraph is mastered. The reader then wonders that such an obviously intelligible page can have offered any opposition whatever. What surprises us is that this fourth stage can last so long as it does. It seems as if it would be so easily passed, and yet, in fact, it is for most persons impassable.

The fifth stage is that of perfection in reading. It is not reached by everybody even in the native language itself. The reader who has attained it sees the contents of a page and catches their meaning at a glance even before he has had time to read the sentences.

This condition of extreme lucidity in a language comes, when it comes at all, long after the mere acquisition of it. I have said that it does not always come even in the native tongue. Some educated people take a much longer time than others to make themselves acquainted with the contents of a newspaper. A clever newspaper reader sees in one minute if there is anything of importance. He knows what articles and telegrams are worth reading before he separates the words.

These five stages refer only to reading, because educated people learn to read first and to speak afterwards. Uneducated people learn foreign languages by ear in a most confused and blundering way. I need not add that they never master them, as only the educated ever master their native tongue. It is unnecessary to go through the stages of progress in conversation, as they are in a great degree dependent upon reading, though they lag behind it; but I will say briefly that the greatest of all difficulties in using foreign languages is to become really insensible to the absurdities that they contain. All languages, I believe, abound in absurd expressions; and a foreigner, with his inconveniently fresh perceptions, can hardly avoid being tickled by them. He cannot use the language seriously without having first become unconscious of these things, and it is inexpressibly difficult to become unconscious of something that has once provoked us to laughter. Again, it is most difficult to arrive at that stage when foreign expressions of politeness strike us no more and no less than they strike the native; or, in other words, it is most difficult for us to attach to them the exact value which they have in the country where they prevail. French forms seem absurdly ceremonious to Englishmen; in reality, they are only convenient, but the difficulty for an Englishman is to feel that they are convenient. There are in every foreign tongue two classes of absurdities,—the real inherent absurdities to which the natives are blinded by habit, though they are seen at once to be comical when attention is directed to them, and the expressions that are not absurd in themselves but only seem so to us because they are not like our own.

The difficulty of becoming insensible to these things must be especially great for humorous people, who are constantly on the look-out for subjects of odd remarks. I have a dear friend who is gifted with a delightful genius for humor, and he knows a little French. All that he has acquired of that language is used by him habitually as material for fun, and as he is quite incapable of regarding the language as anything but a funny way of talking, he cannot make any progress in it. If he were asked to read prayers in French the idea would seem to him incongruous, a mingling of frivolous with sacred things. Another friend is serious in French because he knows it well, and therefore has become unconscious of its real or apparent absurdities, but when he is in a merry mood he talks Italian, with which he is much less intimately acquainted, so that it still seems droll and amusing.

Many readers will be already familiar with the idea of a universal language, which has often been the subject of speculation in recent times, and has even been discussed in a sort of informal congress connected with one of the universal exhibitions. Nobody now looks forward to anything so unlikely, or so undesirable, as the abandonment of all the languages in the world except one. What is considered practicable is the selection of one language as the recognized international medium, and the teaching of that language everywhere in addition to the mother tongue, so that no two educated men could ever meet without possessing the means of communication. To a certain degree we have this already in French, but French is not known so generally, or so perfectly, as to make it answer the purpose. It is proposed to adopt modern Greek, which has several great advantages. The first is that the old education has familiarized us sufficiently with ancient Greek to take away the first sense of strangeness in the same language under its modern form. The second is that everything about modern arts and sciences, and political life, and trade, can be said easily in the Greek of the present day, whilst it has its own peculiar interest for scholars. The third reason is of great practical importance. Greece is a small State, and therefore does not awaken those keen international jealousies that would be inevitably aroused by proposing the language of a powerful State to be learned, without reciprocity, by the youth of the other powerful States. It may be some time before the Governments of great nations agree to promote the study of modern Greek, or any other living language, amongst their peoples; but if all who feel the immense desirableness of a common language for international intercourse would agree to prepare the way for its adoption, the time might not be very far distant when statesmen would begin to consider the question within the horizon of the practical. Let us try to imagine the difference between the present Babel-confusion of tongues, which makes it a mere chance whether we shall be able to communicate with a foreigner or not, and the sudden facility that would result from the possession of a common medium of intercourse! If it were once agreed by a union of nations (of which the present Postal Union may be the forerunner) that the learning of the universal language should be encouraged, that language would be learned with a zest and eagerness of which our present languid linguistic attempts give but a faint idea. There would be such powerful reasons for learning it! All those studies that interest men in different nations would lead to intercommunication in the common tongue. Many books would be written in it, to be circulated everywhere, without being enfeebled and falsified by translation. International commerce would be transacted by its means. Travelling would be enormously facilitated. There would be such a gain to human intercourse by language that it might be preferred, in many cases, to the old-fashioned international intercourse by means of bayonets and cannon-balls.

ESSAY XII
THE OBSTACLE OF RELIGION

HUMAN intercourse, on equal terms, is difficult or impossible for those who do not belong to that religion which is dominant in the country where they live. The tendency has always been either to exclude such persons from human intercourse altogether (a fate so hard to bear during a whole life-time that they have often compromised the matter by outward conformity), or else to maintain some degree of intercourse with them in placing them at a social disadvantage. In barbarous times such persons, when obstinate, are removed by taking away their lives; or if somewhat less obstinate they are effectually deterred from the profession of heretical opinions by threats of the most pitiless punishments. In semi-barbarous times they are paralyzed, so far as public action is concerned, by political disabilities expressly created for their inconvenience. In times which pride themselves on having completely emerged from barbarism political disabilities are almost entirely removed, but certain class-exclusions still persist, by which it is arranged (whilst avoiding all appearance of persecution) that although heretics are no longer banished from their native land they may be excluded from their native class, and either deprived of human intercourse altogether, or left to seek it in classes inferior to their own.

The religious obstacle differs from all other obstacles in one remarkable characteristic. It is maintained only against honest and truth-speaking persons. Exemption from its operation has always been, and is still, uniformly pronounced in favor of all heretics who will consent to lie. The honorable unbeliever has always been treated harshly; the unbeliever who had no sense of honor has been freely permitted, in every age, to make the best use of his abilities for his own social advancement. For him the religious obstacle is simply non-existent. He has exactly the same chances of preferment as the most orthodox Christian. In Pagan times, when public religious functions were a part of the rank of great laymen, unbelief in the gods of Olympus did not hinder them from seeking and exercising those functions. Since the establishment of Christianity as a State religion, the most stringently framed oaths have never prevented an unscrupulous infidel from attaining any position that lay within reach of his wits and his opportunities. He has sat in the most orthodox Parliaments, he has been admitted to Cabinet councils, he has worn royal crowns, he has even received the mitre, the Cardinal's hat, and the Papal tiara. We can never sufficiently admire the beautiful order of society by which heretic-plus-liar is so graciously admitted everywhere, and heretic-plus-honest man is so cautiously and ingeniously kept out. It is, indeed, even more advantageous to the dishonest unbeliever than at first sight appears; for not only does it open to him all positions accessible to the orthodox, but it even gives him a noteworthy advantage over honest orthodoxy itself by training him daily and hourly in dissimulation. To be kept constantly in the habit of dissimulation on one subject is an excellent discipline in the most serviceable of social arts. An atheist who reads prayers with a pious intonation, and is exemplary in his attendance at church, and who never betrays his real opinions by an unguarded word or look, though always preserving the appearance of the simplest candor, the most perfect openness, is, we may be sure, a much more formidable person to contend with in the affairs of this world than an honest Christian who has never had occasion to train himself in habitual imposture. Yet good Christians willingly admit these dangerous, unscrupulous rivals, and timidly exclude those truthful heretics who are only honest, simple people like themselves.

After religious liberty has been nominally established in a country by its lawgivers, its enemies do not consider themselves defeated, but try to recover, through the unwritten law of social customs and observances, the ground they have lost in formal legislation. Hence we are never sure that religious liberty will exist within the confines of a class even when it is loudly proclaimed in a nation as one of the most glorious conquests of the age. It is often enjoyed very imperfectly, or at a great cost of social and even pecuniary sacrifice. In its perfection it is the liberty to profess openly, and in their full force, those opinions on religious subjects which a man holds in his own conscience, and without incurring any kind of punishment or privation on account of them, legal or social. For example, a really sincere member of the Church of England enjoys perfect religious liberty in England.[12] He can openly say what he thinks, openly take part in religious services that his conscience approves, and without incurring the slightest legal or social penalty for so doing. He meets with no hindrance, no obstacle, placed in the path of his worldly life on account of his religious views. True liberty is not that which is attainable at some cost, some sacrifice, but that which we can enjoy without being made to suffer for it in any way. It is always enjoyed, to the full, by every one whose sincere convictions are heartily on the side of authority. Sincere Roman Catholics enjoyed perfect religious liberty in Spain under Ferdinand and Isabella, and in England under Mary Tudor. Even a Trappist who loves the rule of his order enjoys the best kind of liberty within the walls of his monastery. He is not allowed to neglect the prescribed services and other obligations; but as he feels no desire to neglect them he is a free agent, as free as if he dwelt in the Abbaye de Thélème of Rabelais, with its one rule, "Fay ce que vouldras." We may go farther, and say that not only are people whose convictions are on the side of authority perfectly free agents, but, like successful artists, they are rewarded for doing what they themselves prefer. They are always rewarded by the approval of their superiors and very frequently by opportunities for social advancement that are denied to those who think differently from persons in authority.

There are cases in which liberty is less complete than this, yet is still spoken of as liberty. A man is free to be a Dissenter in England and a Protestant in France. By this we mean that he will incur no legal disqualification for his opinions; but does he incur no social penalty? The common answer to this question is that the penalty is so slight that there is nothing to complain of. This depends upon the particular situation of the Dissenter, because the penalty is applied very differently in different cases, and may vary between an unperceived hindrance to an undeveloped ambition and an insurmountable obstacle to an eager and aspiring one. To understand this thoroughly, let us ask whether there are any positions in which a member of the Church of England would incur a penalty for leaving it. Are there any positions that are socially considered to be incompatible with the religious profession of a Dissenter?

It will be generally admitted that royal personages do not enjoy any religious liberty at all. A royal personage *must* profess the State religion of his country, and it is so well understood that this is obligatory and has nothing to do with the convictions of the conscience that such personages are hardly expected to have any conscience in the matter. They take up a religion as part of their situation in the world. A princess may abjure her faith for that of an imperial lover, and if he dies before marriage she may abjure her adopted faith; and if she is asked again in marriage she may abjure the religion of her girlhood a second time without exciting comment, because it is well understood that her private convictions may remain undisturbed by such changes, and that she submits to them as a necessity for which she has no personal responsibility.[13] And whilst princes are compelled to take up the religion which best suits their worldly interests, they are not allowed simply to bear the name of the State Church but must also conform to its services with diligent regularity. In many cases they probably have no objection to this, as they may be really conscientious members of the State Church, or they may accept it in a general way as an expression of duty towards God (without going into dogmatic details), or they may be ready and willing to conform to it for political reasons, as the best means of conciliating public opinion; but however this may be, all human fellowship, so far as religion is concerned, must, for them, be founded on deference to the State religion and a conciliatory attitude towards its ministers. The Court circulars of different countries register the successive acts of outward conformity by which the prince acknowledges the power of the national priesthood, and it would be impossible for him to suspend these acts of conformity for any reason except illness. The daily account of the life of a French sovereign during the hunting season used to be, "His Majesty heard mass; His Majesty went out to hunt." Louis XVIII. had to hear mass like his ancestors; but after the long High Mass which he was compelled to listen to on Sundays, and which he found extremely wearisome, he enjoyed a compensation and a consolation in talking impiously to his courtiers, and was maliciously pleased in shocking pious people and in forcing them to laugh against their conscience, as by courtly duty bound, at the blasphemous royal jests. This is one of the great evils of a compulsory conformity. It drives the victim into a reaction against the religion that tyrannizes over him, and makes him *anti*-religious, when without pressure he would have been simply and inoffensively *non*-religious. To understand the pressure that weighs upon royal personages in this respect, we have only to remember that there is not a sovereign in the whole world who could venture to say openly that he was a conscientious Unitarian, and would attend a Unitarian place of worship. If a King of England held Unitarian opinions, and was at the same time scrupulously honest, he would have no resource but abdication, for not only is the King a member of the Anglican Church, but he is its living head. The sacerdotal position of the Emperor of Russia is still more marked, and he can no more avoid taking part in the fatiguing ceremonies of the orthodox Greek religion than he can avoid sitting on horseback and reviewing troops.

The religious slavery of princes is, however, exclusively in ceremonial acts and verbal professions. With regard to the moral side of religion, with regard to every religious doctrine that is practically favorable to good conduct, exalted personages have always enjoyed an astonishing amount of liberty. They are not free to hold themselves aloof from public ceremonies, but they are free to give themselves up to every kind of private self-indulgence, including flagrant sexual immoralities, which are readily forgiven them by a loyal priesthood and an admiring populace, if only they show an affable condescension in their manners. Surely morality is a part of Christianity; surely it is as unchristian an act to commit adultery as to walk out during service-time on Sunday morning; yet adultery is far more readily forgiven in a prince, and far easier for him, than the merely negative religious sin of abstinence from church-going. Amongst the great criminal sovereigns of the world, the Tudors, Bourbons, Bonapartes, there has never been any neglect of ceremonies, but they have treated the entire moral code of Christianity as if it were not binding on persons of their degree.

Every hardship is softened, at least in some measure, by a compensation; and when in modern times a man is so situated that he has no outward religious liberty it is perfectly understood that his conformity is official, like that of a soldier who is ordered to give the Host a military salute without regard for his private opinion about transubstantiation. This being understood, the religious slavery of a royal personage is far from being the hardest of such slaveries. The hardest cases are those in which there is every appearance of liberty, whilst some subtle secret force compels the slave to acts that have the appearance of the most voluntary submission. There are many positions of this kind in the world. They abound in countries where the right of private judgment is loudly proclaimed, where a man is told that he may act in religious matters quite freely according to the dictates of his conscience, whilst he well knows, at the same time, that unless his conscience happens to be in unison with the opinions of the majority, he will incur some kind of disability, some social paralysis, for having obeyed it.

The rule concerning the ceremonial part of religion appears to be that a man's liberty is in inverse proportion to his rank. A royal personage has none; he must conform to the State Church. An English nobleman has two churches to choose from: he may belong to the Church of England or the Church of Rome. A simple private gentleman, a man of good family and moderate independent fortune, living in a country where the laws are so liberal as they are in England, and where on the whole there is so little bitterness of religious hatred, might be supposed to enjoy perfect religious liberty, but he finds, in a practical way, that it is scarcely possible for him to do otherwise than the nobility. He has the choice between Anglicanism and Romanism, because, though untitled, he is still a member of the aristocracy.

As we go down lower in the social scale, to the middle classes, and particularly to the lower middle classes, we find a broader liberty, because in these classes the principle is admitted that a man may be a good Christian beyond the pale of the State Churches. The liberty here is real, so far as it goes, for although these persons are not obliged by their own class opinion to be members of a State Church, as the aristocracy are, they are not compelled, on the other hand, to be Dissenters. They may be good Churchmen, if they like, and still be middle-class Englishmen, or they may be good Methodists, Baptists, Independents, and still be respectable middle-class Englishmen. This permits a considerable degree of freedom, yet it is still by no means unlimited freedom. The middle-class Englishman allows dissent, but he does not encourage honesty in unbelief.

There is, however, a class in English society in which for some time past religious liberty has been as nearly as possible absolute,—I mean the working population in the large towns. A working-man may belong to the Church of England, or to any one of the dissenting communities; or, if he does not believe in Christianity, he may say so and abstain from religious hypocrisy of all kinds. Whatever his opinions, he will not be regarded very coldly on account of them by persons of his own class, nor prevented from marrying, nor hindered from pursuing his trade.

We find, therefore, that amongst the various classes of society, from the highest to the humblest, religious liberty increases as we go lower. The royal family is bound to conform to whatever may be the dominant religion for the time being; the nobility and gentry have the choice between the present dominant faith and its predecessor; the middle class has, in addition, the liberty of dissent; the lower class has the liberty, not only of dissent, but also of abstinence and negation. And in each case the increase of liberty is real; it is not that illusory kind of extension which loses in one direction the freedom that it wins in another. All the churches are open to the plebeian secularist if he should ever wish to enter them.

We have said that religious liberty increases as we go lower in the social scale. Let us consider, now, how it is affected by locality. The rule may be stated at once. *Religious liberty diminishes with the number of inhabitants in a place.*

However humble may be the position of the dweller in a small village at a distance from a town, he must attend the dominant church because no other will be represented in the place. He may be in heart a Dissenter, but his dissent has no opportunity of expressing itself by a different form of worship. The laws of his country may be as liberal as you please; their liberality is of no practical service in such a case as this because religious profession requires public worship, and an isolated family cannot institute a cult.

If, indeed, there were the liberty of abstinence the evil would not be so great. The liberty of rejection is a great and valuable liberty. If a particular kind of food is unsuited to my constitution, and only that kind of food is offered me, the permission to fast is the safeguard of my health and comfort. The loss of this negative liberty is terrible in convivial customs, when the victim is compelled to drink against his will.

The Dissenter in the country can be forced to conform by his employer or by public opinion, acting indirectly. The master may avoid saying, "I expect you to go to Church," but he may say, "I expect you to attend a place of worship," which attains precisely the same end with an appearance of greater liberality. Public opinion may be really liberal enough to tolerate many different forms of religion, but if it does not tolerate abstinence from public services the Dissenter has to conform to the dominant worship in places where there is no other. In England it may seem that there is not very much hardship in this, as the Church is not extreme in doctrine and is remarkably tolerant of variety, yet even in England a conscientious Unitarian might feel some difficulty about creeds and prayers which were never intended for him. There are, however, harder cases than those of a Dissenter forced to conform to the Church of England. The Church of Rome is far more extreme and authoritative, far more sternly repressive of human reason; yet there are thousands of rural places on the Continent where religious toleration is supposed to exist, and where, nevertheless, the inhabitants are compelled to hear mass to avoid the imputation of absolute irreligion. A man like Wesley or Bunyan would, in such a position, have to choose between apparent Romanism and apparent Atheism, if indeed the village opinion did not take good care that he should have no choice in the matter.

It may be said that people should live in places where their own form of worship is publicly practised. No doubt many do so. I remember an Englishman belonging to a Roman Catholic family who would not spend a Sunday in an out-of-the-way place in Scotland because he could not hear mass. Such a person, having the means to choose his place of residence, and a faith so strong that religious considerations always came first with him, would compel everything to give way to the necessity for having mass every Sunday, but this is a very exceptional case. Ordinary people are the victims of circumstances and not their masters.

If a villager has little religious freedom he does not greatly enlarge it when he becomes a soldier. He has the choice between the Church of England and the Church of Rome. In some countries even this very moderate degree of liberty is denied. Within the present century Roman Catholic soldiers were compelled to attend Protestant services in Prussia. The truth is that the genuine military spirit is strongly opposed to individual opinion in matters of religion. Its ideal is that every detail in a soldier's existence should be settled by the military authorities, his religious belief amongst the rest.

What may be truly said about military authority in religious matters is that as the force employed is perfectly well known,—as it is perfectly well known that soldiers take part in religious services under compulsion,— there is no hypocrisy in their case, especially where the conscription exists, and therefore but slight moral hardship. Certainly the greatest hardship of all is to be compelled to perform acts of conformity with all the appearance of free choice. The tradesman who must go to mass to have customers is in a harder position than the soldier. For this reason, it is better for the moral health of a nation, when there is to be compulsion of some kind, that it should be boldly and openly tyrannical; that its work should be done in the face of day; that it should be outspoken, uncompromising, complete. To tyranny of that kind a man may give way without any loss of self-respect, he yields to *force majeure*; but to that viler and meaner kind of tyranny which keeps a man in constant alarm about the means of earning his living, about the maintenance of some wretched little peddling position in society, he yields with a sense of far deeper humiliation, with a feeling of contempt for the social power that uses such miserable means, and of contempt for himself also.

ESSAY XIII
PRIESTS AND WOMEN

Part I.—Sympathy

WOMEN hate the Inexorable. They like a condition of things in which nothing is so surely fixed but that the rule may be broken in their favor, or the hard decision reversed. They like concession for concession's sake, even when the matter is of slight importance. A woman will ask a favor from a person in authority when a man will shrink from the attempt; and if the woman gains her point by entreaty she will have a keen and peculiar feminine satisfaction in having successfully exercised what she feels to be her own especial power, to which the strong, rough creature, man, may often be made to yield. A woman will go forth on the most hopeless errands of intercession and persuasion, and in spite of the most adverse circumstances will not infrequently succeed. Scott made admirable use of this feminine tendency in the "Heart of Mid-Lothian." Jeanie Deans, with a woman's feelings and perseverance, had a woman's reliance on her own persuasive powers, and the result proved that she was right. All things in a woman combine to make her mighty in persuasion. Her very weakness aids her; she can assume a pitiful, childlike tenderness. Her ignorance aids her, as she seems never to know that a decision can be fixed and final; then she has tears, and besides these pathetic influences she has generally some magnetism of sex, some charm or attraction, at least, in voice or manner, and sometimes she has that marvellous—that all but irresistible—gift of beauty which has ruled and ruined the masters of the world.

Having constantly used these powers of persuasion with the strongest being on this planet, and used them with such wonderful success that it is even now doubtful whether the occult feminine government is not mightier than the open masculine government, whilst it is not a matter of doubt at all, but of assured fact, that society is ruled by queens and ladies and not by kings and lords,—with all these evidences of their influence in this world, it is intelligible that women should willingly listen to those who tell them that they have similar influence over supernatural powers, and, through them, on the destinies of the universe. Far less willingly would they listen to some hard scientific teacher who should say, "No, you have no influence beyond this planet, and that which you exercise upon its surface is limited by the force that you are able to set in motion. The Empress Eugénie had no supernatural influence through the Virgin Mary, but she had great and dangerous natural influence through her husband; and it may be true, what is asserted, that she caused in this way a disastrous war." An exclusively *originating* Intelligence, acting at the beginning of Evolution,—a setter-in-motion of a prodigious self-acting machinery of cause producing effect, and effects in their turn becoming a new complexity of causes,—an Intelligence that we cannot persuade because we are born millions of years too late for the first impulse that started all things,—this may be the God of the future, but it will be a distant future before the world of women will acknowledge him.

There is another element in the feminine nature that urges women in the same direction. They have a constant sense of dependence in a degree hardly ever experienced by men except in debilitating illness; and as this sense of dependence is continual with them and only occasional with us, it becomes, from habit, inseparable from their mental action, whereas even in sickness a man looks forward to the time when he will act again freely for himself. Men choose a course of action; women choose an adviser. They feel themselves unable to continue the long conflict without help, and in spite of their great patience and courage they are easily saddened by solitude, and in their distress of mind they feel an imperious need for support and consolation. "Our valors are our best gods," is a purely masculine sentiment, and to a woman such self-reliance seems scarcely distinguishable from impiety. The feminine counterpart of that would be, "In our weakness we seek refuge in Thy strength, O Lord!"

A woman is not satisfied with merely getting a small share in a vast bounty for the general good; she is kind and affectionate herself, she is personally attentive to the wants of children and animals, and cares for each of them separately, and she desires to be cared for in the same way. The philosopher does not give her any assurance of this whatever; but the priest, on the contrary, gives it in the most positive form. It is not merely one of the doctrines of religion, but the central doctrine, the motive for all religious exercises, that God cares for every one of us individually; that he knows Jane Smith by name, and what she is earning a week, and how much of it she devotes to keeping her poor paralyzed old mother. The philosopher says, "If you are prudent and skilful in your conformity to the laws of life you will probably secure that amount of mental and physical satisfaction which is attainable by a person of your organization." There is nothing in this about personal interest or affection; it is a bare statement of natural cause and consequence. The priest holds a very different language; the use of the one word *love* gives warmth and color to his discourse. The priest says, "If you love God with all your soul and with all your strength He will love and cherish you in return, and be your own true and tender Father. He will watch over every detail and every minute of your existence, guard you from all real evil, and at last, when this earthly pilgrimage shall be over, He will welcome you in His eternal kingdom." But this is not all; God may still seem at too unapproachable a distance. The priest then says that means have been divinely appointed to bridge over that vast abyss. "The Father has given us the Son, and Christ has instituted the Church, and the Church has appointed *me* as her representative in this place, — *me*, to whom you may come always for guidance and consolation that will never be refused you."

This is the language for which the ears of a woman thirst as parched flowers thirst for the summer rain. Instead of a great, blank universe with fixed laws, interesting to *savans* but not to her, she is told of love and affection that she thoroughly understands. She is told of an affectionate Creator, of His beloved and loving Son, of the tender care of the maternal Church that He instituted; and finally all this chain of affectionate interest ends close to her in a living link, — a man with soft, engaging manners, with kind and gentle voice, who takes her hand, talks to her about all that she really cares for, and overflows with the readiest sympathy for all her anxieties. This man is so different from common men, so very much better and purer, and, above all, so much more accessible, communicative, and consolatory! He seems to have had so much spiritual experience, to know so well what trouble and sorrow are, to sympathize so completely with the troubles and sorrows of a woman! With him, the burden of life is ten times easier to bear; without his precious fellowship, that burden would be heavy indeed!

It may be objected to this, that the clergy do not entirely teach a religion of love; that, in fact, they curse as well as bless, and foretell eternal punishment for the majority. All this, it may be thought, must be as painful to the feelings of women as Divine kindness and human felicity must be agreeable to them. Whoever made this objection would show that he had not quite understood the feminine nature. It is at the same time kinder and tenderer than the masculine nature, and more absolute in vindictiveness. Women do not generally like the infliction of pain that they believe to be undeserved;[14] they are not generally advocates for vivisection; but as their feelings of indignation against evil-doers are very easily aroused, and as they are very easily persuaded that severe punishments are just, they have often heartily assented to them even when most horrible. In these cases their satisfaction, though it seems to us ferocious, may arise from feeling themselves God's willing allies against the wicked. When heretics were burnt in Spain the great ladies gazed calmly from their windows and balconies on the grotesque procession of miserable *morituri* with flames daubed on their tabards, so soon to be exchanged for the fiery reality. With the influence that women possess they could have stopped those horrors; but they countenanced them; and yet there is no reason to believe that they were not gentle, tender, affectionate. The most relentless persecutor who ever sat on the throne of England was a woman. Nor is it only in ages of fierce and cruel persecution that women readily believe God to be on the side of the oppressor. Other ages succeed in which human injustice is not so bold and bloodthirsty, not so candid and honest, but more stealthily pursues its end by hampering and paralyzing the victim that it dares not openly destroy. It places a thousand little obstacles in his way, the well-calculated effect of which is to keep him alive in impotent insignificance. In those ages of weaker malevolence the heretic is quietly but carefully excluded from the best educational and social advantages, from public office, from political power. Wherever he turns, whatever he desires to do, he feels the presence of a mysterious invisible force that quietly pushes him aside or keeps him in shadow. Well, in this milder, more coldly cruel form of wrong, vast numbers of the gentlest and most amiable women have always been ready to acquiesce.[15]

I willingly pass from this part of the subject, but it was impossible not to make one sad reference to it, for of all the sorrowful things in the history of the world I see none more sorrowful than this,—that the enormous influence of women should not have been more on the side of justice. It is perhaps too much to expect that they should have placed themselves in advance of their age, but they have been innocent abettors and perpetuators of the worst abuses, and all from their proneness to support any authority, however corrupt, if only it can succeed in confounding itself with goodness.

As the representatives of a Deity who tenderly cares for every one of His creatures, the clergy themselves are bound to cultivate all their own powers and gifts of sympathy. The best of them do this with the important result that after some years spent in the exercise of their profession they become really and unaffectedly more sympathetic than laymen generally are. The power of sympathy is a great power everywhere, but it is so particularly in those countries where the laity are not much in the habit of cultivating the sympathetic feelings, and timidly shrink from the expression of them even when they exist. I remember going with a French gentleman to visit a lady who had very recently lost her father; and my friend made her a little speech in which he said no more than what he felt, but he said it so elegantly, so delicately, so appropriately, and in such feeling terms, that I envied him the talent of expressing condolence in that way. I never knew an English layman who could have got through such an expression of feeling, but I have known English clergymen who could have done it. Here is a very great and real superiority over us, and especially with women, because women are exquisitely alive to everything in which the feelings are concerned, and we often seem to them dead in feeling when we are only awkward, and dumb by reason of our awkwardness.

I think it probable that most readers of this page will find, on consulting their own recollections, that they have received warmer and kinder expressions of sympathy from clerical friends than from laymen. It is certainly so in my own case. On looking back to the expressions of sympathy that have been addressed to me on mournful occasions, and of rejoicing on happy ones, I find that the clearest and most ample and hearty utterances of these feelings have generally come either from clergymen of the Church of England, or priests of the Church of Rome.

The power of sympathy in clergymen is greatly increased by their easy access to all classes of society. They are received everywhere on terms which may be correctly defined as easily respectful; for their sacred character gives them a status of their own, which is neither raised by association with rich people nor degraded by friendliness with the poor or with that lower middle class which, of all classes, is the most perilous to the social position of a layman. They enter into the joys and sorrows of the most different orders of parishioners, and in this way, if there is any natural gift of sympathy in the mind of a clergyman, it is likely to be developed and brought to perfection.

Partly by arrangements consciously devised by ecclesiastical authorities, and partly by the natural force of circumstances, the work of the Church is so ordered that her representatives are sure to be present on the most important occasions in human life. This gives them some influence over men, but that which they gain by it over women is immeasurably greater, because the minds of women are far more closely and exclusively bound up in domestic interests and events.

Of these the most visibly important is marriage. Here the priest has his assured place and conspicuous function, and the wonderful thing is that this function seems to survive the religious beliefs on which it was originally founded. It seems to be not impossible that a Church might still survive for an indefinite length of time in the midst of surrounding scepticism simply for the purpose of performing marriage and funeral rites. The strength of the clerical position with regard to marriage is so great, even on the Continent, that, although a woman may have scarcely a shred of faith in the doctrines of the Church, it is almost certain that she will desire the services of a priest, and not feel herself to be really married without them.

Although the civil ceremony may be the only one recognized by the law, the woman openly despises it, and reserves all her feelings and emotions for the pompous ceremony at the church. On such occasions women laugh at the law, and will even sometimes declare that the law itself is not legal. I once happened to say that civil marriage was obligatory in France, but only legal in England; on which an English lady attacked me vehemently, and stoutly denied that civil marriage was legal in England at all. I asked if she had never heard of marriages in a Registrar's office. "Yes, I have," she answered, with a shocked expression of countenance, "but they are not legal. The Church of England does not recognize them, and that is the legal church."

As soon as a child is born the mother begins to think about its baptism; and at a time of life when the infant is treated by laymen as a little being whose importance lies entirely in the future the clergyman gives it consequence in the present by admitting it, with solemn ceremony, to membership in the Church of Christ. It is not possible to imagine anything more likely to gratify the feelings of a mother than this early admission of her unconscious offspring to the privileges of a great religious community. Before this great initiation it was alone in the world, loved only by her, and with all its prospects darkened by original sin; now it is purified, blessed, admitted into the fellowship of the holy and the wise. A certain relationship of a peculiar kind is henceforth established between priest and infant. In after years he prepares it for confirmation, another ceremony touching to the heart of a mother when she sees her son gravely taking upon himself the responsibilities of a thinking being. The marriage of a son or daughter renews in the mother all those feelings towards the friendly, consecrating power of the Church which were excited at her own marriage.

Then come those anxious occasions when the malady of one member of the family casts a shadow on the happiness of all. In these cases any clergyman who unites natural kindness of heart with the peculiar training and experience of his profession can offer consolation incomparably better than a layman; he is more accustomed to it, more *authorized*. A friendly physician is a great help and a great stay so long as the disease is not alarming, but when he begins to look very grave (the reader knows that look), and says that recovery is not probable, by which physicians mean that death is certain and imminent, the clergyman says there is hope still, and speaks of a life beyond the grave in which human existence will be delivered from the evils that afflict it here. When death has come, the priest treats the dead body with respect and the survivors with sympathy, and when it is laid in the ground he is there to the last moment with the majesty of an ancient and touching form of words already pronounced over the graves of millions who have gone to their everlasting rest.[16]

Part II. Art

I have not yet by any means exhausted the advantages of the priestly position in its influence upon women. If the reader will reflect upon the feminine nature as he has known it, especially in women of the best kind, he will at once admit that not only are women more readily moved by the expression of sympathy than men, and more grateful for it, but they are also more alive to poetical and artistic influences. In our sex the æsthetic instinct is occasionally present in great strength, but more frequently it is altogether absent; in the female sex it seldom reaches much creative force, but it is almost invariably present in minor degrees. Almost all women take an interest in furniture and dress; most of them in the comfortable classes have some knowledge of music; drawing has been learned as an accomplishment more frequently by girls than by boys. The clergy have a strong hold upon the feminine nature by its æsthetic side. All the external details of public worship are profoundly interesting to women. When there is any splendor in ritual the details of vestments and altar decorations are a constant occupation for their thoughts, and they frequently bestow infinite labor and pains to produce beautiful things with their own hands to be used in the service of the Church. In cases where the service itself is too austere and plain to afford much scope for this affectionate industry, the slightest pretext is seized upon with avidity. See how eagerly ladies will decorate a church at Christmas, and how they will work to get up an ecclesiastical bazaar! Even in that Church which most encourages or permits æsthetic industry, the zeal of ladies sometimes goes beyond the desires of the clergy, and has to be more or less decidedly repressed. We all can see from the outside how fond women generally are of flowers, though I believe it is impossible for us to realize all that flowers are to them, as there are no inanimate objects that men love with such affectionate and even tender solicitude. However, we see that women surround themselves with flowers, in gardens, in conservatories, and in their rooms; we see that they wear artificial flowers in their dress, and that they paint flowers in water-color and on china. Now observe how the Church of Rome and the Ritualists in England show sympathy with this feminine taste! Innumerable millions of flowers are employed annually in the churches on the Continent; they are also used in England, though in less lavish profusion, and a sermon on flowers is preached annually in London, when every pew is full of them.

It is well known that women take an unfailing interest in dress. The attention they give to it is close, constant, and systematic, like an orderly man's attention to order. Women are easily affected by official costumes, and they read what great people have worn at levees and drawing-rooms. The clergy possess, in ecclesiastical vestments, a very powerful help to their influence. That many of them are clearly aware of this is proved by their boldness and perseverance in resuming ornamental vestments; and (as might be expected) that Church which has the most influence over women is at the same time the one whose vestments are most gorgeous and most elaborate. Splendor, however, is not required to make a costume impressive. It is enough that it be strikingly peculiar, even in simplicity, like the white robe of the Dominican friars.

Costume naturally leads our minds to architecture. I am not the first to remark that a house is only a cloak of a larger size. The gradation is insensible from a coat to a cathedral: first, the soldier's heavy cloak which enabled the Prussians to dispense with the little tent, then the tent, hut, cottage, house, church, cathedral, heavier and larger as we ascend the scale. "He has clothed himself with his church," says Michelet of the priest; "he has wrapped himself in this glorious mantle, and in it he stands in triumphant state. The crowd comes, sees, admires. Assuredly, if we judge the man by his covering, he who clothes himself with a *Notre Dame de Paris*, or with a Cologne Cathedral, is, to all appearance, the giant of the spiritual world. What a dwelling such an edifice is, and how vast the inhabitant must be! All proportions change; the eye is deceived and deceives itself again. Sublime lights, powerful shadows, all help the illusion. The man who in the street looked like a village schoolmaster is a prophet in this place. He is transfigured by these magnificent surroundings; his heaviness becomes power and majesty; his voice has formidable echoes. Women and children are overawed."

To a mind that does not analyze but simply receives impressions, magnificent architecture is a convincing proof that the words of the preacher are true. It appears inconceivable that such substantial glories, so many thousands of tons of masonry, such forests of timber, such acres of lead and glass, all united in one harmonious work on which men lavished wealth and toil for generations,—it appears inconceivable that such a monument can perpetuate an error or a dream. The echoing vaults bear witness. Responses come from storied window and multitudinous imagery. When the old cosmogony is proclaimed to be true in York Minster, the scientists sink into insignificance in their modern ordinary rooms; when the acolyte rings his bell in Rouen Cathedral, and the Host is lifted up, and the crowd kneels in silent adoration on the pavement, who is to deny the Real Presence? Does not every massive pillar stand there to affirm sturdily that it is true; and do not the towers outside announce it to field and river, and to the very winds of heaven?

The musical culture of women finds its own special interest in the vocal and instrumental parts of the church service. Women have a direct influence on this part of the ritual, and sometimes take an active share in it. Of all the arts music is the most closely connected with religion, and it is the only one that the blessed are believed to practise in a future state. A suggestion that angels might paint or carve is so unaccustomed that it seems incongruous; yet the objection to these arts cannot be that they employ matter, since both poets and painters give musical instruments to the angels,—

> "And angels meeting us shall sing
> To their citherns and citoles."

Worship naturally becomes musical as it passes from the prayer that asks for benefits to the expression of joyful praise; and though the austerity of extreme Protestantism has excluded instruments and encouraged reading instead of chanting, I am not aware that it has ever gone so far as to forbid the singing of hymns.

I have not yet touched upon pulpit eloquence as one of the means by which the clergy gain a great ascendency over women. The truth is that the pulpit is quite the most advantageous of all places for any one who has the gift of public speaking. He is placed there far more favorably than a Member of Parliament in his place in the House, where he is subject to constant and contemptuous interruptions from hearers lounging with their hats on. The chief advantage is that no one present is allowed either to interrupt or to reply; and this is one reason why some men will not go to church, as they say, "We may hear our principles misrepresented and not be permitted to defend them." A Bishop, in my hearing, touched upon this very point. "People say," he remarked, "that a preacher is much at his ease because no one is allowed to answer him; but I invite discussion. If any one here present has doubts about the soundness of my reasoning, I invite him to come to me at the Episcopal Palace, and we will argue the question together in my study." This sounded unusually liberal, but how the advantages were still on the side of the Bishop! His attack on heresy was public. It was uttered with long-practised professional eloquence, it was backed by a lofty social position, aided by a peculiar and dignified costume, and mightily aided also by the architecture of a magnificent cathedral. The doubter was invited to answer, but not on equal terms. The attack was public, the answer was to be private, and the heretic was to meet the Bishop in the Episcopal Palace, where, again, the power of rank and surroundings would be all in the prelate's favor.

Not only are clergymen privileged speakers, in being as secure from present contradiction as a sovereign on the throne, but they have the grandest of all imaginable subjects. In a word, they have the subject of Dante,—they speak to us *del Inferno, del Purgatorio, del Paradiso*. If they have any gift of genius, any power of imagination, such a subject becomes a tremendous engine in their hands. Imagine the difference between a preacher solemnly warning his hearers that the consequences of inattention may be everlasting torment, and a politician warning the Government that inattention may lead to a deficit! The truth is, that however terrible may be the earthly consequences of imprudence and of sin, they sink into complete insignificance before the menaces of the Church; nor is there, on the other hand, any worldly success that can be proposed as a motive comparable to the permanent happiness of Paradise. The good and the bad things of this world have alike the fatal defect, as subjects for eloquence, that they equally end in death; and as death is near to all of us, we see the end to both. The secular preacher is like a man who predicts a more or less comfortable journey, which comes to the same end in any case. A philosophic hearer is not very greatly elated by the promise of comforts so soon to be taken away, nor is he overwhelmed by the threat of evils that can but be temporary. Hence, in all matters belonging to this world only, the tone of quiet advice is the reasonable and appropriate tone, and it is that of the doctor and lawyer; but in matters of such tremendous import as eternal happiness and misery the utmost energy of eloquence can never be too great for the occasion; so that if a preacher can threaten like peals of thunder, and appal like flashes of lightning, he may use such terrible gifts without any disproportionate excess. On the other hand, if he has any charm of language, any brilliancy of imagination, there is nothing to prevent him from alluring his hearers to the paths of virtue by the most lavish and seductive promises. In short, his opportunities in both directions are of such a nature that exaggeration is impossible; and all his power, all his charm, are as free to do their utmost as an ocean wave in a tempest or the nightingale in the summer woods.

I cannot quit the subject of clerical oratory without noticing one of its marked characteristics. The priest is not in a position of disinterested impartiality, like a man of science, who is ready to renounce any doctrine when he finds evidence against it. The priest is an advocate whose life-long pleading must be in favor of the Church as he finds her, and in opposition to her adversaries. To attack adversaries is therefore one of the recognized duties of his profession; and if he is not a man of uncommon fairness, if he has not an inborn love of justice which is rare in human nature, he will not only attack his adversaries but misrepresent them. There is even a worse danger than simple misrepresentation. A priest may possibly be a man of a coarse temper, and if he is so he will employ the weapons of outrage and vituperation, knowing that he can do so with impunity. One would imagine that these methods must inevitably repel and displease women, but there is a very peculiar reason why they seldom have this effect. A highly principled woman is usually so extremely eager to be on the side of what is right that suspension of judgment is most difficult for her. Any condemnation uttered by a person she is accustomed to trust has her approval on the instant. She cannot endure to wait until the crime is proved, but her feelings of indignation are at once aroused against the supposed criminal on the ground that there must be clear distinctions between right and wrong. The priest, for her, is the good man,—the man on the side of God and virtue; and those whom he condemns are the bad men,—the men on the side of the Devil and vice. This being so, he may deal with such men as roughly as he pleases. Nor have these men the faintest chance of setting themselves right in her opinion. She quietly closes the avenues of her mind against them; she declines to read their books; she will not listen to their arguments. Even if one of them is a near relation whose opinions inflict upon her what she calls "the deepest distress of mind," she will positively prefer to go on suffering such distress until she dies, rather than allow him to remove it by a candid exposition of his views. She prefers the hostile misrepresentation that makes her miserable, to an authentic account of the matter that would relieve her anguish.

Part III.—Association.

The association of clergymen with ladies in works of charity affords continual opportunities for the exercise of clerical influence over women. A partnership in good works is set up which establishes interesting and cordial relations, and when the lady has accomplished some charitable purpose she remembers for long afterwards the clergyman without whose active assistance her project might have fallen to the ground. She sees in the clergyman a reflection of her own goodness, and she feels grateful to him for lending his masculine sense and larger experience to the realization of her ideas. There are other cases of a different nature in which the self-esteem of the lady is deeply gratified when she is selected by the clergyman as being more capable of devoted effort in a sacred cause than women of inferior piety and strength of mind. This kind of clerical selection is believed to be very influential in furthering clerical marriages. The lady is told that she will serve the highest of all causes by lending a willing ear to her admirer. Every reader will remember how thoroughly this idea is worked out in "Jane Eyre," where St. John urges Jane to marry him on the plain ground that she would be a valuable fellow-worker with a missionary. Charlotte Brontë was, indeed, so strongly impressed with this aspect of clerical influence that she injured the best and strongest of her novels by an almost wearisome development of that episode.

Clerical influence is immensely aided by the possession of leisure. Without underrating the self-devotion of hard-working clergymen (which is all the more honorable to them that they might take life more easily if they chose), we see a wide distinction, in point of industry, between the average clergyman and the average solicitor, for example. The clergyman has leisure to pay calls, to accept many invitations, and to talk in full detail about the interests that he has in common with his female friends. The solicitor is kept to his office by strictly professional work requiring very close application and allowing no liberty of mind.

Much might be said about the effect of clerical leisure on clerical manners. Without leisure it is difficult to have such quiet and pleasant manners as the clergy generally have. Very busy men generally seem preoccupied with some idea of their own which is not what you are talking about, but a leisurely man will give hospitality to your thought. A busy man wants to get away, and fidgets you; a man of leisure dwells with you, for the time, completely. Ladies are exquisitely sensitive to these differences, and besides, they are generally themselves persons of leisure. Overworked people often confound leisure with indolence, which is a great mistake. Leisure is highly favorable to intelligence and good manners; indolence is stupid, from its dislike to mental effort, and ill-bred, from the habit of inattention.

The feeling of women towards custom draws them strongly to the clergy, because a priesthood is the instinctive upholder of ancient customs and ceremonies, and steadily maintains external decorum. Women are naturally more attracted by custom than we are. A few men have an affectionate regard for the sanctities of usage, but most men only submit to them from an idea that they are generally helpful to the "maintenance of order;" and if women could be supposed absent from a nation for a time, it is probable that external observances of all kinds would be greatly relaxed. Women do not merely submit passively to custom; they uphold it actively and energetically, with a degree of faith in the perfect reasonableness of it which gives them great decision in its defence. It seems to them the ultimate reason from which there is no appeal. Now, in the life of every organized Church there is much to gratify this instinct, especially in those which have been long established. The recurrence of holy seasons, the customary repetition of certain forms of words, the observance at stated intervals of the same ceremonies, the adherence to certain prescribed decencies or splendors of dress, the reservation of sacred days on which labor is suspended, give to the religious life a charm of customariness which is deeply gratifying to good, order-loving women. It is said that every poet has something feminine in his nature; and it is certainly observable that poets, like women, are tenderly affected by the recurrence of holy seasons, and the observance of fixed religious rites. I will only allude to Keble's "Christian Year," because in this instance it might be objected that the poet was secondary to the Christian; but the reader will find instances of the same sentiment in Tennyson, as, for example, in the profoundly affecting allusions to the return of Christmas in "In Memoriam." I could not name another occupation so closely and visibly bound up with custom as the clerical profession, but for the sake of contrast I may mention one or two others that are completely disconnected from it. The profession of painting is an example, and so is that of literature. An artist, a writer, has simply nothing whatever to do with custom, except as a private man. He may be an excellent and a famous workman without knowing Sunday from week-day or Easter from Lent. A man of science is equally unconnected with traditional observances.

It may be a question whether a celibate or a married clergy has the greater influence over women.

There are two sides to this question. The Church of Rome is, from the worldly point of view, the most astute body of men who have ever leagued themselves together in a corporation; and that Church has decided for celibacy, rejecting thereby all the advantages to be derived from rich marriages and good connections. In a celibate church the priest has a position of secure dignity and independence. It is known from the first that he will not marry, so there is no idle and damaging gossip about his supposed aspirations after fortune, or tender feelings towards beauty. Women can treat him with greater confidence than if he were a possible suitor, and then can confess to him, which is felt to be difficult with a married or a marriageable clergy. By being decidedly celibate the clergy avoid the possible loss of dignity which might result from allying themselves with families in a low social position. They are simply priests, and escape all other classification. A married man is, as it were, made responsible for the decent appearance, the good manners, and the proper conduct of three different sets of people. There is the family he springs from, there is his wife's family, and, lastly, there is the family in his own house. Any one of these may drag a man down socially with almost irresistible force. The celibate priest is only affected by the family he springs from, and is generally at a distance from that. He escapes the invasion of his house by a wife's relations, who might possibly be vulgar, and, above all, he escapes the permanent degradation of a coarse and ill-dressed family of his own. No doubt, from the Christian point of view, poverty is as honorable as wealth; but from the worldly point of view its visible imperfections are mean, despicable, and even ridiculous. In the early days of English Protestants the liberty to marry was ruinous to the social position of the clergy. They generally espoused servant-girls or "a lady's maid whose character had been blown upon, and who was therefore forced to give up all hope of catching the steward."[17] Queen Elizabeth issued "special orders that no clergyman should presume to marry a servant-girl without the consent of the master or mistress." "One of the lessons most earnestly inculcated on every girl of honorable family was to give no encouragement to a lover in orders; and if any young lady forgot this precept she was almost as much disgraced as by an illicit amour." The cause of these low marriages was simply poverty, and it is needless to add that they increased the evil. "As children multiplied and grew, the household of the priest became more and more beggarly. Holes appeared more and more plainly in the thatch of his parsonage and in his single cassock. His boys followed the plough, and his girls went out to service."

When clergymen can maintain appearances they gain one advantage from marriage which increases their influence with women. The clergyman's wife is almost herself in holy orders, and his daughter often takes an equally keen interest in ecclesiastical matters. These "clergywomen," as they have been called, are valuable allies, through whom much may be done that cannot be effected directly. This is the only advantage on the side of marriage, and it is but relative; for a celibate clergy has also its female allies who are scarcely less devoted; and in the Church of Rome there are great organized associations of women entirely under the control of ecclesiastics. Again, there is a lay element in a clergyman's family which brings the world into his own house, to the detriment of its religious character. The sons of the clergy are often anything but clerical in feeling. They are often strongly laic, and even sceptical, by a natural reaction from ecclesiasticism. On the whole, therefore, it seems certain that an unmarried clergy more easily maintains both its own dignity and the distinction between itself and the laity.

Auricular confession is so well known as a means of influencing women that I need scarcely do more than mention it; but there is one characteristic of it which is little understood by Protestants. They fancy (judging from Protestant feelings of antagonism) that confession must be felt as a tyranny. A Roman Catholic woman does not feel it to be an infliction that the Church imposes, but a relief that she affords. Women are not naturally silent sufferers. They like to talk about their anxieties and interests, especially to a patient and sympathetic listener of the other sex who will give them valuable advice. There is reason to believe that a good deal of informal confession is done by Protestant ladies; in the Church of Rome it is more systematic and leads to a formal absolution. The subject which the speaker has to talk about is that most interesting of all subjects, self. In any other place than a confessional to talk about self at any length is an error; in the confessional it is a virtue. The truth is that pious Roman Catholic women find happiness in the confessional and try the patience of the priests by minute accounts of trifling or imaginary sins. No doubt confession places an immense power in the hands of the Church, but at an incalculable cost of patience. It is not felt to weigh unfairly on the laity, because the priest who to-day has forgiven your faults will to-morrow kneel in penitence and ask forgiveness for his own. I do not see in the confessional so much an oppressive institution as a convenience for both parties. The woman gets what she wants, — an opportunity of talking confidentially about herself; and the priest gets what he wants, — an opportunity of learning the secrets of the household.

Nothing has so powerfully awakened the jealousy of laymen as this institution of the confessional. The reasons have been so fully treated by Michelet and others, and are in fact so obvious, that I need not repeat them.

The dislike for priests that is felt by many Continental laymen is increased by a cause that helps to win the confidence of women. "Observe," the laymen say, "with what art the priest dresses so as to make women feel that he is without sex, in order that they may confess to him more willingly. He removes every trace of hair from his face, his dress is half feminine, he hides his legs in petticoats, his shoulders under a tippet, and in the higher ranks he wears jewelry and silk and lace. A woman would never confess to a man dressed as we are, so the wolf puts on sheep's clothing."

Where confession is not the rule the layman's jealousy is less acrid and pungent in its expression, but it often manifests itself in milder forms. The pen that so clearly delineated the Rev. Charles Honeyman was impelled by a layman's natural and pardonable jealousy. A feeling of this kind is often strong in laymen of mature years. They will say to you in confidence, "Here is a man about the age of one of my sons, who knows no more concerning the mysteries of life and death than I do, who gets what he thinks he knows out of a book which is as accessible to me as it is to him, and yet who assumes a superiority over me which would only be justifiable if I were ignorant and he enlightened. He calls me one of his sheep. I am not a sheep relatively to him. I am at least his equal in knowledge, and greatly his superior in experience. Nobody but a parson would venture to compare me to an animal (such a stupid animal too!) and himself to that animal's master. His one real and effective superiority is that he has all the women on his side."

You poor, doubting, hesitating layman, not half so convinced as the ladies of your family, who and what are you in the presence of a man who comes clothed with the authority of the Church? If you simply repeat what he says, you are a mere echo, a feeble repetition of a great original, like the copy of a famous picture. If you try to take refuge in philosophic indifference, in silent patience, you will be blamed for moral and religious inertia. If you venture to oppose and discuss, you will be the bad man against the good man, and as sure of condemnation as a murderer when the judge is putting on the black cap. There is no resource for you but one, and that does not offer a very cheering or hopeful prospect. By the exercise of angelic patience, and of all the other virtues that have been preached by good men from Socrates downwards, you may in twenty or thirty years acquire some credit for a sort of inferior goodness of your own,—a pinchbeck goodness, better than nothing, but not in any way comparable to the pure golden goodness of the priest; and when you come to die, the best that can be hoped for your disembodied soul will be mercy, clemency, indulgence; not approbation, welcome, or reward.

ESSAY XIV
WHY WE ARE APPARENTLY
BECOMING LESS RELIGIOUS

IT has happened to me on more than one occasion to have to examine papers left by ladies belonging to the last generation, who had lived in the manner most esteemed and respected by the general opinion of their time, and who might, without much risk of error, be taken for almost perfect models of English gentlewomen as they existed before the present scientific age. The papers left by these ladies consisted either of memoranda of their private thoughts, or of thoughts by others which seemed to have had an especial interest for them. I found that all these papers arranged themselves naturally and inevitably under two heads: either they concerned family interests and affections, or they were distinctly religious in character, like the religious meditations we find in books of devotion.

There may be nothing extraordinary in this. Thousands of other ladies may have left religious memoranda; but consider what a preponderance of religious ideas is implied when written thoughts are entirely confined to them! The ladies in question lived in the first half of the nineteenth century, a period of great intellectual ferment, of the most important political and social changes, and of wonderful material progress; but they did not seem to have taken any real interest in these movements. The Bible and the commentaries of the clergy satisfied not only their spiritual but also their intellectual needs. They seem to have desired no knowledge of the universe, or of the probable origin and future of the human race, which the Bible did not supply. They seem to have cared for no example of human character and conduct other than the scriptural examples.

This restfulness in Biblical history and philosophy, this substitution of the Bible for the world as a subject of study and contemplation, this absence of desire to penetrate the secrets of the world itself, this want of aspiration after any ideal more recent than the earlier ages of Christianity, permitted a much more constant and uninterrupted dwelling with what are considered to be religious ideas than is possible to any active and inquiring mind of the present day. Let it be supposed, for example, that a person to whom the Bible was everything desired information about the origin of the globe, and of life upon it; he would refer to the Book of Genesis as the only authority, and this reference would have the character of a religious act, and he would get credit for piety on account of it; whilst a modern scientific student would refer to some great modern paleontologist, and his reference would not have the character of a religious act, nor bring him any credit for piety; yet the prompting curiosity, the desire to know about the remote past, would be exactly the same in both cases. And I think it may be easily shown that if the modern scientific student appears to be less religious than others think he ought to be, it is often because he possesses and uses more abundant sources of information than those which were accessible to the ancient Jews. It is not his fault if knowledge has increased; he cannot be blamed if he goes where information is most copious and most exact; yet his preference for such information gives an unsanctified aspect to his studies. The study of the most ancient knowledge wears a religious aspect, but the study of modern knowledge appears to be non-religious.

Again, when we come to the cultivation of the idealizing faculties, of the faculties which do not seek information merely, but some kind of perfection, we find that the very complexity of modern life, and the diversity of the ideal pleasures and perfections that we modern men desire, have a constant tendency to take us outside of strictly religious ideals. As long as the writings which are held to be sacred supply all that our idealizing faculties need, so long will our imaginative powers exercise themselves in what is considered to be a religious manner, and we shall get credit for piety; but when our minds imagine what the sacred writers could not or did not conceive, and when we seek help for our imaginative faculty in profane writers, we appear to be less religious. So it is with the desire to study and imitate high examples of conduct and character. There is no nobler or more fruitful instinct in man than a desire like this, which is possible only to those who are at once humble and aspiring. An ancient Jew who had this noble instinct could satisfy it by reading the sacred books of the Hebrews, and so his aspiration appeared to be wholly religious. It is not so with an active-minded young Englishman of the present day. He cannot find the most inspiriting models amongst the ancient Hebrews, for the reason that their life was altogether so much simpler and more primitive than ours. They had nothing that can seriously be called science; they had not any organized industry; they had little art, and hardly any secular literature, so that in these directions they offer us no examples to follow. Our great inspiriting examples in these directions are to be found either in the Renaissance or in recent times, and therefore in profane biography. From this it follows that an active modern mind seems to study and follow non-religious examples, and so to differ widely, and for the worse, from the simpler minds of old time, who were satisfied with the examples they found in their Bibles. This appearance is misleading; it is merely on the surface; for if we go deeper and do not let ourselves be deceived by the words "sacred" and "profane," we shall find that when a simple mind chooses a model from a primitive people, and a cultivated one chooses a model from an advanced people, and from the most advanced class in it, they are both really doing the same thing, namely, seeking ideal help of the kind which is best for each. Both of them are pursuing the same object, — a mental discipline and elevation which may be comprised under the general term *virtue*; the only difference being that one is studying examples of virtue in the history of the ancient Jews, whilst the other finds examples of virtue more to his own special purpose in the lives of energetic Englishmen, Frenchmen, or Germans.

A hundred such examples might be mentioned, for every occupation worth following has its own saints and heroes; but I will confine myself to two. The first shall be a French gentleman of the eighteenth century, to whom life offered in the richest profusion everything that can tempt a man to what is considered an excusable and even a respectable form of idleness. He had an independent fortune, excellent health, a good social position, and easy access to the most lively, the most entertaining, the most amiable society that ever was, namely, that of the intelligent French nobility before the Revolution. There is no merit in renouncing what we do not enjoy; but he enjoyed all pleasant things, and yet renounced them for a higher and a harder life. At the age of thirty-two he retired to the country, made a rule of early rising and kept it, sallied forth from his house every morning at five, went and shut himself up in an old tower with a piece of bread and a glass of water for his breakfast, worked altogether eleven or twelve hours a day in two sittings, and went to bed at nine. This for eight months in the year, regularly, the remaining four being employed in scientific and administrative work at the Jardin des Plantes. He went on working in this way for forty years, and in the whole course of that time never let pass an ill-considered page or an ill-constructed sentence, but always did his best, and tried to make himself able to do better.

Such was the great life of Buffon; and in our own time another great life has come to its close, inferior to that of Buffon only in this, that as it did not begin in luxury, the first renunciation was not so difficult to make. Yet, however austere his beginnings, it is not a light or easy thing for a man to become the greatest intellectual worker of his time, so that one of his days (including eight hours of steady nocturnal labor) was equivalent to two or more of our days. No man of his time in Europe had so vast a knowledge of literature and science in combination; yet this knowledge was accompanied by perfect modesty and by a complete indifference to vulgar distinctions and vain successes. For many years he was the butt of coarse and malignant misrepresentation on the part of enemies who easily made him odious to a shallow society; but he bore it with perfect dignity, and retained unimpaired the tolerance and charity of his nature. His way of living was plain and frugal; he even contented himself with narrow dwellings, though the want of space must have occasioned frequent inconvenience to a man of his pursuits. He scrupulously fulfilled his domestic duties, and made use of his medical education in ministering gratuitously to the poor. Such was his courage that when already advanced in life he undertook a gigantic task, requiring twenty years of incessant labor; and such were his industry and perseverance that he brought it to a splendidly successful issue. At length, after a long life of duty and patience, after bearing calumny and ridicule, he was called to endure another kind of suffering,—that of incessant physical pain. This he bore with perfect fortitude, retaining to the last his mental serenity, his interest in learning, and a high-minded patriotic thoughtfulness for his country and its future, finding means in the midst of suffering to dictate long letters to his fellow-citizens on political subjects, which, in their calm wisdom, stood in the strongest possible contrast to the violent party writing of the hour.

Such was the great life of Littré; and now consider whether he who studies lives like these, and wins virtue from their austere example, does not occupy his thoughts with what would have been considered religious aspirations, if these two men, instead of being Frenchmen of the eighteenth and nineteenth centuries, had happened to be ancient Jews. If it had been possible for so primitive a nation as the Jewish to produce men of such steady industry and so large a culture, we should have read the story of their lives in the Jewish sacred books, and then it would have been a part of the popular religion to study them, whereas now the study of such biography is held to be non-religious, if not (at least in the case of Littré) positively irreligious. Yet surely when we think of the virtues which made these lives so fruitful, our minds are occupied in a kind of religious thought; for are we not thinking of temperance, self-discipline, diligence, perseverance, patience, charity, courage, hope? Were not these men distinguished by their aspiration after higher perfection, by a constant desire to use their talents well, and by a vigilant care in the employment of their time? And are not these virtues and these aspirations held to be parts of a civilized man's religion, and the best parts?

The necessity for an intellectual expansion beyond the limits of the Bible was felt very strongly at the time of the Renaissance, and found ample satisfaction in the study of the Greek and Latin classics. There are many reasons why women appear to be more religious than men; and one of them is because women study only one collection of ancient writings, whilst men have been accustomed to study three; consequently that which women study (if such a word is applicable to devotional, uncritical reading) occupies their minds far more exclusively than it occupies the mind of a classical scholar. But, though the intellectual energies of men were for a time satisfied with classical literature, they came at length to look outside of that as their fathers had looked outside of the Bible. Classical literature was itself a kind of religion, having its own sacred books; and it had also its heretics,—the students of nature,—who found nature more interesting than the opinions of the Greeks and Romans. Then came the second great expansion of the human mind, in the midst of which we ourselves are living. The Renaissance opened for it a world of mental activity which had the inappreciable intellectual advantage of lying well outside of the popular beliefs and ideas, so that cultivated men found in it an escape from the pressure of the uneducated; but the new scientific expansion offers us a region governed by laws of a kind peculiar to itself, which protect those who conform to them against every assailant. It is a region in which authority is unknown, for, however illustrious any great man may appear in it, every statement that he makes is subject to verification. Here the knowledge of ancient writers is continually superseded by the better and more accurate knowledge of their successors; so that whereas in religion and learning the most ancient writings are the most esteemed, in science it is often the most recent, and even these have no authority which may not be called in question freely by any student. The new scientific culture is thus encouraging a habit of mind different from old habits, and which in our time has caused such a degree of separation that the most important and the most interesting of all topics are those upon which we scarcely dare to venture for fear of being misunderstood.

If I had to condense in a short space the various reasons why we are apparently becoming less religious, I should say that it is because knowledge and feeling, embodied or expressed in the sciences and arts, are now too fully and too variously developed to remain within the limits of what is considered sacred knowledge or religious emotion. It was possible for them to remain well within those limits in ancient times, and it is still possible for a mind of very limited activity and range to dwell almost entirely in what was known or felt at the time of Christ; but this is not possible for an energetic and inquiring mind, and the consequence is that the energetic mind will seem to the other, by contrast, to be negligent of holy things, and too much occupied with purely secular interests and concerns. A great misunderstanding arises from this, which has often had a lamentable effect on intercourse between relations and friends. Pious ladies, to whom theological writings appear to contain almost everything that it is desirable to know, often look with secret misgiving or suspicion on young men of vigorous intellect who cannot rest satisfied with the old knowledge, and what such ladies vaguely hear of the speculations of the famous scientific leaders inspires them with profound alarm. They think that we are becoming less religious because theological writings do not occupy the same space in our time and thoughts as they do in theirs; whereas, if such a matter could be put to any kind of positive test, it would probably be found that we know more, even of their own theology, than they do, and that, instead of being indifferent to the great problems of the universe, we have given to such problems an amount of careful thought far surpassing, in mental effort, their own simple acquiescence. The opinions of a thoughtful and studious man in the present day have never been lightly come by; and if he is supposed to be less religious than his father or his grandfather it may be that his religion is different from theirs, without being either less earnest or less enlightened. There is, however, one point of immense importance on which I believe that we really are becoming less religious, indeed on that point we seem to be rapidly abandoning the religious principle altogether; but the subject is of too much consequence to be treated at the end of an Essay.

ESSAY XV
HOW WE ARE REALLY BECOMING
LESS RELIGIOUS

THE reader may remember how, after the long and unsuccessful siege of Syracuse, the Athenian general Nikias, seeing his discouraged troops ill with the fever from the marshes, determined to raise the siege; and that, when his soldiers were preparing to retreat, and striking their tents for the march, there occurred an eclipse of the moon. Nikias, in his anxiety to know what the gods meant by this with reference to him and his army, at once consulted a soothsayer, who told him that he would incur the Divine anger if he did not remain where he was for three times nine days. He remained, doing nothing, allowing his troops to perish and his ships to be shut up by a line of the enemy's vessels chained together across the entrance of the port. At length the three times nine days came to an end, and what was left of the Athenian army had to get out of a situation that had become infinitely more difficult during its inaction. The ships tried to get out in vain; the army was able to retreat by land, but only to be harassed by the enemy, and finally placed in such distress that it was compelled to surrender. Most of the remnant died miserably in the old quarries of Syracuse.

The conduct of Nikias throughout these events was in the highest degree religious. He was fully convinced that the gods concerned themselves about him and his doings, that they were watching over him, and that the eclipse was a communication from them not to be neglected without a breach of religious duty. He, therefore, in the spirit of the most perfect religious faith, which we are compelled to admire for its sincerity and thoroughness, shut his eyes resolutely to all the visible facts of a situation more disastrous every day, and attended only to the invisible action of the invisible gods, of which nothing could be really known by him. For twenty-seven days he went on quietly sacrificing his soldiers to his faith, and only moved at last when he believed that the gods allowed it.

In contrast with this, let us ask what we think of an eclipse ourselves, and how far any religious emotion, determinant of action or of inaction, is connected with the phenomenon in our experience. We know, in the first place, that eclipses belong to the natural order, and we do not feel either grateful to the supernatural powers, or ungrateful, with regard to them. Even the idea that eclipses demonstrate the power of God is hardly likely to occur to us, for we constantly see terrestrial objects eclipsed by cast shadows; and the mere falling of a shadow is to us only the natural interruption of light by the intervention of any opaque object. In the true theory of eclipses there is absolutely no ground whatever for religious emotion, and accordingly the phenomenon is now entirely disconnected from religious ideas. The consequence is that where the Athenian general had a strong motive for religious emotion, a motive so strong that he sacrificed his army to the supposed will of Heaven, a modern general in the same situation would feel no emotion and make no sacrifice.

If this process stopped at eclipses the result would be of little importance, as eclipses of the celestial bodies are not frequently visible, and to lose the opportunity of emotion which they present is not a very sensible loss. But so far is the process from stopping at eclipses, that exactly the same process is going on with regard to thousands of other phenomena which are one by one, yet with increasing rapidity, ceasing to be regarded as special manifestations of Divine will, and beginning to be regarded as a part of that order of nature with which, to quote Professor Huxley's significant language, "nothing interferes." Every one of these transferrences from supernatural government to natural order deprives the religious sentiment of one special cause or motive for its own peculiar kind of emotion, so that we are becoming less and less accustomed to such emotion (as the opportunities for it become less frequent), and more and more accustomed to accept events and phenomena of all kinds as in that order of nature "with which nothing interferes."

This single mental conception of the unfailing regularity of nature is doing more in our time to affect the religious condition of thoughtful people than could be effected by many less comprehensive conceptions.

It has often been said, not untruly, that merely negative arguments have little permanent influence over the opinions of men, and that institutions which have been temporarily overthrown by negation will shortly be set up again, and flourish in their old vigor, unless something positive can be found to supply their place. But here is a doctrine of a most positive kind. "The order of nature is invariably according to regular sequences." It is a doctrine which cannot be proved, for we cannot follow all the changes which have ever taken place in the universe; but, although incapable of demonstration, it may be accepted until something happens to disprove it; and it *is* accepted, with the most absolute faith, by a constantly increasing number of adherents.

To show how this doctrine acts in diminishing religious emotion by taking away the opportunity for it, let me narrate an incident which really occurred on a French line of railway in the winter of 1882. The line, on which I had travelled a few days before, passes between a river and a hill. The river has a rocky bed and is torrential in winter; the hill is densely covered with a pine forest coming down to the side of the line. The year 1882 had been the rainiest known in France for two centuries, and the roots of the trees on the edge of this pine forest had been much loosened by the rain. In consequence of this, two large pine-trees fell across the railway early one morning, and soon afterwards a train approached the spot by the dim light of early dawn. There was a curve just before the engine reached the trees, and it had come rapidly for several miles down a decline. The driver reversed his steam, the engine and tender leaped over the trees, and then went over the embankment to a place within six feet of the rapid river. The carriages remained on the line, but were much broken. Nobody was killed; nobody was seriously injured. The remarkable escape of the passengers was accounted for as follows by the religious people in the neighborhood. There happened to be a priest in the train, and at the time when the shock took place he made what is called "a pious ejaculation." This, it was said, had saved the lives of the passengers. In the ages of faith this explanation would have been received without question; but the notion of natural sequences— Professor Huxley's "order with which nothing interferes"—had obtained such firm hold on the minds of the townsmen generally that they said the priest was trying to make ecclesiastical capital out of an occurrence easily explicable by natural causes. They saw nothing supernatural either in the production of the accident or its comparative harmlessness. The trickling of much water had denuded the roots of the trees, which fell because they could not stand with insufficient roothold; the lives of the passengers were saved because they did not happen to be in the most shattered carriage; and the men on the engine escaped because they fell on soft ground, made softer still by the rain. It was probable, too, they said, that if any beneficent supernatural interference had taken place it would have maintained the trees in an erect position, by preventive miracle, and so spared the slight injuries which really were inflicted, and which, though treated very lightly by others because there were neither deaths nor amputations, still caused suffering to those who had to bear them.

Now if we go a little farther into the effects of this accident on the minds of the people who shared in it, or whose friends had been imperilled by it, we shall see very plainly the effect of the modern belief in the regularity of natural sequences. Those who believed in supernatural intervention would offer thanksgivings when they got home, and probably go through some special religious thanksgiving services for many days afterwards; those who believed in the regularity of natural sequences would simply feel glad to have escaped, without any especial sense of gratitude to supernatural powers. So much for the effect as far as thanksgiving is concerned; but there is another side of the matter at least equally important from the religious point of view,—that of prayer. The believers in supernatural interference would probably, in all their future railway journeys, pray to be supernaturally protected in case of accident, as they had been in 1882; but the believers in the regularity of natural sequences would only hope that no trees had fallen across the line, and feel more than usually anxious after long seasons of rainy weather. Can there be a doubt that the priest's opinion, that he had won safety by a pious ejaculation, was highly favorable to his religious activity afterwards, whilst the opinion of the believers in "the natural order with which nothing interferes" was unfavorable both to prayer and thanksgiving in connection with railway travelling?

Examples of this kind might easily be multiplied, for there is hardly any enterprise that men undertake, however apparently unimportant, which cannot be regarded both from the points of view of naturalism and supernaturalism; and in every case the naturalist manner of regarding the enterprise leads men to study the probable influence of natural causes, whilst the supernaturalist opinion leads them to propitiate supernatural powers. Now, although some new sense may come to be attached to the word "religion" in future ages, so that it may come to mean scientific thoroughness, intellectual ingenuousness, or some other virtue that may be possessed by a pure naturalist, the word has always been understood, down to the present time, to imply a constant dependence upon the supernatural; and when I say that we are becoming less religious, I mean that from our increasing tendency to refer everything to natural causes the notion of the supernatural is much less frequently present in our minds than it was in the minds of our forefathers. Even the clergy themselves seem to be following the laity towards the belief in natural law, at least so far as matter is concerned. The Bishop of Melbourne, in 1882, declined to order prayers for rain, and gave his reason honestly, which was that material phenomena were under the control of natural law, and would not be changed in answer to prayer. The Bishop added that prayer should be confined to spiritual blessings. Without disputing the soundness of this opinion, we cannot help perceiving that if it were generally received it would put an end to one half of the religious activity of the human race; for half the prayers and half the thanksgivings addressed to the supernatural powers are for material benefits only. It is possible that, in the future, religious people will cease to pray for health, but take practical precautions to preserve it; that they will cease to pray for prosperity, but study the natural laws which govern the wealth of nations; that they will no longer pray for the national fleets and armies, but see that they are well supplied and intelligently commanded. All this and much more is possible; but when it comes to pass the world will be less religious than it was when men believed that every pestilence, every famine, every defeat, was a chastisement specially, directly, and intentionally inflicted by an angry Deity. Even now, what an immense step has been made in this direction! In the fearful description of the pestilence at Florence, given with so much detail by Boccaccio, he speaks of "l'ira di Dio a punire la iniquità degli uomini con quella pestilenza;" and he specially implies that those who sought to avoid the plague by going to healthier places in the country deceived themselves in supposing that the wrath of God would not follow them whithersoever they went. That is the old belief expressing itself in prayers and humiliations. It is still recognized officially. If the plague could occur in a town on the whole so well cared for as modern London, the language of Boccaccio would still be used in the official public prayers; but the active-minded practical citizens would be thinking how to destroy the germs, how to purify air and water. An instance of this divergence occurred after the Egyptian war of 1882. The Archbishop of York, after the battle of Tel-el-Kebir, ordered thanksgivings to be offered in the churches, on the ground that God was in Sir Garnet Wolseley's camp and fought with him against the Egyptians, which was a survival of the antique idea that national deities fought with the national armies. On this a Member of Parliament, Mr. George Palmer, said to his constituents in a public meeting at Reading, "At the same time I cannot agree with the prayers that have been made in churches. Though I respect the consciences of other men, I must say that it was not by Divine interference, but from the stuff of which our army was made and our great ironclads, that victory was achieved." I do not quote this opinion for any originality in itself, as there have always been men who held that victory was a necessary result of superior military efficiency, but I quote it as a valuable test of the change in general opinion. It is possible that such views may have been expressed in private in all ages of the world; but I doubt if in any age preceding ours a public man, at the very time when he was cultivating the good graces of his electors, would have refused to the national Deity a special share in a military triumph. To an audience imbrued with the old conception of incessant supernatural interferences, the doctrine that a victory was a natural result would have sounded impious; and such an audience, if any one had ventured to say what Mr. Palmer said, would have received him with a burst of indignation. But Mr. Palmer knew the tendencies of the present age, and was quite correct in thinking that he might safely express his views. His hearers were not indignant, they were not even grave and silent, as Englishmen are when they simply disapprove, but they listened willingly, and marked their approbation by laughter and cheers. Even a clergyman may hold Mr. Palmer's opinion. Soon after his speech at Reading the Rev. H. R. Haweis said the same thing in the pulpit. "Few people," he said, "really doubt that we have conquered the Egyptians, not because we were in the right and they were in the wrong, but because we had the heaviest hand." The preacher went on to say that the idea of God fighting on one side more than another in particular battles seemed to him to be a Pagan or at most a Jewish one. How different was the old sentiment as expressed by Macaulay in the stirring ballad of Ivry! "We of the religion" had no doubt about the Divine interference in the battle,

"For our God hath crushed the tyrant, our God hath raised the slave,
And mocked the counsel of the wise, and the valor of the brave;
Then glory to his holy name from whom all glories are,
And glory to our Sovereign Lord, King Henry of Navarre!"

The way in which the great mental movement of our age towards a more complete recognition of natural order is affecting human intercourse may be defined in a few words. If the movement were at an equal rate of advance for all civilized people they would be perfectly agreed amongst themselves at any one point of time, as it would be settled which events were natural in their origin and which were due to the interposition of Divine or diabolical agency. Living people would differ in opinion from their predecessors, but they would not differ from each other. The change, however, though visible and important, is not by any means uniform, so that a guest sitting at dinner may have on his right hand a lady who sees supernatural interferences in many things, and on his left a student of science who is firmly convinced that there are no supernatural interferences in the present, and that there never have been any in the past. Private opinion, out of which public opinion slowly and gradually forms itself, is in our time in a state of complete anarchy, because two opposite doctrines are held loosely, and one or the other is taken up as it happens to seem appropriate. The interpositions of Providence are recognized or rejected according to political or personal bias. The French Imperialists saw the Divine vengeance in the death of Gambetta, whilst in their view the death of Napoleon III. was the natural termination of his disease, and that of the Prince Imperial a simple accident, due to the carelessness of his English companions. Personal bias shows itself in the belief, often held by men occupying positions of importance, that they are necessary, at least for a time, to fulfil the intentions of Providence. Napoleon III. said in a moment of emotion, "So long as I am needed I am invulnerable; but when my hour comes I shall be broken like glass!" Even in private life a man will sometimes think, "I am so necessary to my wife and family that Providence will not remove me," though every newspaper reports the deaths of fathers who leave their families destitute. Sometimes men believe that Providence takes the same view of their enterprises that they themselves take; and when a great enterprise is drawing near to its termination they feel assured that supernatural power will protect them till it is quite concluded, but they believe that the enterprises of other men are exposed to all the natural risks. When Mr. Gifford Palgrave was wrecked in the sea of Oman, he was for some time in an open boat, and thus describes his situation: "All depended on the steerage, and on the balance and support afforded by the oars, and even more still on the Providence of Him who made the deep; nor indeed could I get myself to think that He had brought me thus far to let me drown just at the end of my journey, and in so very unsatisfactory a way too; for had we then gone down, what news of the event off Sowadah would ever have reached home, or when?—so that altogether I felt confident of getting somehow or other on shore, though by what means I did not exactly know." Here the writer thinks of his own enterprise as deserving Divine solicitude, but does not attach the same importance to the humbler enterprises of the six passengers who went down with the vessel. I cannot help thinking, too, of the poor passenger Ibraheem, who swam to the boat and begged so piteously to be taken in, when a sailor "loosened his grasp by main force and flung him back into the sea, where he disappeared forever." Neither can I forget the four who imprudently plunged from the boat and perished. We may well believe that these lost ones would have been unable to write such a delightful and instructive book as Mr. Palgrave's "Travels in Arabia," yet they must have had their own humble interests in life, their own little objects and enterprises.

The calculation that Providence would spare a traveller towards the close of a long journey may be mistaken, but it is pious; it affords an opportunity for the exercise of devout emotion which the scientific thinker would miss. If Mr. Herbert Spencer had been placed in the same situation he would, no doubt, have felt the most perfect confidence that the order of nature would not be disturbed, that even in such a turmoil of winds and waters the laws of buoyancy and stability would be observed in every motion of the boat to the millionth of an inch; but he would not have considered himself likely to escape death on account of the important nature of his undertakings. Mr. Spencer's way of judging the situation as one of equal peril for himself and his humble companions would have been more reasonable, but at the same time he would have lost that opportunity for special and personal gratitude which Mr. Palgrave enjoyed when he believed himself to be supernaturally protected. The curious inconsistency of the common French expression, "C'est un hasard providentiel" is another example of the present state of thought on the question. A Frenchman is upset from a carriage, breaks no bones, and stands up, exclaiming, as he dusts himself, "It was un hasard vraiment providentiel that I was not lamed for life." It is plain that if his escape was providential it could not be accidental at the same time, yet in spite of the obvious inconsistency of his expression there is piety in his choice of an adjective.

The distinction, as it has usually been understood hitherto, between religious and non-religious explanations of what happens, is that the religious person believes that events happen by supernatural direction, and he is only thinking religiously so long as he thinks in that manner; whilst the non-religious theory is that events happen by natural sequence, and so long as a person thinks in this manner, his mind is acting non-religiously, whatever may be his religious profession. "To study the universe as it is manifested to us; to ascertain by patient inquiry the order of the manifestations; to discover that the manifestations are connected with one another after regular ways in time and space; and, after repeated failures, to give up as futile the attempt to understand the power manifested, is condemned as irreligious. And meanwhile the character of religious is claimed by those who figure to themselves a Creator moved by motives like their own; who conceive themselves as seeing through His designs, and who even speak of Him as though He laid plans to outwit the Devil!"

Yes, this is a true account of the way in which the words irreligious and religious have always been used and there does not appear to be any necessity for altering their signification. Every event which is transferred, in human opinion, from supernatural to natural action is transferred from the domain of religion to that of science; and it is because such transferrences have been so frequent in our time that we are becoming so much less religious than our forefathers were. In how many things is the modern man perfectly irreligious! He is so in everything that relates to applied science, to steam, telegraphy, photography, metallurgy, agriculture, manufactures.

He has not the slightest belief in spiritual intervention, either for or against him, in these material processes. He is beginning to be equally irreligious in government. Modern politicians have been accused of thinking that God cannot govern, but that is not a true account of their opinion. What they really think is that government is an application of science to the direction of national life, in which no invisible powers will either thwart a ruler in that which he does wisely, or shield him from the evil consequences of his errors.

But though we are less religious than our ancestors because we believe less in the interferences of the supernatural, do we deserve censure for our way of understanding the world? Certainly not. Was Nikias a proper object of praise because the eclipse seen by him at Syracuse seemed a warning from the gods; and was Wolseley a proper object of blame because the comet seen by him on the Egyptian plain was without a Divine message? Both these opinions are quite outside of merit, although the older opinion was in the highest degree religious, and the later one is not religious in the least. Such changes simply indicate a gradual revolution in man's conception of the universe, which is the result of more accurate knowledge. So why not accept the fact, why not admit that we have really become less religious? Possibly we have a compensation, a gain equivalent to our loss. If the gods do not speak to us by signs in the heavens; if the entrails of victims and the flight of birds no longer tell us when to march to battle and where to remain inactive in our tents; if the oracle is silent at Delos, and the ark lost to Jerusalem; if we are pilgrims to no shrine; if we drink of no sacred fountain and plunge into no holy stream; if all the special sanctities once reverenced by humanity are unable any longer to awaken our dead enthusiasm, have we gained nothing in exchange for the many religious excitements that we have lost? Yes, we have gained a keener interest in the natural order, and a knowledge of it at once more accurate and more extensive, a gain that Greek and Jew might well have envied us, and which a few of their keener spirits most ardently desired. Our passion for natural knowledge is not a devout emotion, and therefore it is not religious; but it is a noble and a fruitful passion nevertheless, and by it our eyes are opened. The good Saint Bernard had his own saintly qualities; but for us the qualities of a De Saussure are not without their worth. Saint Bernard, in the perfection of ancient piety, travelling a whole day by the lake of Geneva without seeing it, too much absorbed by devout meditation to perceive anything terrestrial, was blinded by his piety, and might with equal profit have stayed in his monastic cell. De Saussure was a man of our own time. Never, in his writings, do you meet with any allusion to supernatural interferences (except once or twice in pity for popular superstitions); but fancy De Saussure passing the lake of Geneva, or any other work of nature, without seeing it! His life was spent in the continual study of the natural world; and this study was to him so vigorous an exercise for the mind, and so strict a discipline, that he found in it a means of moral and even of physical improvement. There is no trace in his writings of what is called devout emotion, but the bright light of intelligent admiration illumines every page; and when he came to die, if he could not look back, like Saint Bernard, upon what is especially supposed to be a religious life, he could look back upon many years wisely and well spent in the study of that nature of which Saint Bernard scarcely knew more than the mule that carried him.

ESSAY XVI
ON AN UNRECOGNIZED FORM OF UNTRUTH

IN the art of painting there are two opposite ways of dealing with natural color. It may be intensified, or it may be translated by tints of inferior chromatic force. In either case the picture may be perfectly harmonious, provided only that the same principle of interpretation be consistently followed throughout.

The first time that I became acquainted with the first of these two methods of interpretation was in my youth, when I met with a Scottish painter who has since become eminent in his art. He was painting studies from nature; and I noticed that whenever in the natural object there was a trace of dull gold, as in some lichen, he made it a brighter gold, and whenever there was a little rusty red he made it a more vivid red. So it was with every other tint. His eye seemed to become excited by every hue, and he translated it by one of greater intensity and power.

Now that is a kind of exaggeration which is very commonly recognized as a departure from the sober truth. People complain that the sky is too blue, the fields too green, and so on.

Afterwards I saw French painters at work, and I noticed that they (in those days) interpreted natural color by an intentional lowering of the chromatic force. When they had to deal with the splendors of autumnal woods against a blue sky they interpreted the azure by a blue-gray, and the flaming gold by a dull russet. They even refused themselves the more quiet brightness of an ordinary wheat-field, and translated the yellow of the wheat by an earthy brown.

Unlike falsehood by exaggeration, this other kind of falsehood (by diminution) is very seldom recognized as a departure from the truth. Such coloring as this French coloring excited but few protests, and indeed was often praised for being "modest" and "subdued."

Both systems are equally permissible in the fine arts, if consistently followed, because in art the unity and harmony of the work are of greater importance than the exact imitation of nature. It is not as an art-critic that I should have any fault to find with a well-understood and thoroughly consistent conventionalism in the interpretation of nature; but the two kinds of falsity we have noticed are constantly found in action outside of the fine arts, and yet only one of them is recognized in its true character, the other being esteemed as a proof of modesty and moderation.

The general opinion, in our own country, condemns falsehood by exaggeration, but it does not blame falsehood by diminution. Overstatement is regarded as a vice, and understatement as a sort of modest virtue, whilst in fact they are both untruthful, exactly in the degree of their departure from perfect accuracy.

If a man states his income as being larger than it really is, if he adopts a degree of ostentation which (though he may be able to pay for it) conveys the idea of more ample means than he really possesses, and if we find out afterwards what his income actually is, we condemn him as an untruthful person; but lying by diminution with reference to money matters is looked upon simply as modesty.

I remember a most respectable English family who had this modesty in perfection. It was their great pleasure to represent themselves as being much less rich than they really were. Whenever they heard of anybody with moderate or even narrow means, they pretended to think that he had quite an ample income. If you mentioned a man with a family, struggling on a pittance, they would say he was "very comfortably provided for," and if you spoke of another whose expenses were the ordinary expenses of gentlemen, they wondered by what inventions of extravagance he could get through so much money. They themselves pretended to spend much less than they really spent, and they always affected astonishment when they heard how much it cost other people to live exactly in their own way. They considered that this was modesty; but was it not just as untruthful as the commoner vice of assuming a style more showy than the means warrant?

In France and Italy the departure from the truth is almost invariably in the direction of overstatement, unless the speaker has some distinct purpose to serve by adopting the opposite method, as when he desires to depreciate the importance of an enemy. In England people habitually understate, and the remarkable thing is that they believe themselves to be strictly truthful in doing so. The word "lying" is too harsh a term to be applied either to the English or the Continental habit in this matter; but it is quite fair to say that both of them miss the truth, one in falling short of it, the other in going beyond it.

An English family has seen the Alps for the first time. A young lady says Switzerland is "nice;" a young gentleman has decided that it is "jolly." This is what the habit of understatement may bring us down to,—absolute inadequacy. The Alps are not "nice," and they are not "jolly;" far more powerful adjectives are only the precise truth in this instance. The Alps are stupendous, overwhelming, magnificent, sublime. A Frenchman in similar circumstances will be embarrassed, not by any timidity about using a sufficiently forcible expression, but because he is eager to exaggerate; and one scarcely knows how to exaggerate the tremendous grandeur of the finest Alpine scenery. He will have recourse to eloquent phraseology, to loudness of voice, and finally, when he feels that these are still inadequate, he will employ energetic gesture. I met a Frenchman who tried to make me comprehend how many English people there were at Cannes in winter. "Il y en a—des Anglais—il y en a,"—then he hesitated, whilst seeking for an adequate expression. At last, throwing out both his arms, he cried, "Il y en a plus qu'en Angleterre!"

The English love of understatement is even more visible in moral than in material things. If an Englishman has to describe any person or action that is particularly admirable on moral grounds, he will generally renounce the attempt to be true, and substitute for the high and inspiring truth some quiet little conventional expression that will deliver him from what he most dreads,—the appearance of any noble enthusiasm. It does not occur to him that this inadequacy, this insufficiency of expression, is one of the forms of untruth; that to describe noble and admirable conduct in commonplace and non-appreciative language is to pay tribute of a kind especially acceptable to the Father of Lies. If we suppose the existence of a modern Mephistopheles watching the people of our own time and pleased with every kind of moral evil, we may readily imagine how gratified he must be to observe the moral indifference which uses exactly the same terms for ordinary and heroic virtue, which never rises with the occasion, and which always seems to take it for granted that there are neither noble natures nor high purposes in the world. The dead mediocrity of common talk, too timid and too indolent for any expression equivalent either to the glory of external nature or the intellectual and moral grandeur of great and excellent men, has driven many of our best minds from conversation into literature, because in literature it is not thought extraordinary for a man to express himself with a degree of force and clearness equivalent to the energy of his feelings, the accuracy of his knowledge, and the importance of his subject. The habit of using inadequate expression in conversation has led to the strange result that if an Englishman has any power of thought, any living interest in the great problems of human destiny, you will know hardly anything of the real action of his mind unless he becomes an author. He dares not express any high feelings in conversation, because he dreads what Stuart Mill called the "sneering depreciation" of them; and if such feelings are strong enough in him to make expression an imperative want, he has to utter them on paper. By a strange result of conventionalism, a man is admired for using language of the utmost clearness and force in literature, whilst if he talked as vigorously as he wrote (except, perhaps, in extreme privacy and even secrecy with one or two confidential companions) he would be looked upon as scarcely civilized. This may be one of the reasons why English literature, including the periodical, is so abundant in quantity and so full of energy. It is a mental outlet, a *dérivatif*.

The kind of untruthfulness which may be called *untruthfulness by inadequacy* causes many strong and earnest minds to keep aloof from general society, which seems to them insipid. They find frank and clear expression in books, they find it even in newspapers and reviews, but they do not find it in social intercourse. This deficiency drives many of the more intelligent of our countrymen into the strange and perfectly unnatural position of receiving ideas almost exclusively through the medium of print, and of communicating them only by writing. I remember an Englishman of great learning and ability who lived almost entirely in that manner. He received his ideas through books and the learned journals, and whenever any thought occurred to him he wrote it immediately on a slip of paper. In society he was extremely absent, and when he spoke it was in an apologetic and timidly suggestive manner, as if he were always afraid that what he had to say might not be interesting to the hearer, or might even appear objectionable, and as if he were quite ready to withdraw it. He was far too anxious to be well-behaved ever to venture on any forcible expression of opinion or to utter any noble sentiment; and yet his convictions on all important subjects were very serious, and had been arrived at after deep thought, and he was capable of real elevation of mind. His writings are the strongest possible contrast to his oral expression of himself. They are bold in opinion, very clear and decided in statement, and full of well-ascertained knowledge.

ESSAY XVII
ON A REMARKABLE ENGLISH PECULIARITY

IN De Tocqueville's admirable book on "Democracy in America" there is an interesting chapter on the behavior of Englishmen to each other when they meet in a foreign country: —

> "Two Englishmen meet by chance at the antipodes; they are surrounded by foreigners whose language and mode of life are hardly known to them.

> "These two men begin by studying each other very curiously and with a kind of secret uneasiness; they then turn away, or, if they meet, they are careful to speak only with a constrained and absent air, and to say things of little importance.

> "And yet they know nothing of each other; they have never met, and suppose each other to be perfectly honorable. Why, then, do they take such pains to avoid intercourse?"

De Tocqueville was a very close observer, and I hardly know a single instance in which his faculty of observation shows itself in greater perfection. In his terse style of writing every word tells; and even in my translation, unavoidably inferior to the original, you actually see the two Englishmen and the minute details of their behavior.

Let me now introduce the reader to a little scene at a foreign *table d'hôte*, as described with great skill and truth by a well-known English novelist, Miss Betham-Edwards: —

> "The time, September; the scene, a *table d'hôte* dinner in a much-frequented French town. For the most part nothing can be more prosaic than these daily assemblies of English tourists bound for Switzerland and the South, and a slight sprinkling of foreigners, the two elements seldom or never blending; a visitant from another planet might, indeed, suppose that between English and French-speaking people lay such a gulf as divides the blond New Englander from the swarth African, so icy the distance, so unbroken the

reserve. Nor is there anything like cordiality between the English themselves. Our imaginary visitant from Jupiter would here find matter for wonder also, and would ask himself the reason of this freezing reticence among the English fellowship. What deadly feud of blood, caste, or religion could thus keep them apart? Whilst the little knot of Gallic travellers at the farther end of the table straightway fall into friendliest talk, the long rows of Britons of both sexes and all ages speak only in subdued voices and to the members of their own family."

Next, let me give an account of a personal experience in a Parisian hotel. It was a little, unpretending establishment that I liked for its quiet and for the honest cookery. There was a *table d'hôte*, frequented by a few French people, generally from the provinces, and once there came some English visitors who had found out the merits of the little place. It happened that I had been on the Continent a long time without revisiting England, so when my fellow-countrymen arrived I had foolish feelings of pleasure on finding myself amongst them, and spoke to them in our common English tongue. The effect of this bold experiment was extremely curious, and to me, at the time, almost inexplicable, as I had forgotten that chapter by De Tocqueville. The new-comers were two or three young men and one in middle life. The young men seemed to be reserved more from timidity than pride. They were quite startled and frightened when spoken to, and made answer with grave brevity, as if apprehensive of committing themselves to some compromising statement. With an audacity acquired by habits of intercourse with foreigners, I spoke to the older Englishman. His way of putting me down would have been a charming study for a novelist. His manner resembled nothing so much as that of a dignified English minister,—Mr. Gladstone for example, when he is questioned in the House by some young and presumptuous member of the Opposition. A few brief words were vouchsafed to me, accompanied by an expression of countenance which, if not positively stern, was intentionally divested of everything like interest or sympathy. It then began to dawn upon me that perhaps this Englishman was conscious of some august social superiority; that he might even know a lord; and I thought, "If he does really know a lord we are very likely to hear his lordship's name." My expectation was not fulfilled to the letter, but it was quite fulfilled in spirit; for in talking to a Frenchman (for me to hear) our Englishman shortly boasted that he knew an English duchess, giving her name and place of abode. "One day when I was at — — House I said to the Duchess of — —," and he repeated what he had said to Her Grace; but it would have no interest for the reader, as it probably had none for the great lady herself. Shade of Thackeray! why wast thou not there to add a paragraph to the "Book of Snobs"?

The next day came another Englishman of about fifty, who distinguished himself in another way. He did not know a duchess, or, if he did, we were not informed of his good fortune; but he assumed a wonderful air of superiority to his temporary surroundings, that filled me, I must say, with the deepest respect and awe. The impression he desired to produce was that he had never before been in so poor a little place, and that our society was far beneath what he was accustomed to. He criticised things disdainfully, and when I ventured to speak to him he condescended, it is true, to enter into conversation, but in a manner that seemed to say, "Who and what are you that you dare to speak to a gentleman like me, who am, as you must perceive, a person of wealth and consideration?"

This account of our English visitors is certainly not exaggerated by any excessive sensitiveness on my part. Paris is not the Desert; and one who has known it for thirty years is not dependent for society on a chance arrival from beyond the sea. For me these Englishmen were but actors in a play, and perhaps they afforded me more amusement with their own peculiar manners than if they had been pleasant and amiable. One result, however, was inevitable. I had been full of kindly feeling towards my fellow-countrymen when they came, but this soon gave place to indifference; and their departure was rather a relief. When they had left Paris, there arrived a rich French widow from the south with her son and a priest, who seemed to be tutor and chaplain. The three lived at our *table d'hôte*; and we found them most agreeable, always ready to take their share in conversation, and, although far too well-bred to commit the slightest infraction of the best French social usages, either through ignorance or carelessness, they were at the same time perfectly open and easy in their manners. They set up no pretensions, they gave themselves no airs, and when they returned to their own southern sunshine we felt their departure as a loss.

The foreign idea of social intercourse under such conditions (that is, of intercourse between strangers who are thrown together accidentally) is simply that it is better to pass an hour agreeably than in dreary isolation. People may not have much to say that is of any profound interest, but they enjoy the free play of the mind; and it sometimes happens, in touching on all sorts of subjects, that unexpected lights are thrown upon them. Some of the most interesting conversations I have ever heard have taken place at foreign *tables d'hôte*, between people who had probably never met before and who would separate forever in a week. If by accident they meet again, such acquaintances recognize each other by a bow, but there is none of that intrusiveness which the Englishman so greatly dreads.

Besides these transient acquaintanceships which, however brief, are by no means without their value to one's experience and culture, the foreign way of understanding a *table d'hôte* includes the daily and habitual meeting of regular subscribers, a meeting looked forward to with pleasure as a break in the labors of the day, or a mental refreshment when they are over. Nothing affords such relief from the pressure of work as a free and animated conversation on other subjects. Of this more permanent kind of *table d'hôte*, Mr. Lewes gave a lively description in his biography of Goethe:—

> "The English student, clerk, or bachelor, who dines at an eating-house, chop-house, or hotel, goes there simply to get his dinner, and perhaps look at the 'Times.' Of the other diners he knows nothing, cares little. It is rare that a word is interchanged between him and his neighbor. Quite otherwise in Germany. There the same society is generally to be found at the same table. The *table d'hôte* is composed of a circle of *habitués*, varied by occasional visitors who in time become, perhaps, members of the circle. *Even with strangers conversation is freely interchanged*; and in a little while friendships are formed over these dinner-tables, according as natural tastes and likings assimilate, which, extending beyond the mere hour of dinner, are carried into the current of life. Germans do not rise so hastily from the table as we, for time with them is not so precious; life is not so crowded; time can be found for quiet after-dinner talk. The cigars and coffee, which appear before the cloth is removed, keep the company together; and in that state of suffused comfort which quiet digestion creates, they hear without anger the opinions of antagonists."

In this account of German habits we see the repast made use of as an opportunity for human intercourse, which the Englishman avoids except with persons already known to him or known to a private host. The reader has noticed the line I have italicized,—"Even with strangers conversation is freely interchanged." The consequence is that the stranger does not feel himself to be isolated, and if he is not an Englishman he does not take offence at being treated like an intelligent human being, but readily accepts the welcome that is offered to him.

The English peculiarity in this respect does not, however, consist so much in avoiding intercourse with foreigners as in shunning other English people. It is true that in the description of a *table d'hôte* by Miss Betham-Edwards, the English and foreign elements are represented as separated by an icy distance, and the description is strikingly accurate; but this shyness and timidity as regards foreigners may be sufficiently accounted for by want of skill and ease in speaking their language. Most English people of education know a little French and German, but few speak those languages freely, fluently, and correctly. When it does happen that an Englishman has mastered a foreign tongue, he will generally talk more readily and unreservedly with a foreigner than with one of his own countrymen. This is the notable thing, that if English people do not really dislike and distrust one another, if there is not really "a deadly feud of blood, caste, or religion" to separate them, they expose themselves to the accusation of John Stuart Mill, that "everybody acts as if everybody else was either an enemy or a bore."

This English avoidance of English people is so remarkable and exceptional a characteristic that it could not but greatly interest and exercise so observant a mind as that of De Tocqueville. We have seen how accurately he noticed it; how exactly the conduct of shy Englishmen had fixed itself in his memory. Let us now see how he accounted for it.

Is it a mark of aristocracy? Is it because our race is more aristocratic than other races?

De Tocqueville's theory was, that it is *not* the mark of an aristocratic society, because, in a society classed by birth, although people of different castes hold little communication with each other, they talk easily when they meet, without either fearing or desiring social fusion. "Their intercourse is not founded on equality, but it is free from constraint."

This view of the subject is confirmed by all that I know, through personal tradition, of the really aristocratic time in France that preceded the Revolution. The old-fashioned facility and directness of communication between ranks that were separated by wide social distances would surprise and almost scandalize a modern aspirant to false aristocracy, who has assumed the *de*, and makes up in *morgue* what is wanting to him in antiquity of descent. I believe, too, that when England was a far more aristocratic country than it is at present, manners were less distant and not so cold and suspicious.

If the blame is not to be laid on the spirit of aristocracy, what is the real cause of the indisputable fact that an Englishman avoids an Englishman? De Tocqueville believed that the cause was to be found in the uncertainty of a transition state from aristocratic to plutocratic ideas; that there is still the notion of a strict classification; and yet that this classification is no longer determined by blood, but by money, which has taken its place, so that although the ranks exist still, as if the country were really aristocratic, it is not easy to see clearly, and at the first glance, who occupies them. Hence there is a *guerre sourde* between all the citizens. Some try by a thousand artifices to edge their way in reality or apparently amongst those above them; others fight without ceasing to repel the usurpers of their rights; or rather, the same person does both; and whilst he struggles to introduce himself into the upper region he perpetually endeavors to put down aspirants who are still beneath him.

"The pride of aristocracy," said De Tocqueville, "being still very great with the English, and the limits of aristocracy having become doubtful, every one fears that he may be surprised at any moment into undesirable familiarity. Not being able to judge at first sight of the social position of those they meet, the English prudently avoid contact. They fear, in rendering little services, to form in spite of themselves an ill-assorted friendship; they dread receiving attention from others; and they withdraw themselves from the indiscreet gratitude of an unknown fellow-countryman as carefully as they would avoid his hatred."

This, no doubt, is the true explanation, but something may be added to it. An Englishman dreads acquaintances from the apprehension that they may end by coming to his house; a Frenchman is perfectly at his ease on that point by reason of the greater discretion of French habits. It is perfectly understood, in France, that you may meet a man at a *café* for years, and talk to him with the utmost freedom, and yet he will not come near your private residence unless you ask him; and when he meets you in the street he will not stop you, but will simply lift his hat,—a customary salutation from all who know your name, which does not compromise you in any way. It might perhaps be an exaggeration to say that in France there is absolutely no struggling after a higher social position by means of acquaintances, but there is certainly very little of it. The great majority of French people live in the most serene indifference as regards those who are a little above them socially. They hardly even know their titles; and when they do know them they do not care about them in the least.[18]

It may not be surprising that the conduct of Americans should differ from that of Englishmen, as Americans have no titles; but if they have not titles they have vast inequalities of wealth, and Englishmen can be repellent without titles. Yet, in spite of pecuniary differences between Americans, and notwithstanding the English blood in their veins, they do not avoid one another. "If they meet by accident," says De Tocqueville, "they neither seek nor avoid one another; their way of meeting is natural, frank, and open; it is evident that they hope or fear scarcely anything from each other, and that they neither try to exhibit nor to conceal the station they occupy. If their manner is often cold and serious, it is never either haughty or stiff; and when they do not speak it is because they are not in the humor for conversation, and not because they believe it their interest to be silent. In a foreign country two Americans are friends at once, simply because they are Americans. They are separated by no prejudice, and their common country draws them together. In the case of two Englishmen the same blood is not enough; there must be also identity of rank."

The English habit strikes foreigners by contrast, and it strikes Englishmen in the same way when they have lived much in foreign countries. Charles Lever had lived abroad, and was evidently as much struck by this as De Tocqueville himself. Many readers will remember his brilliant story, "That Boy of Norcott's," and how the young hero, after finding himself delightfully at ease with a society of noble Hungarians, at the Schloss Hunyadi, is suddenly chilled and alarmed by the intelligence that an English lord is expected. "When they shall see," he says, "how my titled countryman will treat me,—the distance at which he will hold me, and the measured firmness with which he will repel, not my familiarities, for I should not dare them, *but simply the ease of my manner*,—the foreigners will be driven to regard me as some ignoble upstart who has no pretension whatever to be amongst them."

Lever also noted that a foreigner would have had a better chance of civil treatment than an Englishman. "In my father's house I had often had occasion to remark that while Englishmen freely admitted the advances of a foreigner and accepted his acquaintance with a courteous readiness, with each other they maintained a cold and studied reserve, as though no difference of place or circumstance was to obliterate that insular code which defines class, and limits each man to the exact rank he belongs to."

These readings and experiences, and many others too long to quote or narrate, have led me to the conclusion that it is scarcely possible to attempt any other manner with English people than that which the very peculiar and exceptional state of national feeling appears to authorize. The reason is that in the present state of feeling the innovator is almost sure to be misunderstood. He may be perfectly contented with his own social position; his mind may be utterly devoid of any desire to raise himself in society; the extent of his present wishes may be to wile away the tedium of a journey or a repast with a little intelligent conversation; yet if he breaks down the barrier of English reserve he is likely to be taken for a pushing and intrusive person who is eager to lift himself in the world. Every friendly expression on his part, even in a look or the tone of his voice, "simply the ease of his manner," may be repelled as an impertinence. In the face of such a probable misinterpretation one feels that it is hardly possible to be too distant or too cold. When two men meet it is the colder and more reserved man who always has the advantage. He is the rock; the other is the wave that comes against the rock and falls shattered at its foot.

It would be wrong to conclude this Essay without a word of reference to the exceptional Englishman who can pass an hour intelligently with a stranger, and is not constantly preoccupied with the idea that the stranger is plotting how to make some ulterior use of him. Such Englishmen are usually men of ripe experience, who have travelled much and seen much of the world, so that they have lost our insular distrust. I have met with a few of them,—they are not very numerous,—and I wish that I could meet the same fellow-countrymen by some happy accident again. There is nothing stranger in life than those very short friendships that are formed in an hour between two people born to understand each other, and cut short forever the next day, or the next week, by an inevitable separation.[19]

ESSAY XVIII
OF GENTEEL IGNORANCE

ALL virtue has its negative as well as its positive side, and every ideal includes not having as well as having. Gentility, for those who aspire to it and value it, is an ideal condition of humanity, a superior state which is maintained by selection amongst the things that life offers to a man who has the power to choose. He is judged by his selection. The genteel person selects in his own way, not only amongst things that can be seen and handled, such as the material adjuncts of a high state of civilization, but also amongst the things of the mind, including all the varieties of knowledge.

That a selection of this kind should be one of the marks of gentility is in itself no more than a natural consequence of the idealizing process as we see it continually exercised in the fine arts. Every work of fine art is a result of selection. The artist does not give us the natural truth as it is, but he purposely omits very much of it, and alters that which he recognizes. The genteel person is himself a work of art, and, as such, contains only partial truth.

This is the central fact about gentility, that it is a narrow ideal, impoverishing the mind by the rejection of truth as much as it adorns it by elegance; and it is for this reason that gentility is disliked and refused by all powerful and inquiring intellects. They look upon it as a mental condition with which they have nothing to do, and they pursue their labors without the slightest deference or condescension to it. They may, however, profitably study it as one of the states of human life, and a state towards which a certain portion of humanity, aided by wealth, appears to tend inevitably.

The misfortune of the genteel mind is that it is carried by its own idealism so far away from the truth of nature that it becomes divorced from fact and unable to see the movement of the actual world; so that genteel people, with their narrow and erroneous ideas, are sure to find themselves thrust aside by men of robust intelligence, who are not genteel, but who have a stronger grip upon reality. There is, consequently, a pathetic element in gentility, with its fallacious hopes, its certain disappointments, so easily foreseen by all whom it has not blinded, and its immense, its amazing, its ever invincible ignorance.

There is not a country in Europe more favorable than France for the study of the genteel condition of mind. There you have it in its perfection in the class *qui n'a rien appris et rien oublié*, and in the numerous aspirants to social position who desire to mix themselves and become confounded with that class. It has been in the highest degree fashionable, since the establishment of the Republic, to be ignorant of the real course of events. In spite of overwhelming evidence to the contrary, genteel people either really believed or universally professed to believe during the life-time of the Count de Chambord, that his restoration was not only probable but imminent. No belief could have been more destitute of foundation in fact; and if genteel people had not been compelled by gentility to shut their eyes against what was obvious to everybody else, they might have ascertained the truth with the utmost facility. The truth was simply this, that the country was going away further and further from divine right every day, and from every sort of real monarchy, or one-man government, and was becoming more and more attached to representative institutions and an elective system everywhere; and what made this truth glaringly evident was not only the steadily increasing number of republican elections, but the repeated return to power of the very ministers whom the party of divine right most bitterly execrated. The same class of genteel French people affected to believe that the end of the temporal power of the Papacy by the foundation of the Italian kingdom was but a temporary crisis, probably of short duration; though the process which had brought the Papacy to nothing as a temporal sovereignty had been slow, gradual, and natural,—the progressive enfeeblement of a theocracy unable to defend itself against its own subjects, and dependent on foreign soldiers for every hour of its artificial survival. Such is genteel ignorance in political matters. It is a polite shutting of the eyes against all facts and tendencies that are disagreeable to people of fashion. It is unpleasant to people of fashion to be told that the France of the future is more likely to be governed by men of business than by kings and cardinals; it is disagreeable to them to hear that the Pope is not to do what he likes with the Roman people; and so, to please them, we are to pretend that we do not understand the course of recent history, which is obvious to everybody who thinks. The course of events has always proved the blindness of the genteel world, its incapacity to understand the present and forecast the future; yet still it goes on in the old way, shutting its eyes resolutely against surrounding facts, and making predictions that are sure to be falsified by the event. Such a state of mind is unintelligent to the last degree, but then it is genteel; and there is always, in every country, a large class of persons who would rather be gentlemanly than wise.

In religion, genteel ignorance is not less remarkable than in politics. Here the mark of gentility is to ignore the unfashionable churches, and generally to underestimate all those forces of opinion that are not on the side of the particular form of orthodoxy which is professed by the upper class. In France it is one of the marks of high breeding not to know anything about Protestantism. The fact that there are such people as Protestants is admitted, and it is believed that some of them are decent and respectable people in their line of life, who may follow an erroneous religion with an assiduity praiseworthy in itself, but the nature of their opinions is not known, and it is thought better not to inquire into them.

In England the gentry know hardly anything about Dissenters. As to the organization of dissenting communities, nobody ever hears of any of them having bishops, and so it is supposed that they must have some sort of democratic system. Genteel knowledge of dissenting faith and practice is confined to a very few points,—that Unitarians do not believe in the Trinity, that Baptists have some unusual practice about baptism, and that Methodists are fond of singing hymns. This is all, and more than enough; as it is inconceivable that an aristocratic person can have anything to do with Dissent, unless he wants the Nonconformist vote in politics. If Dissenters are to be spoken of at all, it should be in a condescending tone, as good people in their way, who may be decent members of the middle and lower classes, of some use in withstanding the tide of infidelity.

I remember a lady who condemned some eminent man as an atheist, on which I ventured to object that he was a deist only. "It is exactly the same thing," she replied. Being at that time young and argumentative, I maintained that there existed a distinction: that a deist believed in God, and an atheist had not that belief. "That is of no consequence," she rejoined; "what concerns us is that we should know as little as possible about such people." When this dialogue took place the lady seemed to me unreasonable and unjust, but now I perceive that she was genteel. She desired to keep her soul pure from the knowledge which gentility did not recognize; she wanted to know nothing about the shades and colors of heresy.

There is a delightful touch of determined ignorance in the answer of the Russian prelates to Mr. William Palmer, who went to Russia in 1840 with a view to bring about a recognition of Anglicanism by Oriental orthodoxy. In substance, according to Cardinal Newman, it amounted to this: "We know of no true Church besides our own. We are the only Church in the world. The Latins are heretics, or all but heretics; you are worse; *we do not even know your name.*" It would be difficult to excel this last touch; it is the perfection of uncontaminated orthodoxy, of the pure Russian religious *comme il faut.* We, the holy, the undefiled, the separate from heretics and from those lost ones, worse than heretics, into whose aberrations we never inquire, "*we do not even know your name.*"

Of all examples of genteel ignorance, there are none more frequent than the ignorance of those necessities which are occasioned by a limited income. I am not, at present, alluding to downright poverty. It is genteel to be aware that the poor exist; it is genteel, even, to have poor people of one's own to pet and patronize; and it is pleasant to be kind to such poor people when they receive our kindness in a properly submissive spirit, with a due sense of the immense distance between us, and read the tracts we give them, and listen respectfully to our advice. It is genteel to have to do with poor people in this way, and even to know something about them; the real genteel ignorance consists in not recognizing the existence of those impediments that are familiar to people of limited means. "I cannot understand," said an English lady, "why people complain about the difficulties of housekeeping. Such difficulties may almost always be included under one head,—insufficiency of servants; people have only to take more servants, and the difficulties disappear." Of course the cost of maintaining a troup of domestics is too trifling to be taken into consideration. A French lady, in my hearing, asked what fortune had such a family. The answer was simple and decided, they had no fortune at all. "No fortune at all! then how can they possibly live? How can people live who have no fortune?" This lady's genteel ignorance was enlightened by the explanation that when there is no fortune in a family it is generally supported by the labor of one or more of its members. "I cannot understand," said a rich Englishman to one of my friends, "why men are so imprudent as to allow themselves to sink into money embarrassments. There is a simple rule that I follow myself, and that I have always found a great safeguard,—it is, *never to let one's balance at the banker's fall below five thousand pounds.* By strictly adhering to this rule one is always sure to be able to meet any unexpected and immediate necessity." Why, indeed, do we not all follow a rule so evidently wise? It may be especially recommended to struggling professional men with large families. If only they can be persuaded to act upon it they will find it an unspeakable relief from anxiety, and the present volume will not have been penned in vain.

Genteel ignorance of pecuniary difficulties is conspicuous in the case of amusements. It is supposed, if you are inclined to amuse yourself in a certain limited way, that you are stupid for not doing it on a much more expensive scale. Charles Lever wrote a charming paper for one of the early numbers of the "Cornhill Magazine," in which he gave an account of the dangers and difficulties he had encountered in riding and boating, simply because he had set limits to his expenditure on those pastimes, an economy that seemed unaccountably foolish to his genteel acquaintances. "Lever will ride such screws! Why won't he give a proper price for a horse? It's the stupidest thing in the world to be under-horsed; and bad economy besides." These remarks, Lever said, were not sarcasms on his skill or sneers at his horsemanship, but they were far worse, they were harsh judgments on himself expressed in a manner that made reply impossible. So with his boating. Lever had a passion for boating, for that real boating which is perfectly distinct from yachting and incomparably less costly; but richer acquaintances insisted on the superior advantages of the more expensive amusement. "These cockle-shells, sir, must go over; they have no bearings, they lee over, and there you are,—you fill and go down. Have a good decked boat,—I should say five-and-thirty or forty tons; *get a clever skipper and a lively crew.*" Is not this exactly like the lady who thought people stupid for not having an adequate establishment of servants?

Another form of genteel ignorance consists in being so completely blinded by conventionalism as not to be able to perceive the essential identity of two modes of life or habits of action when one of them happens to be in what is called "good form," whilst the other is not accepted by polite society. My own tastes and pursuits have often led me to do things for the sake of study or pleasure which in reality differ but very slightly from what genteel people often do; yet, at the same time, this slight difference is sufficient to prevent them from seeing any resemblance whatever between my practice and theirs. When a young man, I found a wooden hut extremely convenient for painting from nature, and when at a distance from other lodging I slept in it. This was unfashionable; and genteel people expressed much wonder at it, being especially surprised that I could be so imprudent as to risk health by sleeping in a little wooden house. Conventionalism made them perfectly ignorant of the fact that they occasionally slept in little wooden houses themselves. A railway carriage is simply a wooden hut on wheels, generally very ill-ventilated, and presenting the alternative of foul air or a strong draught, with vibration that makes sleep difficult to some and to others absolutely impossible. I have passed many nights in those public wooden huts on wheels, but have never slept in them so pleasantly as in my own private one.[20] Genteel people also use wooden dwellings that float on water. A yacht's cabin is nothing but a hut of a peculiar shape with its own special inconveniences. On land a hut will remain steady; at sea it inclines in every direction, and is tossed about like Gulliver's large box. An Italian nobleman who liked travel, but had no taste for dirty Southern inns, had four vans that formed a square at night, with a little courtyard in the middle that was covered with canvas and served as a spacious dining-room. The arrangement was excellent, but he was considered hopelessly eccentric; yet how slight was the difference between his vans and a train of saloon carriages for the railway! He simply had saloon carriages that were adapted for common roads.

It is difficult to see what advantage there can be in genteel ignorance to compensate for its evident disadvantages. Not to be acquainted with unfashionable opinions, not to be able to imagine unfashionable necessities, not to be able to perceive the real likeness between fashionable and unfashionable modes of life on account of some external and superficial difference, is like living in a house with closed shutters. Surely a man, or a woman either, might have as good manners, and be as highly civilized in all respects, with accurate notions of things as with a head full of illusions. To understand the world as it really is, to see the direction in which humanity is travelling, ought to be the purpose of every strong and healthy intellect, even though such knowledge may take it out of gentility altogether.

The effect of genteel ignorance on human intercourse is such a deduction from the interest of it that men of ability often avoid genteel society altogether, and either devote themselves to solitary labors, cheered principally by the companionship of books, or else keep to intimate friends of their own order. In Continental countries the public drinking-places are often frequented by men of culture, not because they want to drink, but because they can talk freely about what they think and what they know without being paralyzed by the determined ignorance of the genteel. In England, no doubt, there is more information; and yet Stuart Mill said that "general society as now carried on in England is so insipid an affair, even to the persons who make it what it is, that it is kept up for any reason rather than the pleasure it affords. All serious discussion on matters in which opinions differ being considered ill-bred, and the national deficiency in liveliness and sociability having prevented the cultivation of the art of talking agreeably on trifles, the sole attraction of what is called society to those who are not at the top of the tree is the hope of being aided to climb a little higher. To a person of any but a very common order in thought or feeling, such society, unless he has personal objects to serve by it, must be supremely unattractive; and most people in the present day of any really high class of intellect make their contact with it so slight and at such long intervals as to be almost considered as retiring from it altogether." The loss here is distinctly to the genteel persons themselves. They may not feel it, they may be completely insensible of it, but by making society insipid they eliminate from it the very men who might have been its most valuable elements, and who, whether working in solitude or living with a few congenial spirits, are really the salt of the earth.

ESSAY XIX
PATRIOTIC IGNORANCE

PATRIOTIC ignorance is maintained by the satisfaction that we feel in ignoring what is favorable to another nation. It is a voluntary closing of the mind against the disagreeable truth that another nation may be on certain points equal to our own, or even, though inferior, in some degree comparable to our own.

The effect of patriotic ignorance as concerning human intercourse is to place any one who knows the exact truth in the unpleasant dilemma of having either to correct mistakes which are strongly preferred to truth, or else to give assent to them against his sense of justice. International intercourse is made almost impossible by patriotic ignorance, except amongst a few highly cultivated persons who are superior to it. Nothing is more difficult than to speak about one's own country with foreigners who are perpetually putting forward the errors which they have imbibed all their lives, and to which they cling with such tenacity that it seems as if those errors were, in some mysterious way, essential to their mental comfort and well-being. If, on the other hand, we have any really intimate knowledge of a foreign country, gained by long residence in it and studious observation of the inhabitants, then we find a corresponding difficulty in talking reasonably about it and them with our own countrymen, because they, too, have their patriotic ignorance which they prize and value as foreigners value theirs.

At the risk of turning this Essay into a string of anecdotes, I intend to give a few examples of patriotic ignorance, in order to show to what an astonishing degree of perfection it may attain. When we fully understand this we shall also understand how those who possess such a treasure should be anxious for its preservation. Their anxiety is the more reasonable that in these days there is a difficulty in keeping things when they are easily injured by light.

A French lady who possessed this treasure in its perfection gave, in my hearing, as a reason why French people seldom visited England, that there were no works of art there, no collections, no architecture, nothing to gratify the artistic sense or the intelligence; and that it was only people specially interested in trade and manufactures who went to England, as the country had nothing to show but factories and industrial products. On hearing this statement, there suddenly passed before my mind's eye a rapid vision of the great works of architecture, sculpture, and painting that I had seen in England, and a confused recollection of many minor examples of these arts not quite unworthy of a studious man's attention. It is impossible to contradict a lady; and any statement of the simple truth would, in this instance, have been a direct and crushing contradiction. I ventured on a faint remonstrance, but without effect; and my fair enemy triumphed. There were no works of art in England. Thus she settled the question.

This little incident led me to take note of French ideas about England with reference to patriotic ignorance; and I discovered that there existed a very general belief that there was no intellectual light of any kind in England. Paris was the light of the world, and only so far as Parisian rays might penetrate the mental fog of the British Islands was there a chance of its becoming even faintly luminous. It was settled that the speciality of England was trade and manufacture, that we were all of us either merchants or cotton-spinners, and I discovered that we had no learned societies, no British Museum, no Royal Academy of Arts.

An English painter, who for many years had exhibited on the line of the Royal Academy, happened to be mentioned in my presence and in that of a French artist. I was asked by some French people who knew him personally whether the English painter had a good professional standing. I answered that he had a fair though not a brilliant reputation; meanwhile the French artist showed signs of uneasiness, and at length exploded with a vigorous protest against the inadmissible idea that a painter could be anything whatever who was not known at the French *Salon*. "Il n'est pas connu au Salon de Paris, donc, il n'existe pas—il n'existe pas. Les réputations dans les beaux-arts se font au Salon de Paris et pas ailleurs." This Frenchman had no conception whatever of the simple fact that artistic reputations are made in every capital of the civilized world. That was a truth which his patriotism could not tolerate for a moment.

A French gentleman expressed his surprise that I did not have my books translated into French, "because," said he, "no literary reputation can be considered established until it has received the consecration of Parisian approval." To his unfeigned astonishment I answered that London and not Paris was the capital city of English literature, and that English authors had not yet fallen so low as to care for the opinion of critics ignorant of their language.

I then asked myself why this intense French patriotic ignorance should continue so persistently; and the answer appeared to be that there was something profoundly agreeable to French patriotic sentiment in the belief that England had no place in the artistic and intellectual world. Until quite recently the very existence of an English school of painting was denied by all patriotic Frenchmen, and English art was rigorously excluded from the Louvre.[21] Even now a French writer upon art can scarcely mention English painting without treating it *de haut en bas,* as if his Gallic nationality gave him a natural right to treat uncivilized islanders with lofty disdain or condescending patronage.

My next example has no reference to literature or the fine arts. A young French gentleman of superior education and manners, and with the instincts of a sportsman, said in my hearing, "There is no game in England." His tone was that of a man who utters a truth universally acknowledged.

It might be a matter of little consequence, as touching our national pride, whether there was game in England or not. I have no doubt that some philosophers would consider, and perhaps with reason, that the non-existence of game, where it can only be maintained by an army of keepers and a penal code of its own, would be the sign of an advancing social state; but my young Frenchman was not much of a philosopher, and no doubt he considered the non-existence of game in England a mark of inferiority to France. There is something in the masculine mind, inherited perhaps from ancestors who lived by the chase, which makes it look upon an abundance of wild things that can be shot at, or run after with horses and dogs, as a reason for the greatest pride and glorification. On reflection, it will be found that there is more in the matter than at first sight appears. As there is no game in England, of course there are no sportsmen in that country. The absence of game means the absence of shooters and huntsmen, and consequently an inferiority in manly exercises to the French, thousands of whom take shooting licenses and enjoy the invigorating excitement of the chase. For this reason it is agreeable to French patriotic sentiment to be perfectly certain that there is no game in England. When I inquired what reason my young friend had for holding his conviction on the subject, he told me that in a country like England, so full of trade and manufactures, there could not be any room for game.

One of the most popular of French songs is that charming one by Pierre Dupont in praise of his vine. Every Frenchman who knows anything knows that song, and believes that he also knows the tune. The consequence is that when one of them begins to sing it his companions join in the refrain or chorus, which is as follows:—

"Bons Français, quand je vois mon verre
Plein de ce vin couleur de feu
Je songe en remerciant Dieu
Qu'ils n'en ont pas dans l'Angleterre!"

The singers repeat "qu'ils n'en ont pas," and besides this the whole of the last line is repeated with triumphant emphasis.

We need not feel hurt by this little outburst of patriotism. There is no real hatred of England at the bottom of it, only a little "malice" of a harmless kind, and the song is sometimes sung good-humoredly in the presence of Englishmen. It is, however, really connected with patriotic ignorance. The common French belief is that as vines are not grown in England, we have no wine in our cellars, so that English people hardly know the taste of wine; and this belief is too pleasing to the French mind to be readily abandoned by those who hold it. They feel that it enhances the delightfulness of every glass they drink. The case is precisely the same with fruit. The French enjoy plenty of excellent fruit, and they enjoy it all the more heartily from a firm conviction that there is no fruit of any kind in England. "Pas un fruit," said a countryman of Pierre Dupont in writing about our unfavored island, "pas un fruit ne mûrit dans ce pays." What, not even a gooseberry? Were the plums, pears, strawberries, apples, apricots, that we consumed in omnivorous boyhood every one of them unripe? It is lamentable to think how miserably the English live. They have no game, no wine, no fruit (it appears to be doubtful, too, whether they have any vegetables), and they dwell in a perpetual fog where sunshine is totally unknown. It is believed, also, that there is no landscape-beauty in England,—nothing but a green field with a hedge, and then another green field with another hedge, till you come to the bare chalk cliffs and the dreary northern sea. The English have no Devonshire, no valley of the Severn, no country of the Lakes. The Thames is a foul ditch, without a trace of natural beauty anywhere.[22]

It would be easy to give many more examples of the patriotism of our neighbors, but perhaps for the sake of variety it may be desirable to turn the glass in the opposite direction and see what English patriotism has to say about France. We shall find the same principle at work, the same determination to believe that the foreign country is totally destitute of many things on which we greatly pride ourselves. I do not know that there is any reason to be proud of having mountains, as they are excessively inconvenient objects that greatly impede agriculture and communication; however, in some parts of Great Britain it is considered, somehow, a glory for a nation to have mountains; and there used to be a firm belief that French landscape was almost destitute of mountainous grandeur. There were the Highlands of Scotland, but who had ever heard of the Highlands of France? Was not

France a wearisome, tame country that unfortunately had to be traversed before one could get to Switzerland and Italy? Nobody seemed to have any conception that France was rich in mountain scenery of the very grandest kind. Switzerland was understood to be the place for mountains, and there was a settled but erroneous conviction that Mont Blanc was situated in that country. As for the Grand-Pelvoux, the Pointe des Écrins, the Mont Olan, the Pic d'Arsine, and the Trois Ellions, nobody had ever heard of them. If you had told any average Scotchman that the most famous Bens would be lost and nameless in the mountainous departments of France, the news would have greatly surprised him. He would have been astonished to hear that the area of mountainous France exceeded the area of Scotland, and that the height of its loftiest summits attained three times the elevation of Ben Nevis.

It may be excusable to feel proud of mountains, as they are noble objects in spite of their inconvenience, but it seems less reasonable to be patriotic about hedges, which make us pay dearly for any beauty they may possess by hiding the perspective of the land. A hedge six feet high easily masks as many miles of distance. However, there is a pride in English hedges, accompanied by a belief that there are no such things in France. The truth is that regions of large extent are divided by hedges in France as they are in England Another belief is that there is little or no wood in France, though wood is the principal fuel, and vast forests are reserved for its supply. I have heard an Englishman proudly congratulating himself, in the spirit of Dupont's song, on the supposed fact that the French had neither coal nor iron; and yet I have visited a vast establishment at the Creuzot, where ten thousand workmen are continually employed in making engines, bridges, armor-plates, and other things from iron found close at hand, by the help of coal fetched from a very little distance. I have read in an English newspaper that there were no singing birds in France; and by way of commentary a hundred little French songsters kept up a merry din that would have gladdened the soul of Chaucer. It happened, too, to be the time of the year for nightingales, which filled the woods with their music in the moonlight.

Patriotic ignorance often gets hold of some partial truth unfavorable to another country, and then applies it in such an absolute manner that it is truth no longer. It is quite true, for example, that athletic exercises are not so much cultivated in France, nor held in such high esteem, as they are in England, but it is not true that all young Frenchmen are inactive. They are often both good swimmers and good pedestrians, and, though they do not play cricket, many of them take a practical interest in gymnastics and are skilful on the bar and the trapeze. The French learn military drill in their boyhood, and in early manhood they are inured to fatigue in the army, besides which great numbers of them learn fencing on their own account, that they may hold their own in a duel. Patriotic ignorance likes to shut its eyes to all inconvenient facts of this kind, and to dwell on what is unfavorable. A man may like a glass of absinthe in a *café* and still be as energetic as if he drank port wine at home. I know an old French officer who never misses his daily visit to the *café*, and so might serve as a text for moralizing, but at the same time he walks twenty kilomètres every day. Patriotic ignorance has its opportunity in every difference of habit. What can be apparently more indolent, for an hour or two after *déjeûner*, than a prosperous man of business in Paris? Very possibly he may be caught playing cards or dominoes in the middle of the day, and severely blamed by a foreign censor. The difference between him and his equal in London is simply in the arrangement of time. The Frenchman has been at his work early, and divides his day into two parts, with hours of idleness between them.

Many examples of those numerous international criticisms that originate in patriotic ignorance are connected with the employment of words that are apparently common to different nations, yet vary in their signification. One that has given rise to frequent patriotic criticisms is the French word *univers*. French writers often say of some famous author, such as Victor Hugo, "Sa renommée remplit l'univers;" or of some great warrior, like Napoleon, "Il inquiéta l'univers." English critics take up these expressions and then say, "Behold how bombastic these French writers are, with their absurd exaggerations, as if Victor Hugo and Napoleon astonished the universe, as if they were ever heard of beyond our own little planet!" Such criticism only displays patriotic ignorance of a foreign language. The French expression is perfectly correct, and not in the least exaggerated. Napoleon did not disquiet the universe, but he disquieted *l'univers*. Victor Hugo is not known beyond the terrestrial globe, but he is known, by name at least, throughout *l'univers*. The persistent ignorance of English writers on this point would be inexplicable if it were not patriotic; if it did not afford an opportunity for deriding the vanity of foreigners. It is the more remarkable that the deriders themselves constantly use the word in the same restricted sense as an adjective or an adverb. I open Mr. Stanford's atlas, and find that it is called "The London Atlas of *Universal Geography*," though it does not contain a single map of any planet but our own, not even one of the visible hemisphere of the moon, which might easily have been given. I take a newspaper, and I find that the late President of the Royal Society died *universally* respected, though he was known only to the cultivated inhabitants of a single planet. Such is the power of patriotic ignorance that it is able to prevent men from understanding a foreign word when they themselves employ a nearly related word in identically the same sense.[23]

The word *univers* reminds me of universities, and they recall a striking example of patriotic ignorance in my own countrymen. I wonder how many Englishmen there are who know anything about the University of France. I never expect an Englishman to know anything about it; and, what is more, I am always prepared to find him impervious to any information on the subject. As the organization of the University of France differs essentially from that of English universities, each of which is localized in one place, and can be seen in its entirety from the top of a tower, the Englishman hears with contemptuous inattention any attempt to make him understand an institution without a parallel in his own country. Besides this, the Universities of Oxford and Cambridge are venerable and wealthy institutions, visibly beautiful, whilst the University of France is of comparatively recent origin; and, though large sums are expended in its service, the result does not strike the eye because the expenditure is distributed over the country. I remember having occasion to mention the Academy of Lyons to a learned doctor of Oxford who was travelling in France, and I found that he had never heard of the Academy of Lyons, and knew nothing about the organization of the national university of which that academy forms a part. From a French point of view this is quite as remarkable an example of patriotic ignorance as if some foreigner had never heard of the diocese of York, or the episcopal organization of the Church of England. Every Frenchman who has any education at all knows the functions of academies in the university, and which of the principal cities are the seats of those learned bodies.

As Englishmen ignore the University of France, they naturally at the same time ignore the degrees that it confers. They never know what a *Licencié* is, they have no conception of the *Agrégation*, or of the severe ordeal of competitive examination through which an *Agrégé* must have passed. Therefore, if a Frenchman has attained either of these grades, his title is unintelligible to an Englishman.

There is, no doubt, great ignorance in France on the subject of the English universities, but it is neither in the same degree nor of the same kind. I should hardly call French ignorance of the classes at Oxford patriotic ignorance, because it does not proceed from the belief that a foreign university is unworthy of a Frenchman's attention. I should call French ignorance of the Royal Academy, for example, genuine patriotic ignorance, because it proceeds from a conviction that English art is unworthy of notice, and that the French *Salon* is the only exhibition that can interest an enlightened lover of art. That is the essence of patriotism in ignorance, —to be ignorant of what is done in another nation, because we believe our own to be first and the rest nowhere; and so the English ignorance of the University of France is genuine patriotic ignorance. It is caused by the existence of Oxford and Cambridge, as the French ignorance of the Royal Academy is caused by the French *Salon*.

Patriotic ignorance is one of the most serious impediments to conversation between people of different nationality, because occasions are continually arising when the national sentiments of the one are hurt by the ignorance of the other. But we may also wound the feelings of a foreigner by assuming a more complete degree of ignorance on his part than that which is really his. This is sometimes done by English people towards Americans, when English people forget that their national literature is the common possession of the two countries. A story is told by Mr. Grant White of an English lady who informed him that a novel (which she advised him to read) had been written about Kenilworth, by Sir Walter Scott; and he expected her to recommend a perusal of the works of William Shakespeare. Having lived much abroad, I am myself occasionally the grateful recipient of valuable information from English friends. For example, I remember an Englishman who kindly and quite seriously informed me that Eton College was a public school where many sons of the English aristocracy were educated.

There is a very serious side to patriotic ignorance in relation to war. There can be no doubt that many of the most foolish, costly, and disastrous wars ever undertaken were either directly due to patriotic ignorance, or made possible only by the existence of such ignorance in the nation that afterwards suffered by them. The way in which patriotic ignorance directly tends to produce war is readily intelligible. A nation sees its own soldiers, its own cannons, its own ships, and becomes so proud of them as to remain contentedly and even wilfully ignorant of the military strength and efficiency of its neighbors. The war of 1870-71, so disastrous to France, was the direct result of patriotic ignorance. The country and even the Emperor himself were patriotically ignorant of their own inferior military condition and of the superior Prussian organization. One or two isolated voices were raised in warning, but it was considered patriotic not to listen to them. The war between Turkey and Russia, which cost Turkey Bulgaria and all but expelled her from Europe, might easily have been avoided by the Sultan; but he was placed in a false position by the patriotic ignorance of his own subjects, who believed him to be far more powerful than he really was, and who would have probably dethroned or murdered him if he had acted rationally, that is to say, in accordance with the degree of strength that he possessed. In almost every instance that I am able to remember, the nations that have undertaken imprudent and easily avoidable wars have done so because they were blinded by patriotic ignorance, and therefore either impelled their rulers into a foolish course against their better knowledge, or else were themselves easily led into peril by the temerity of a rash master, who would risk the well-being of all his subjects that he might attain some personal and private end. The French have been cured of their most dangerous patriotic ignorance,—that concerning the military strength of the country,—by the war of 1870, but the cure was of a costly nature.

Patriotism has been so commonly associated with a wilful closing of the eyes against unpleasant facts, that those who prefer truth to illusion are often considered unpatriotic. Yet surely ignorance has not the immense advantage over knowledge of having all patriotism on her side. There is a far higher and better patriotism than that of ignorance; there is a love of country that shows itself in anxiety for its best welfare, and does not remain satisfied with the vain delusion of a fancied superiority in everything. It is the interest of England as a nation to be accurately informed about all that concerns her position in the world, and it is impossible for her to receive this information if a stupid national vanity is always ready to take offence when it is offered. It is desirable for England to know exactly in what degree she is a military power, and also how she stands with reference to the naval armaments of other nations, not as they existed in the days of Nelson, but as they will exist next year. It is the interest of England to know by what tenure she holds India, just as in the reign of George the Third it would have been very much the interest of England to know accurately both the rights of the American colonists and their strength. I cannot imagine any circumstances that might make ignorance more desirable for a free people than knowledge. With enslaved peoples the case is different: the less they know and the greater, perhaps, are their chances of enjoying the dull kind of somnolent happiness which alone is attainable by them; but this is a kind of happiness that no citizen of a free country would desire.

ESSAY XX
CONFUSIONS

SURELY the analytical faculty must be very rare, or we should not so commonly find people confounding together things essentially distinct. Any one who possesses that faculty naturally, and has followed some occupation which strengthens it, must be continually amused if he has a humorous turn, or irritated if he is irascible, by the astounding mental confusions in which men contentedly pass their lives. To be just, this account ought to include both sexes, for women indulge in confusions even more frequently than men, and are less disposed to separate things when they have once been jumbled together.

A confusion of ideas in politics which is not uncommon amongst the enemies of all change is to believe that whoever desires the reform of some law wants to do something that is not legal, and has a rebellious, subversive spirit. Yet the reformer is not a rebel; it is indeed the peculiar distinction of his position not to be a rebel, for there has never been a real reformer (as distinguished from a revolutionist) who wished to do anything illegal. He desires, certainly, to do something which is not legal just at present, but he does not wish to do it so long as it remains in the condition of illegality. He wishes first to make it legal by obtaining legislative sanction for his proposal, and then to do it when it shall have become as legal as anything else, and when all the most conservative people in the kingdom will be strenuous in its defence as "part and parcel of the law of the land."

Another confusion in political matters which has always been extremely common is that between private and public liberty. Suppose that a law were enacted to the effect that each British subject without exception should go to Mass every Sunday morning, on pain of death, and should take the Roman Catholic Sacrament of Holy Communion, involving auricular confession, at Easter; such a law would not be an infringement of the sensible liberty of Roman Catholics, because they do these things already. Then they might say, "People talk of the tyranny of the law, yet the law is not tyrannical at all; we enjoy perfect liberty in England, and it is most unreasonable to say that we do not." The Protestant part of the community would exclaim that such a law was an intolerable infringement of liberty, and would rush to arms to get rid of it. This is the distinction between private and public liberty. There is private liberty when some men are not interfered with in the ordinary habits of their existence; and there has always been much of such private liberty under the worst of despotisms; but there is not public liberty until every man in the country may live according to his own habits, so long as he does not interfere with the rights of others. Here is a distinction plain enough to be evident to a very commonplace understanding; yet the admirers of tyrants are often successful in producing a confusion between the two things, and in persuading people that there was "ample liberty" under some foreign despot, because they themselves, when they visited the country that lay prostrate under his irresistible power, were allowed to eat good dinners, and drive about unmolested, and amuse themselves by day and by night according to every suggestion of their fancy.

Many confusions have been intentionally maintained by political enemies in order to cast odium on their adversaries; so that it becomes of great importance to a political cause that it should not bear a name with two meanings, or to which it may be possible to give another meaning than that which was originally intended. The word "Radical" is an instance of this. According to the enemies of radicalism it has always meant a political principle that strikes at the root of the constitution; but it was not that meaning of the word which induced the first Radicals to commit the imprudence of adopting it. The term referred to agriculture rather than tree-felling, the original idea being to uproot abuses as a gardener pulls weeds up by the roots. I distinctly remember my first boyish notion of the Radicals. I saw them in a sort of sylvan picture,—violent savage men armed with sharp axes, and hewing away at the foot of a majestic oak that stood for the glory of England. Since then I have become acquainted with another instance of the unfortunate adoption of a word which may be plausibly perverted from its meaning. The French republican motto is *Liberté, Égalité, Fraternité*, and to this day there is hardly an English newspaper that does not from time to time sneer at the French Republicans for aspiring to equality, as if equality were not impossible in the nature of things, and as if, supposing an unnatural equality to be established to-day, the operation of natural causes would not bring about inequality to-morrow. We are told that some men would be stronger, or cleverer, or more industrious than others, and earn more and make themselves leaders; that children of the same parents, starting in life with the same fortunes, never remain in precisely the same positions; and much more to the same purpose. All this trite and familiar reasoning is without application here. The word *Égalité* in the motto means something which *can* be attained, and which, though it did not exist in France before the Revolution, is now almost a perfect reality there,—it means equality before the law; it means that there shall not be privileged classes exempt from paying taxes, and favored with such scandalous partiality that all posts of importance in the government, the army, the magistracy, and the church are habitually reserved for them. If it meant absolute equality, no Republican could aim at wealth, which is the creation of inequality in his own favor; neither would any Republican labor for intellectual reputation, or accept honors. There would not even be a Republican in the gymnastic societies, where every member strives to become stronger and more agile than his fellows, and knows that, whether in his favor or against him, the most striking inequalities will be manifested in every public contest. There would be no Republicans in the University, for has it not a hierarchy with the most marked gradations of title, and differences of consideration and authority? Yet the University is so full of Republicans that it is scarcely too much to say that it is entirely composed of them. I am aware that there are dreamers in the working classes, both in France and elsewhere, who look forward to a social state when all men will work for the same wages,— when the Meissonier of the day will be paid like a sign-painter, and the sign-painter like a white-washer, and all three perform each other's tasks by turns for equality of agreeableness in the work; but these dreams are only possible in extreme ignorance, and lie quite outside of any theories to be seriously considered.

Religious intolerance, when quite sincere and not mixed up with social contempt or political hatred, is founded upon a remarkable confusion of ideas, which is this. The persecutor assumes that the heretic knowingly and maliciously resists the will of God in rejecting the theology which he knows that God desires him to receive. This is a confusion between the mental states of the believer and the unbeliever, and it does not accurately describe either, for the believer of course accepts the doctrine, and the unbeliever does not reject it as coming from God, but precisely because he is convinced that it has a purely human origin.

"Are you a Puseyite?" was a question put to a lady in my hearing; and she at once answered, "Certainly not, I should be ashamed of being a Puseyite." Here was a confusion between her present mental state and her supposed possible mental state as a Puseyite; for it is impossible to be a real Puseyite and at the same time to think of one's belief with an inward sense of shame. A believer always thinks that his belief is simply the truth, and nobody feels ashamed of believing what is true. Even concealment of a belief does not imply shame; and those who have been compelled, in self-defence, to hide their real opinions, have been ashamed, if at all, of hiding and not of having them.

A confusion common to all who do not think, and avoided only with the greatest difficulty by those who do, is that between their own knowledge and the knowledge possessed by another person who has different tastes, different receptive powers, and other opportunities. They cannot imagine that the world does not appear the same to him that it appears to them. They do not really believe that he can feel quite differently from themselves and still be in every respect as sound in mind and as intelligent as they are. The incapacity to imagine a different mental condition is strikingly manifested in what we call the Philistine mind, and is one of its strongest characteristics. The true Philistine thinks that every form of culture which opens out a world that is closed against himself leaves the votary exactly where he was before. "I cannot imagine why you live in Italy," said a Philistine to an acquaintance; "nothing could induce *me* to live in Italy." He did not take into account the difference of gifts and culture, but supposed the person he addressed to have just his own mental condition, the only one that he was able to conceive, whereas, in fact, that person was so endowed and so educated as to enjoy Italy in the supreme degree. He spoke the purest Italian with perfect ease; he had a considerable knowledge of Italian literature and antiquities; his love of natural beauty amounted to an insatiable passion; and from his youth he had delighted in architecture and painting. Of these gifts, tastes, and acquirements the Philistine was simply destitute. For him Italy could have had no meaning. Where the other found unfailing interest he would have suffered from unrelieved *ennui*, and would have been continually looking back, with the intolerable longing of nostalgia, to the occupations of his English home. In the same spirit a French *bourgeois* once complained in my hearing that too much space was given to foreign affairs in the newspapers, "car, vous comprenez, cela n'intéresse pas." This was simply an attribution of his personal apathy to everybody else. Certainly, as a nation, the French take less interest in foreign affairs than we do, but they do take some interest, and the degree of it is exactly reflected by the importance given to foreign affairs in their journals, always greatest in the best of them. An Englishman said, also in my hearing, that to have a library was a mistake, as a library was of no use; he admitted that a few books might be useful if the owner read them through. Here, again, is the attribution of one person's experience to all cases. This man had never himself felt the need of a library, and did not know how to use one. He could not realize the fact that a few books only allow you to read, whilst a library allows you to pursue a study. He could not at all imagine what the word "library" means to a scholar,—that it means the not being stopped at every turn for want of light, the not being exposed to scornful correction by men of inferior ability and inferior industry, whose only superiority is the great and terrible one of living within a cabfare of the British Museum. I remember reading an account of the establishment of a Greek professorship in a provincial town, and it was wisely proposed, by one who understood the difficulties of a scholar remote from the great libraries, that provision should be made for the accumulation of books for the use of the future occupants of the chair, but the trustees (honest men of business, who had no idea of a scholar's wants and necessities) said that each professor must provide his own library, just as road commissioners advertise that a surveyor must have his own horse.

One of the most serious reasons why it is imprudent to associate with people whose opinions you do not wish to be made responsible for is that others will confound you with them. There is an old Latin proverb, and also a French one, to the effect that if a man knows what your friends are, he knows what you are yourself. These proverbs are not true, but they well express the popular confusion between having something in common and having everything in common. If you are on friendly terms with clergymen, it is inferred that you have a clerical mind; when the reason may be that you are a scholar living in the country, and can find no scholarship in your neighborhood except in the parsonage houses. You associate with foreigners, and are supposed to be unpatriotic; when in truth you are as patriotic as any rational and well-informed creature can be, but have a faculty for languages that you like to exercise in conversation. This kind of confusion takes no account of the indisputable fact that men constantly associate together on the ground of a single pursuit that they have in common, often a mere amusement, or because, in spite of every imaginable difference, they are drawn together by one of those mysterious natural affinities which are so obscure in their origin and action that no human intelligence can explain them.

Not only are a man's tastes liable to be confounded with those of his personal acquaintances, but he may find some trade attributed to him, by a perfectly irrational association of ideas, because it happens to be prevalent in the country where he lives. I have known instances of men supposed to have been in the cotton trade simply because they had lived in Lancashire, and of others supposed to be in the mineral oil trade for no other reason than because they had lived in a part of France where mineral oil is found.

Professional men are usually very much alive to the danger of confusion as affecting their success in life. If you are known to do two things, a confusion gets established between the two, and you are no longer classed with that ease and decision which the world finds to be convenient. It therefore becomes a part of worldly wisdom to keep one of the occupations in obscurity, and if that is not altogether possible, then to profess as loudly and as frequently as you can that it is entirely secondary and only a refreshment after more serious toils. Many years ago a well-known surgeon published a set of etchings, and the merit of them was so dangerously conspicuous, so superior, in fact, to the average of professional work, that he felt constrained to keep those too clever children in their places by a quotation from Horace,—

"O laborum
Dulce lenimen!"

To present one's self to the world always in one character is a great help to success, and maintains the stability of a position. The kings in the story-books and on playing cards who have always their crowns on their heads and sceptres in their hands, appear to enjoy a decided advantage over modern royalty, which dresses like other people and enters into common interests and pursuits. Literary men admire the prudent self-control of our literary sovereign, Tennyson, who by his rigorous abstinence from prose takes care never to appear in public without his singing robes and his crown of laurel. Had he carelessly and familiarly employed the commoner vehicle of expression, there would have been a confusion of two Tennysons in the popular idea, whilst at present his name is as exclusively associated with the exquisite music of his verse as that of Mozart with another kind of melody.

The great evil of confusions, as they affect conversation, is that they constantly place a man of accurate mental habits in such trying situations that, unless he exercises the most watchful self-control, he is sure to commit the sin of contradiction. We have all of us met with the lady who does not think it necessary to distinguish between one person and another, who will tell a story of some adventure as having happened to A, when in reality it happened to B; who will attribute sayings and opinions to C, when they properly belong to D; and deliberately maintain that it is of no consequence whatever, when some suffering lover of accuracy undertakes to set her right. It is in vain to argue that there really does exist, in the order of the universe, a distinction between one person and another, though both belong to the human race; and that organisms are generally isolated, though there has been an exception in the case of the Siamese twins. The death of the wonderful swimmer who attempted to descend the rapids of Niagara afforded an excellent opportunity for confounders. In France they all confounded him with Captain Boyton, who swam with an apparatus; and when poor Webb was sucked under the whirlpool they said, "You see that, after all, his inflated dress was of no avail." Fame of a higher kind does not escape from similar confusions. On the death of George Eliot, French readers of English novels lamented that they would have nothing more from the pen that wrote "John Halifax," and a cultivated Frenchman expressed his regret for the author of "Adam Bede" and "Uncle Tom's Cabin."[24]

Men who have trained themselves in habits of accurate observation often have a difficulty in realizing the confused mental condition of those who simply receive impressions without comparison and classification. A fine field for confused tourists is architecture. They go to France and Italy, they talk about what they have seen, and leave you in bewilderment, until you make the discovery that they have substituted one building for another, or, better still, mixed two different edifices inextricably together. Foreigners of this class are quite unable to establish any distinction between the Houses of Parliament and Westminster Abbey, because both have towers; and they are not clear about the difference between the British Museum and the National Gallery, because there are columns in the fronts of both. [25] English tourists will stay some time in Paris, and afterwards not be able to distinguish between photographs of the Louvre and the Hôtel de Ville. We need not be surprised that people who have never studied architecture at all should not be sure whether St. Paul's is a Gothic building or not, but the wonder is that they seem to retain no impressions received merely by the eye. One would think that the eye alone, without knowledge, would be enough to establish a distinction between one building and another altogether different from it; yet it is not so.

I cannot close this chapter without some allusion to a crafty employment of words only too well understood already by those who influence the popular mind. There is such a natural tendency to confusion in all ordinary human beings that if you repeatedly present to them two totally distinct things at the same time, they will, before long, associate them so closely as to consider them inseparable by their very nature. This is the reason why all those branches of education that train the mind in analysis are so valuable. To be able to distinguish between accidental connections of things or characteristics and necessary connections, is one of the best powers that education bestows upon us. By far the greater number of erroneous popular notions are due simply to the inability to make this distinction which belongs to all undisciplined minds. Calumnies, that have great influence over such minds, must lose their power as the habit of analysis enables people to separate ideas which the uncultivated mingle together.

Insufficient analysis leads to a very common sort of confusion between the defectiveness of a part only and a defect pervading the whole. An invention (as often happens) does not visibly succeed on the first trial, and then the whole of the common public will at once declare the invention to be bad, when, in reality, it may be a good invention with a local defect, easily remediable. Suppose that a yacht misses stays, the common sort of criticism would be to say that she was a bad boat, when, in fact, her hull and everything else might be thoroughly well made, and the defect be due only to a miscalculation in the placing of her canvas. I have myself seen a small steel boat sink at her anchorage, and a crowd laugh at her as badly contrived, when her only defect was the unobserved starting of a rivet. The boat was fished up, the rivet replaced, and she leaked and sank no more. When Stephenson's locomotive did not go because its wheels slid on the rails, the vulgar spectators were delighted with the supposed failure of a benefactor of the human species, and set up a noise of jubilant derision. The invention, they had decided, was of no good, and they sang their own foolish *gaudeamus igitur*. Stephenson at once perceived that the only defect was want of weight, and he immediately proceeded to remedy it by loading the machine with ballast. So it is in thousands of cases. The common mind, untrained in analysis, condemns the whole as a failure, when the defect lies in some small part which the specialist, trained in analysis, seeks for and discovers.

I have not touched upon the confusions due to the decline of the intellectual powers. In that case the reason is to be sought for in the condition of the brain, and there is, I believe, no remedy. In healthy people, enjoying the complete vigor of their faculties, confusions are simply the result of carelessness and indolence, and are proper subjects for sarcasm. With senile confusions the case is very different. To treat them with hard, sharp, decided correction, as is so often done by people of vigorous intellect, is a most cruel abuse of power. Yet it is difficult to say what ought to be done when an old person falls into manifest errors of this kind. Simple acquiescence is in this case a pardonable abandonment of truth, but there are situations in which it is not possible. Then you find yourself compelled to show where the confusion lies. You do it as gently as may be, but you fail to convince, and awaken that tenacious, unyielding opposition which is a characteristic of decline in its earlier stages. All that can be said is, that when once it has become evident that confusions are not careless but senile, they ought to be passed over if possible, and if not, then treated with the very utmost delicacy and gentleness.

ESSAY XXI
THE NOBLE BOHEMIANISM

AMONGST the common injustices of the world there have been few more complete than its reprobation of the state of mind and manner of life that have been called Bohemianism; and so closely is that reprobation attached to the word that I would gladly have substituted some other term for the better Bohemianism had the English language provided me with one. It may, however, be a gain to justice itself that we should be compelled to use the same expression, qualified only by an adjective, for two states of existence that are the good and the bad conditions of the same, as it will tend to make us more charitable to those whom we must always blame, and yet may blame with a more or less perfect understanding of the causes that led them into error.

The lower forms of Bohemianism are associated with several kinds of vice, and are therefore justly disliked by people who know the value of a well-regulated life, and, when at the worst, regarded by them with feelings of positive abhorrence. The vices connected with these forms of Bohemianism are idleness, irregularity, extravagance, drunkenness, and immorality; and besides these vices the worst Bohemianism is associated with many repulsive faults that may not be exactly vices, and yet are almost as much disliked by decent people. These faults are slovenliness, dirt, a degree of carelessness in matters of business, often scarcely to be distinguished from dishonesty, and habitual neglect of the decorous observances that are inseparable from a high state of civilization.

After such an account of the worst Bohemianism, in which, as the reader perceives, I have extenuated nothing, it may seem almost an act of temerity to advance the theory that this is only the bad side of a state of mind and feeling that has its good and perfectly respectable side also. If this seems difficult to believe, the reader has only to consider how certain other instincts of humanity have also their good and bad developments. The religious and the sexual instincts, in their best action, are on the side of national and domestic order, but in their worst action they produce sanguinary quarrels, ferocious persecutions, and the excesses of the most degrading sensuality. It is therefore by no means a new theory that a human instinct may have a happy or an unfortunate development, and it is not a reason for rejecting Bohemianism, without unprejudiced examination, that the worst forms of it are associated with evil.

Again, before going to the *raison d'être* of Bohemianism, let me point to one consideration of great importance to us if we desire to think quite justly. It is, and has always been, a characteristic of Bohemianism to be extremely careless of appearances, and to live outside the shelter of hypocrisy; so its vices are far more visible than the same vices when practised by men of the world, and incomparably more offensive to persons with a strong sense of what is called "propriety." At the time when the worst form of Bohemianism was more common than it is now, its most serious vices were also the vices of the best society. If the Bohemian drank to excess, so did the nobility and gentry; if the Bohemian had a mistress, so had the most exalted personages. The Bohemian was not so much blamed for being a sepulchre as for being an ill-kept sepulchre, and not a whited sepulchre like the rest. It was far more his slovenliness and poverty than his graver vices that made him offensive to a corrupt society with fine clothes and ceremonious manners.

Bohemianism and Philistinism are the terms by which, for want of better, we designate two opposite ways of estimating wealth and culture. There are two categories of advantages in wealth,—the intellectual and the material. The intellectual advantages are leisure to think and read, travel, and intelligent conversation. The material advantages are large and comfortable houses, tables well served and abundant, good coats, clean linen, fine dresses and diamonds, horses, carriages, servants, hot-houses, wine-cellars, shootings. Evidently the most perfect condition of wealth would unite both classes of advantages; but this is not always, or often, possible, and it so happens that in most situations a choice has to be made between them. The Bohemian is the man who with small means desires and contrives to obtain the intellectual advantages of wealth, which he considers to be leisure to think and read, travel, and intelligent conversation. The Philistine is the man who, whether his means are small or large, devotes himself wholly to the attainment of the other set of advantages,—a large house, good food and wine, clothes, horses, and servants.

The Philistine gratifies his passion for comfort to a wonderful extent, and thousands of ingenious people are incessantly laboring to make his existence more comfortable still, so that the one great inconvenience he is threatened with is the super-multiplication of conveniences. Now there is a certain noble Bohemianism which perceives that the Philistine life is not really so rich as it appears, that it has only some of the advantages which ought to belong to riches, and these not quite the best advantages; and this noble Bohemianism makes the best advantages its first aim, being contented with such a small measure of riches as, when ingeniously and skilfully employed, may secure them.

A highly developed material luxury, such as that which fills our modern universal exhibitions and is the great pride of our age, has in itself so much the appearance of absolute civilization that any proposal to do without it may seem like a return to savagery; and Bohemianism is exposed to the accusation of discouraging arts and manufactures. There is a physical side to Bohemianism to be considered later; and there may, indeed, be some connection between Bohemianism and the life of a red Indian who roams in his woods and contents himself with a low standard of physical well-being. The fair statement of the case between Bohemianism and the civilization of arts and manufactures is as follows: the intelligent Bohemian does not despise them; on the contrary, when he can afford it, he encourages them and often surrounds himself with beautiful things; but he will not barter his mental liberty in exchange for them, as the Philistine does so readily. If the Bohemian simply prefers sordid idleness to the comfort which is the reward of industry, he has no part in the higher Bohemianism, but combines the Philistine fault of intellectual apathy with the Bohemian fault of standing aloof from industrial civilization. If a man abstains from furthering the industrial civilization of his country he is only excusable if he pursues some object of at least equal importance. Intellectual civilization really is such an object, and the noble Bohemianism is excusable for serving it rather than that other civilization of arts and manufactures which has such numerous servants of its own. If the Bohemian does not redeem his negligence of material things by superior intellectual brightness, he is half a Philistine, he is destitute of what is best in Bohemianism (I had nearly written of all that is worth having in it), and his contempt for material perfection has no longer any charm, because it is not the sacrifice of a lower merit to a higher, but the blank absence of the lower merit not compensated or condoned by the presence of anything nobler or better.

Bohemianism and Philistinism are alike in combining self-indulgence with asceticism, but they are ascetic or self-indulgent in opposite directions. Bohemianism includes a certain self-indulgence, on the intellectual side, in the pleasures of thought and observation and in the exercise of the imaginative faculties, combining this with a certain degree of asceticism on the physical side, not a severe religious asceticism, but a disposition, like that of a thorough soldier or traveller, to do without luxury and comfort, and take the absence of them gayly when they are not to be had. The self-indulgence of Philistinism is in bodily comfort, of which it has never enough; its asceticism consists in denying itself leisure to read and think, and opportunities for observation.

The best way of describing the two principles will be to give an account of two human lives that exemplified them. These shall not be described from imagination, but from accurate memory; and I will not have recourse to the easy artifice of selecting an unfavorable example of the class with which I happen to have a minor degree of personal sympathy. My Philistine shall be one whom I sincerely loved and heartily respected. He was an admirable example of everything that is best and most worthy in the Philistine civilization; and I believe that nobody who ever came into contact with him, or had dealings with him, received any other impression than this, that he had a natural right to the perfect respect which surrounded him. The younger son of a poor gentleman, he began life with narrow means, and followed a profession in a small provincial town. By close attention and industry he saved a considerable sum of money, which he lost entirely through the dishonesty of a trusted but untrustworthy acquaintance. He had other mishaps, which but little disturbed his serenity, and he patiently amassed enough to make himself independent. In every relation of life he was not only above reproach, he was much more than that: he was a model of what men ought to be, yet seldom are, in their conduct towards others. He was kind to every one, generous to those who needed his generosity, and, though strict with himself, tolerant towards aberrations that must have seemed to him strangely unreasonable. He had great natural dignity, and was a gentleman in all his ways, with an old-fashioned grace and courtesy. He had no vanity; there may have been some pride as an ingredient in his character, but if so it was of a kind that could hurt nobody, for he was as simple and straightforward in his intercourse with the poor as he was at ease with the rich.

After this description (which is so far from being overcharged that I have omitted, for the sake of brevity, many admirable characteristics), the reader may ask in what could possibly consist the Philistinism of a nature that had attained such excellence. The answer is that it consisted in the perfect willingness with which he remained outside of every intellectual movement, and in the restriction of his mental activity to riches and religion. He used to say that "a man must be contentedly ignorant of many things," and he lived in this contented ignorance. He knew nothing of the subjects that awaken the passionate interest of intellectual men. He knew no language but his own, bought no books, knew nothing about the fine arts, never travelled, and remained satisfied with the life of his little provincial town. Totally ignorant of all foreign literatures, ancient or modern, he was at the same time so slightly acquainted with that of his own country that he had not read, and scarcely even knew by name, the most famous authors of his own generation. His little bookcase was filled almost exclusively with evangelical sermons and commentaries. This is Philistinism on the intellectual side, the mental inertness that remains "contentedly ignorant" of almost everything that a superior intellect cares for. But, besides this, there is also a Philistinism on the physical side, a physical inertness; and in this, too, my friend was a real Philistine. In spite of great natural strength, he remained inexpert in all manly exercises, and so had not enjoyed life on that side as he might have done, and as the Bohemian generally contrives to do. He belonged to that class of men who, as soon as they reach middle age, are scarcely more active than the chairs they sit upon, the men who would fall from a horse if it were lively, upset a boat if it were light, and be drowned if they fell into the water. Such men can walk a little on a road, or they can sit in a carriage and be dragged about by horses. By this physical inertia my friend was deprived of one set of impressions, as he was deprived by his intellectual inertia of another. He could not enjoy that close intimacy with nature which a Bohemian generally finds to be an important part of existence.

I wonder if it ever occurred to him to reflect, in the tedious hours of too tranquil age, how much of what is best in the world had been simply *missed* by him; how he had missed all the variety and interest of travel, the charm of intellectual society, the influences of genius, and even the physical excitements of healthy out-door amusements. When I think what a magnificent world it is that we inhabit, how much natural beauty there is in it, how much admirable human work in literature and the fine arts, how many living men and women there are in each generation whose acquaintance a wise man would travel far to seek, and value infinitely when he had found it, I cannot avoid the conclusion that my friend might have lived as he did in a planet far less richly endowed than ours, and that after a long life he went out of the world without having really known it.

I have said that the intelligent Bohemian is generally a man of small or moderate means, whose object is to enjoy the *best* advantages (not the most visible) of riches. In his view these advantages are leisure, travel, reading, and conversation. His estimate is different from that of the Philistine, who sets his heart on the lower advantages of riches, sacrificing leisure, travel, reading, and conversation, in order to have a larger house and more servants. But how, without riches, is the Bohemian to secure the advantages that he desires, for they also belong to riches? There lies the difficulty, and the Bohemian's way of overcoming it constitutes the romance of his existence. In absolute destitution the intelligent Bohemian life is not possible. A little money is necessary for it, and the art and craft of Bohemianism is to get for that small amount of money such an amount of leisure, reading, travel, and good conversation as may suffice to make life interesting. The way in which an old-fashioned Bohemian usually set about it was this: he treated material comfort and outward appearances as matters of no consequence, accepting them when they came in his way, but enduring the privation of them gayly. He learned the art of living on a little.

"Je suis pauvre, très pauvre, et vis pourtant fort bien
C'est parce que je vis comme les gens de rien."[26]

He spent the little that he had, first for what was really necessary, and next for what really gave him pleasure, but he spent hardly anything in deference to the usages of society. In this way he got what he wanted. His books were second-hand and ill bound, but he *had* books and read them; his clothes were shabby, yet still they kept him warm; he travelled in all sorts of cheap ways and frequently on foot; he lived a good deal in some unfashionable quarters in a capital city, and saw much of art, nature, and humanity.

To exemplify the true theory of Bohemianism let me describe from memory two rooms, one of them inhabited by an English lady, not at all Bohemian, the other by a German of the coarser sex who was essentially and thoroughly Bohemian. The lady's room was not a drawing-room, being a reasonable sort of sitting-room without any exasperating inutilities, but it was extremely, excessively comfortable. Half hidden amongst its material comforts might be found a little rosewood bookcase containing a number of pretty volumes in purple morocco that were seldom, if ever, opened. My German Bohemian was a steady reader in six languages; and if he had seen such a room as that he would probably have criticised it as follows. He would have said, "It is rich in superfluities, but has not what is necessary. The carpet is superfluous; plain boards are quite comfortable enough. One or two cheap chairs and tables might replace this costly furniture. That pretty rosewood bookcase holds the smallest number of books at the greatest cost, and is therefore contrary to true economy; give me, rather, a sufficiency of long deal shelves all innocent of paint. What is the use of fine bindings and gilt edges? This little library is miserably poor. It is all in one language, and does not represent even English literature adequately; there are a few novels, books of poems, and travels, but I find neither science nor philosophy. Such a room as that, with all its comfort, would seem to me like a prison. My mind needs wider pastures." I remember his own room, a place to make a rich Englishman shudder. One climbed up to it by a stone corkscrew-stair, half-ruinous, in an old mediæval house. It was a large room, with a bed in one corner, and it was wholly destitute of anything resembling a carpet or a curtain. The remaining furniture consisted of two or three rush-bottomed chairs, one large cheap lounging-chair, and two large plain tables. There were plenty of shelves (common deal, unpainted), and on them an immense litter of books in different languages, most of them in paper covers, and bought second-hand, but in readable editions. In the way of material luxury there was a pot of tobacco; and if a friend dropped in for an evening a jug of ale would make its appearance. My Bohemian was shabby in his dress, and unfashionable; but he had seen more, read more, and passed more hours in intelligent conversation than many who considered themselves his superiors. The entire material side of life had been systematically neglected, in his case, in order that the intellectual side might flourish. It is hardly necessary to observe that any attempt at luxury or visible comfort, any conformity to fashion, would have been incompatible, on small means, with the intellectual existence that this German scholar enjoyed.

Long ago I knew an English Bohemian who had a small income that came to him very irregularly. He had begun life in a profession, but had quitted it that he might travel and see the world, which he did in the oddest, most original fashion, often enduring privation, but never ceasing to enjoy life deeply in his own way, and to accumulate a mass of observations which would have been quite invaluable to an author. In him the two activities, physical and mental, were alike so energetic that they might have led to great results had they been consistently directed to some private or public end; but unfortunately he remained satisfied with the existence of an observant wanderer who has no purpose beyond the healthy exercise of his faculties. In usefulness to others he was not to be compared with my good and admirable Philistine, but in the art of getting for himself what is best in the world he was by far the more accomplished of the two. He fully enjoyed both the physical and the intellectual life; he could live almost like a red Indian, and yet at the same time carry in his mind the most recent results of European thought and science. His distinguishing characteristic was a heroic contempt for comfort, in which he rather resembled a soldier in war-time than any self-indulgent civilian. He would sleep anywhere,—in his boat under a sail, in a hayloft, under a hedge if belated, and he would go for days together without any regular meal. He dressed roughly, and his clothes became old before he renewed them. He kept no servant, and lived in cheap lodgings in towns, or hired one or two empty rooms and adorned them with a little portable furniture. In the country he contrived to make very economical arrangements in farmhouses, by which he was fed and lodged quite as well as he ever cared to be. It would be difficult to excel him in simple manliness, in the quiet courage that accepts a disagreeable situation or faces a dangerous one; and he had the manliness of the mind as well as that of the body; he estimated the world for what it is worth, and cared nothing for its transient fashions either in appearances or opinion. I am sorry that he was a useless member of society,—if, indeed, such an eccentric is to be called a member of society at all, —but if uselessness is blamable he shares the blame, or ought in justice to share it, with a multitude of most respectable gentlemen and ladies who receive nothing but approbation from the world.

Except this fault of uselessness there was nothing to blame in this man's manner of life, but his want of purpose and discipline made his fine qualities seem almost without value. And now comes the question whether the fine qualities of the useless Bohemian may not be of some value in a life of a higher kind. I think it is evident that they may, for if the Bohemian can cheerfully sacrifice luxury for some mental gain he has made a great step in the direction of the higher life, and only requires a purpose and a discipline to attain it. Common men are completely enslaved by their love of comfort, and whoever has emancipated himself from this thraldom has gained the first and most necessary victory. The use that he will make of it depends upon himself. If he has high purposes, his Bohemianism will be ennobled by them, and will become a most precious element in his character; and if his purposes are not of the highest, the Bohemian element may still be very valuable if accompanied by self-discipline. Napoleon cannot be said to have had high purposes, but his Bohemianism was admirable. A man who, having attained success, with boundless riches at his disposal, could quit the luxury of his palaces and sleep anywhere, in any poor farmhouse, or under the stars by the fire of a bivouac, and be satisfied with poor meals at the most irregular hours, showed that, however he may have estimated luxury, he was at least entirely independent of it. The model monarch in this respect was Charles XII. of Sweden, who studied his own personal comfort as little as if he had been a private soldier. Some royal commanders have carried luxury into war itself, but not to their advantage. When Napoleon III. went in his carriage to meet his fate at Sedan the roads were so encumbered by wagons belonging to the Imperial household as to impede the movements of the troops.

There is often an element of Bohemianism where we should least expect to find it. There is something of it in our English aristocracy, though it is not *called* Bohemianism here because it is not accompanied by poverty; but the spirit that sacrifices luxury to rough travelling is, so far, the true Bohemian spirit. In the aristocracy, however, such sacrifices are only temporary; and a rough life accepted for a few weeks or months gives the charm of a restored freshness to luxury on returning to it. The class in which the higher Bohemianism has most steadily flourished is the artistic and literary class, and here it is visible and recognizable because there is often poverty enough to compel the choice between the objects of the intelligent Bohemian and those of ordinary men. The early life of Goldsmith, for example, was that of a genuine Bohemian. He had scarcely any money, and yet he contrived to get for himself what the intelligent Bohemian always desires, namely, leisure to read and think, travel, and interesting conversation. When penniless and unknown he lounged about the world thinking and observing; he travelled in Holland, France, Switzerland, and Italy, not as people do in railway carriages, but in leisurely intercourse with the inhabitants. Notwithstanding his poverty he was received by the learned in different European cities, and, notably, heard Voltaire and Diderot talk till three o'clock in the morning. So long as he remained faithful to the true principles of Bohemianism he was happy in his own strange and eccentric way, and all the anxieties, all the slavery of his later years were due to his apostasy from those principles. He no longer estimated leisure at its true value when he allowed himself to be placed in such a situation that he was compelled to toil like a slave in order to clear off work that had been already paid for, such advances having been rendered necessary by expenditure on Philistine luxuries. He no longer enjoyed humble travel but on his later tour in France with Mrs. Horneck and her two beautiful daughters, instead of enjoying the country in his own old simple innocent way, he allowed his mind to be poisoned with Philistine ideas, and constantly complained of the want of physical comfort, though he lived far more expensively than in his youth. The new apartments, taken on the success of the "Good-natured Man," consisted, says Irving, "of three rooms, which he furnished with mahogany sofas, card-tables, and bookcases; with curtains, mirrors, and Wilton carpets." At the same time he went even beyond the precept of Polonius, for his garments were costlier than his purse could buy, and his entertainments were so extravagant as to give pain to his acquaintances. All this is a desertion of real Bohemian principles. Goldsmith ought to have protected his own leisure, which, from the Bohemian point of view, was incomparably more precious to himself than Wilton carpets and coats "of Tyrian bloom."

Corot, the French landscape-painter, was a model of consistent Bohemianism of the best kind. When his father said, "You shall have £80 a year, your plate at my table, and be a painter; or you shall have £4,000 to start with if you will be a shop-keeper," his choice was made at once. He remained always faithful to true Bohemian principles, fully understanding the value of leisure, and protecting his artistic independence by the extreme simplicity of his living. He never gave way to the modern rage for luxuries, but in his latter years, when enriched by tardy professional success and hereditary fortune, he employed his money in acts of fraternal generosity to enable others to lead the intelligent Bohemian life.

Wordsworth had in him a very strong element of Bohemianism. His long pedestrian rambles, his interest in humble life and familiar intercourse with the poor, his passion for wild nature, and preference of natural beauty to fine society, his simple and economical habits, are enough to reveal the tendency. His "plain living and high thinking" is a thoroughly Bohemian idea, in striking opposition to the Philistine passion for rich living and low thinking. There is a story that he was seen at a breakfast-table to cut open a new volume with a greasy butter-knife. To every lover of books this must seem horribly barbarous, yet at the same time it was Bohemian, in that Wordsworth valued the thought only and cared nothing for the material condition of the volume. I have observed a like indifference to the material condition of books in other Bohemians, who took the most lively interest in their contents. I have also seen "bibliophiles" who had beautiful libraries in excellent preservation, and who loved to fondle fine copies of books that they never read. That is Philistine, it is the preference of material perfection to intellectual values.

The reader is, I hope, fully persuaded by this time that the higher Bohemianism is compatible with every quality that deserves respect, and that it is not of necessity connected with any fault or failing. I may therefore mention as an example of it one of the purest and best characters whom it was ever my happiness to know. There was a strong element of noble Bohemianism in Samuel Palmer, the landscape-painter. "From time to time," according to his son, "he forsook his easel, and travelled far away from London smoke to cull the beauties of some favorite country side. His painting apparatus was complete, but singularly simple, his dress and other bodily requirements simpler still; so he could walk from village to hamlet easily carrying all he wanted, and utterly indifferent to luxury. With a good constitution it mattered little to him how humble were his quarters or how remote from so-called civilization. 'In exploring wild country,' he writes, 'I have been for a fortnight together, uncertain each day whether I should get a bed under cover at night; and about midsummer I have repeatedly been walking all night to watch the mystic phenomena of the silent hours.' He enjoyed to the full this rough but not uncomfortable mode of travelling, and was better pleased to take his place, after a hard day's work, in some old chimney corner—joining on equal terms the village gossip—than to mope in the dull grandeur of a private room."

Here are two of my Bohemian elements,—the love of travel and the love of conversation. As for the other element,—the love of leisure to think and read,—it is not visible in this extract (though the kind of travel described is leisurely), but it was always present in the man. During the quiet, solitary progress by day and night there were ample opportunities for thinking, and as for reading we know that Palmer never stirred without a favorite author in his pocket, most frequently Milton or Virgil. To complete the

Bohemian we only require one other characteristic,—contentment with a simple material existence; and we are told that "the painting apparatus was singularly simple, the dress and other bodily requirements simpler still." So here we have the intelligent Bohemian in his perfection.

All this is the exact opposite of Philistine "common sense." A Philistine would not have exposed himself, voluntarily, to the certainty of poor accommodation. A Philistine would not have remained out all night "to watch the mystic phenomena of the silent hours." In the absence of a railway he would have hired a carriage, and got through the wild country rapidly to arrive at a good dinner. Lastly, a Philistine would not have carried either Milton or Virgil in his pocket; he would have had a newspaper.

Some practical experience of the higher Bohemianism is a valuable part of education. It enables us to estimate things at their true worth, and to extract happiness from situations in which the Philistine is both dull and miserable. A true Bohemian, of the best kind, knows the value of mere shelter, of food enough to satisfy hunger, of plain clothes that will keep him sufficiently warm; and in the things of the mind he values the liberty to use his own faculties as a kind of happiness in itself. His philosophy leads him to take an interest in talking with human beings of all sorts and conditions, and in different countries. He does not despise the poor, for, whether poor or rich in his own person, he understands simplicity of life, and if the poor man lives in a small cottage, he, too, has probably been lodged less spaciously still in some small hut or tent. He has lived often, in rough travel, as the poor live every day. I maintain that such tastes and experiences are valuable both in prosperity and in adversity. If we are prosperous they enhance our appreciation of the things around us, and yet at the same time make us really know that they are not indispensable, as so many believe them to be; if we fall into adversity they prepare us to accept lightly and cheerfully what would be depressing privations to others. I know a painter who in consequence of some change in the public taste fell into adversity at a time when he had every reason to hope for increased success. Very fortunately for him, he had been a Bohemian in early life,—a respectable Bohemian, be it understood,—and a great traveller, so that he could easily dispense with luxuries. "To be still permitted to follow art is enough," he said; so he reduced his expenses to the very lowest scale consistent with that pursuit, and lived as he had done before in the old Bohemian times. He made his old clothes last on, he slung a hammock in a very simple painting-room, and cooked his own dinner on the stove. With the canvas on his easel and a few books on a shelf he found that if existence was no longer luxurious it had not yet ceased to be interesting.

ESSAY XXII
OF COURTESY IN EPISTOLARY
COMMUNICATION

THE universal principle of courtesy is that the courteous person manifests a disposition to sacrifice something in favor of the person whom he desires to honor; the opposite principle shows itself in a disposition to regard our own convenience as paramount over every other consideration.

Courtesy lives by a multitude of little sacrifices, not by sacrifices of sufficient importance to impose any burdensome sense of obligation. These little sacrifices may be both of time and money, but more of time, and the money sacrifice should be just perceptible, never ostentatious.

The tendency of a hurried age, in which men undertake more work or more pleasure (hardest work of all!) than they are able properly to accomplish, is to abridge all forms of courtesy because they take time, and to replace them by forms, if any forms survive, which cost as little time as possible. This wounds and injures courtesy itself in its most vital part, for the essence of it is the willingness to incur that very sacrifice which modern hurry avoids.

The first courtesy in epistolary communication is the mere writing of the letter. Except in cases where the letter itself is an offence or an intrusion, the mere making of it is an act of courtesy towards the receiver. The writer sacrifices his time and a trifle of money in order that the receiver may have some kind of news.

It has ever been the custom to commence a letter with some expression of respect, affection, or good will. This is graceful in itself, and reasonable, being nothing more than the salutation with which a man enters the house of his friend, or his more ceremonious act of deference in entering that of a stranger or a superior. In times and seasons where courtesy has not given way to hurry, or a selfish dread of unnecessary exertion, the opening form is maintained with a certain amplitude, and the substance of the letter is not reached in the first lines, which gently induce the reader to proceed.

Afterwards these forms are felt to involve an inconvenient sacrifice of time, and are ruthlessly docked.

In justice to modern poverty in forms it is fair to take into consideration the simple truth, so easily overlooked, that we have to write thirty letters where our ancestors wrote one; but the principle of sacrifice in courtesy always remains essentially the same; and if of our more precious and more occupied time we consecrate a smaller portion to forms, it is still essential that there should be no appearance of a desire to escape from the kind of obligation which we acknowledge.

The most essentially modern element of courtesy in letter-writing is the promptitude of our replies. This promptitude was not only unknown to our remote ancestors, but even to our immediate predecessors. They would postpone answering a letter for days or weeks, in the pure spirit of procrastination, when they already possessed all the materials necessary for the answer. Such a habit would try our patience very severely, but our fathers seem to have considered it a part of their dignity to move slowly in correspondence. This temper even yet survives in official correspondence between sovereigns, who still notify to each other their domestic events long after the publication of them in the newspapers.

A prompt answer equally serves the purpose of the sender and the receiver. It is a great economy of time to answer promptly, because the receiver of the letter is so much gratified by the promptitude itself that he readily pardons brevity in consideration of it. An extremely short but prompt letter, that would look curt without its promptitude, is more polite than a much longer one written a few days later.

Prompt correspondents save all the time that others waste in excuses. I remember an author and editor whose system imposed upon him the tax of perpetual apologizing. He always postponed writing until the delay had put his correspondent out of temper, so that when at last he *did* write, which somehow happened ultimately, the first page was entirely occupied with apologies for his delay, as he felt that the necessity had arisen for soothing the ruffled feelings of his friend. It never occurred to him that the same amount of pen work which these apologies cost him would, if given earlier, have sufficed for a complete answer. A letter-writer of this sort must naturally be a bad man of business, and this gentleman was so, though he had excellent qualities of another order.

I remember receiving a most extraordinary answer from a correspondent of this stamp. I wrote to him about a matter which was causing me some anxiety, and did not receive an answer for several weeks. At last the reply came, with the strange excuse that as he knew I had guests in my house he had delayed writing from a belief that I should not be able to attend to anything until after their departure. If such were always the effect of entertaining friends, what incalculable perturbation would be caused by hospitality in all private and public affairs!

The reader may, perhaps, have met with a collection of letters called the "Plumpton Correspondence," which was published by the Camden Society in 1839. I have always been interested in this for family reasons, and also because the manuscript volume was found in the neighborhood where I lived in youth;[27] but it does not require any blood connection with the now extinct house of Plumpton of Plumpton to take an interest in a collection of letters which gives so clear an insight into the epistolary customs of England in the fifteenth and sixteenth centuries. The first peculiarity that strikes the modern reader is the extreme care of almost all the writers, even when near relations, to avoid a curt and dry style, destitute of the ambages which were in those days esteemed an essential part of politeness. The only exception is a plain, straightforward gentleman, William Gascoyne, who heads his letters, "To my Uncle Plumpton be these delivered," or "To my Uncle Plumpton this letter be delivered in hast." He begins, "Uncle Plumpton, I recommend me unto you," and finishes, "Your nephew," simply, or still more laconically, "Your." Such plainness is strikingly rare. The rule was, to be deliberately perfect in all epistolary observances, however near the relationship. Not that the forms used were hard forms, entirely fixed by usage and devoid of personal feeling and individuality. They appear to have been more flexible and living than our own, as they were more frequently varied according to the taste and sentiment of the writers. Sometimes, of course, they were perfunctory, but often they have an original and very graceful turn. One letter, which I will quote at length, contains curious evidence of the courtesy and discourtesy of those days. The forms used in the letter itself are perfect, but the writer complains that other letters have not been answered.

In the reign of Henry VII. Sir Robert Plumpton had a daughter, Dorothy, who was in the household of Lady Darcy (probably as a sort of maid of honor to her ladyship), but was not quite pleased with her position, and wanted to go home to Plumpton. She had written to her father several times, but had received no answer, so she now writes again to him in these terms. The date of the letter is not fully given, as the year is wanting; but her parents were married in 1477, and her father died in 1523, at the age of seventy, after a life of strange vicissitudes. The reader will observe two leading characteristics in this letter, — that it is as courteous as if the writer were not related to the receiver, and as affectionate as if no forms had been observed. As was the custom in those days, the young lady gives her parents their titles of worldly honor, but she always adds to them the most affectionate filial expressions:

*To the right worshipfull and my most entyerly beloved, good,
kind father, Sir Robart Plompton, knyght, lying at Plompton in
Yorkshire, be thes delivered in hast.*

Ryght worshipfull father, in the most humble manner
that I can I recommend me to you, and to my lady my
mother, and to all my brethren and sistren, whom I besech
almyghtie God to mayntayne and preserve in prosperus
health and encrese of worship, entyerly requiering you
of your daly blessing; letting you wyt that I send to you
mesuage, be Wryghame of Knarsbrugh, of my mynd,
and how that he should desire you in my name to send
for me to come home to you, and as yet I had no answere
agane, the which desire my lady hath gotten knowledg.
Wherefore, she is to me more better lady than ever she
was before, insomuch that she hath promysed me hir good
ladyship as long as ever she shall lyve; and if she or ye
can fynd athing meyter for me in this parties or any other,
she will helpe to promoote me to the uttermost of her
puyssaunce. Wherefore, I humbly besech you to be so good
and kind father unto me as to let me know your pleasure,
how that ye will have me ordred, as shortly as it shall like
you. And wryt to my lady, thanking hir good ladyship
of hir so loving and tender kyndnesse shewed unto me,
beseching hir ladyship of good contynewance thereof. And
therefore I besech you to send a servant of yours to my lady
and to me, and show now by your fatherly kyndnesse that
I am your child; for I have sent you dyverse messuages and
wryttings, and I had never answere againe. Wherefore yt
is thought in this parties, by those persones that list better
to say ill than good, that ye have litle favor unto me; the
which error ye may now quench yf yt will like you to be
so good and kynd father unto me. Also I besech you to
send me a fine hatt and some good cloth to make me some
kevercheffes. And thus I besech *Jesu* to have you in his
blessed keeping to his pleasure, and your harts desire and
comforth. Wryten at the Hirste, the xviii day of Maye.

      By your loving daughter,
       Dorythe Plompton.

It may be worth while, for the sake of contrast, and that we may the better perceive the lost fragrance of the antique courtesy, to put the substance of this letter into the style of the present day. A modern young lady would probably write as follows:—

Hirst, *May 18.*

Dear Papa,—Lady Darcy has found out that I want to leave her, but she has kindly promised to do what she can to find something else for me. I wish you would say what you think, and it would be as well, perhaps, if you would be so good as to drop a line to her ladyship to thank her. I have written to you several times, but got no answer, so people here say that you don't care very much for me. Would you please send me a handsome bonnet and some handkerchiefs? Best love to mamma and all at home.

Your affectionate daughter,
Dorothy Plumpton.

This, I think, is not an unfair specimen of a modern letter.[28] The expressions of worship, of humble respect, have disappeared, and so far it may be thought that there is improvement, yet that respect was not incompatible with tender feeling; on the contrary, it was closely associated with it, and expressions of sentiment have lost strength and vitality along with expressions of respect. Tenderness may be sometimes shown in modern letters, but it is rare; and when it occurs it is generally accompanied by a degree of familiarity which our ancestors would have considered in bad taste. Dorothy Plumpton's own letter is far richer in the expression of tender feeling than any modern letter of the courteous and ceremonious kind, or than any of those pale and commonplace communications from which deep respect and strong affection are almost equally excluded. Please observe, moreover, that the young lady had reason to be dissatisfied with her father for his neglect, which does not in the least diminish the filial courtesy of her style, but she chides him in the sweetest fashion,—"*Show now by your futherly kindness that I am your child.*" Could anything be prettier than that, though the reproach contained in it is really one of some severity?

Dorothy's father, Sir Robert, puts the following superscription on a letter to his wife, "To my entyrely and right hartily beloved wife, Dame Agnes Plumpton, be this Letter delivered." He begins his letter thus, "My deare hart, in my most hartily wyse, I recommend mee unto you;" and he ends tenderly, "By your owne lover, Robert Plumpton, Kt." She, on the contrary, though a faithful and brave wife, doing her best for her husband in a time of great trial, and enjoying his full confidence, begins her letters, "Right

worshipful Sir," and ends simply, "By your wife, Dame Agnes Plumpton."
She is so much absorbed by business that her expressions of feeling are rare
and brief. "Sir, I am in good health, and all your children prays for your daly
blessing. And all your servants is in good health and prays diligently for
your good speed in your matters."

The generally courteous tone of the letters of those days may be judged
of by the following example. The reader will observe how small a space is
occupied with the substance of the letter in comparison with the expressions
of pure courtesy, and how simply and handsomely regret for the trespass
is expressed:—

To his worshipful Cosin, Sir Robart Plompton, Kt.

Right reverend and worshipful Cosin, I commend me unto
you as hertyly as I can, evermore desiring to heare of your
welfare, the which I besech *Jesu* to continew to his pleasure,
and your herts desire. Cosin, please you witt that I am
enformed, that a poor man somtyme belonging to mee,
called Umfrey Bell, hath trespased to a servant of youres,
which I am sory for. Wherefore, Cosin, I desire and hartily
pray you to take upp the matter into your own hands for
my sake, and rewle him as it please you; and therein you
wil do, as I may do that may be plesur to you, and my
contry, the which I shalbe redy too, by the grace of God,
who preserve you.

By your own kynsman,
Robart Warcopp, of Warcoppe.

The reader has no doubt by this time enough of these old letters, which
are not likely to possess much charm for him unless, like the present writer,
he is rather of an antiquarian turn.[29]

The quotations are enough to show some of the forms used in
correspondence by our forefathers, forms that were right in their own day,
when the state of society was more ceremonious and deferential, but no one
would propose to revive them. We may, however, still value and cultivate
the beautifully courteous spirit that our ancestors possessed and express it
in our own modern ways.

I have already observed that the essentially modern form of courtesy is
the rapidity of our replies. This, at least, is a virtue that we can resolutely
cultivate and maintain. In some countries it is pushed so far that telegrams
are very frequently sent when there is no need to employ the telegraph. The

Arabs of Algeria are extremely fond of telegraphing for its own sake: the notion of its rapidity pleases and amuses them; they like to wield a power so wonderful. It is said that the Americans constantly employ the telegraph on very trivial occasions, and the habit is increasing in England and France. The secret desire of the present age is to find a plausible excuse for excessive brevity in correspondence, and this is supplied by the comparative costliness of telegraphing. It is a comfort that it allows you to send a single word. I have heard of a letter from a son to a father consisting of the Latin word *Ibo*, and of a still briefer one from the father to the son confined entirely to the imperative *I*. These miracles of brevity are only possible in letters between the most intimate friends or relations, but in telegraphy they are common.

It is very difficult for courtesy to survive this modern passion for brevity, and we see it more and more openly cast aside. All the long phrases of politeness have been abandoned in English correspondence for a generation, except in formal letters to official or very dignified personages; and the little that remains is reduced to a mere shred of courteous or affectionate expression. We have not, it is true, the detestable habit of abridging words, as our ancestors often did, but we cut our phrases short, and sometimes even words of courtesy are abridged in an unbecoming manner. Men will write Dr. Sir for Dear Sir. If I am dear enough to these correspondents for their sentiments of affection to be worth uttering at all, why should they be so chary of expressing them that they omit two letters from the very word which is intended to affect my feelings?

"If I be dear, if I be dear,"

as the poet says, why should my correspondent begrudge me the four letters of so brief an adjective?

The long French and Italian forms of ceremony at the close of letters are felt to be burdensome in the present day, and are gradually giving place to briefer ones; but it is the very length of them, and the time and trouble they cost to write, that make them so courteous, and no brief form can ever be an effective substitute in that respect.

I was once placed in the rather embarrassing position of having suddenly to send telegrams in my own name, containing a request, to two high foreign authorities in a corps where punctilious ceremony is very strictly observed. My solution of the difficulty was to write two full ceremonious letters, with all the formal expressions unabridged, and then have these letters telegraphed *in extenso*. This was the only possible solution, as an ordinary telegram would have been entirely out of the question. It being rather expensive to telegraph a very formal letter, the cost added to the appearance of deference, so I had the curious but very real advantage on my side that I made a telegram seem even more deferential than a letter.

The convenience of the letter-writer is consulted in inverse ratio to the appearances of courtesy. In the matter of sealing, for example, that seems so slight and indifferent a concern, a question of ceremony and courtesy is involved. The old-fashioned custom of a large seal with the sender's arms or cipher added to the importance of the contents both by strictly guarding the privacy of the communication and by the dignified assertion of the writer's rank. Besides this, the time that it costs to take a proper impression of a seal shows the absence of hurry and the disposition to sacrifice which are a part of all noble courtesy; whilst the act of rapidly licking the gum on the inside of an envelope and then giving it a thump with your fist to make it stick is neither dignified nor elegant. There were certain beautiful associations with the act of sealing. There was the taper that had to be lighted, and that had its own little candlestick of chased or gilded silver, or delicately painted porcelain; there was the polished and graven stone of the seal, itself more or less precious, and enhanced in value by an art of high antiquity and noble associations, and this graven signet-stone was set in massive gold. The act of sealing was deliberate, to secure a fair impression, and as the wax caught flame and melted it disengaged a delicate perfume. These little things may be laughed at by a generation of practical men of business who know the value of every second, but they had their importance, and have it still, amongst those who possess any delicacy of perception.[30] The reader will remember the sealing of Nelson's letter to the Crown Prince of Denmark during the battle of Copenhagen. "A wafer was given him," says Southey, "but he ordered a candle to be brought from the cockpit, and sealed the letter with wax, *affixing a larger seal than he ordinarily used*. 'This,' said he, 'is no time to appear hurried and informal.'" The story is usually told as a striking example of Nelson's coolness in a time of intense excitement, but it might be told with equal effect as a proof of his knowledge of mankind and of the trifles which have a powerful effect on human intercourse. The preference of wax to a wafer, and especially the deliberate choice of a larger seal as more ceremonious and important, are clear evidence of diplomatic skill. No doubt, too, the impression of Nelson's arms was very careful and clear.

In writing to French Ministers of State it is a traditional custom to employ a certain paper called "papier ministre," which is very much larger than that sent to ordinary mortals. Paper is by no means a matter of indifference.

It is the material costume under which we present ourselves to persons removed from us by distance; and as a man pays a call in handsome clothes as a sign of respect to others, and also of self-respect, so he sends a piece of handsome paper to be the bearer of his salutation. Besides, a letter is in itself a gift, though a small one, and however trifling a gift may be it must never be shabby. The English understand this art of choosing good-looking letter-paper, and are remarkable for using it of a thickness rare in other nations. French love of elegance has led to charming inventions of tint and texture, particularly in delicate gray tints, and these papers are now often decorated with embossed initials of heraldic devices on a large scale, but that is carrying prettiness too far. The common American habit of writing letters on ruled paper is not to be recommended, as the ruling reminds us of copy-books and account-books, and has a mechanical appearance that greatly detracts from what ought to be the purely personal air of an autograph.

Modern love of despatch has led to the invention of the post-card, which, from our present point of view, that of courtesy, deserves unhesitating condemnation. To use a post-card is as much as to say to your correspondent, "In order to save for myself a very little money and a very little time, I will expose the subject of our correspondence to the eyes of any clerk, postman, or servant, who feels the slightest curiosity about it; and I take this small piece of card, of which I am allowed to use one side only, in order to relieve myself from the obligation, and spare myself the trouble, of writing a letter." To make the convenience absolutely perfect, it is customary in England to omit the opening and concluding salutations on post-cards, so that they are the *ne plus ultra*, I will not say of positive rudeness, but of that negative rudeness which is not exactly the opposite of courtesy, but its absence. Here again, however, comes the modern principle; and promptitude and frequency of communication may be accepted as a compensation for the sacrifice of formality. It may be argued, and with reason, that when a man of our own day sends a post-card his ancestors would have been still more laconic, for they would have sent nothing at all, and that there are a thousand circumstances in which a post-card may be written when it is not possible to write a letter. A husband on his travels has a supply of such cards in a pocket-book. With these, and his pencil, he writes a line once or twice a day in train or steamboat, or at table between two dishes, or on the windy platform of a railway station, or in the street when he sees a letter-box. He sends fifty such communications where his father would have written three letters, and his grandfather one slowly composed and slowly travelling epistle.

Many modern correspondents appreciate the convenience of the postcard, but their conscience, as that of well-bred people, cannot get over the fault of its publicity. For these the stationers have devised several different substitutes. There is the French plan of what is called "Un Mot à la Poste," a piece of paper with a single fold, gummed round the other three edges, and perforated like postage-stamps for the facility of the opener.[31] There is the miniature sheet of paper that you have not to fold, and there is the card that you enclose in an envelope, and that prepares the reader for a very brief communication. Here, again, is a very curious illustration of the sacrificial nature of courtesy. A card is sent; why a card? Why not a piece of paper of the same size which would hold as many words? The answer is that a card is handsomer and more costly, and from its stiffness a little easier to take out of the envelope, and pleasanter to hold whilst reading, so that a small sacrifice is made to the pleasure and convenience of the receiver, which is the essence of courtesy in letter-writing. All this brief correspondence is the offspring of the electric telegraph. Our forefathers were not used to it, and would have regarded it as an offence. Even at the present date (1884) it is not quite safe to write in our brief modern way to persons who came to maturity before the electric telegraph was in use.

There is a wide distinction between brevity and hurry; in fact, brevity, if of the intelligent kind, is the best preservative against hurry. Some men write short letters, but are very careful to observe all the forms; and they have the great advantage that the apparent importance of the formal expressions is enhanced by the shortness of the letter itself. This is the case in Robert Warcopp's letter to Sir Robert Plumpton.

When hurry really exists, and it is impossible to avoid the appearance of it, as when a letter *cannot* be brief, yet must be written at utmost speed, the proper course is to apologize for hurry at the beginning and not at the end of the letter. The reader is then propitiated at once, and excuses the slovenly penmanship and style.

It is remarkable that legibility of handwriting should never have been considered as among the essentials of courtesy in correspondence. It is obviously for the convenience of the reader that a letter should be easily read; but here another consideration intervenes. To write very legibly is the accomplishment of clerks and writing-masters, who are usually poor men, and, as such, do not hold a high social position. Aristocratic pride has always had it for a principle to disdain, for itself, the accomplishments of professional men; and therefore a careless scrawl is more aristocratic than a clean handwriting, if the scrawl is of a fashionable kind. Perhaps the historic origin of this feeling may be the scorn of the ignorant mediæval baron for writing of all kinds as beneath the attention of a warrior. In a cultured age there may be a reason of a higher order. It may be supposed that attention to mechanical excellence is incompatible with the action of the intellect; and people are curiously ready to imagine incompatibilities where they do not really exist. As a matter of fact, some men of eminent intellectual gifts write with as exquisite a clearness in the formation of their letters as in the elucidation of their ideas. It is easily forgotten, too, that the same person may use different kinds of handwriting, according to circumstances, like the gentleman whose best hand some people could read, whose middling hand the writer himself could read, and whose worst neither he nor any other human being could decipher. Legouvé, in his exquisite way, tells a charming story of how he astonished a little girl by excelling her in calligraphy. His scribble is all but illegible, and she was laughing at it one day, when he boldly challenged her to a trial. Both sat down and formed their letters with great patience, as in a writing class, and it turned out, to the girl's amazement, that the scribbling Academician had by far the more copperplate-like hand of the two. He then explained that his bad writing was simply the result of speed. Frenchmen provokingly reserve their very worst and most illegible writing for the signature. You are able to read the letter but not the signature, and if there is not some other means of ascertaining the writer's name you are utterly at fault.

The old habit of crossing letters, now happily abandoned, was a direct breach of real, though not of what in former days were conventional, good manners. To cross a letter is as much as to say, "In order to spare myself the cost of another sheet of paper or an extra stamp, I am quite willing to inflict upon you, my reader, the trouble of disengaging one set of lines from another." Very economical people in the past generation saved an occasional penny in another way at the cost of the reader's eyes. They diluted their ink with water, till the recipient of the letter cried, "Prithee, why so pale?"

The modern type-writing machine has the advantage of making all words equally legible; but the receiver of the printed letter is likely to feel on opening it a slight yet perceptible shock of the kind always caused by a want of consideration. The letter so printed is undoubtedly easier to read than all but the very clearest manuscript, and so far it may be considered a politeness to use the instrument; but unluckily it is impersonal, so that the performer on the instrument seems far removed from the receiver of the letter and not in that direct communication with him which would be apparent in an autograph. The effect on the mind is almost like that of a printed circular, or at least of a letter which has been dictated to a short-hand writer.

The dictation of letters is allowable in business, because men of business have to use the utmost attainable despatch, and (like the use of the lead pencil) it is permitted to invalids, but with these exceptions it is sure to produce a feeling of distance almost resembling discourtesy. In the first place, a dictated letter is not strictly private, its contents being already known to the amanuensis; and besides this it is felt that the reason for dictating letters is the composer's convenience, which he ought not to consult so obviously. If he dictates to a short-hand writer he is evidently chary of his valuable time, whereas courtesy always at least *seems* willing to sacrifice time to others. These remarks, I repeat, have no reference to business correspondence, which has its own code of good manners.

The most irritating letters to receive are those which, under a great show of courtesy, with many phrases and many kind inquiries about your health and that of your household, and even with some news adapted to your taste, contain some short sentence which betrays the fact that the whole letter was written with a manifestly selfish purpose. The proper answer to such letters is a brief business answer to the one essential sentence that revealed the writer's object, not taking any notice whatever of the froth of courteous verbiage.

Is it a part of necessary good breeding to answer letters at all? Are we really, in the nature of things, under the obligation to take a piece of paper and write phrases and sentences thereupon because it has pleased somebody at a distance to spend his time in that manner?

This requires consideration; there can be no general rule. It seems to me that people commit the error of transferring the subject from the region of oral conversation to the region of written intercourse. If a man asked me the way in the street it would be rudeness on my part not to answer him, because the answer is easily given and costs no appreciable time, but in written correspondence the case is essentially different. I am burdened with work; every hour, every minute of my day is apportioned to some definite duty or necessary rest, and three strangers make use of the post to ask me questions. To answer them I must make references; however brief the letters may be they will take time,—altogether the three will consume an hour. Have these correspondents any right to expect me to work an hour for them? Would a cabman drive them about the streets of London during an hour for nothing? Would a waterman pull them an hour on the Thames for nothing? Would a shoe-black brush their boots and trousers an hour for nothing? And why am I to serve these men gratuitously and be called an ill-bred, discourteous person if I tacitly decline to be their servant? We owe sacrifices—occasional sacrifices—of this kind to friends and relations, and we can afford them to a few, but we are under no obligation to answer everybody. Those whom we do answer may be thankful for a word on a post-card in Gladstone's brief but sufficient fashion. I am very much of the opinion of Rudolphe in Ponsard's "L'Honneur et l'Argent." A friend asks him what he does about letters:—

> *Rudolphe.*   Je les mets
> Soigneusement en poche et ne réponds jamais.
> *Premier Ami.*   Oh! vous raillez.
> *Rudolphe.* Non pas. Je ne puis pas admettre
> Qu'un importun m'oblige à répondre à sa lettre,
> Et, parcequ'il lui plaît de noircir du papier
> Me condamne moi-même à ce fâcheux métier.

ESSAY XXIII
LETTERS OF FRIENDSHIP

IF the art of writing had been unknown till now, and if the invention of it were suddenly to burst upon the world as did that of the telephone, one of the things most generally said in praise of it would be this. It would be said, "What a gain to friendship, now that friends can communicate in spite of separation by the very widest distances!"

Yet we have possessed this means of communication, the fullest and best of all, from remote antiquity, and we scarcely make any use of it—certainly not any use at all responding to its capabilities, and as time goes on, instead of developing those capabilities by practice in the art of friendly correspondence, we allow them to diminish by disuse.

The lowering of cost for the transport of letters, instead of making friendly correspondents numerous, has made them few. The cheap postage-stamp has increased business correspondence prodigiously, but it has had a very different effect on that of friendship. Great numbers of men whose business correspondence is heavy scarcely write letters of friendship at all. Their minds produce the business letter as by a second nature, and are otherwise sterile.

As for the facilities afforded by steam communication with distant countries, they seem to be of little use to friendship, since a moderate distance soon puts a stop to friendly communication. Except in cases of strong affection the Straits of Dover are an effectual though imaginary bar to intercourse of this kind, not to speak of the great oceans.

The impediment created by a narrow sea is, as I have said, imaginary, but we may speculate on the reasons for it; and my own reflections have ended in the somewhat strange conclusion that it must have something to do with sea-sickness. It must be that people dislike the idea of writing a letter that will have to cross a narrow channel of salt-water, because they vaguely and dimly dread the motion of the vessel. Nobody would consciously avow to himself such a sympathy with a missive exempt from all human ills, but the feeling may be unconsciously present. How else are we to account for the remarkable fact that salt-water breaks friendly communication by letter?

If you go to live anywhere out of your native island your most intimate friends cease to give any news of themselves. They do not even send printed announcements of the marriages and deaths in their families. This does not imply any cessation of friendly feeling on their part. If you appeared in England again they would welcome you with the utmost kindness and hospitality, but they do not like to post anything that will have to cross the sea. The news-vendors have not the same delicate imaginative sympathy with the possible sufferings of rag-pulp, so you get your English journals and find therein, by pure accident, the marriage of one intimate old friend and the death of another. You excuse the married man, because he is too much intoxicated with happiness to be responsible for any omission; and you excuse the dead man, because he cannot send letters from another world. Still you think that somebody not preoccupied by bridal joys or impeded by the last paralysis might have sent you a line directly, were it only a printed card.

Not only do the writers of letters feel a difficulty in sending their manuscript across the sea, but people appear to have a sense of difficulty in correspondence proportionate to the distance the letter will have to traverse. One would infer that they really experience, by the power of imagination, a feeling of fatigue in sending a letter on a long journey. If this is not so, how are we to account for the fact that the rarity of letters from friends increases in exact proportion to our remoteness from them? A simple person without correspondence would naturally imagine that it would be resorted to as a solace for separation, and that the greater the distance the more the separated friends would desire to be drawn together occasionally by its means, but in practice this rarely happens. People will communicate by letter across a space of a hundred miles when they will not across a thousand.

The very smallest impediments are of importance when the desire for intercourse is languid. The cost of postage to colonies and to countries within the postal union is trifling, but still it is heavier than the cost of internal postage, and it may be unconsciously felt as an impediment. Another slight impediment is that the answer to a letter sent to a great distance cannot arrive next day, so that he who writes in hope of an answer is like a trader who cannot expect an immediate return for an investment.

To prevent friendships from dying out entirely through distance, the French have a custom which seems, but is not, an empty form. On or about New Year's Day they send cards to *all* friends and many acquaintances, however far away. The useful effects of this custom are the following:—

1. It acquaints you with the fact that your friend is still alive,—pleasing information if you care to see him again.

2. It shows you that he has not forgotten you.

3. It gives you his present address.

4. In case of marriage, you receive his wife's card along with his own; and if he is dead you receive no card at all, which is at least a negative intimation.[32]

This custom has also an effect upon written correspondence, as the printed card affords the opportunity of writing a letter, when, without the address, the letter might not be written. When the address is well known the card often suggests the idea of writing.

When warm friends send visiting-cards they often add a few words of manuscript on the card itself, expressing friendly sentiments and giving a scrap of brief but welcome news.

Here is a suggestion to a generation that thinks friendly letter-writing irksome. With a view to the sparing of time and trouble, which is the great object of modern life (sparing, that is, in order to waste in other ways), cards might be printed as forms of invitation are, leaving only a few blanks to be filled up; or there might be a public signal-book in which the phrases most likely to be useful might be represented by numbers.

The abandonment of letter-writing between friends is the more to be regretted that, unless our friends are public persons, we receive no news of them indirectly; therefore, when we leave their neighborhood, the separation is of that complete kind which resembles temporary death. "No word comes from the dead," and no word comes from those silent friends. It is a melancholy thought in leaving a friend of this kind, when you shake hands at the station and still hear the sound of his voice, that in a few minutes he will be dead to you for months or years. The separation from a corresponding friend is shorn of half its sorrows. You know that he will write, and when he writes it requires little imagination to hear his voice again.

To write, however, is not all. For correspondence to reach its highest value, both friends must have the natural gift of friendly letter-writing, which may be defined as the power of talking on paper in such a manner as to represent their own minds with perfect fidelity in their friendly aspect.

This power is not common. A man may be a charming companion, full of humor and gayety, a well of knowledge, an excellent talker, yet his correspondence may not reveal the possession of these gifts. Some men are so constituted that as soon as they take a pen their faculties freeze. I remember a case of the same congelation in another art. A certain painter had exuberant humor and mimicry, with a marked talent for strong effects in talk; in short, he had the gifts of an actor, and, as Pius VII. called Napoleon I., he was both *commediante* and *tragediante*. Any one who knew him, and did not know his paintings, would have supposed at once that a man so gifted must have painted the most animated works; but it so happened (from some cause in the deepest mysteries of his nature) that whenever he took up a brush or a pencil his humor, his tragic power, and his love of telling effects all suddenly left him, and he was as timid, slow, sober, and generally ineffectual in his painting as he was full of fire and energy in talk. So it is in writing. That which ought to be the pouring forth of a man's nature often liberates only a part of his nature, and perhaps that part which has least to do with friendship. Your friend delights you by his ease and affectionate charm of manner, by the happiness of his expressions, by his wit, by the extent of his information, all these being qualities that social intercourse brings out in him as colors are revealed by light. The same man, in dull solitude at his desk, may write a letter from which every one of these qualities may be totally absent, and instead of them he may offer you a piece of perfunctory duty-writing which, as you see quite plainly, he only wanted to get done with, and in which you do not find a trace of your friend's real character. Such correspondence as that is worth having only so far as it informs you of your friend's existence and of his health.

Another and a very different way in which a man may represent himself unfairly in correspondence, so that his letters are not his real self, is when he finds that he has some particular talent as a writer, and unconsciously cultivates that talent when he holds a pen, whereas his real self has many other qualities that remain unrepresented. In this way humor may become the dominant quality in the letters of a correspondent whose conversation is not dominantly humorous.

Habits of business sometimes produce the effect that the confirmed business correspondent will write to his friend willingly and promptly on any matter of business, and will give him excellent advice, and be glad of the opportunity of rendering him a service, but he will shrink from the unaccustomed effort of writing any other kind of letter.

There is a strong temptation to blame silent friends and praise good correspondents; but we do not reflect that letter-writing is a task to some and a pleasure to others, and that if people may sometimes be justly blamed for shirking a *corvée* they can never deserve praise for indulging in an amusement. There is a particular reason why, when friendly letter-writing is a task, it is more willingly put off than many other tasks that appear far heavier and harder. It is either a real pleasure or a feigned pleasure, and feigned pleasures are the most wearisome things in life, far more wearisome than acknowledged work. For in work you have a plain thing to do and you see the end of it, and there is no need for ambages at the beginning or for a graceful retiring at the close; but a feigned pleasure has its own observances that must be gone through whether one has any heart for them or not. The groom who cleans a rich man's stable, and whistles at his work, is happier than the guest at a state dinner who is trying to look other than what he is,—a wearied victim of feigned and formal pleasure with a set false smile upon his face. In writing a business letter you have nothing to affect; but a letter of friendship, unless you have the real inspiration for it, is a narrative of things you have no true impulse to narrate, and the expression of feelings which (even if they be in some degree existent) you do not earnestly desire to utter.

The sentiment of friendship is in general rather a quiet feeling of regard than any lively enthusiasm. It may be counted upon for what it is,—a disposition to receive the friend with a welcome or to render him an occasional service, but there is not, commonly, enough of it to be a perennial warm fountain of literary inspiration. Therefore the worst mistake in dealing with a friend is to reproach him for not having been cordial and communicative enough. Sometimes this reproach is made, especially by women, and the immediate effect of it is to close whatever communicativeness there may be. If the friend wrote little before being reproached he will write less after.

The true inspiration of the friendly letter is the perfect faith that all the concerns of the writer will interest his friend. If James, who is separated by distance from John, thinks that John will not care about what James has been doing, hoping, suffering, the fount of friendly correspondence is frozen at its source. James ought to believe that John loves him enough to care about every little thing that can affect his happiness, even to the sickness of his old horse or the accident that happened to his dog when the scullery-maid threw scalding water out of the kitchen window; then there will be no lack, and James will babble on innocently through many a page, and never have to think.

The believer in friendship, he who has the true undoubting faith, writes with perfect carelessness about great things and small, avoiding neither serious interests, as a wary man would, nor trivial ones that might be passed over by a writer avaricious of his time. William of Orange, in his letters to Bentinck, appears to have been the model of friendly correspondents; and he was so because his letters reflected not a part only of his thinking and living, but the whole of it, as if nothing that concerned him could possibly be without interest for the man he loved. Familiar as it must be to many readers, I cannot but quote a passage from Macaulay:

"The descendants of Bentinck still preserve many letters written by William to their master, and it is not too much to say that no person who has not studied those letters can form a correct notion of the Prince's character. He whom even his admirers generally accounted the most frigid and distant of men here forgets all distinctions of rank, and pours out all his thoughts with the ingenuousness of a schoolboy. He imparts without reserve secrets of the highest moment. He explains with perfect simplicity vast designs affecting all the governments of Europe. Mingled with his communications on such subjects are other communications of a very different but perhaps not of a less interesting kind. All his adventures, all his personal feelings, his long runs after enormous stags, his carousals on St. Hubert's Day, the growth of his plantations, the failure of his melons, the state of his stud, his wish to procure an easy pad-nag for his wife, his vexation at learning that one of his household, after ruining a girl of good family, refused to marry her, his fits of sea-sickness, his coughs, his headaches, his devotional moods, his gratitude for the Divine protection after a great escape, his struggles to submit himself to the Divine will after a disaster, are described with an amiable garrulity hardly to have been expected from the most discreetly sedate statesman of his age. Still more remarkable is the careless effusion of his tenderness, and the brotherly interest which he takes in his friend's domestic felicity."

Friendly letters easily run over from sheet to sheet till they become ample and voluminous. I received a welcome epistle of twenty pages recently, and have seen another from a young man to his comrade which exceeded fifty; but the grandest letter that I ever heard of was from Gustave Doré to a very old lady whom he liked. He was travelling in Switzerland, and sent her a letter eighty pages long, full of lively pen-sketches for her entertainment. Artists often insert sketches in their letters,—a graceful habit, as it adds to their interest and value.

The talent for scribbling friendly letters implies some rough literary power, but may coexist with other literary powers of a totally different kind, and, as it seems, in perfect independence of them. There is no apparent connection between the genius in "Childe Harold," "Manfred," "Cain," and the talent of a lively letter-writer, yet Byron was the best careless letter-writer in English whose correspondence has been published and preserved.

He said "dreadful is the exertion of letter-writing," but by this he must have meant the first overcoming of indolence to begin the letter, for when once in motion his pen travelled with consummate naturalness and ease, and the exertion is not to be perceived. The length and subject of his communications were indeterminate. He scribbled on and on, every passing mood being reflected and fixed forever in his letters, which complete our knowledge of him by showing us the action of his mind in ordinal times as vividly as the poems display its power in moments of highest exaltation. We follow his mental phases from minute to minute. He is not really in one state and pretending to be in another for form's sake, so you have all his moods, and the letters are alive. The transitions are quick as thought. He darts from one topic to another with the freedom and agility of a bird, dwelling on each just long enough to satisfy his present need, but not an instant longer, and this without any reference to the original subject or motive of the letter. He is one of those perfect correspondents *qui causent avec la plume.* Men, women, and things, comic and tragic adventures, magnificent scenery, historical cities, all that his mind spontaneously notices in the world, are touched upon briefly, yet with consummate power. Though the sentences were written in the most careless haste and often in the strangest situations, many a paragraph is so dense in its substance, so full of matter, that one could not abridge it without loss. But the supreme merit of Byron's letters is that they record his own sensations with such fidelity. What do I, the receiver of a letter, care for second-hand opinions about anything? I can hear the fashionable opinions from echoes innumerable. What I *do* want is a bit of my friend himself, of his own peculiar idiosyncrasy, and if I get *that* it matters nothing that his feelings and opinions should be different from mine; nay, the more they differ from mine the more freshness and amusement they bring me. All Byron's correspondents might be sure of getting a bit of the real Byron. He never describes anything without conveying the exact effect upon himself. Writing to his publisher from Rome in 1817, he gives in a single paragraph a powerful description of the execution of three robbers by the guillotine (rather too terrible to quote), and at the end of it comes the personal effect:—

> "The pain seems little, and yet the effect to the spectator
> and the preparation to the criminal are very striking and
> chilling. The first turned me quite hot and thirsty, and
> made me shake so that I could hardly hold the opera-
> glass (I was close, but was determined to see as one
> should see everything once, with attention); the second
> and third (which shows how dreadfully soon things grow

indifferent), I am ashamed to say, had no effect on me as a horror, though I would have saved them if I could."

How accurately this experience is described with no affectation of impassible courage (he trembles at first like a woman) or of becoming emotion afterwards, the instant that the real emotion ceased! Only some pity remains,—"I would have saved them if I could."

The bits of frank criticism thrown into his letters, often quite by chance, were not the least interesting elements in Byron's correspondence. Here is an example, about a book that had been sent him:—

> "Modern Greece—good for nothing; written by some one who has never been there, and, not being able to manage the Spenser stanza, has invented a thing of his own, consisting of two elegiac stanzas, an heroic line and an Alexandrine, twisted on a string. Besides, why *modern*? You may say *modern Greeks*, but surely *Greece* itself is rather more ancient than ever it was."

The carelessness of Byron in letter-writing, his total indifference to proportion and form, his inattention to the beginning, middle, and end of a letter, considered as a literary composition, are not to be counted for faults, as they would be in writings of any pretension. A friendly letter is, by its nature, a thing without pretension. The one merit of it which compensates for every defect is to carry the living writer into the reader's presence, such as he really is, not such as by study and art he might make himself out to be. Byron was energetic, impetuous, impulsive, quickly observant, disorderly, generous, open-hearted, vain. All these qualities and defects are as conspicuous in his correspondence as they were in his mode of life. There have been better letter-writers as to literary art,—to which he gave no thought,—and the literary merits that his letters possess (their clearness, their force of narrative and description, their conciseness) are not the results of study, but the characteristics of a vigorous mind.

The absolutely best friendly letter writer known to me is Victor Jacquemont. He, too, wrote according to the inspiration of the moment, but it was so abundant that it carried him on like a steadily flowing tide. His letters are wonderfully sustained, yet they are not *composed*; they are as artless as Byron's, but much more full and regular. Many scribblers have facility, a flux of words, but who has Jacquemont's weight of matter along with it? The development of his extraordinary epistolary talent was due to another talent deprived of adequate exercise by circumstances. Jacquemont was by nature a brilliant, charming, amiable talker, and the circumstances were various situations in which this talker was deprived of an audience, being often, in long wanderings, surrounded by dull or ignorant people. Ideas accumulated in his mind till the accumulation became difficult to bear, and he relieved himself by talking on paper to friends at a distance, but intentionally only to one friend at a time. He tried to forget that his letters were passed round a circle of readers, and the idea that they would be printed never once occurred to him:—

> "En écrivant aujourd'hui aux uns et aux autres, j'ai cherché à oublier ce que tu me dis de l'échange que chacun fait des lettres qu'il reçoit de moi. Cette pensée m'aurait retenu la plume, ou du moins, *ne l'aurait pas laissée couler assez nonchalamment sur le papier pour en noircir, en un jour, cinquante-huit feuilles*, comme je l'ai fait.... *Je sais et j'aime beaucoup causer à deux; à trois, c'est autre chose; il en est de même pour écrire.* Pour parler comme je pense et sans blague, *il me faut la persuasion que je ne serai lu que de celui à qui j'écris.*"

To read these letters, in the four volumes of them which have been happily preserved, is to live with the courageous observer from day to day, to share pleasures enjoyed with the freshness of sensation that belongs to youth and strength, and privations borne with the cheerfulness of a truly heroic spirit.

This Essay would run to an inordinate length if I even mentioned the best of the many letter-writers who are known to us; and it is generally by some adventitious circumstance that they have ever been known at all. A man wins fame in something quite outside of letter-writing, and then his letters are collected and given to the world, but perfectly obscure people may have been equal or superior to him as correspondents. Occasionally the letters of some obscure person are rescued from oblivion. Madame de Rémusat passed quietly through life, and is now in a blaze of posthumous fame. Her son decided upon the publication of her letters, and then it became at once apparent that this lady had extraordinary gifts of the observing and recording order, so that her testimony, as an eye-witness of rare intelligence, must affect all future estimates of the conqueror of Austerlitz. There may be at this moment, there probably are, persons to whom the world attributes no literary talent, yet who are cleverly preserving the very best materials of history in careless letters to their friends.

It seems an indiscretion to read private letters, even when they are in print, but it is an indiscretion we cannot help committing. What can be more private than a letter from a man to his wife on purely family matters? Surely it is wrong to read such letters; but who could repent having read that exquisite one from Tasso's father, Bernardo Tasso, written to his wife about the education of their children during an involuntary separation? It shows to what a degree a sheet of paper may be made the vehicle of a tender affection. In the first page he tries, and, lover-like, tries again and again, to find words that will draw them together in spite of distance. "Not merely often," he says, "but continually our thoughts must meet upon the road." He expresses the fullest confidence that her feelings for him are as strong and true as his own for her, and that the weariness of separation is painful alike for both, only he fears that she will be less able to bear the pain, not because she is wanting in prudence but by reason of her abounding love. At length the tender kindness of his expressions culminates in one passionate outburst, "poi ch' io amo voi in quello estremo grado che si possa amar cosa mortale."

It would be difficult to find a stronger contrast than that between Bernardo Tasso's warmth and the tranquil coolness of Montaigne, who just says enough to save appearances in that one conjugal epistle of his which has come down to us. He begins by quoting a sceptical modern view of marriage, and then briefly disclaims it for himself, but does not say exactly what his own sentiments may be, not having much ardor of affection to express, and honestly avoiding any feigned declarations:—

> "Ma Femme vous entendez bien que ce n'est pas le tour
> d'vn galand homme, aux reigles de ce temps icy, de vous
> courtiser & caresser encore. Car ils disent qu'vn habil
> homme peut bien prendre femme: mais que de l'espouser
> c'est à faire à vn sot. Laissons les dire: ie me tiens de
> ma part à la simple façon du vieil aage, aussi en porte-
> ie tantost le poil. Et de vray la nouuelleté couste si cher
> iusqu'à ceste heure à ce pauure estat (& si ie ne sçay si nous
> en sommes à la dernière enchere) qu'en tout & par tout i'en
> quitte le party. Viuons ma femme, vous & moy, à la vieille
> Françoise."

If friendship is maintained by correspondence, it is also liable to be imperilled by it. Not unfrequently have men parted on the most amiable terms, looking forward to a happy meeting, and not foreseeing the evil effects of letters. Something will be written by one of them, not quite acceptable to the other, who will either remonstrate and cause a rupture in that way, or take his trouble silently and allow friendship to die miserably of her wound. Much experience is needed before we entirely realize the danger of friendly intercourse on paper. It is ten times more difficult to maintain a friendship by letter than by personal intercourse, not for the obvious reason that letter-writing requires an effort, but because as soon as there is the slightest divergence of views or difference in conduct, the expression of it or the account of it in writing cannot be modified by kindness in the eye or gentleness in the tone of voice. My friend may say almost anything to me in his private room, because whatever passes his lips will come with tones that prove him to be still my friend; but if he wrote down exactly the same words, and a postman handed me the written paper, they might seem hard, unkind, and even hostile. It is strange how slow we are to discover this in practice. We are accustomed to speak with great freedom to intimate friends, and it is only after painful mishaps that we completely realize the truth that it is perilous to permit ourselves the same liberty with the pen. As soon as we *do* realize it we see the extreme folly of those who timidly avoid the oral expression of friendly censure, and afterwards write it all out in black ink and send it in a missive to the victim when he has gone away. He receives the letter, feels it to be a cold cruelty, and takes refuge from the vexations of friendship in the toils of business, thanking Heaven that in the region of plain facts there is small place for sentiment.

ESSAY XXIV
LETTERS OF BUSINESS

THE possibilities of intercourse by correspondence are usually underestimated.

That there are great natural differences of talent for letter-writing is certainly true; but it is equally true that there are great natural differences of talent for oral explanation, yet, although we constantly hear people say that this or that matter of business cannot be treated by correspondence, we *never* hear them say that it cannot be treated by personal interviews. The value of the personal interview is often as much over-estimated as that of letters is depreciated; for if some men do best with the tongue, others are more effective with the pen.

It is presumed that there is nothing in correspondence to set against the advantages of pouring forth many words without effort, and of carrying on an argument rapidly; but the truth is, that correspondence has peculiar advantages of its own. A hearer seldom grasps another person's argument until it has been repeated several times, and if the argument is of a very complex nature the chances are that he will not carry away all its points even then. A letter is a document which a person of slow abilities can study at his leisure, until he has mastered it; so that an elaborate piece of reasoning may be set forth in a letter with a fair chance that such a person will ultimately understand it. He will read the letter three or four times on the day of its arrival, then he will still feel that something may have escaped him, and he will read it again next day. He will keep it and refer to it afterwards to refresh his memory. He can do nothing of all this with what you say to him orally. His only resource in that case is to write down a memorandum of the conversation on your departure, in which he will probably make serious omissions or mistakes. Your letter is a memorandum of a far more direct and authentic kind.

Appointments are sometimes made in order to settle a matter of business by talking, and after the parties have met and talked for a long time one says to the other, "I will write to you in a day or two;" and the other instantly agrees with the proposal, from a feeling that the matter can be settled more clearly by letter than by oral communication.

In these cases it may happen that the talking has cleared the way for the letter,—that it has removed subjects of doubt, hesitation, or dispute, and left only a few points on which the parties are very nearly agreed.

There are, however, other cases, which have sometimes come under my own observation, in which men meet by appointment to settle a matter, and then seem afraid to cope with it, and talk about indifferent subjects with a half-conscious intention of postponing the difficult one till there is no longer time to deal with it on that day. They then say, when they separate, "We will settle that matter by correspondence," as if they could not have done so just as easily without giving themselves the trouble of meeting. In such cases as these the reason for avoiding the difficult subject is either timidity or indolence. Either the parties do not like to face each other in an opposition that may become a verbal combat, or else they have not decision and industry enough to do a hard day's work together; so they procrastinate, that they may spread the work over a larger space of time.

The timidity that shrinks from a personal encounter is sometimes the cause of hostile letter-writing about matters of business even when personal interviews are most easy. There are instances of disputes by letter between people who live in the same town, in the same street, and even in the same house, and who might quarrel with their tongues if they were not afraid, but fear drives them to fight from a certain distance, as it requires less personal courage to fire a cannon at an enemy a league away than to face his naked sword.

Timidity leads people to write letters and to avoid them. Some timorous people feel bolder with a pen; others, on the contrary, are extremely afraid of committing anything to paper, either because written words remain and may be referred to afterwards, or because they may be read by eyes they were never intended for, or else because the letter-writer feels doubtful about his own powers in composition, grammar, or spelling.

Of these reasons against doing business by letter the second is really serious. You write about your most strictly private affairs, and unless the receiver of the letter is a rigidly careful and orderly person, it may be read by his clerks or servants. You may afterwards visit the recipient and find the letter lying about on a disorderly desk, or stuck on a hook suspended from a wall, or thrust into a lockless drawer; and as the letter is no longer your property, and you have not the resource of destroying it, you will keenly appreciate the wisdom of those who avoid letter-writing when they can.

The other cause of timidity, the apprehension that some fault may be committed, some sin against literary taste or grammatical rule, has a powerful effect as a deterrent from even necessary business correspondence. The fear which a half-educated person feels that he will commit faults causes a degree of hesitation which is enough of itself to produce them; and besides this cause of error there is the want of practice, also caused by timidity, for persons who dread letter-writing practise it as little as possible.

The awkwardness of uneducated letter-writers is a most serious cause of anxiety to people who are compelled to intrust the care of things to uneducated dependants at a distance. Such care-takers, instead of keeping you regularly informed of the state of affairs as an intelligent correspondent would, write rarely, and they have such difficulty in imagining the necessary ignorance of one who is not on the spot, that the information they give you is provokingly incomplete on some most important points.

An uneducated agent will write to you and tell you, for example, that damage has occurred to something of yours, say a house, a carriage, or a yacht, but he will not tell you its exact nature or extent, and he will leave you in a state of anxious conjecture. If you question him by letter, he will probably miss what is most essential in your questions, so that you will have great difficulty in getting at the exact truth. After much trouble you will perhaps have to take the train and go to see the extent of damage for yourself, though it might have been described to you quite accurately in a short letter by an intelligent man of business.

Nothing is more wonderful than the mistakes in following written directions that can be committed by uneducated men. With clear directions in the most legible characters before their eyes they will quietly go and do something entirely different, and appear unfeignedly surprised when you show them the written directions afterwards. In these cases it is probable that they have unconsciously substituted a notion of their own for your idea, which is the common process of what the uneducated consider to be understanding things.

The extreme facility with which this is done may be illustrated by an example. The well-known French *savant* and inventor, Ruolz, whose name is famous in connection with electro-plating, turned his attention to paper for roofing and, as he perceived the defects of the common bituminous papers, invented another in which no bitumen was employed. This he advertised constantly and extensively as the "Carton *non* bitumé Ruolz," consequently every one calls it the "Carton bitumé Ruolz." The reason here is that the notion of papers for roofs was already so associated in the French mind with bitumen, that it was absolutely impossible to effect the disjunction of the two ideas.

Instances have occurred to everybody in which the consequence of warning a workman that he is not to do some particular thing, is that he goes and does it, when if nothing had been said on the subject he might, perchance, have avoided it. Here are two good instances of this, but I have met with many others. I remember ordering a binder to bind some volumes with red edges, specially stipulating that he was not to use aniline red. He therefore carefully stained the edges with aniline. I also remember writing to a painter that he was to stain some new fittings of a boat with a transparent glaze of raw sienna, and afterwards varnish them, and that he was to be careful *not* to use opaque paint anywhere. I was at a great distance from the boat and could not superintend the work. In due time I visited the boat and discovered that a foul tint of opaque paint had been employed everywhere on the new fittings, without any glaze or varnish whatever, in spite of the fact that old fittings, partially retained, were still there, with mellow transparent stain and varnish, in the closest juxtaposition with the hideous thick new daubing.

It is the evil of mediocrity in fortune to have frequently to trust to uneducated agents. Rich men can employ able representatives, and in this way they can inform themselves accurately of what occurs to their belongings at a distance. Without riches, however, we may sometimes have a friend on the spot who will see to things for us, which is one of the kindest offices of friendship. The most efficient friend is one who will not only look to matters of detail, but will take the trouble to inform you accurately about them, and for this he must be a man of leisure. Such a friend often spares one a railway journey by a few clear lines of report or explanation. Judging from personal experience, I should say that retired lawyers and retired military officers were admirably adapted to render this great service efficiently, and I should suppose that a man who had retired from busy commercial life would be scarcely less useful, but I should not hope for precision in one who had always been unoccupied, nor should I expect many details from one who was much occupied still. The first would lack training and experience; the second would lack leisure.

The talent for accuracy in affairs may be distinct from literary talent and education, and though we have been considering the difficulty of corresponding on matters of business with the uneducated, we must not too hastily infer that because a man is inaccurate in spelling, and inelegant in phraseology, he may not be an agreeable and efficient business correspondent. There was a time when all the greatest men of business in England were uncertain spellers. Clear expression and completeness of statement are more valuable than any other qualities in a business correspondent. I sometimes have to correspond with a tradesman in Paris who rose from an humble origin and scarcely produces what a schoolmaster would consider a passable letter; yet his letters are models in essential qualities, as he always removes by plain statements or questions every possibility of a mistake, and if there is any want of absolute precision in my orders he is sure to find out the deficiency, and to call my attention to it sharply.

The habit of *not acknowledging orders* is one of the worst negative vices in business correspondence. It is most inconveniently common in France, but happily much rarer in England. Where this vice prevails you cannot tell whether the person you wish to employ has read your order or not; and if you suppose him to have read it, you have no reason to feel sure that he has understood it, or will execute it in time.

It is a great gain to the writer of letters to be able to make them brief and clear at the same time, but as there is obscurity in a labyrinth of many words so there may be another kind of obscurity from their paucity,—that kind which Horace alluded to with reference to poetry,—

> "Brevis esse laboro
> Obscurus fio."

Sometimes one additional word would spare the reader a doubt or a misunderstanding. This is likely to become more and more the dominant fault of correspondence as it imitates the brevity of the telegram.

Observe the interesting use of the word *laboro* by Horace. You may, in fact, *labor* to be brief, although the result is an appearance of less labor than if you had written at ease. It may take more time to write a very short letter than one of twice the length, the only gain in this case being to the receiver.

Letters of business often appear to be written in the most rapid and careless haste; the writing is almost illegible from its speed, the composition slovenly, the letter brief. And yet such a letter may have cost hours of deliberate reflection before one word of it was committed to paper. It is the rapid registering of a slowly matured decision.

It is a well-known principle of modern business correspondence that if a letter refers only to one subject it is more likely to receive attention than if it deals with several; therefore if you have several different orders or directions to give it is bad policy to write them all at once, unless you are absolutely compelled to do so because they are all equally pressing. Even if there is the same degree of urgency for all, yet a practical impossibility that all should be executed at the same time, it is still the best policy to give your orders successively and not more quickly than they can be executed. The only danger of this is that the receiver of the orders may think at first that they are small matters in which postponement signifies little, as they can be executed at any time. To prevent this he should be strongly warned at first that the order will be rapidly followed by several others. If there is not the same degree of urgency for all, the best way is to make a private register of the different matters in the order of their urgency, and then to write several short notes, at intervals, one about each thing.

People have such a marvellous power of misunderstanding even the very plainest directions that a business letter never *can* be made too clear. It will, indeed, frequently happen that language itself is not clear enough for the purposes of explanation without the help of drawing, and drawing may not be clear to one who has not been educated to understand it, which compels you to have recourse to modelling. In these cases the task of the letter-writer is greatly simplified, as he has nothing to do but foresee and prevent any misunderstanding of the drawing or model.

Every material thing constructed by mankind may be explained by the three kinds of mechanical drawing,—plan, section, and elevation,—but the difficulty, is that so many people are unable to understand plans and sections; they only understand elevations, and not always even these. The special incapacity to understand plans and sections is common in every rank of society, and it is not uncommon even in the practical trades. All letter-writing that refers to material construction would be immensely simplified if, by a general rule in popular and other education, every future man and woman in the country were taught enough about mechanical drawing to be able at least to *read* it.

It is delightful to correspond about construction with any trained architect or engineer, because to such a correspondent you can explain everything briefly, with the perfect certainty of being accurately understood. It is terrible toil to have to explain construction by letter to a man who does not understand mechanical drawing; and when you have given great labor to your explanation, it is the merest chance whether he will catch your meaning or not. The evil does not stop at mechanical drawing. Not only do uneducated people misunderstand a mechanical plan or section, but they are quite as liable to misunderstand a perspective drawing, as the great architect and draughtsman Viollet-le-Duc charmingly exemplified by the work of an intelligent child. A little boy had drawn a cat as he had seen it in front with its tail standing up, and this front view was stupidly misunderstood by a mature *bourgeois*, who thought the animal was a biped (as the hind-legs were hidden), and believed the erect tail to be some unknown object sticking out of the nondescript creature's head. If you draw a board in perspective (other than isometrical) a workman is quite likely to think that one end of it is to be narrower than the other.

Business correspondence in foreign languages is a very simple matter when it deals only with plain facts, and it does not require any very extensive knowledge of the foreign tongue to write a common order; but if any delicate or complicated matter has to be explained, or if touchy sensitiveness in the foreigner has to be soothed by management and tact, then a thorough knowledge of the shades of expression is required, and this is extremely rare. The statement of bare facts, or the utterance of simple wants, is indeed only a part of business correspondence, for men of business, though they are not supposed to display sentiment in affairs, are in reality just as much human beings as other men, and consequently they have feelings which are to be considered. A correspondent who is able to write a foreign language with delicacy and tact will often attain his object when one with a ruder and more imperfect knowledge of the language would meet with certain failure, though he asked for exactly the same thing.

It is surety possible to be civil and even polite in business correspondence without using the deplorable commercial slang which exists, I believe, in every modern language. The proof that such abstinence is possible is that some of the most efficient and most active men of business never have recourse to it at all. This commercial slang consists in the substitution of conventional terms originally intended to be more courteous than plain English, French, etc., but which, in fact, from their mechanical use, become wholly destitute of that best politeness which is personal, and does not depend upon set phrases that can be copied out of a tradesman's model letter-writer. Anybody but a tradesman calls your letter a letter; why should an English tradesman call it "your favor," and a French one *"votre honorée"*? A gentleman writing in the month of May speaks of April, May, and June, when a tradesman carefully avoids the names of the months, and calls them *ultimo, courant,* and *proximo*; whilst instead of saying "by" or "according to," like other Englishmen, he says *per*. This style was touched upon by Scott in Provost Crosbie's letter to Alexander Fairford: "Dear Sir—Your *respected favor* of 25th *ultimo, per* favor of Mr. Darsie Latimer, reached me in safety." This is thought to be a finished commercial style. One sometimes meets with the most astonishing and complicated specimens of it, which the authors are evidently proud of as proofs of their high commercial training. I regret not to have kept some fine examples of these, as their perfections are far beyond all imitation. This is not surprising when we reflect that the very worst commercial style is the result of a striving by many minds, during several generations, after a preposterous ideal.

Tradesmen deserve credit for understanding the one element of courtesy in letter-writing which has been neglected by gentlemen. They value legible handwriting, and they print clear names and addresses on their letter-paper, by which they spare much trouble.

Before closing this chapter let me say something about the reading of business letters as well as the writing of them. It is, perhaps, a harder duty to read such letters with the necessary degree of attention than to compose them, for the author has his head charged with the subject, and writing the letter is a relief to him; but to the receiver the matter is new, and however lucid may be the exposition it always requires some degree of real attention on his part. How are you, being at a distance, to get an indolent man to bestow that necessary attention? He feels secure from a personal visit, and indulges his indolence by neglecting your concerns, even when they are also his own. Long ago I heard an English Archdeacon tell the following story about his Bishop. The prelate was one of that numerous class of men who loathe the sight of a business letter; and he had indulged his indolence in that respect to such a degree that, little by little, he had arrived at the fatal stage where one leaves letters unopened for days or weeks. At one particular time the Archdeacon was aware of a great arrear of unopened letters, and impressed his lordship with the necessity for taking some note of their contents. Yielding to a stronger will, the Bishop began to read; and one of the first communications was from a wealthy man who offered a large sum for church purposes (I think for building), but if the offer was not accepted within a certain lapse of time he declared his intention of making it to that which a Bishop loveth not—a dissenting community. The prelate had opened the letter too late, and he lost the money. I believe that the Archdeacon's vexation at the loss was more than counterbalanced by gratification that his hierarchical superior had received such a lesson for his neglect. Yet he did but imitate Napoleon, of whom Emerson says, "He directed Bourrienne to leave all letters unopened for three weeks, and then observed with satisfaction how large a part of the correspondence had disposed of itself and no longer required an answer." This is a very unsafe system to adopt, as the case of the Bishop proves. Things may "dispose of themselves" in the wrong way, like wine in a leaky cask, which, instead of putting itself carefully into a sound cask, goes trickling into the earth.

The indolence of some men in reading and answering letters of business would be incredible if they did not give clear evidence of it. The most remarkable example that ever came under my notice is the following. A French artist, not by any means in a condition of superfluous prosperity, exhibited a picture at the *Salon*. He waited in Paris till after the opening of the exhibition and then went down into the country. On the day of his departure he received letters from two different collectors expressing a desire to purchase his work, and asking its price. Any real man of business would have seized upon such an opportunity at once. He would have answered both letters, stayed in town, and contrived to set the two amateurs bidding against each other. The artist in question was one of those unaccountable mortals who would rather sacrifice all their chances of life than indite a letter of business, so he left both inquiries unanswered, saying that if the men had really wanted the picture they would have called to see him. He never sold it, and some time afterwards was obliged to give up his profession, quite as much from the lack of promptitude in affairs as from any artistic deficiency.

Sometimes letters of business are *read*, but read so carelessly that it would be better if they were thrown unopened into the fire. I have seen some astounding instances of this, and, what is most remarkable, of repeated and incorrigible carelessness in the same person or firm, compelling one to the conclusion that in corresponding with that person or that firm the clearest language, the plainest writing, and the most legible numerals, are all equally without effect. I am thinking particularly of one case, intimately known to me in all its details, in which a business correspondence of some duration was finally abandoned, after infinite annoyance, for the simple reason that it was impossible to get the members of the firm, or their representatives, to attend to written orders with any degree of accuracy. Even whilst writing this very Essay I have given an order with regard to which I foresaw a probable error. Knowing by experience that a probable error is almost certain if steps are not taken energetically to prevent it, I requested that this error might not be committed, and to attract more attention to my request I wrote the paragraph containing it in red ink,—a very unusual precaution. The foreseen error was accurately committed.

ESSAY XXV
ANONYMOUS LETTERS

PROBABLY few of my mature readers have attained middle age without receiving a number of anonymous letters. Such letters are not always offensive, sometimes they are amusing, sometimes considerate and kind, yet there is in all cases a feeling of annoyance on receiving them, because the writer has made himself inaccessible to a reply. It is as if a man in a mask whispered a word in your ear and then vanished suddenly in a crowd. You wish to answer a calumny or acknowledge a kindness, and you may talk to the winds and streams.

Anonymous letters of the worst kind have a certain value to the student of human nature, because they afford him glimpses of the evil spirit that disguises itself under the fair seemings of society. You believe with childlike simplicity and innocence that, as you have never done any intentional injury to a human being, you cannot have a human enemy, and you make the startling discovery that somewhere in the world, perhaps even amongst the smiling people you meet at dances and dinners, there are creatures who will have recourse to the foulest slanders if thereby they may hope to do you an injury. What *can* you have done to excite such bitter animosity? You may both have done much and neglected much. You may have had some superiority of body, mind, or fortune; you may have neglected to soothe some jealous vanity by the flattery it craved with a tormenting hunger.

The simple fact that you seem happier than Envy thinks you ought to be is of itself enough to excite a strong desire to diminish your offensive happiness or put an end to it entirely. That is the reason why people who are going to be married receive anonymous letters. If they are not really happy they have every appearance of being happy, which is not less intolerable. The anonymous letter-writer seeks to put a stop to such a state of things. He might go to one of the parties and slander the other openly, but it would require courage to do that directly to his face. A letter might be written, but if name and address were given there would come an inconvenient demand for proofs. One course remains, offering that immunity from consequences which is soothing to the nerves of a coward. The envious or jealous man can throw his vitriol in the dark and slip away unperceived—*he can write an anonymous letter.*

Has the reader ever really tried to picture to himself the state of that man's or woman's mind (for women write these things also) who can sit down, take a sheet of paper, make a rough draft of an anonymous letter, copy it out in a very legible yet carefully disguised hand, and make arrangements for having it posted at a distance from the place where it was written? Such things are constantly done. At this minute there are a certain number of men and women in the world who are vile enough to do all that simply in order to spoil the happiness of some person whom they regard with "envy, hatred, malice, and all uncharitableness." I see in my mind's eye the gentleman—the man having all the apparent delicacy and refinement of a gentleman—who is writing a letter intended to blast the character of an acquaintance. Perhaps he meets that acquaintance in society, and shakes hands with him, and pretends to take an interest in his health. Meanwhile he secretly reflects upon the particular sort of calumny that will have the greatest degree of verisimilitude. Everything depends upon his talent in devising the most *credible* sort of calumny,—not the calumny most likely to meet general credence, but that which is most likely to be believed by the person to whom it is addressed, and most likely to do injury when believed. The anonymous calumniator has the immense advantage on his side that most people are prone to believe evil, and that good people are unfortunately the most prone, as they hate evil so intensely that even the very phantom of it arouses their anger, and they too frequently do not stop to inquire whether it is a phantom or a reality. The clever calumniator is careful not to go too far; he will advance something that might be or that might have been; he does not love *le vrai*, but he is a careful student of *le vraisemblable*. He will assume an appearance of reluctance, he will drop hints more terrible than assertions, because they are vague, mysterious, disquieting. When he thinks he has done enough he stops in time; he has inoculated the drop of poison, and can wait till it takes effect.

It must be rather an anxious time for the anonymous letter-writer when he has sent off his missive. In the nature of things he cannot receive an answer, and it is not easy for him to ascertain very soon what has been the result of his enterprise. If he has been trying to prevent a marriage he does not know immediately if the engagement is broken off, and if it is not broken off he has to wait till the wedding-day before he is quite sure of his own failure, and to suffer meanwhile from hope deferred and constantly increasing apprehension. If the rupture occurs he has a moment of Satanic joy, but it *may* be due to some other cause than the success of his own calumny, so that he is never quite sure of having himself attained his object.

It is believed that most people who are engaged to be married receive anonymous letters recommending them to break off the match. Not only are such letters addressed to the betrothed couple themselves, but also to their relations. If there is not a doubt that the statements in such letters are purely calumnious, the right course is to destroy them immediately and never allude to them afterwards; but if there is the faintest shadow of a doubt—if there is the vaguest feeling that there may be *some* ground for the attack—then the only course is to send the letter to the person accused, and to say that this is done in order to afford him an opportunity for answering the anonymous assailant. I remember a case in which this was done with the best results. A professional man without fortune was going to marry a young heiress; I do not mean a great heiress, but one whose fortune might be a temptation. Her family received the usual anonymous letters, and in one of them it was stated that the aspirant's father, who had been long dead, had dishonored himself by base conduct with regard to a public trust in a certain town where he occupied a post of great responsibility towards the municipal authorities. The letter was shown to the son, and he was asked if he knew anything of the matter, and if he could do anything to clear away the imputation. Then came the difficulty that the alleged betrayal of trust was stated to have occurred twenty years before, and that the Mayor was dead, and probably most of the common councillors also. What was to be done? It is not easy to disprove a calumny, and the *onus* of proof ought always to be thrown upon the calumniator, but this calumniator was anonymous and intangible, so the son of the victim was requested to repel the charge. By a very unusual and most fortunate accident, his father had received on quitting the town in question a letter from the Mayor of a most exceptional character, in which he spoke with warm and grateful appreciation of services rendered and of the happy relations of trust and confidence that had subsisted between himself and the slandered man down to the very termination of their intercourse. This letter, again by a most lucky accident, had been preserved by the widow, and by means of it one dead man defended the memory of another. It removed the greatest obstacle to the marriage; but another anonymous writer, or the same in another handwriting, now alleged that the slandered man had died of a disease likely to be inherited by his posterity. Here, again, luck was on the side of the defence, as the physician who had attended him was still alive, so that this second invention was as easily disposed of as the first. The marriage took place; it has been more than usually happy, and the children are pictures of health.

The trouble to which anonymous letter-writers put themselves to attain their ends must sometimes be very great. I remember a case in which some of these people must have contrived by means of spies or agents to procure a private address in a foreign country, and must have been at great pains also to ascertain certain facts in England which were carefully mingled with the lies in the calumnious letter. The nameless writer was evidently well informed, possibly he or she may have been a "friend" of the intended victim. In this case no attention was paid to the attack, which did not delay the marriage by a single hour. Long afterwards the married pair happened to be talking about anonymous letters, and it then appeared that each side had received several of these missives, coarsely or ingeniously concocted, but had given them no more attention than they deserved.

An anonymous letter is sometimes written in collaboration by two persons of different degrees of ability. When this is done one of the slanderers generally supplies the basis of fact necessary to give an appearance of knowledge, and the other supplies or improves the imaginative part of the common performance and its literary style. Sometimes one of the two may be detected by the nature of the references to fact, or by the supposed writer's personal interest in bringing about a certain result.

It is very difficult at the first glance entirely to resist the effect of a clever anonymous letter, and perhaps it is only men of clear strong sense and long experience who at once overcome the first shock. In a very short time, however, the phantom evil grows thin and disappears, and the motive of the writer is guessed at or discerned.

The following brief anonymous letter or one closely resembling it (I quote from memory) was once received by an English gentleman on his travels.

> "Dear Sir,—I congratulate you on the fact that you will be
> a grandfather in about two months. I mention this as you
> may like to purchase baby-linen for your grandchild during
> your absence. I am, Sir, yours sincerely,
>
> "A Well-wisher."

The receiver had a family of grown-up children of whom not one was married. The letter gave him a slight but perceptible degree of disquietude which he put aside to the best of his ability. In a few days came a signed letter from one of his female servants confessing that she was about to become a mother, and claiming his protection as the grandfather of the child. It then became evident that the anonymous letter had been written by the girl's lover, who was a tolerably educated man whilst she was uneducated, and that the pair had entered into this little plot to obtain money. The matter ended by the dismissal of the girl, who then made threats until she was placed in the hands of the police. Other circumstances were recollected proving her to be a remarkably audacious liar and of a slanderous disposition.

The torture that an anonymous letter may inflict depends far more on the nature of the person who receives it than on the circumstances it relates. A jealous and suspicious nature, not opened by much experience or knowledge of the world, is the predestined victim of the anonymous torturer. Such a nature jumps at evil report like a fish at an artificial fly, and feels the anguish of it immediately. By a law that seems really cruel such natures seize with most avidity on those very slanders that cause them the most pain.

A kind of anonymous letter of which we have heard much in the present disturbed state of European society is the letter containing threats of physical injury. It informs you that you will be "done for" or "disabled" in a short time, and exhorts you in the meanwhile to prepare for your awful doom. The object of these letters is to deprive the receiver of all feeling of security or comfort in existence. His consolation is that a real intending murderer would probably be thinking too much of his own perilous enterprise to indulge in correspondence about it, and we do not perceive that the attacks on public men are at all proportionate in number to the menaces addressed to them.

As there are malevolent anonymous letters intended to inflict the most wearing anxiety, so there are benevolent ones written to save our souls. Some theologically minded person, often of the female sex, is alarmed for our spiritual state because she fears that we have doubts about the supernatural, and so she sends us books that only make us wonder at the mental condition for which such literature can be suitable. I remember one of my female anonymous correspondents who took it for granted that I was like a ship drifting about without compass or rudder (a great mistake on her part), and so she offered me the safe and spacious haven of Swedenborgianism! Others will tell you of the "great pain" with which they have read this or that passage of your writings, to which an author may always reply that as there is no Act of Parliament compelling British subjects to read his books the sufferers have only to let them alone in order to spare themselves the dolorous sensations they complain of.

Some kind anonymous correspondents write to console us for offensive criticism by maintaining the truth of our assertions as supported by their own experience. I remember that when the novel of "Wenderholme" was published, and naturally attacked for its dreadful portraiture of the drinking habits of a past generation, a lady wrote to me anonymously from a locality of the kind described bearing mournful witness to the veracity of the description.[33] In this case the employment of the anonymous form was justified by two considerations. There was no offensive intention, and the lady had to speak of her own relations whose names she desired to conceal. Authors frequently receive letters of gently expressed criticism or remonstrance from readers who do not give their names. The only objection to these communications, which are often interesting, is that it is rather teasing and vexatious to be deprived of the opportunity for answering them. The reader may like to see one of these gentle anonymous letters. An unmarried lady of mature age (for there appears to be no reason to doubt the veracity with which she gives a slight account of herself) has been reading one of my books and thinks me not quite just to a most respectable and by no means insignificant class in English society. She therefore takes me to task,—not at all unkindly.

> "Dear Sir,—I have often wished to thank you for the intense pleasure your books have given me, especially the 'Painter's Camp in the Highlands,' the word-pictures of which reproduced the enjoyment, intense even to pain, of the Scottish scenery.

> "I have only now become acquainted with your 'Intellectual Life,' which has also given me great pleasure, though of another kind. Its general fairness and candor induce me to protest against your judgment of a class of women whom I am sure you underrate from not having a sufficient acquaintance with their capabilities.

> "'Women who are not impelled by some masculine influence are not superior, either in knowledge or in discipline of the mind, at the age of fifty to what they were at twenty-five.... The best illustration of this is a sisterhood of three or four rich old maids.... You will observe that they invariably remain, as to their education, where they were left by their teachers many years before.... Even in what most interests them—theology, they repeat but do not extend their information.'

> "My circle of acquaintance is small, nevertheless I know many women between twenty-five and forty whose culture is always steadily progressing; who keep up an acquaintance with literature for its own sake, and not 'impelled' thereto 'by masculine influence;' who, though without creative power, yet have such capability of reception that they can appreciate the best authors of the day; whose theology is not quite the fossil you represent it, though I confess it is for but a small number of my acquaintance that I can claim the power of judicially estimating the various schools of theology.

"Without being specialists, the more thoughtful of our class have such an acquaintance with current literature that they are able to enter into the progress of the great questions of the day, and may even estimate the more fairly a Gladstone or a Disraeli for being spectators instead of actors in politics.

"I have spoken of my own acquaintances, but they are such as may be met within any middle-class society. For myself, I look back to the painful bewilderment of twenty-five and contrast it with satisfaction with the brighter perceptions of forty, finding out 'a little more, and yet a little more, of the eternal order of the universe.' One reason for your underrating us may be that our receptive powers only are in constant use, and we have little power of expression. I dislike anonymous letters as a rule, but as I write as the representative of a class, I beg to sign myself,

> "Yours gratefully,
> "One of Three or Four Rich Old Maids.

"November 13, 1883."

Letters of this kind give no pain to the receiver, except when they compel him to an unsatisfactory kind of self-examination. In the present case I make the best amends by giving publicity and permanence to this clearly expressed criticism. Something may be said, too, in defence of the passages incriminated. Let me attempt it in the form of a letter which may possibly fall under the eye of the Rich Old Maid.

Dear Madam,—Your letter has duly reached me, and produced feelings of compunction. Have I indeed been guilty of injustice towards a class so deserving of respect and consideration as the Rich Old Maids of England? It has always seemed to me one of the privileges of my native country that such a class should flourish there so much more amply and luxuriantly than in other lands. Married women are absorbed in the cares and anxieties of their own households, but the sympathies of old maids spread themselves over a wider area. Balzac hated them, and described them as having souls overflowing with gall; but Balzac was a Frenchman, and if he was just to the rare old maids of his native country (which I cannot believe) he knew nothing of the more numerous old maids of Great Britain. I am not in Balzac's position. Dear friends of mine, and dearer relations, have belonged to that kindly sisterhood.

The answer to your objection is simple. "The Intellectual Life" was not published in 1883 but in 1873. It was written some time before, and the materials had been gradually accumulating in the author's mind several years before it was written. Consequently your criticism is of a much later date than the work you criticise, and as you are forty in 1883 you were a young maid in the times I was thinking of when writing. It is certainly true that many women of the now past generation, particularly those who lived in celibacy, had a remarkable power of remaining intellectually in the same place. This power is retained by some of the present generation, but it is becoming rarer every day because the intellectual movement is so strong that it is drawing a constantly increasing number of women along with it; indeed this movement is so accelerated as to give rise to a new anxiety, and make us look back with a wistful regret. We are now beginning to perceive that a certain excellent old type of Englishwomen whom we remember with the greatest affection and respect will soon belong as entirely to the past as if they had lived in the days of Queen Elizabeth. From the intellectual point of view their lives were hardly worth living, but we are beginning to ask ourselves whether their ignorance (I use the plain term) and their prejudices (the plain term again) were not essential parts of a whole that commanded our respect. Their simplicity of mind may have been a reason why they had so much simplicity of purpose in well-doing. Their strength of prejudice may have aided them to keep with perfect steadfastness on the side of moral and social order. Their intellectual restfulness in a few clear settled ideas left a degree of freedom to their energy in common duties that may not always be possible amidst the bewildering theories of an unsettled and speculative age.

Faithfully yours,
The Author of "The Intellectual Life."

ESSAY XXVI
AMUSEMENTS

ONE of the most unexpected discoveries that we make on entering the reflective stage of existence is that amusements are social obligations.

The next discovery of this kind is that the higher the rank of the person the more obligatory and the more numerous do his so-called "amusements" become, till finally we reach the princely life which seems to consist almost exclusively of these observances.

Why should it ever be considered obligatory upon a man to amuse himself in some way settled by others? There appear to be two principal reasons for this. The first is, that when amusements are practised by many persons in common it appears unsociable and ungracious to abstain. Even if the amusement is not interesting in itself it is thought that the society it leads us into ought to be a sufficient reason for following it.

The second reason is that, like all things which are repeated by many people together, amusements soon become fixed customs, and have all the weight and authority of customs, so that people dare not abstain from observing them for fear of social penalties.

If the amusements are expensive they become not only a sign of wealth but an actual demonstration and display of it, and as nothing in the world is so much respected as wealth, or so efficient a help to social position, and as the expenditure which is visible produces far more effect upon the mind than that which is not seen, it follows that all costly amusements are useful for self-assertion in the world, and become even a means of maintaining the political importance of great families.

On the other hand, not to be accustomed to expensive amusements implies that one has lived amongst people of narrow means, so that most of those who have social ambition are eager to seize upon every opportunity for enlarging their experience of expensive amusements in order that they may talk about them afterwards, and so affirm their position as members of the upper class.

The dread of appearing unsociable, of seeming rebellious against custom, or inexperienced in the habits of the rich, are reasons quite strong enough for the maintenance of customary amusements even when there is very little real enjoyment of them for their own sake.

But, in fact, there are always *some* people who practise these amusements for the sake of the pleasure they give, and as these people are likely to excel the others in vivacity, activity, and skill, as they have more *entrain* and gayety, and talk more willingly and heartily about the sports they love, so they naturally come to lead opinion upon the subject and to give it an appearance of earnestness and warmth that is beyond its real condition. Hence the tone of conversation about amusements, though it may accurately represent the sentiments of those who enjoy them, does not represent all opinion fairly. The opposite side of the question found a witty exponent in Sir George Cornewall Lewis, when he uttered that immortal saying by which his name will endure when the recollection of his political services has passed away, — "How tolerable life would be were it not for its pleasures!" There you have the feeling of the thousands who submit and conform, but who would have much to say if it were in good taste to say anything against pleasures that are offered to us in hospitality.

Amusements themselves become work when undertaken for an ulterior purpose such as the maintenance of political influence. A great man goes through a certain regular series of dinners, balls, games, shooting and hunting parties, races, wedding-breakfasts, visits to great houses, excursions on land and water, and all these things have the outward appearance of amusement, but may, in reality, be labors that the great man undertakes for some purpose entirely outside of the frivolous things themselves. A Prime Minister scarcely goes beyond political dinners, but what an endless series of engagements are undertaken by a Prince of Wales! Such things are an obligation for him, and when the obligation is accepted with unfailing patience and good temper, the Prince is not only working, but working with a certain elegance and grace of art, often involving that prettiest kind of self-sacrifice which hides itself under an appearance of enjoyment. Nobody supposes that the social amusements so regularly gone through by the eldest son of Queen Victoria can be, in all cases, very entertaining to him; we suppose them to be accepted as forms of human intercourse that bring him into personal relations with his future subjects. The difference between this Prince and King Louis II. of Bavaria is perhaps the most striking contrast in modern royal existences. Prince Albert Edward is accessible to everybody, and shares the common pleasures of his countrymen; the Bavarian sovereign is never so happy as when in one of his romantic and magnificent residences, surrounded by the sublimity of nature and the embellishments of art, he sits alone and dreams as he listens to the strains of exquisite music. Has he not erected his splendid castle on a rock, like the builder of "The Palace of Art"?

> "A huge crag-platform, smooth as burnish'd brass
> I chose. The ranged ramparts bright
> From level meadow-bases of deep grass
> Suddenly scaled the light.

> "Thereon I built it firm. Of ledge or shelf
> The rock rose clear, or winding stair.
> My soul would live alone unto herself
> In her high palace there."

The life of the King of Bavaria, sublimely serene in its independence, is a long series of tranquil omissions. There may be a wedding-feast in one of his palaces, but such an occurrence only seems to him the best of all reasons why he should be in another. He escapes from the pleasures and interests of daily life, making himself an earthly paradise of architecture, music, and gardens, and lost in his long dream, assuredly one of the most poetical figures in the biographies of kings, and one of the most interesting, but how remote from men! This remoteness is due, in great part, to a sincerity of disposition which declines amusements that do not amuse, and desires only those real pleasures which are in perfect harmony with one's own nature and constitution. We like the sociability, the ready human sympathy, of the Prince of Wales; we think that in his position it is well for him to be able to keep all that endless series of engagements, but has not King Louis some claim upon our indulgence even in his eccentricity? He has refused the weary round of false amusements and made his choice of ideal pleasure. If he condescended to excuse himself, his *Apologia pro vitâ sua* might take a form somewhat resembling this. He might say, "I was born to a great fortune and only ask leave to enjoy it in my own way. The world's amusements are an infliction that I consider myself at liberty to avoid. I love musical or silent solitude, and the enchantments of a fair garden and a lofty dwelling amidst the glorious Bavarian mountains. Let the noisy world go its way with its bitter wranglings, its dishonest politics, its sanguinary wars! I set up no tyranny. I leave my subjects to enjoy their brief human existence in their own fashion, and they let me dream my dream."

These are not the world's ways nor the world's view. The world considers it essential to the character of a prince that he should be at least apparently happy in those pleasures which are enjoyed in society, that he should seem to enjoy them along with others to show his fellow-feeling with common men, and not sit by himself, like King Louis in his theatre, when "Tannhauser" is performed for the royal ears alone.

Of the many precious immunities that belong to humble station there are none more valuable than the freedom from false amusements. A poor man is under one obligation, he must work, but his work itself is a blessed deliverance from a thousand other obligations. He is not obliged to shoot, and hunt, and dance against his will, he is not obliged to affect interest and pleasure in games that only weary him, he has not to receive tiresome strangers in long ceremonious repasts when he would rather have a simple short dinner with his wife. Béranger sang the happiness of beggars with his sympathetic humorous philosophy, but in all seriousness it might be maintained that the poor are happier than they know. They get their easy unrestrained human intercourse by chance meetings, and greetings, and gossipings, and they are spared all the acting, all the feigning, that is connected with the routine of imposed enjoyments.

Avowed work, even when uncongenial, is far less trying to patience than feigned pleasure. You dislike accounts and you dislike balls, but though your dislike may be nearly equal in both cases you will assuredly find that the time hangs less heavily when you are resolutely grappling with the details of your account-books than when you are only wishing that the dancers would go to bed. The reason is that any hard work, whatever it is, has the qualities of a mental tonic, whereas unenjoyed pleasures have an opposite effect, and even though work may be uncongenial you see a sort of result, whilst a false pleasure leaves no result but the extreme fatigue that attends it,—a kind of fatigue quite exceptional in its nature, and the most disagreeable that is known to man.

The dislike for false amusements is often misunderstood to be a puritanical intolerance of all amusement. It is in this as in all things that are passionately enjoyed,—the false thing is most disliked by those who best appreciate the true.

What may be called the truth or falsehood of amusements is not in the amusements themselves, but in the relation between one human idiosyncrasy and them. Every idiosyncrasy has its own strong mysterious affinities, generally distinguishable in childhood, always clearly distinguishable in youth. We are like a lute or a violin, the tuned strings vibrate in answer to certain notes but not in answer to others.

To convert amusements into social customs or obligations, to make it a man's duty to shoot birds or ride after foxes because it is agreeable to others to discharge guns and gallop across fields, is an infringement of individual liberty which is less excusable in the case of amusements than it is in more serious things. For in serious things, in politics and religion, there is always the plausible argument that the repression of the individual conscience is good for the unity of the State; whereas amusements are supposed to exist for the recreation of those who practise them, and when they are not enjoyed they are not amusements but something else. There is no single English word that exactly expresses what they are, but there is a French one, the word *corvée*, which means forced labor, labor under dictation, all the more unpleasant in these cases that it must assume the appearance of enjoyment.[34]

Surely there is nothing in which the independence of the individual ought to be so absolute, so unquestioned, as in amusements. What right have I, because a thing is a pleasant pastime to me, to compel my friend or my son to do that thing when it is a *corvée* to him? No man can possibly amuse himself in obedience to a word of command, the most he can do is to submit, to try to appear amused, wishing all the time that the weary task was over.

To mark the contrast clearly I will describe some amusements from the opposite points of view of those who enjoy them naturally, and those to whom they would be indifferent if they were not imposed, and hateful if they were.

Shooting is delightful to genuine sportsmen in many ways. It renews in them the sensations of the vigorous youth of humanity, of the tribes that lived by the chase. It brings them into contact with nature, gives a zest and interest to hard pedestrian exercise, makes the sportsmen minutely acquainted with the country, and leads to innumerable observations of the habits of wild animals that have the interest without the formal pretensions of a science. Shooting is a delightful exercise of skill, requiring admirable promptitude and perfect nerve, so that any success in it is gratifying to self-esteem. Sir Samuel Baker is always proud of being such a good marksman, and frankly shows his satisfaction. "I had fired three *beautifully correct* shots with No. 10 bullets, and seven drachms of powder in each charge; these were so nearly together that they occupied a space in her forehead of about three inches." He does not aim at an animal in a general way, but always at a particular and penetrable spot, recording each hit, and the special bullet used. Of course he loves his guns. These modern instruments are delightful toys on account of the highly developed art employed in their construction, so that they would be charming things to possess, and handle, and admire, even if they were never used, whilst the use of them gives a terrible power to man. See a good marksman when he takes a favorite weapon in his hand! More redoubtable than Roland with the sword Durindal, he is comparable rather to Apollo with the silver bow, or even to Olympian Zeus himself grasping his thunders. Listen to him when he speaks of his weapon! If he thinks you have the free-masonry of the chase, and can understand him, he talks like a poet and lover. Baker never fails to tell us what weapon he used on each occasion, and how beautifully it performed, and due honor and advertisement are kindly given to the maker, out of gratitude.

> "I accordingly took my trusty little Fletcher double rifle No. 24, and running knee-deep into the water to obtain a close shot I fired exactly between the eyes near the crown of the head. At the reports of the little Fletcher the hippo disappeared."

Then he adds an affectionate foot-note about the gun, praising it for going with him for five years, as if it had had a choice about the matter, and could have offered its services to another master. He believes it to be alive, like a dog.

> "This excellent and handy rifle was made by Thomas Fletcher, of Gloucester, and accompanied me like a faithful dog throughout my journey of nearly five years to the Albert Nyanza, and returned with me to England as good as new."

In the list of Baker's rifles appears his bow of Ulysses, his Child of a Cannon, familiarly called the Baby, throwing a half-pound explosive shell, a lovely little pet of a weapon with a recoil that broke an Arab's collar-bone, and was not without some slight effect even upon that mighty hunter, its master.

> "Bang went the Baby; round I spun like a weather-cock with the blood flowing from my nose, as the recoil had driven the top of the hammer deep into the bridge. My Baby not only screamed but kicked viciously. However I knew the elephant would be bagged, as the half-pound shell had been aimed directly behind the shoulder."

We have the most minute descriptions of the effects of these projectiles in the head of a hippopotamus and the body of an elephant. "I was quite satisfied with my explosive shells," says the enthusiastic sportsman, and the great beasts appear to have been satisfied too.

Now let me attempt to describe the feelings of a man not born with the natural instinct of a sportsman. We need not suppose him to be either a weakling or a coward. There are strong and brave men who can exercise their strength and prove their courage without willingly inflicting wounds or death upon any creature. To some such men a gun is simply an encumbrance, to wait for game is a wearisome trial of patience, to follow it is aimless wandering, to slaughter it is to do the work of a butcher or a poulterer, to wound it is to incur a degree of remorse that is entirely destructive of enjoyment. The fact that somewhere on mountain or in forest poor creatures are lying with festering flesh or shattered bones to die slowly in pain and hunger, and the terrible thirst of the wounded, and all for the pleasure of a gentleman,—such a fact as that, when clearly realized, is not to be got over by anything less powerful than the genuine instinct of the sportsman who is himself one of Nature's own born destroyers, as panthers and falcons are. The feeling of one who has not the sporting instinct has been well expressed as follows by Mr. Lewis Morris, in "A Cynic's Daydream:"—

> "Scant pleasure should I think to gain
> From endless scenes of death and pain;
> 'Twould little profit me to slay
> A thousand innocents a day;
> I should not much delight to tear
> With wolfish dogs the shrieking hare;
> With horse and hound to track to death
> A helpless wretch that gasps for breath;
> To make the fair bird check its wing,
> And drop, a dying, shapeless thing;
> To leave the joy of all the wood
> A mangled heap of fur and blood,
> Or else escaping, but in vain,
> To pine, a shattered wretch, in pain;
> Teeming, perhaps, or doomed to see
> Its young brood starve in misery."

Hunting may be classed with shooting and passed over, as the instinct is the same for both, with this difference only that the huntsman has a natural passion for horsemanship that may be wanting to the pedestrian marksman. An amusement entirely apart from every other, and requiring a special instinct, is that of sailing.

If you have the nautical passion it was born with you, and no reasoning can get it out of you. Every sheet of navigable water draws you with a marvellous attraction, fills you with an indescribable longing. Miles away from anything that can be sailed upon, you cannot feel a breeze upon your cheek without wishing to be in a sailing-boat to catch it in a spread of canvas. A ripple on a duck-pond torments you with a teazing reminder of larger surfaces, and if you had no other field for navigation you would want to be on that duck-pond in a tub. "I would rather have a plank and a handkerchief for a sail," said Charles Lever, "than resign myself to give up boating." You have pleasure merely in being afloat, even without motion, and all the degrees of motion under sail have their own peculiar charm for you, from an insensible gliding through glassy waters to a fight against opposite winds and raging seas. You have a thorough, intimate, and affectionate knowledge of all the details of your ship. The constant succession of little tasks and duties is an unfailing interest, a delightful occupation. You enjoy the manual labor, and acquire some skill not only as a sailor but as ship's carpenter and painter. You take all accidents and disappointments cheerfully, and bear even hardship with a merry heart. Nautical exercise, though on the humble scale of the modest amateur, has preserved or improved your health and activity, and brought you nearer to Nature by teaching you the habits of the winds and waters and by displaying to you an endless variety of scenes, always with some fresh interest, and often of enchanting beauty.

Now let us suppose that you are simple enough to think that what pleases you, who have the instinct, will gratify another who is destitute of it. If you have power enough to make him accompany you, he will pass through the following experiences.

Try to realize the fact that to him the sailing-boat is only a means of locomotion, and that he will refer to his watch and compare it with other means of locomotion already known to him, not having the slightest affectionate prejudice in its favor or gentle tolerance of its defects. If you could always have a steady fair wind he would enjoy the boat as much as a coach or a very slow railway train, but he will chafe at every delay. None of the details that delight you can have the slightest interest for him. The sails, and particularly the cordage, seem to him an irritating complication which, he thinks, might be simplified, and he will not give any mental effort to master them. He cares nothing about those qualities of sails and hull which have been the subject of such profound scientific investigation, such long and passionate controversy. You cannot speak of anything on board without employing technical terms which, however necessary, however unavoidable, will seem to him a foolish and useless affectation by which an amateur tries to give himself nautical airs. If you say "the mainsheet" he thinks you might have said more rationally and concisely "the cord by which you pull towards you that long pole which is under the biggest of the sails," and if you say "the starboard quarter," he thinks you ought to have said, in simple English, "that part of the vessel's side that is towards the back end of it and to your right hand when you are standing with your face looking forwards." If you happen to be becalmed he suffers from an infinite *ennui*. If you have to beat to windward he is indifferent to the wonderful art and vexed with you because, as his host, you have not had the politeness and the forethought to provide a favorable breeze. If you are a yachtsman of limited means and your guest has to take a small share in working the vessel, he will not perform it with any cheerful alacrity, but consider it unfit for a gentleman. If this goes on for long it is likely that there will be irritation on both sides, snappish expressions, and a quarrel. Who is in fault? Both are excusable in the false situation that has been created, but it ought not to have been created at all. You ought not to have invited a man without nautical instincts, or he ought not to have accepted the invitation. He was a charming companion on land, and that misled you both. Meet him on land again, receive him hospitably at your house. I would say "forgive him!" if there were anything to forgive, but it is not any fault of his or any merit of yours if, by the irrevocable fate of congenital idiosyncrasy, the amusement that you were destined to seek and enjoy is the *corvée* that he was destined to avoid.

I find no language strong enough to condemn the selfishness of those who, in order that they may enjoy what is a pleasure to themselves, deliberately and knowingly inflict a *corvée* upon others. This objection does not apply to paid service, for that is the result of a contract. Servants constantly endure the tedium of waiting and attendance, but it is their form of work, and they have freely undertaken it. Work of that kind is not a *corvée*, it is not forced labor. Real *corvées* are inflicted by heads of families on dependent relations, or by patrons on humble friends who are under some obligation to them, and so bound to them as to be defenceless. The father or patron wants, let us say, his nightly game at whist; he must and will have it, if he cannot get it he feels that the machine of the universe is out of gear. He singles out three people who do not want to play, perhaps takes for his partner one who thoroughly dislikes the game, but who has learned something of it in obedience to his orders. They sit down to their board of green cloth. The time passes wearily for the principal victim, who is thinking of something else and makes mistakes. The patron loses his temper, speaks with increasing acerbity, and finally either flies into a passion and storms (the old-fashioned way), or else adopts, with grim self-control, a tone of insulting contempt towards his victim that is even more difficult to endure. And this is the reward for having been unselfish and obliging, these are the thanks for having sacrificed a happy evening!

If this is often done by individuals armed with some kind of power and authority, it is done still more frequently by majorities. The tyranny of majorities begins in our school-days, and the principal happiness of manhood is in some measure to escape from it. Many a man in after-life remembers with bitterness the weary hours he had to spend for the gratification of others in games that he disliked. The present writer has a vivid recollection of what, to him, was the infinite dulness of cricket. He was not by any means an inactive boy, but it so happened that cricket never had the slightest interest for him, and to this day he cannot pass a cricket-ground without a feeling of strong antipathy to its level surface of green, and of thankfulness that he is no longer compelled to go through the irksome old *corvée* of his youth. One of the many charms, to his taste, of a rocky mountain-side in the Highlands is that cricket is impossible there. At the same time he quite believes and admits everything that is so enthusiastically claimed for cricket by those who have a natural affinity for the game.

There are not only sports and pastimes, but there is the long reverberating echo of every sport in endless conversations. Here it may be remarked that the lovers of a particular amusement, when they happen to be a majority, possess a terrible power of inflicting *ennui* upon others, and they often exercise it without mercy. Five men are dining together, and three are fox-hunters. Evidently they ought to keep fox-hunting to themselves in consideration for the other two, but this requires an almost superhuman self-discipline and politeness, so there is a risk that the minority may have to submit in silence to an inexhaustible series of details about horses and foxes and dogs. Indeed you are never safe from this kind of conversation, even when you have numbers on your side. Sporting talk may be inflicted by a minority when that minority is incapable of any other conversation and strong in its own incapacity. Here is a case in point that was narrated to me by one of the three *convives*. The host was a country gentleman of great intellectual attainments, one guest was a famous Londoner, and the other was a sporting squire who had been invited as a neighbor. Fox-hunting was the only subject of talk, because the squire was garrulous and unable to converse about any other topic.

Ladies are often pitiable sufferers from this kind of conversation. Sometimes they have the instinct of masculine sport themselves, and then the subject has an interest for them; but an intelligent woman may find herself in a wearisome position when she would rather avoid the subject of slaughter, and all the men around her talk of nothing but killing and wounding.

It is natural that men should talk much about their amusements, because the mere recollection of a true amusement (that for which we have an affinity) is in itself a renewal of it in imagination, and an immense refreshment to the mind. In the midst of a gloomy English winter the yachtsman talks of summer seas, and whilst he is talking he watches, mentally, his well-set sails, and hears the wash of the Mediterranean wave.

There are three pleasures in a true amusement, first anticipation, full of hope, which is

> "A feast for promised triumph yet to come,"

often the best banquet of all. Then comes the actual fruition, usually dashed with disappointments that a true lover of the sport accepts in the most cheerful spirit. Lastly, we go through it all over again, either with the friends who have shared our adventures or at least with those who could have enjoyed them had they been there, and who (for vanity often claims her own delights) know enough about the matter to appreciate our own admirable skill and courage.

In concluding this Essay I desire to warn young readers against a very common mistake. It is very generally believed that literature and the fine arts can be happily practised as amusements. I believe this to be an error due to the vulgar notion that artists and literal people do not work but only display talent, as if anybody could display talent without toil. Literary and artistic pursuits are in fact *studies* and not amusements. Too arduous to have the refreshing quality of recreation, they put too severe a strain upon the faculties, they are too troublesome in their processes, and too unsatisfactory in their results, unless a natural gift has been developed by earnest and long-continued labor. It does indeed occasionally happen that an artist who has acquired skill by persistent study will amuse himself by exercising it in sport. A painter may make idle sketches as Byron sometimes broke out into careless rhymes, or as a scholar will playfully compose doggerel in Greek, but these gambols of accomplished men are not to be confounded with the painful efforts of amateurs who fancy that they are going to dance in the Palace of Art and shortly discover that the muse who presides there is not a smiling hostess but a severe and exigent schoolmistress. An able French painter, Louis Leloir, wrote thus to a friend about another art that he felt tempted to practise:—

> "Etching tempts me much. I am making experiments and hope to show you something soon. Unhappily life is too short; we do a little of everything and then perceive that each branch of art would of itself consume the life of a man, to practise it very imperfectly after all.... We get angry with ourselves and struggle, but too late. It was at the beginning that we ought to have put on blinkers to hide from ourselves everything that is not art."

If we mean to amuse ourselves let us avoid the painful wrestling against insuperable difficulties, and the humiliation of imperfect results. Let us shun all ostentation, either of wealth or talent, and take our pleasures happily like poor children, or like the idle angler who stands in his old clothes by the purling stream and watches the bobbing of his float, or the glancing of the fly that his guileful industry has made.

INDEX

a mark of?

Norman influence

antipathy, to Dissent

sent to Eton

and Bohemianism

dislike of scholarship

(See *Rank* .)

Aristophilus, fictitious character

Armies: national ignorance

monopoly of places in French

(See *War* .)

Art: detached from religion

affecting friendship

Claude and Turner

chance acquaintances

purposes lowered

penetrated by love

affecting fraternity

friendship

lifts above mercenary motives

literary

adaptability of Greek language

preferences of artists rewarded

affecting relations of Priests and Women (Essay XIII. part ii.), , *passim;*

exaggeration and diminution, both admissible

result of selection

French ignorance of English

antagonized by Philistinism

not mere amusement

(See *Painting* , *Sculpture* , *Turner* , etc.)

Asceticism, tinges both the Philistine and Bohemian

(See *Priesthood*, *Roman Catholicism*, etc.)

Association: pleasurable or not

    affected by opinions

    by tastes

    London

    of a certain French painter

    between Priests and Women (Essay XIII. part iii.), *passim;*

    among travellers (Essay XVII)

    leads to misapprehension of opinions

    (See *Companionship*, *Friendship*, *Society*, etc.)

Atavism, puzzling to parents

Atheism: reading prayers

    apparent

    confounded with Deism

    (See *God*, *Religion*, etc.)

Attention: how directed in the study of language

    want of

Austerlitz, battle

    (See *Napoleon I.*)

Austria, Empress

Authority, of fathers (Essay VI), *passim*

    (See *Priests* .)

Authors: illustration

    indebtedness to humbler classes

    relations of several to women, *et seq.;*

    sensitiveness to family indifference

    in society and with the pen

    a procrastinating correspondent

    anonymous letters

    (See *Hamerton*, etc.)

Authorship, illustrating interdependence

the Brights

money affairs

generosity and meanness

refinement an obstacle

lack of fraternal interest

riches and poverty

(See *Boys* , *Friendship* , *Sons* , etc.)

Buffon, Georges Louis Leclerc de, his noble life

Buildings, literary illustration

Bulgaria, lost to Turkey, .

Bull-fights, women's presence

(See *Cruelty*.)

Bunyan, John: choice in religion

imprisoned

Business: affecting family ties

affecting letter-writing

Letters of (Essay XXIV)

orally conducted or written

stupid agents

talent for accuracy

acknowledging orders

apparent carelessness, one subject best

knowledge of drawing important to explanations on paper

acquaintance with languages a help

commercial slang

indolence in letter-reading has disastrous results

(See *Correspondence* .)

Byron, Lord: on Friendship

Haidée

marriage relations

as a letter-writer

careless rhymes, .

Chinese mandarins

Chirography, in letters

Christ: his divinity a past issue

    Church instituted

    Dr. Macleod on

    limits of knowledge in Jesus' day

    (See *Church* , *Religion* , etc.)

Christianity: as affecting intercourse

    its early disciples

    preferment for adherence

    morality a part of

    state churches

    in poetry

    early ideal

    (See *Roman Catholicism* , etc.)

Christmas: decorations

    in Tennyson

    (See *Clergy* , *Priesthood* , *Women* .)

Church: attendance of hypocrites

    compulsory

    instituted by God in Christ

    influence at all stages of life

    æsthetic industry

    dress

    buildings

    menaces

    partisanship

    power of custom

    authority

    (See *Religion, Roman Catholicism,* etc.)

Church of England: as affecting friendship

freedom of members in their own country, instance of Dissenting tyranny

 dangers of forsaking

 bondage of royalty

 adherence of nobility

 of working-people

 compulsory attendance, liberality

 ribaldry sanctioned by its head

 priestly consolation

 the *legal* church

 ritualistic art

 a bishop's invitation to a discussion

 story of a bishop's indolence

 French ignorance of

 (See *England* , *Christ* , etc.)

Cipher, in letters

Civility. (See *Hospitality* .)

Civilization: liking for

 antagonism to nature in love-matters

 lower state

 affected by hospitality

 material adjuncts

 physical

 duty to further

 forsaken

 (See *Barbarism* , *Bohemianism* , *Philistinism* , etc.)

Classes: Differences of Rank (Essay X), *passim;*

 affected by religion (Essay XII)

 limits

 in connection with Gentility (Essay XVIII), *passim*

 (See *Caste* , *Ceremonies* , *Rank* , etc.)

Classics, study of, in the Renaissance

Claude, helps Turner. (See *Painters* , etc.)

Clergy: mercenary motives

more tolerant of immorality than of heresy

belief in natural law

dangers of association with

(See *Priesthood* , *Religion* , etc.)

Clergywomen

Clerks, their knowledge an aid to national intercourse

(See *Business* , *Languages* , etc.)

Coats-of-arms: usurped

in letters

(See *Rank* .)

Cockburn, Sir Alexander, knowledge of French

Cock Robin, boat

(See *Boating* .)

Coffee, satire on trade

Cologne Cathedral

Colors, in painting

Columbus, Voltaire's allusion

Comet, in Egyptian war

(See *Superstition* .)

Comfort, pursuit of,

(See *Philistinism* .)

Commerce, affected by language,

(See *Business* , *Languages* , etc.)

Communism, threats

Como, Italy, solitude

Companionship: how decided

affected by opinions

by tastes

feminine liking

Confessional, the: influencing women

    a supposititious compulsion

    (See *Religion* , etc.)

Confirmation, priestly connection with

    (See *Women* .)

Confusion: (Essay XX)

    masculine and feminine

    political

    rebels and reformers

    private and public liberty

    Radicals

    égalité

    religious

    Philistines and Bohemians

    confounding people with their associates

    vocations

    persons

    foreign buildings

    inducing calumny

    caused by insufficient analysis

    about inventions

    result of carelessness, indolence, or senility

Consolation, of clergy

    (See *Religion* .)

Construing, different from reading

    (See *Languages* .)

Continent, the: family ties

    friendship broken by marriage

    religious liberality

    marriage

post-cards

un mot à la poste

brevity and hurry

handwriting

crossed lines, ink, type-writers

dictation, outside courtesy

to reply or not reply? ;

Letters of Friendship (Essay XXIII)

a supposed gain to friendship

neglected

impediments

French cards

abandonment to be regretted

letter-writing a gift

real self wanted in letters

letters of business and friendship

familiarity best

lengthy letters

Byron's

Jacquemont's

the Rémusat letters

Bernardo Tasso's, Montaigne's

perils of plain speaking

Letters of Business (Essay XXIV)

differences of talent

repeated perusals

refuge of timidity

letters exposed, literary faults, omissions

directions misunderstood

acknowledging orders

slovenly writing, one subject in each letter

foreign forms

by telegraph

in little things

in stationery

affected by postal cards

in chirography

affected by type-writers

for show merely

requiring answers

(See *Manners*, *Classes*, etc.)

Cousins: French proverb, general relationship

lack of friendly interest

(See *Brothers*, etc.)

Creuzot, French foundry

Cricket: not played in France

author's dislike

(See *Amusements*.)

Crimean War, caused by ignorance

(See *War*.)

Criticism: intolerant of certain features in books

in Byron's letters

in anonymous letters

explained by a date

Cromwell, Oliver, contrasted with his son

Culture and Philistinism

Customs: upheld by clergy

amusements changed into,

(See *Ceremonies, Courtesy, Rank*, etc.)

Daily News, London, illustration of natural law *vs.* religion

Dancing: French quotation about

religious aversion

    not compulsory to the poor

    (See *Amusements*, etc.)

Dante, his subjects

Daughters, their respectful and impertinent letters

    (See *Fathers, Sons, Women* , etc.)

Death: termination of intercourse

    from love

    Byron's lines

    ingratitude expressed in a will

    of wife's relations

    of Friendship (Essay VIII)

    not personal

    of a French gentleman

    priestly connection with

    of absent friends

    French customs

    silence

    (See *Priests, Religion* .)

Debauchery, destructive of love

Deference, why liked

    (See *Rank* , etc.)

Deism, confounded with Atheism

    (See *God, Religion* , etc.)

Delos, oracle of

Democracies, illustration of broken friendships

Democracy: accusation of

    confounded with Dissent

    (See *Nationality* , etc.)

Denmark, the crown-prince of

Dependence, of one upon all

De Saussure, Horace Benedict, his life study

Despotism, provincial and social

    (See *Tyranny* .)

De Tocqueville, Alexis Charles Henri Clerel: allusion

    translation

    on English unsociability (Essay XVII), *passim*

Devil: priestly opposition

    belief in agency

    God's relation to

    (See *Clergy, Superstition, Religion* , etc.)

Devonshire, Eng., its beauty

Dickens, Charles: his middle-class portraitures

    his indebtedness to the poor

    humor

Dictionary, references

    (See *Languages* .)

Diderot, Denis, Goldsmith's interview

Dignity, to be maintained in middle-life

Diminution, habit in art and life (Essay XVI)

    (See *Exaggeration* .)

Diogenes, his philosophy

Discipline: of children, *passim;*

    delegated

    mental

    of self

Discord, the result of high taste

Dishonesty, part of Bohemianism

Disraeli, Benjamin, female estimate

Dissenters: French estimate

    English exclusion

    liberty in religion

position not compulsory

small towns

(See *Church of England* , etc.)

Dissipation: among working-men

in France

(See *Wine* , etc.)

Distinctions forgotten (Essay XX), *passim*

(See *Confusion* .)

Divorce, causes of

(See *Marriage, Women* , etc.)

Dobell, Sidney, social exclusion

Dog, rifle compared to

(See *Amusements* .)

Dominicans, dress

(See *Religion* , etc.)

Dominoes in France

(See *Amusements*.)

Don Quixote, illustration of paternal satire

Doré, Gustave, his kind and long letter

Double, Léopold, home

Dover Straits

Drama: power of adaptation

amateur actors

Drawing: a French church

aid to business letters

(See *Painters* , etc.)

Dreams, outgrown

Dress: connection with manners

ornaments to indicate wealth

feminine interest

clerical vestments

sexless

of the Philistines

Bohemian,

(See *Women* .)

Driving, sole exercise

Drunkenness: part of Bohemianism

in best society

(See *Table, Wine* , etc.)

Duelling, French

Du Maurier, George, his satire on coffee-dealers

Dupont, Pierre, song about wine,

Ear, learning languages by

(See *Languages* .)

Easter: allusion

confession

Eccentricity: high intellect

in an artist

claims indulgence

Eclipse, superstitious view

Economy, necessitated by marriage

(See *Wealth* .)

Edinburgh Review, editor

Editor, a procrastinating correspondent

Education: similarity

affecting idiosyncrasy

conventional

effect upon humor

literary, derived from the poor

affected by change in filial obedience

home, *et seq.;*

a most relentless monarch

women during reign of Charles II

marriage rites

aristocracy

A Remarkable Peculiarity (Essay XVII)

meeting abroad

reticence in each other's company

anecdotes

dread of intrusion

freedom with foreigners and with compatriots

not a mark of aristocracy

fear of meddlers

interest in rank

reticence outgrown

Lever's illustration

exceptions

Saxon and Norman influence

Dissenters ignored

general information

French ignorance of art and literature in

game

mountains

landscapes

Church

supposed law about attending the Mass

homes longed for

the architectural blunders of tourists

Philistine lady

painter and Philistine

letters in the fifteenth and sixteenth centuries

use of telegraph

letters shortened

letter-paper ;

post-cards

communication with France

trade habits

reading of certain books not compulsory

old maids

winter

(See *Church of England, France* , etc.)

English Language: ignorance of, a misfortune

familiar knowledge unusual in France

forms of courtesy

conversation abroad

Bohemian

literature

bad spelling

no synonym for *corvée*

nautical terms

(See *England* , etc.)

English People: Continental repulsion

artistic attraction

undervaluation of chance conversations

looseness of family ties

ashamed of sentiment

feeling about heredity

one lady's empty rooms

another's incivility

a merchant's loss of wealth

deteriorated aristocrat

letters by ladies

no consoling power

latest thought

cities

William of Orange, on complications

communistic disturbances

(See *England, France* , etc.)

Evangelicism, English peculiarities

(See *Dissenters* , etc.)

Evans, Marian. (See *George Eliot* .)

Evolution, theory of

Exaggeration, the habit in art and life (Essay XVI)

(See *Diminution* .)

Exercise: love of

in the young and the old

(See *Amusements* .)

Experience: value

needed to avoid dangers in letter-writing

Extravagance: part of Bohemianism

Goldsmith's

Family: Ties (Essay V)

looseness in England

brotherly coolness

domestic jealousies

laws of primogeniture

instances of strong attachment

illustrations of kindness

pecuniary relations

parsimony

discomfort of refinement

cousins

wife's relations

political criticism

noisy card-players

disregard of titles

adage about riches

English ideas slowly received

travel in Southern

religious freedom

marriage

railway accident

the Imperialists

feudal fashions

obstinacy of the old régime

mountains

vigor of young men

universities

equality attained by Revolution

bourgeois complaint of newspapers

mineral oil

confusion of tourists

Goldsmith's travels

landscape painter

end of Plumpton family

use of telegraph

letters shortened

letter-paper

post-cards

chirography

New Year's cards

carton non bitumé

habits of tradesmen

the *Salon*

old maids

a *corvée*

Leloir the painter

(See *Continent* , etc.)

Fraternity, *fraternité*

(See *Brothers* .)

Freedom: national

public and private liberty confounded

French Language: teaching

ignorance a misfortune

rare knowledge of, by Englishmen

letters by English ladies

forms of courtesy

prayers

as the universal tongue

English knowledge of

univers

(See *Languages* .)

French People: excellence in painting, and relations to Americans and English

an ideal of *good form*

old conventionality

love in fiction

family ties

proverb about cousins

unbelieving sons

bourgeois table manners formerly

state apartments

incivility towards, at an English table

girls

a woman's clever retort

literature condemned by wholesale

royal daily life

power of consolation

examples of virtue

old nobility

Buffon and Littré

hazard providentiel

painters

overstatement

   sociability with strangers contrasted with the English want of it
(Essay XVII), *passim;*

a widow and suite

discreet social habits

a disregard of titles

a weak question about fortune

ignorance of English matters

wine-song

fuel and iron

seeming vanity of language

conceit cured by war

communist dreamers

proverb

confusion of persons

Friendship: supposed impossible in a given case

real

how formed

not confined to the same class

affected by art and religion

by taste and nationality

by likeness

with those with whom we have not much in common

affection overflows in long letters

fault-finding dangerous

journeys saved

(See *Association, Companionship, Family* , etc.)

Fruit, ignorance about English

Fruition, pleasure of

Fuel, French

Furniture: feminine interest in

regard and disregard (Essay XXI), *passim;*

Goldsmith's extravagance

(See *Women.*)

Gambetta, his death

Game: in England

elephant and hippopotamus

(See *Sports* .)

Games, connection with amusement

(See *Cards* , etc.)

Garden, illustration

Gascoyne, William, letters

Generosity: affecting family ties

of a Philistine

Geneva Lake, as seen by different eyes

Genius, enjoyment of

Gentility: Genteel Ignorance (Essay XVIII)

an ideal condition

misfortune

French noblesse

ignores differing forms of religion

poverty

inferior financial conditions

real differences

  genteel society avoided

  because stupid

Geography: London Atlas

  work of Reclus

  (See *Ignorance* .)

Geology, allusion

  (See *Science* .)

George III., colonial tenure

Germany: models of virtue

  hotel fashions

  a Bohemian and scholar

German Language, English knowledge

Gladstone, William E.: the probable effect of a French training

  indebtedness to trade

  Lord

  foreign troubles ending in inkshed

  allusion

  use of post-cards

  female estimate

Glasgow, steamer experience

Gloucester, Eng., manufactory of rifles

God: of the future

  personal care

  against wickedness

  Divine love

   interference with law (Essay XV), *passim;*

  human motives

  (See *Religion* , etc.)

Gods: our valors the best

  siege of Syracuse

conversation in Scotland

in a steamer

acquaintance with a painter

belief in Nature's promises, *et seq.;*

what a sister said

the love of two brothers

delightful experience with wife's relations

experience of hospitable tyranny, *et seq.;*

Parisian dinner

experience with friendship

noisy French farmers

Scotch dinner

country incident

questioning a Parisian lady

Waterloo letters

how Italian seems to him

incident of Scotch travel

visit to a bereaved French lady

travel in France

lesson from a painter

snubbed at a hotel

a French widow on her travels

a lady's ignorance about religious distinctions

personal anecdotes about ignorance between the English and French, *passim;*

translations into French

Puseyite anecdote

conversations heard

boat incident

life-portraits

experience with procrastinators

enjoyment of

Jews: not the only subjects of useful study

God of Battles

advance of knowledge

(See *Bible* .)

John, an imaginary friend

Jones, an imaginary gentleman

Justice: feminine disregard

connection with priesthood

Keble, John, Christian Year

Kempis, Thomas à, his great work

Kenilworth, anecdote

Kindness, how to be received

Kindred: affected by incompatibility

Family Ties (Essay V)

given by Fate

(See *Sons* , etc.)

Kings: divine right

on cards

courtesy in correspondence

a poetic figure

(See *Rank* , etc.)

Knarsbrugh, Eng

Knyghton, Henry, quotation

Lakes, English

Lancashire, Eng.: all residents not in cotton-trade

residence

drinking-habits

Land-ownership

corrogata

Laws: difficult to ascertain

human resignation to

of Human Intercourse (Essay I)

fixed knowledge difficult

common belief

similarity of interest

may breed antagonism

national prejudices

likeness begets friendship

idiosyncrasy and adaptability

intimacy slow

law of the pleasure of human intercourse still hidden

fixed

feminine disregard

quiet tone

regularity and interference (Essay XV), *passim;*

legal distinctions

Laymen, contrasted with clergy

Lectures, one-sided

Legouvé, M.: on filial relations

religious question

anecdote of chirography

Leisure: its connection with refinement

varying in different professions

Leloir, Louis, fondness for etching

Lent, allusion

Letters. (See *Correspondence* .)

Lever, Charles: quotation from That Boy of Norcott's

finances misunderstood

boating

Morris, Lewis, A Cynic's Day-dream

Mothers, "loud-tongued,"

(See *Children, Women* , etc.)

Mountains: climbing affected by railways

quotation from Byron

in pictures

glory in England and France

Mont Blanc, where situated

Mozart, Johann Chrysostom Wolfgang Amadeus, allusion

Muloch, Dinah Maria, confounded with George Eliot

Music: detached from religion

voice of love

affecting fraternity

connection with religion

illustration of harmony

Nagging, by parents

Napoleon I.: and the Universe

privations

mot of the Pope

Rémusat letters

Napoleon III.: death, son

ignorance of German power

losing Sedan

Nationality: prejudices

to be respected at table

different languages an obstacle to intercourse (Essay XI)

mutual ignorance (Essay XIX) *passim*

National Gallery, London

Nature: compensations

causes

Poetry: detached from religion

   of love

   dulness to

   Shelley's

   Byron's

   Goethe's

   and science

   Tennyson on Brotherhood

   lament

   art

   music in heaven

   Keble

   Battle of Ivry

   French

   Latin, loyalty of Tennyson

   French couplet

   in a library

   "If I be dear,"

   Horace

   Palace of Art

   quotation from Morris

   line about anticipation

Poets: ideas about the harmlessness of love

   avoidance of practical difficulties

   love in natural scenery

Politics: conventional

   French narrowness

   coffee-house

   inherited opinions

   opinions of guests to be respected

   affecting friendship

war and God

natural order

Providence

salvation from shipwreck

un hazard providentiel

irreligion

less piety

devotion and science

wise expenditure of time

feuds

genteel ignorance of established churches

French ignorance of English Church

distinctions confounded

intolerance mixed with social contempt

activity limited to religion and riches

in old letters

female interest in the author's welfare

in theology

(See *Church of England, Methodism, Protestantism* , etc.)

Rémusat, Mme. de, letters

Renaissance, expansion of study in the

Renan, Ernest, one objection to trade

Republic, French

Residence, affecting friendship

Respect: the road to filial love

why liked

in correspondence

Restraints, of marriage and love

Retrospection, pleasures of

Revolution, French

(See *France* .)

Protestantism ignored

Romanism ignored by the Greek Church

compulsory attendance

(See *Priesthood, Religion* , etc.)

Romance: like or dislike for

glamour of love

Rome: people not subjected to the papacy

Byron's letter

Rossetti, on Mrs. Harriett Shelley

Rouen Cathedral

Royal Academy, London

Royal Society, London

Royalty, its religious bondage

Rugby, residence of a father

Ruolz, the inventor, his bituminous paper

Russell, Lord Arthur, his knowledge of French

Russia: religious position of the Czar

orthodoxy

war with Turkey

(See *Greek Church* .)

Sabbath, its observance

Sacredness, definition of

Sacrifices: demanded by courtesy

in letter-writing

to indolence

Sahara, love-simile

Saint Bernard, qualities

Saint Hubert's Day, carousal

Saints, in every occupation

Salon, French

literary and artistic

Subjugation, the motive of display of wealth

Suez Canal, and superstition

Sunbeam, yacht

Sunday: French incident

    allusion

    supposed law

    (See *Sabbath* .)

Sunset, allusion

Supernaturalism (Essay XV) *passim*;

    doubts about

Superstition and religion (Essay XV) *passim*

Surgeon, an artistic

Sweden, king of

Swedenborgianism, commended to the author

Swift, Jonathan, Gulliver's box

Swimming: affected by railways

    in France

Switzerland: epithets applied to

    tourists

    Alps

    Goldsmith's travels

    Doré's travels

Sympathy: with an author

    one of two great powers deciding human intercourse

    of a married man with a single

    between parents and children (Essay VI) *passim*;

    between Priests and Women (Essay XIII. part i.) *passim*

Symposium, antique, allusion

Syracuse, siege

Understatement. (See *Untruth* .)

Union of languages and peoples

Unitarianism: no European sovereign dare profess

    difficulty with creeds

    ignorance about

United States, advantage of having the same language as England

Universe*univers*

Universities: degrees

    French and English

    Radical members

Untruth: an Unrecognized Form of (Essay XVI)

    two methods in painting

    exaggeration and diminution

    self-misrepresentation

    overstatement and understatement illustrated in travelling epithets

    dead mediocrity in conversation

    inadequacy

    illustration

Vanity: national (Essay XIX) *passim*;

    taking offence

    absence

Vice: of classes

    devilish

    part of Bohemianism

    of best society

Victoria, Queen: quotation from her diary

    her oldest son

Violin, illustration

Viollet-le-Duc, anecdote

Virgil, Palmer's constant companion

Footnotes:

[1] An expression used to me by a learned Doctor of Oxford.

[2] The causes of this curious repulsion are inquired into elsewhere in this volume.

[3] The exact degree of blame due to Shelley is very difficult to determine. He had nothing to do with the suicide, though the separation was the first in a train of circumstances that led to it. It seems clear that Harriett did not desire the separation, and clear also that she did nothing to assert her rights. Shelley ought not to have left her, but he had not the patience to accept as permanent the consequences of a mistaken marriage.

[4] Lewes's "Life of Goethe."

[5] Only a poet can write of his private sorrows. In prose one cannot sing, —

> "A dirge for her, the doubly dead, in that she died so
> young."

[6] Schuyler's "Peter the Great."

[7] That valiant enemy of false pretensions, Mr. Punch, has often done good service in throwing ridicule on unreal distinctions. In "Punch's Almanack" for 1882 I find the following exquisite conversation beneath one of George Du Maurier's inimitable drawings:

> *Grigsby.* Do you know the Joneses?
>
> *Mrs. Brown.* No, we—er—don't care to
> know *Business* people, as a rule, although my husband's in
> business; but then he's in the *Coffee* business,—and they're
> all Gentlemen in the *Coffee* business, you know!
>
> *Grigsby* (who always suits himself to his company). *Really,*
> now! Why, that's more than can be said of the Army, the
> Navy, the Church, the Bar, or even the *House of Lords*! I
> don't *wonder* at your being rather *exclusive*!

[8] I am often amused by the indignant feelings of English journalists on this matter. Some French newspaper calls an Englishman a lord when he is not a lord, and our journalists are amazed at the incorrigible ignorance of the French. If Englishmen cared as little about titles they would be equally ignorant, and two or three other things are to be said in defence of the French journalist that English critics *never* take into account. They suppose that because Gladstone is commonly called Mr. a Frenchman ought to know that he cannot be a lord. That does not follow. In France a man may be called Monsieur and be a baron at the same time. A Frenchman may answer, "If Gladstone is not a lord, why do you call him one? English almanacs not only say that Gladstone is a lord, but that he is the very First Lord of the Treasury. Again, why am I not to speak of Sir Chamberlain? I have seen a printed letter to him beginning with 'Sir,' which is plain evidence that your 'Sir' is the equivalent of our *Monsieur*." A Frenchman is surely not to be severely blamed if he is not aware that the First Lord of the Treasury is not a lord at all, and that a man who is called a "Sir" inside every letter addressed to him has no right to that title on the envelope.

[9] That of M. Léopold Double.

[10] I need hardly say that this is not intended as a description of poor men's hospitality generally, but only of the effects of poverty on hospitality in certain cases. The point of the contrast lies in the difference between this uncomfortable hospitality, which a lover of pleasant human intercourse avoids, with the easy and agreeable hospitality that the very same people would probably have offered if they had possessed the conveniences of wealth.

[11] Italian, to me, seems Latin made natural.

[12] So far as the State and society generally are concerned; but there are private situations in which even a member of the State Church does not enjoy perfect religious liberty. Suppose the case (I am describing a real case) of a lady left a widow and in poverty. Her relations are wealthy Dissenters. They offer to provide for her handsomely if she will renounce the Church of England and join their own sect. Does she enjoy religious liberty? The answer depends upon the question whether she is able to earn her own living or not. If she is, she can secure religious freedom by incessant labor; if she is unable to earn her living she will have no religious freedom, although she belongs, in conscience, to the most powerful religion in the State. In the case I am thinking of, the lady had the honorable courage to open a little shop, and so remained a member of the Church of England; but her

freedom was bought by labor and was therefore not the same thing as the best freedom, which is unembittered by sacrifice.

[13] The phrase adopted by Court journalists in speaking of such a conversion is, "The Princess has received instruction in the religion which she will adopt on her marriage," or words to that effect, just as if different and mutually hostile religions were not more contradictory of each other than sciences, and as if a person could pass from one religion to another with no more twisting and wrenching of previous beliefs than he would incur in passing from botany to geology.

[14] The word "generally" is inserted here because women do apparently sometimes enjoy the infliction of undeserved pain on other creatures. They grace bull-fights with their presence, and will see horses disembowelled with apparent satisfaction. It may be doubted, too, whether the Empress of Austria has any compassion for the sufferings of a fox.

[15] I have purposely omitted from the text another cause for feminine indifference to the work of persecutors, but it may be mentioned incidentally. At certain times those women whose influence on persons in authority might have been effectively employed in favor of the oppressed were too frivolous or even too licentious for their thoughts to turn themselves to any such serious matter. This was the case in England under Charles II. The contrast between the occupations of such women as these and the sufferings of an earnest man has been aptly presented by Macaulay:—

> "The ribaldry of Etherege and Wycherley was, in the
> presence and under the special sanction of the head of
> the Church, publicly recited by female lips in female ears,
> while the author of the 'Pilgrim's Progress' languished in
> a dungeon, for the crime of proclaiming the gospel to the
> poor."

This is deplorable enough; but on the whole I do not think that the frivolity of light-minded women has been so harmful to noble causes as the readiness with which serious women place their immense influence at the service of constituted authorities, however wrongfully those authorities may act. Ecclesiastical authorities especially may quietly count upon this kind of support, and they always do so.

[16] Since this Essay was written I have met with the following passage in Her Majesty's diary, which so accurately describes the consolatory influence of clergymen, and the natural desire of women for the consolation ·

given by them, that I cannot refrain from quoting it. The Queen is speaking of her last interview with Dr. Norman Macleod:—

> "He dwelt then, as always, on the love and goodness of God, and on his conviction that God would give us, in another life, the means to perfect ourselves and to improve gradually. No one ever felt so convinced, and so anxious as he to convince others, that God was a loving Father who wished all to come to Him, and to preach of a living personal Saviour, One who loved us as a brother and a friend, to whom all could and should come with trust and confidence. No one ever raised and strengthened one's faith more than Dr. Macleod. His own faith was so strong, his heart so large, that all—high and low, weak and strong, the erring and the good—*could alike find sympathy, help, and consolation from him.*"

> "*How I loved to talk to him, to ask his advice, to speak to him of my sorrows and anxieties.*"

A little farther on in the same diary Her Majesty speaks of Dr. Macleod's beneficial influence upon another lady:—

> "He had likewise a marvellous power of winning people of all kinds, and of sympathizing with the highest and with the humblest, and of soothing and comforting the sick, the dying, the afflicted, the erring, and the doubting. *A friend of mine told me that if she were in great trouble, or sorrow, or anxiety, Dr. Norman Macleod was the person she would wish to go to.*"

The two points to be noted in these extracts are: first, the faith in a loving God who cares for each of His creatures individually (not acting only by general laws); and, secondly, the way in which the woman goes to the clergyman (whether in formal confession or confidential conversation) to hear consolatory doctrine from his lips in application to her own personal needs. The faith and the tendency are both so natural in women that they could only cease in consequence of the general and most improbable acceptance by women of the scientific doctrine that the Eternal Energy is invariably regular in its operations and inexorable, and that the priest has no clearer knowledge of its inscrutable nature than the layman.

[17] These quotations (I need hardly say) are from Macaulay's History, Chapter III.

[18] The difference of interest as regards people of rank may be seen by a comparison of French and English newspapers. In an English paper, even on the Liberal side, you constantly meet with little paragraphs informing you that one titled person has gone to stay with another titled person; that some old titled lady is in poor health, or some young one going to be married; or that some gentleman of title has gone out in his yacht, or entertained friends to shoot grouse,—the reason being that English people like to hear about persons of title, however insignificant the news may be in itself. If paragraphs of the same kind were inserted in any serious French newspaper the subscribers would wonder how they got there, and what possible interest for the public there could be in the movements of mediocrities, who had nothing but titles to distinguish them.

[19] Since this Essay was written I have come upon a passage quoted from Henry Knyghton by Augustin Thierry in his "History of the Norman Conquest:"—

> "It is not to be wondered at if the difference of nationality (between the Norman and Saxon races) produces a difference of conditions, or that there should result from it an excessive distrust of natural love; and that the separateness of blood should produce a broken confidence in mutual trust and affection."

Now, the question suggests itself, whether the reason why Englishman shuns Englishman to-day may not be traceable, ultimately, to the state of feeling described by Knyghton as a result of the Norman Conquest. We must remember that the avoidance of English by English is quite peculiar to us; no other race exhibits the same peculiarity. It is therefore probably due to some very exceptional fact in English history. The Norman Conquest was exactly the exceptional fact we are in search of. The results of it may be traceable as follows:—

1. Norman and Saxon shun each other.

2. Norman has become aristocrat.

3. Would-be aristocrat (present representative of Norman) shuns possible plebeian (present representative of Saxon).

[20] It so happens that I am writing this Essay in a rough wooden hut of my own, which is in reality a most comfortable little building, though "stuffy luxury" is rigorously excluded.

[21] At present it is most inadequately represented by a few unimportant gifts. The donors have desired to break the rule of exclusion, and have succeeded so far, but that is all.

[22] These, of course, are only examples of vulgar patriotic ignorance. A few Frenchmen who have really *seen* what is best in English landscape are delighted with it; but the common impression about England is that it is an ugly country covered with *usines*, and on which the sun never shines.

[23] The French word *univers* has three or four distinct senses. It may mean all that exists, or it may mean the solar system, or it may mean the earth's surface, in whole or in part. Voltaire said that Columbus, by simply looking at a map of our *univers*, had guessed that there must be another, that is, the western hemisphere. "Paris est la plus belle ville de l'univers" means simply that Paris is the most beautiful city in the world.

[24] A French critic recently observed that his countrymen knew little of the tragedy of "Macbeth" except the familiar line "To be or not to be, that is the question!"

[25] I never make a statement of this kind without remembering instances, even when it does not seem worth while to mention them particularly. It is not of much use to quote what one has heard in conversation, but here are two instances in print. Reclus, the French geographer, in "La Terre à Vol d'Oiseau," gives a woodcut of the Houses of Parliament and calls it "L'Abbaye de Westminster." The same error has even occurred in a French art periodical.

[26] Rodolphe, in "L'Honneur et l'Argent."

[27] In the library at Towneley Hall in Lancashire.

[28] In Prosper Mérimée's "Correspondence" he gives the following as the authentic text of the letter in which Lady Florence Paget announced her elopement with the last Marquis of Hastings to her father:—

> "Dear Pa, as I knew you would never consent to my
> marriage with Lord Hastings, I was wedded to him to-day.
> I remain yours, etc."

[29] For those who take an interest in such matters I may say that the last representative of the Plumptons died in France unmarried in 1749, and Plumpton Hall was barbarously pulled down by its purchaser, an ancestor of the present Earls of Harewood. The history of the family is very

interesting, and the more so to me that it twice intermarried with my own. Dorothy Plumpton was a niece of the first Sir Stephen Hamerton.

[30] Sir Walter Scott had sympathy enough with the courtesy of old time to note its minutiæ very closely:—

> "After inspecting the cavalry, Sir Everard again
> conducted his nephew to the library, where he produced
> a letter, *carefully folded, surrounded by a little stripe of*
> *flox-silk, according to ancient form,* and sealed with *an*
> *accurate impression* of the Waverley coat-of-arms. It was
> addressed, *with great formality,* 'To Cosmo Comyne
> Bradwardine, Esq., of Bradwardine, at his principal
> mansion of Tully-Veolan, in Perthshire, North Britain.
> These—by the hands of Captain Edward Waverley,
> nephew of Sir Everard Waverley, of Waverley-Honour,
> Bart.'" —*Waverley,* chap. vi.

I had not this passage in mind when writing the text of this Essay, but the reader will notice how closely it confirms what I have said about deliberation and care to secure a fair impression of the seal.

[31] A very odd but very real objection to the employment of these missives is that the receiver does not always know how to open them, and may burn them unread. I remember sending a short letter in this shape from France to an English lady. She destroyed my letter without opening it; and I got for answer that "if it was a French custom to send blank post-cards she did not know what could be the signification of it." Such was the result of a well-meant attempt to avoid the non-courteous post-card!

[32] Besides which, in the case of a French friend, you are sure to have notice of such events by printed *lettres de faire part.*

[33] I need hardly say that there has been immense improvement in this respect, and that such descriptions have no application to the Lancashire of to-day; indeed, they were never true, in that extreme degree, of Lancashire generally, but only of certain small localities which were at one time like spots of local disease on a generally vigorous body.

[34] Littré derives *corvée* from the Low-Latin *corrogata*, from the Latin *cum* and *rogare.*